William Richard Morfill, Richard Williams

Ballads from Manuscripts.

Vol. II.

William Richard Morfill, Richard Williams

Ballads from Manuscripts.
Vol. II.

ISBN/EAN: 9783744786997

Printed in Europe, USA, Canada, Australia, Japan

Cover: Foto ©Andreas Hilbeck / pixelio.de

More available books at **www.hansebooks.com**

Ballads from Manuscripts.

Vol. II.

Ballads from Manuscripts.

Ballads from Manuscripts.
Vol. II.

PART I. A POORE MANS PITTANCE,

BY

RICHARD WILLIAMS.

EDITED FROM THE AUTOGRAPH MS. BY

F. J. FURNIVALL, M.A.

PART II. BALLADS RELATING CHIEFLY TO THE REIGN OF QUEEN ELIZABETH.

EDITED, WITH INTRODUCTION AND NOTES TO THE WHOLE VOLUME,

BY

W. R. MORFILL, M.A.,

ORIEL COLLEGE, OXFORD.

PRINTED FOR

The Ballad Society,

BY STEPHEN AUSTIN AND SONS,

HERTFORD.

1873.

3 and 10

HERTFORD:
STEPHEN AUSTIN AND SONS, PRINTERS.

CONTENTS.

PREFACE.

It will not be necessary that I should say much by way of preface to the miscellaneous collection included in the present volume. The notices appended to each of the pieces will speak for them. Although for the most part deficient in poetical merit, they will have their value to the antiquarian and historical student. Many of the most life-like sketches and photographic portraits by Macaulay were drawn from the contemporaneous broadsides which he laid under contribution, and we have all, no doubt, felt surprise on running our eyes over the notes to his invaluable works when we have realized the strange sources whence his information was frequently drawn. The immortal chapter on the condition of England and the manners of the English in the time of Charles II. could only have been written by one who had made an exhaustive study of the fugitive literature of the Caroline period.

Several of the pieces included in this book have unfortunately been already printed; but as they have

made their appearance in works which have now
become excessively rare, their reproduction cannot be
unwelcome to the reader.

In conclusion, I must thank Mr. (Adams) Cokayne,
formerly Rouge Dragon, now Somerset Herald, for
some valuable information on the personages named
in Teshe's poem. For the Introduction and Notes
on the Campion poems I am indebted to Mr. Richard
Simpson, the author of an exhaustive biography of
the unfortunate priest.

Mr. Furnivall edited the text of Richard Williams's
Poor Mans Pittance from the author's MS. for the
Society in 1868. I have now added, at his request,
an Introduction and Notes to it. He wishes to correct
the date [1604] in the last line of p. 2 to [1605], as
Williams miscalled the third year of James I. "The
seconde yeare." I must thank him for many valuable
suggestions, and the kind interest he has taken in the
book throughout.

W. R. MORFILL.

OXFORD.

INTRODUCTION.

The cruel policy adopted by Elizabeth towards the Roman Catholics, her unjust detention in prison of Mary Queen of Scots, and the loud and frequent anathemas hurled against her by Pope and Spaniard, caused her reign to be fertile in plots and intrigues. The position of the Papists during this time had become very anomalous. In consequence of the Bull issued against her by Pius V. declaring that she was never at any time the true Queen of England, and absolving all her subjects from their allegiance, the Government resolved to take even more stringent measures than had been adopted previously. By 13 Eliz. it was treason to call the Queen heretic, schismatic or usurper, to introduce a Papal Bull, or to send relief to the fugitives over sea.

Even the most private practice of their religion was forbidden to Romanists; at any hour they might be hurried before the Courts of High Commission, where they could be interrogated as to how often they had been at church, and were in consequence liable to fines and imprisonment. Their houses were constantly being searched, and even foreign ambassadors complained that their chapels were visited by informers.

In 1581 a severe statute was passed, which was entitled " An Act to retain the Queen's Majesty's subjects in their due obedience " (23 Eliz. c. 1). It is thereby provided that any person perverting another to the Romish religion should be treated as a traitor, and the person reconciled incur the penalty of misprision of treason. Saying mass was to be punished by a fine of 200 marks; hearing it by a fine of 100 marks, with, in each case, a year's imprisonment. Absence from church was to be visited with the infliction of a fine of £20 a month; and if it continued for a year or more, two sureties of £200 each were to be given for future good behaviour.

The kingdom was now full of spies, and the rack and gallows daily claimed their victims. The country saw something very like a renewal of the far-famed Marian persecutions, which form so dark a page in our national fasti, and have earned a very disagreeable epithet for their supposed anthorizer. Although the English Roman Catholics showed considerable loyalty at the time of the Armada, yet within three months after its defeat, when leniency might have become cheap from so unsuspected a triumph, more than thirty persons—laity and clergy included—were put to death on account of their creed.

A statute was enacted, compelling those Catholics not possessing 20 marks a year to abjure the realm within three months after conviction, under the penalty of felony without benefit of clergy. In 1593 a very severe Act was passed against Popish recusants—as the Conrt phrase was. They were now not to travel a distance of more than five miles from their houses.

It can be readily imagined that these Draconian enactments produced an average quota of victims. The names of the unhappy victims are duly paraded before us by Lingard. To the man who reads history in an unprejudiced spirit they prove—if any proof were needed—how very little the doctrine of religious toleration was understood, obviously a growth of far later times. In pp. 157-191 of this book mention is made of the sufferings of Campion. But perhaps one of the saddest instances of this injudicious severity is furnished by the fate of Robert Southwell.

This unfortunate man was a Romish priest, who was apprehended in 1592, while domiciled in the house of the Countess of Arundel. He was thrown into the Tower, and frequently put to the torture. After three years' imprisonment, he was, on his own application, brought to trial, and so eager were his judges to carry out his sentence, that he was even consigned to the executioner on the following day. Lord Burghley, who had been implored to make some settlement of his case, and release him from the dungeon in which he was languishing, brutally remarked, that "if he was in such haste to be hanged, he should have his desire." His poems, many of which are of great beauty, are well known to the lovers of our older English literature.[1]

Of the various plots attempted in this reign, the most important, from its fatal effects upon the captive Queen of Scots, and the romantic character of some of those implicated in it, was unquestionably that of Anthony Babington and his followers, whose dismal fate forms the subject of the poem printed on pages 5-22.

In this remarkable conspiracy three distinct elements may be traced : first, that of the enthusiasts sent into the country by the Pope, who aimed at nothing less than the assassination of the Queen ; secondly, some English Catholics, who joined with a view to better the condition of their co-religionists, but probably with no design upon the person of their Sovereign ; and thirdly, the counterplot inaugurated by Walsingham and his spies, who hoped so far to implicate Mary that her detection should involve the loss of her life. Anthony Babington, the chief figure in this web of threads and cross-threads, —a hot-headed youth, with a handsome figure, well-stored purse, and little discretion,—was the son of a certain Henry Babington, of Dethick, in Derbyshire, an opulent landowner. The estate had come into the family by the marriage of Thomas, second son of Sir John Babington, of Chilwell, with Isabella, daughter and heiress of Robert Dethick, who died in 1467.

---

[1] Thus how solemnly funereal and mournfully quaint are the stanzas beginning, "Before my face the picture hangs," to be found, it is true, in almost every book . of extracts, but none the worse for being somewhat hackneyed, as we cannot hear such choice poems too often. When we read this poem, we seem to be gazing into an open grave. There is something very fine, too, about Southwell's prose, especially his "Marie Magdalen's Funerall Teares."

The unfortunate Anthony was born in 1569, and lost his father ten years after his birth. During his minority his mother married again : her second husband being Henry Foljambe, who seems to have treated his step-son with great kindness. This circumstance is alluded to in the poem (pp. 10, 11) :—

> "But in the state of widowhode not longe shee tarried,
>   For with that good gentleman, Henrye Foliambe she married.
>   Whoe loved vs all tenderlie as wee had bene his owne,
>   And was verye carefull of oure education."

In favour of this gentleman Anthony charged his estates with 100 marks per annum, as a token of his gratitude. Besides himself, his father had left two daughters and three sons, Francis, George, and Charles. The latter is said to have committed suicide in prison, probably because implicated in the conspiracy for which his brother suffered. On the 25th September, 1587, among the prisoners in the Clink, we find Charles Babington.

The early youth of Anthony seems to have been spent in gaiety and the various amusements of the town. Being too early master of himself, and with abundance of means at his disposal, he led a wild and reckless existence, no doubt frequenting the theatres, where certainly his morals would not be improved, if Stubbes has given us a correct account in his Anatomie of Abuses, 1584) : " . . . . Marke the flockyng and runnyng to Theaters and Curteins, daylie and hourelie, night and daie, tyme and tide, to see Plaies and Enterludes, where suche wanton gestures, suche bawdie speeohes, suche laughyng and flearying, such kissyng and bussyng, suche clippyng and culling, such wincking and glauncing of wanton eyes, and the like, is used, as is wonderfull to beholde."—The English Drama and Stage, Roxb. Libr. 1869, p. 223. We feel that we have a picture of him when Dekker is describing the deportment of a gallant in Paul's walks; and the later sketch of Earle [1] will suit him well, when drawing the dandy of his time :—" Hee obserues London trulier

---

[1] Microcosmographie, edited by Arber, p. 39.

then the Termers, and his businesse is the street: the stage, the court, and those places where a proper man is best showne. If hee be qualified in gaming extraordinary, he is so much the more gentle and compleate, and hee learnes the beast [best] oathes for the purpose. These are a great part of his discourse, and he is as curious in their newnesse as the fashion. His other talke is Ladies and such pretty things, or some iests at a Play. His Pick-tooth beares a great part in his discourse, so does his body; the vpper parts whereof are as starcht as his linnen, and perchance vse the same Laundresse. Hee has learnt to ruffle his face from his Boote, and takes great delight in his walke to heare his Spurs gingle. . . . . He is one neuer serious but with his Taylor, when hee is in conspiracie for the next deuice."

Everything shows, however, that the unfortunate youth was of a friendly and genial temperament, and much endeared to his friends. There is something very touching in the words of Chidiock Tichbourne on the scaffold: "Before this thing chanced we lived together in the most flourishing estate. Of whom went report in the Strand, Fleet Street, and elsewhere about London, but of Babington and Tichbourne? No threshold was of force to brave our entry. Thus we lived, and wanted nothing we could wish for, and God knows what less in my head than matters of state! I have always thought it impious, and denied to be a dealer in it; but in regard of my friend I was silent, and so consented."

Babington appears to have made some profession of studying the law. He soon after married Margery, daughter of his guardian, Philip Draycot, of Paynsley or Peinsley, in Staffordshire, by whom he had one daughter, Mary, who died at the age of eight years. It was a Roman Catholic family, and we find Draycot apprehended as a recusant in 1587.

At the persuasion of John Ballard, a priest, who had entered England in disguise, and made a tour through a considerable part of the country to tamper with the disaffected and those who were attached to the old faith, Babington joined the conspiracy, the leading features of which seem to have been the assassination of Elizabeth and the liberation of the Queen of Scots. Two other chief participators were a desperado named Savage, who had served the King of Spain in the war then raging against the revolted Netherlands, and a certain Pooley, who, although to all appearance faithful to tho conspirators, was in reality in secret communication with Walsingham, Elizabeth's minister.

Mary, whose hopes of release had recently become fainter than ever through the treaty which had been concluded between her son James and the English Queen, was induced to become a participator in this plot, although at her trial she steadfastly affirmed that she had consented to nothing but an insurrection, and was in no way privy to the attempt on the life of her persecutor. A secret correspondence was carried on between Mary and Babington. The letters were all written in cipher; but in each instance Walsingham was made acquainted with the sending. The epistles were opened on their transmission, deciphered, and resealed by two experts, named Phelipps and Gregory, and forwarded to their destination, as if they had not been tampered with.

On the 14th of July, 1586, Mary is said to have received an important communication from Babington. It described the projected invasion of the country, the plan for her escape, and for the assassination. "This letter," says Tytler, "was not produced at the trial, and Mary denied ever having received it." The original certainly does not exist at present, but what purports to be a copy in a clerk's hand has been preserved. Besides the contents previously mentioned, Babington apologizes for his long silence, which he attributes to the extreme difficulty of safe communication with her. He tells her that six gentlemen had been selected for the honourable office of assassinating the Queen, and conjures her to be mindful of their posterity should they perish in the attempt. In her reply to this remarkable document, Mary fully accepts the responsibilities of the conspiracy;[1] that is, if the document at present passing for her answer, which does not profess to be any more than a copy, and is preserved in the State Paper Office, has not been tampered with by Walsingham, as was asserted by Camden, and is also insinuated by Tytler.[2] The plan of the wily secretary had now fully succeeded; it only remained to seize his victim, who had never indulged a suspicion that her correspondence had met any other eyes than those for which it was intended.

She was at this time a prisoner at Chartley, in Staffordshire, and Phelipps, who deciphered the letters, was living under the same roof with her. She had remarked the man about the premises, and had a sort of half notion that his mission boded no good. In a letter, still preserved, she has left a description of this fellow as slender, yellow-bearded, pitted in the face with small-pox, and short-sighted; so that we have as it were a photograph of Walsingham's creature transmitted to us—a man fitted for dark passages and by-paths, just such a person as under a despotic government becomes a police-spy.

The Queen of Scots was still fond of and still able to indulge in the pleasures of the chase. On the morning of the 8th of August her keeper, Sir Amias Paulet—the same who had, with such virtue or prudence, resisted the dark hints given him by Elizabeth about poisoning his captive—invited her to hunt on

---

[1] The mention of the design of the six gentlemen exists only in a postscript to the letter, and the defenders of Mary—notably Prince Labanoff and latterly M. Petit ["History of Mary Stuart, Queen of Scots." Translated from Professor Petit by Charles de Flandre. London, 1874.]—consider it to have been fabricated by Phelipps. The subject is also cleverly handled in the new work of Father Morris ("The Letter-books of Sir Amias Poulet," 1874), who considers that the passage is inconsistent with other parts of the letter, where Mary is apprehensive of the punishment which Elizabeth will probably inflict upon her friends, if she succeeds in effecting her escape. She could therefore hardly have contemplated the immediate assassination of her enemy. The question is too intricate to admit of being discussed here, and I cannot do better than refer the reader to the above-mentioned work of Morris (pp. 227-242), where he will find the specious argument of Mr. Froude demolished with much ingenuity.

[2] "History of Scotland," vol. iv. p. 127. Edin. 1864.

the neighbouring estate of Tixall. She rode with a small retinue, including her two secretaries, Nau and Curle, from Chartley, but on her way was stopped by a Mr. Thomas Gorges, who informed her of the detection of the conspiracy, and further that she was to be conveyed to Tixall, and not to be allowed to return to Chartley. At first she abandoned herself to a paroxysm of rage and despair, and called upon her companions to rescue their mistress from the traitors who had ventured to lay hands upon her. Her passion, however, lasted but for a moment. Reflecting how useless all opposition must be, she allowed herself to be carried off; while her attendants Nau and Curle were detained, and her desk and papers rifled and ransacked by the obsequious emissaries of Elizabeth.

Leaving, however, the unfortunate Queen, over whom already the shadow of the scaffold was looming, let us trace the fate of the foolish men who had linked themselves to this insane enterprise.

On the following day Ballard, the priest, was arrested, and Babington now suddenly found that Pooley had betrayed them. Being closely watched and hotly pursued upon the faintest trace of their presence being indicated, he and his fellow conspirators hid themselves in the neighbourhood of Harrow and St. John's Wood.[1] The search became more and more careful. Indeed we have a letter from Lord Burghley himself, stimulating the zeal of the pursuers, and finding fault with their inadequate caution, because, instead of dispersing, they hunted their victims in gangs, thereby arousing suspicion. Moreover, as he tells them, their ideas of the persons who were to be arrested were far from accurate. They seem only to have known that one of the leading malefactors "had a hooked nose." Perhaps Babington was the gentleman (to follow the direction) "talle of stature, of whitely complexion, somewhat rownde faced, his beard flaxen

---

[1] These circumstances are narrated minutely by Mr. Froude, who has treated the whole subject somewhat sensationally, and perhaps drawn too much upon an exuberant imagination.

and cut shorte, having a doublett and hose of yeallowe fustian
and a russet cloake."

Williams is very explicit in giving the names of all those who
were apprehended and suffered. They were finally, fourteen in
number, brought to trial. The indictment charged them with
a two-fold conspiracy, one plot to murder the Queen, and another
to raise a rebellion within the realm in favour of Mary Stuart.
Many of the prisoners had been apprehended in the house of
a farmer, named Bellamy, who was destined to pay dear for his
mistaken hospitality. He is alluded to in the poem—

"Lastlie Bellamye, our hoste, that made us all the chere."

Babington, Ballard, Savage, Barnewell, Tichebourne, and Donne,
admitted their guilt: the remaining pleaded not guilty, and
of these five were convicted as accomplices on the authority
of passages extracted from the confessions of the others, and
two, Gage and Bellamy, as accessories after the fact, because
they had assisted the conspirators after the proclamation issued
against them.[1]

---

[1] "Jerome Bellamye attaynted by verdict of xij men. His offence was in that
he ayded and releyved Babington, Barnewell, and Dune in the woods and in his
mother's haye barne, after that he vnderstood that searche was made for them
as traytors, for conspiring the deathe of the Queene's Majestie."—Quoted from
the *Reliquary*, vol. ii. p. 177. "In his examination Richard Mascall, servant
to Mrs. Bellamy, stated that Ierome Bellamy appoynted him to guide the
parties, and willed him to carry meat to these parties; he met with them in
the wood & knew Donne, for that Donne had been divers times at Mrs.
Bellamy's house: he saw them first lying on the grouud in the woods, and
then he went to his Mistress' house; when in the house he saw Donne and
Ierome. Ierome delivered unto this party (Mascall) the meat & 3 loaves of
bread, which this party carried at night: they ran to the hay barn on Thursday
night & all five lay there. The meat was dressed in his Mistress' house. Upon
Sunday at night they were altogether in the woods. Donne and Gage were
taken upon Sunday night between 8 & 9 of the clock at night, and this party
being with them fled from the watchmen. Mr. Donne hath a son at Windsor,
dwelling in a farm called Shawe, who is servant to the Master of the Rolls (Sir
Gilbert Gerard). Dolman & one Walle came of late to his Mistress' house.
Donne told this party that all these other parties did seek to save themselves for
religion's sake."—The *Reliquary*, vol. ii. p. 181.

On the day of his execution, Sept. 20th, Babington acknowledged and subscribed before the Privy Council the document (still preserved in the State Paper Office) in which he confessed his secret correspondence with the Scotch Queen. "This last is the alphabet by which only I have written with the Queene of Scotts, or receaved letters from her."

The wretched men were led to death according to the order and in the manner described in the ballad. Lincoln's Inn Fields was the place appointed for this melancholy spectacle, because they had been accustomed to meet there to concoct their conspiracy. Ballard suffered first, and after him Babington. He is said to have maintained a haughty demeanour on the scaffold, refusing either to kneel or to take off his hat. The curious reader may see the full details of his death in Howell's State Trials; but the account is too harrowing for transcription here. The cruel mode of execution which prevailed at this time, and lasted, we must remember, till the middle of the eighteenth century, caused the miserable prisoner to be almost embowelled and quartered alive. Strong as was the feeling against these misguided men, and sluggish as were all public demonstrations at this time, the sickening butchery met with such reprobation from the people that it was considered injudicious to attempt to repeat it on the following day, although we are told that the Queen was particularly anxious that the culprits should pay their penalty to the full.

Those who suffered on the 21st of September were simply hanged: the disgusting accessories of their punishment being omitted.

A touching letter was written by poor Babington, just before he suffered. A copy of it is preserved among the Ashmolean MSS. (Ash. MS. 781, leaf 73.) "The Coppie of Anthony Babington's let^r written to Queene Eliza: being in Prison for high treason committed against her Matie." I here add it from the *Reliquary*, vol. i. p. 3:

"Most gratious Souvraigne, yf either bitter teares, a pensive contrite harte, ore any dutyfull sight of the wretched Synner might work any pitty in your royall brest, I would wringe out of my drayned eyes as much bloode as in bemoaninge my drery tragedye shold lamentably bewayll my faulte, & somewhat (no dought) move you to compassion, but synnce there is no proportione betwixte the qualitye of my crimes and any human commiseration, Showe sweet Queene, some mirakle on a wretch that lyethe prostrate in yr prison, most grivously bewaylinge his offence, and imploringe such comforte at your anoynted hande as my poore wives misfortunes doth begge, my childe innocente doth crave, my gyltless family doth wishe, and my heynous trecheryo dothe leaste deserve, So shall your divine mersy make your glorye shyne as far above all princes, as my most horrible practices are more detestable amongst your beste subjectes, whom lovinglye and happiclye to governe,

"I humbly beseche the mercye Master himself to grante for his sweet Sonnes sake, Iesus Christe.

"Yor maties moste unfortunate, bicause most disloyall subiecte,

"Anthonyc Babington." [1]

---

[1] I extract the following from the *Reliquary*, vol. i. pp. 52–53:—"Stowe, in his 'Summarie of the Chronicles of England' in 1604, speaking of the execution, says: 'On the 15th September other 7 were likewise arraigned, who pleaded not guiltie, were found guilty by Iury, and had judgement. These traytors, 14 in number, were executed in Lincoln's Inne-fields, on a stage or scaffold of timber, strongly made for that purpose; even in the place where they had used to meete, & to conferre of their trayterous practices, there were they hanged, bowelled, and quartered, 7 of them on the 20 of Sep. to wit—J. Ballard, priest; A. Babyngton, Esquire; J. Savadge, Gent.; R. Barnwell, Gen.; Chidiake Tichborn, Esquire; Charles Tilney, Esquire; E. Avington, Esquire. The other 7 were likewise executed on the 21 of September, to wit—T. Salisbury, Esquire; Henrie Dunne, Gent.; Edward Jones, Esquire; I. Traverse, Gent.; I. Charnocke, Gent.; R. Gage, Gen.; Ierome Bellamie, Gent.;' etc.

"In a very rare black-letter tract, 'The Censure of a Loyall Subiect upon certaine noted Speach & behauiours of those fourteene notable Traitors, at the place of their executions, the xx. & xxi. of September, last past,' printed in 1587, in the possession of the Editor, the following account of the execution occurs:—   *   *   *

'Wilk. Next unto this priest, Anthony Babbington was made ready to the Gallowes, and in euery point was handled like unto Ballard.

'West. Little may be the mone, bad was the best; but what observed you in his end?

'Wilk. A signe of his former pride, for whereas the rest, through the cogitation of death, were exercised in praier upon their knees, and bare headed, he whose tourne was next, stode on his feete, with his hat on his head, as if he had been but a beholder of the execution: concerning his religion, he died a papist. His treasons were so odious, as the sting of conscience perswaded him to 'acknowledge himselfe to be a most grievous trespasser against God & the Queen's Majesty.   *   *   *

'Wilk. Next unto Babington, Sauadge was made ready for the execution.'"

Among a curious list of his books and other chattels, given by Mr. Purton Cooper in the "Reliquary," we find many Roman Catholic works of devotion, which were found hidden under a pile of wood. A handsome clock was appropriated by the Queen, who seized on all his estates, except those which were settled, and conferred them upon Sir Walter Raleigh. Of Dethick, the former seat of Babington, nothing at present remains: "all is open field," but we find the name of the family still lingering in "Babington lane" at Derby.

The history of another of the conspirators presents such touching passages that we make a few extracts from it. Chidiock Tichbourne (called Tushbourne in the indictment) seems to have been a young man of handsome fortune and singular promise. He had been unhappily seduced into the conspiracy from his friendship with Babington, no doubt hardly realizing to what extremities the matter would drift. I have already quoted an interesting extract from his address to the spectators while on the scaffold. I will close this short notice with the letter of Tichbourne to his wife, written the night before his execution, and the pathetic verses which he composed on his own most melancholy fate. They were published in the *Reliquiæ Wottonianæ*, but perhaps have obtained more ample notice from their introduction into Isaac Disraeli's Curiosities of Literature.[1]

"A letter written by Chidiock Tichbourne the night before he suffered death, unto his wife, dated anno 1586.

"To the most loving wife alive; I commend me unto her, and desire God to bless her with all happiness; let her pray for her dead husband, and be of good comforte, for I hope in Jesus Christ this morning to see the face of my Maker and Redeemer in the most joyful throne of his glorious kingdome. Commend me to all my friends, and desire them to pray for me, and in all charitie to pardon me, if I have offended them. Commend me to my six sisters, poore desolate soules, advise them to serve God, for without him no goodness is to be expected: were it possible, my little sister Bubb, the darling of my race, might be bred by

---

[1] Disraeli tells us that he discovered them among the Harleian MSS. (36, 50). His account of the conspiracy is pleasantly written. See Curiosities of Literature, vol. ii. p. 171, ed. 1859.

her, God would rewarde her; but I do her wrong I confesse, that hath by my desolate negligence too little for herselfe, to add a further charge unto her. Deere wife, forgive me that have by these means so much impoverished her fortunes; patience and pardon, good wife, I crave—make of these our necessities a virtue, and lay no further burthen on my neck than hath already been. There be certain debts that I owe, and because I knowe not the order of the lawe, pitcous it hath taken from me all, forfeited by my course of offence to her majestie. I cannot advise thee to benefit me herein, but if there fall out, wherewithal, let them be discharged for God's sake. I will not that you trouble yourselfe with the performance of these matters, my own heart, but make it knowne to my uncles, and desire them, for the honour of God, and ease of their souls, to take care of them as they may, and especially care of my sisters bringing up; the burden is now laid on them. Now, sweetcheek, what is left to bestow on thee, a small joynture, a small recompense for thy deservinge, these legacies following to be thine owne. God of his infinite goodness give thee grace alwaies to remain his true and faithful servant, that through the merits of his bitter and blessed passion thou maist become in good time of his kingdom with all the blessed women in heaven. May the Holy Ghost comfort thee with all necessaries for the wealth of thy soul in the world to come, where, until it shall please Almighty God I meete thee, farewell lovinge wife, farewell the dearest to me on all the earth, farewell!

" By the hand from the heart of thy most faithful lovinge husband,
" Chideock Tichebourne."

" Verses

Made by Chidiock Ticheborne of himself in the Tower, the night before he suffered death, who was executed in Lincoln's Inn Fields for treason, 1586.

> " My prime of youth is but a frost of cares,
> My feast of joy is but a dish of pain,
> My crop of corn is but a field of tares,
> And all my goods is but vain hope of gain :
> The day is fled, and yet I saw no sun ;
> And now I live, and now my life is done !
>
> " My spring is past, and yet it hath not sprung ;
> The fruit is dead, and yet the leaves are green ;
> My youth is past, and yet I am but young ;
> I saw the world, and yet I was not seen :
> My thread is cut, and yet it is not spun ;
> And now I live, and now my life is done !
>
> " I sought for death, and found it in the wombe ;
> I lookt for life, and yet it was a shade ;
> I trode the ground, and knew it was my tomb ;
> And now I die, and now I am but made :
> The glass is full, and yet my glass is run ;
> And now I live, and now my life is done ! "[1]

---

[1] Many MSS. exist of this interesting and undoubtedly genuine composition, and besides being printed in the *Reliquiæ Wottonianæ* and by Disraeli, it also appears in Ritson's *Bibliographia Poetica*, page 361. Dr. Hannah, in his " Courtly Poets," 1870, has given us a reply from a MS. in the possession of Mr J. P. Collier, beginning, " Thy flower of youth is with a north wind blasted"—a piece of no value whatsoever.

The poem of Williams, pp. 9-22, it must be confessed, is not of any great poetical merit. It has, however, the freshness of a contemporaneous production, and adds a few facts to our knowledge of Babington's early life. Thus there is something very quaint about little Anthony nearly getting hanged with the chain of the good "Foliambe" (p. 11). Williams is evidently disposed to consider it prophetic of his subsequent fate.

> "But [I] was not suffred there longe to hange,
>   but was nere strangled or I was taken downe."

His gay roystering life in London has been already mentioned, and is duly commented on in the ballad, perhaps with pious exaggeration. If, however, these young gallants frequented the "Curtayne," they were sometimes to be seen at Paul's Cross (p. 13):

> "Yett to the sermons wee woulde often resorte,"

although Williams adds that they only went there in ridicule of religion.

The circumstances of the arrest of Babington are very minutely narrated in verses 39, 40: we see him walking about, accompanied by his serving-man, in the guise of an ostler. One of the watch—a weaver by trade—is on the look-out for him, and is not to be put off by the affected nonchalance of Anthony:

> "We walked throughe the pastures as men without feare."

The ballad represents him as lamenting that he should have drawn his poor friend Tichborne into the conspiracy (p. 21):

> "But o, Tuchborne, Tuchborne! thou makest me full woe!
>   For I was the firste that allurde thee to the same,
>   Thie witts beinge yonge, likewaye I did frame;
>   Thou beinge well Inelinde, throughe me didst consente
>   To conceale the thinge that made vs all repente."

Williams's poem has been previously printed in the *Reliquary*.

An interesting ballad on the subject of Babington's Conspiracy is published by Mr. Payne Collier in his Book of Roxburghe

Ballads (1847), by Thomas Nelson, from which we extract the following lines :—

> "This proude and haughtie Babington, in hope to gaine renowne,
> Did stirre up many wilfull men, in many a shire and towne,
> To ayde him in this devilish act, and for to take in hand
> The spoyle of our renowmed Prince, and people of this land,
> Who did conclude with bloudie blade a slaughter to commit
> Upon her Counsell, as they should within Star Chamber sit,
> Which is a place whereas the Lords, and those of that degree,
> Yeelde justice unto every man that crave it on his knee."

Compare also—

> "And Babington, that cursed wretch, what did bewitch thy minde?
> That to thy Prince and country deere thou shouldst be so vnkinde?
> Thou hopedst (belike) for better hap than euer traitor had,
> But now thou hast thy due desert, which maks our harts ful glad."

—"A Dutiful Invective Against the moste heynous Treasons of Ballard and Babington : with other their adherents, latelie executed. G. W. Kempe, 1587."

Mr. Cooper also cites a ballad by Thomas Deloney, edited by Mr. J. P. Collier, for the Percy Society, in 1840 (Old Ballads, p. 104).

The lines on Babington are :

> "Next Babington, that caitiffe vilde,
> Was hanged for his hier;
> His carcase likewise quartered,
> And hart cast in the fire."

And of those executed on the 21st, he makes Donne and Jones both complain of Babington.

> "The first of them was Salsburie,
> And next to him was Duu,
> Who did complaine most earnestly
> Of proud yong Babington.
>
> "Both Lords and Knights of hye renowne
> He ment for to displace,
> And likewise all the towers and townes
> And cities for to raze :
>
> "So likewise Iones did much complaine
> Of his detested pride,
> And shewed how lewdly he did live
> Before the time he died."

Richard Jones had been licensed on the 27th August to print a Ballad authorized by the Archbishop of Canterbury, "beinge a joyfull songe made by a citizen of London in the behalfe of all Her Maties subjectes touchinge the Ioye for the taking of the Traytors."—Registers of the Stationers' Company, vol. ii. p. 214, but no copy is known to be extant.

THE GUNPOWDER PLOT.

It is well known that the Roman Catholics, who had undergone many cruel persecutions during the reign of Elizabeth, looked forward with hope to her successor; but James, underneath his preposterous pedantry and coarse buffooneries, concealed no little astuteness and all the mendacity of a true Stuart. Before his accession Percy, who afterwards figured in the Gunpowder Plot, was sent by the English Catholics to ascertain what kind of treatment he proposed to extend to them, and received assurances from James that he would tolerate the Mass, "albeit in a corner." Hopes also had been built on the fact that the mother of the new sovereign had been so conspicuous in her adherence to the old worship.[1]

All these expectations were, however, doomed to be dashed to the ground. The inclinations of the new King were clearly shown in his treatment of a Mr. Pound, of Cheshire, who, having ventured to petition against the persecutions to which his co-religionists were subjected, was summoned before the Star Chamber, imprisoned in the Fleet, and fined £1000. A statute was also passed in 1604, requiring Jesuits and Seminary priests to quit the realm by a certain day.

The persecutions undergone by Sir Thomas Tresham, the father of Francis Tresham, one of the conspirators, will be mentioned

---

[1] Throughout this notice I have made considerable use of the interesting facts accumulated by Mr. Jardine in the account given in his Criminal Trials.

afterwards. Edward Rookwood, cousin of Ambrose, also implicated, of Euston Hall, in Suffolk, was committed to prison for "obstinate papistry," and after being reduced to beggary died in gaol. In the parish register of St. James, at Bury St. Edmunds, we have the following curt and melancholy entry: "Mr. Rookwood, from the jail, buried June 4th, 1598." The troops of menial lords and parasitic beggars which had accompanied James from Scotland were deeply interested in discovering any offending Romanists, and acquiring their forfeited estates.

Finding, therefore, their condition rapidly becoming worse, the recusants, as they were called, formed the desperate plot which has become so famous in English history, but is not without its parallel in the annals of other countries, instances having occurred at Stockholm, Lübeck, and Antwerp.[1] The original conspirators—seven in number—were all, as Fawkes said subsequently, "gentlemen of name and blood; and not any were employed in or about this action (no, not so much as in digging and in mining) that was not a gentleman." The chief contriver was Catesby, a man of ancient family long settled at Ashby St. Ledgers, in Northamptonshire, and a descendant of the favourite of Richard III., who fell with his master at Bosworth. There in the quiet village church may be seen the graves and monumental brasses of many of the Catesbys, but not of him who was destined to throw so dark a shade over the family name for all time. The old seat—or what remains of it—has long since passed into the hands of strangers; but the villagers still affect to show the room in which the conspiracy is alleged to have been concocted, grey with age and haunted with the traditions of a crime which has taken so deep a hold of the popular mind.[2]

---

[1] It is probable also that the fate of Darnley may have given them a suggestion.

[2] A history of the Catesby family will be found in Baker's "Northamptonshire" —a very valuable work of its kind. He traces them back to Randle, Earl of Chester, temp. Henry I. and Stephen. The manor of Ashby St. Ledgers passed by marriage to John Catesby, of Ladbrook, in Warwickshire, in 1374, and his descendant was the Sir William Catesby of Richard the Third's time—the "cat" of the doggrel verse, which cost its fabricator his head. His brass may be seen

Catesby gained over Winter, a gentleman of Worcestershire, who had been long a soldier in the Low Countries, and Winter initiated Fawkes, son of Edward Fawkes, a notary of York. This tremendous fanatic, who has long become the conventional stage-ruffian of the whole piece, seems to have been born a Protestant; but his father died in 1578, when he was yet a child, leaving a large family, and his mother, Edith Fawkes, after a widowhood of three years, married one Denis Baynbridge, a Papist, embracing his religion, in which she also caused her children to be educated. Thus young Guy grew up a confirmed Roman Catholic. Inheriting but a small property from his father, he soon dissipated it, and turned his attention to the great struggle then going on between Spain and the revolted Netherlands. As a soldier of fortune, he took service under the Archduke Albert, and, among other achievements, was present at the taking of Calais by the Archduke in 1598. He is described by Father Greenway as a man of great piety, of exemplary temperance, of mild and cheerful demeanour, an enemy of broils and disputes, a faithful friend, and remarkable for his scrupulous observance of all religious duties. He also seems to have been very popular among his co-religionists, for we are told by the same authority that his company was much sought by all those in the Archduke's camp who were most distinguished for nobility and virtue. The desperate fanaticism of the man may be plainly seen in his invariably choosing the most perilous posts, and the

---

in Ashby Church. His son, George Catesby, in 1425, obtained a reversal of his father's attainder and the restitution of his lands. Sir William Catesby, a great-grandson of this George, was on the 15th Nov. 1581, cited before the Court of Star Chamber, with Lord Vaux, of Harrowden, and Sir Thomas Tresham, as elsewhere mentioned. Among the Harleian MSS. is a detailed account of this trial, supposed to be drawn up by Sir Thomas Tresham himself. Robert Catesby, son of Sir William, was the projector of the Gunpowder Plot. I have twice visited this interesting place, under the guidance of a lady fully aware of the glories of her native county, both historical and intellectual—of Naseby, Ashby, Rushton, Fotheringay, and other localities,—and last, but by no means least, of "glorious John," whose name seems to close the roll of Northampton celebrities as with a diapason.

almost ferocious hatred he exhibited to Protestantism. When dragged, smeared with powder and coal-dust, into the presence of James, his manner was unabashed and insolent. "He is no more dismayed," wrote Cecil, "than if he were taken for a poor robbery on the highway." His answer to the King is too well known to need quoting here. The latter, with his own hand, carefully traced out the gradual degrees of torture to which he was to be subjected, as he had done in the case of the unfortunate Scotch quack, Cunningham.[1] We can picture to ourselves how efficacious the royal recipe must have been, by the feeble disjointed signature of the miserable patient.

In a lonely field near St. Clement's Inn, Catesby first revealed under an oath of secresy his desperate plot. An additional oath was afterwards administered to all the conspirators by a Jesuit missionary, Father Gerard, who was perhaps hardly fully aware of what they purposed. They were soon afterwards joined by Winter's brother, the two Wrights, Sir Everard Digby, and others, and lastly by one Francis Tresham, the son of Sir Thomas Tresham, of an old Northamptonshire family at Rushton, who had been frequently in trouble for harbouring recusants, and had been cited on the 15th of November, 1581, before the Star Chamber, with Lord Vaux, of Harrowden, for sheltering Jesuits in his house, and being present at the celebration of mass.

The circumstances of their obtaining an unoccupied building next to the Parliament House: then subsequently finding that they could hire a cellar immediately under it: and the arrest of Fawkes in consequence of the mysterious letter which had been received by Lord Mounteagle: are all well-known matters of history. On the subject of this letter—of which Williams speaks (p. 50)—

"One small letter hathe barde this strife"

---

[1] "Ye maye thinke of this, for it is like to be the laboure of such a desperate fellow as this is; if he will not other wayes confesse, the gentler tortours are to be first usid unto him, *et sic per gradus ad ima tenditur;* and so God speede youre goode worke.—James R."

—there remains still great obscurity. The probability is that Tresham, of whose fidelity there had been doubts from the first, had long before revealed the conspiracy, which was allowed to proceed till it had become fairly ripened. The letter was then written, merely as a blind, and an opportunity was given the British Solomon of making an attitude out of his supposed sagacity. It is not a little curious that Lord Mounteagle himself was one of the persons accused of complicity by Winter in his examination before the Council, and in a State Paper still extant, his name can be read as that of a person implicated, although considerable pains have been taken to obliterate it. It had been arranged that Fawkes was to fire the mine, and as quickly as he could after the catastrophe embark on board a vessel for Flanders. Meanwhile Sir Everard Digby—a hot-headed young man of twenty-four, who had made lavish promises of money to assist the conspiracy—was to assemble a number of Roman Catholic gentlemen at Dunchurch, as if to hunt on Dunsmoor Heath; and as soon as intelligence arrived that King James and his ministers had been blown to the four winds, they were to send a party to seize the Princess Elizabeth. She was at once to be proclaimed Queen, with a regent during her minority, if the Prince of Wales or Duke of York, afterwards Charles I., did not fall into their clutches. Many attempts had been previously made by Tresham to induce Catesby to abandon the plot, and leave the country. The conspirators soon discovered that the letter had been shown to the King, but still followed up their plans with the wildest impetuosity, even though the cellar was visited as if by accident by the Lord Chamberlain and Lord Mounteagle. They saw Fawkes keeping guard, and a great store of coals and wood heaped up. Making a few casual remarks, and noting the ferocious appearance of the man whom they found in the vault, they afterwards retired. Fawkes was not without suspicions of this visit, but still clung to his perilous position, having, as he declared, made up his mind to blow the whole place up on the faintest signal of alarm. About midnight, however, on the eve of the 5th of November, Sir Thomas Knevett, a magistrate, with a party of soldiers, surrounded the vault. Fawkes was arrested instantaneously, before he could execute his desperate plan. He was booted and dressed for a journey. A lantern was discovered in the corner, which is now preserved among the curiosities of the Bodleian Library. Everywhere were to be found the implements of combustion; among others, thirty-six barrels of gunpowder in casks, concealed under billets of wood. The conspirator did not disguise his attempt. He only remarked coolly to Sir Thomas, that if he had had a chance he would have blown him up together with all the premises. The discovery of the plot threw all the conspirators into the greatest consternation. Five of them, including Catesby himself, rode post haste to Ashby. Percy and John Wright even cast off their cloaks and threw them into the hedge, to increase their speed. As soon as the direct objects of the conspirators became known, many of the Roman Catholic gentlemen deserted the cause. Being hotly pursued by the sheriff of Worcestershire and the *posse comitatus* of the county, the conspirators resolved to make a last stand at Holbeach. Here an engagement took place with the authorities. Thomas Winter was hit in the arm by a cross-bow, and disabled. Two more shots mortally wounded both the Wrights; and Catesby and Percy, standing back to back, were pierced by two bullets from one musket, belonging to John Streete, one of the sheriff's men, who in consequence had a pension given him. Catesby feebly crawled to one of the sacred images in the house, clasped it, and instantly expired. Percy died of his wounds on the following day.

Sir Everard Digby was soon after overtaken near Dudley, and captured; and Robert Winter and Stephen Littleton were taken in concealment at Hagley, after having endured many privations, being for some time hidden in a barley-mow.

Tresham was not arrested till the 12th of November. His connexion with the plot has always been a mystery, which will never perhaps be satisfactorily cleared up. Any disagreeable revelations which he may have made were effectually checked by the silence of the grave. He was found dead in the Tower on the 23rd of December. The account of his end is thus given by Sir William Waad, the Lieutenant, in a letter to the Earl of Salisbury: "He died this night, about two of the o'clock after midnight, with very great pain ; for though his spirits were much spent and his body dead, he lay above two hours in departing." There seems, however, some reason to doubt whether after all this unhappy man met with a violent end. It is certain that his wife and servant were constantly with him. It must, however, have been important to many that he especially should be removed.

I have already alluded to the tortures which Fawkes had undergone by the direct recommendation of James himself, although there is very little doubt that the practice was a complete infringement of the law. It only remains to allude briefly to the fate of the prisoners. Some of the more fortunate had died sword in hand, fighting with the ferocity of madmen. Eight were doomed to perish under the knife of the executioner, with all the concomitant horrors which then rendered agonizing the punishment of treason. Sir Everard Digby, Robert Winter, John Grant, and Thomas Bates—the latter only engaged in the conspiracy in a menial capacity—were executed on a scaffold erected at the western end of St. Paul's Churchyard. The unhappy Sir Everard met his fate with firmness, but the deadly pallor of his face did not escape the notice of the bystanders. At the conclusion of his trial he had told his judges that if he could carry their forgiveness with him to the gallows, he should be able to meet his terrible fate more cheerfully. On the following day, being Friday, Thomas Winter, Ambrose Rookwood, Robert Keyes, and Guy or Guido Fawkes, underwent the same fate on a scaffold over against the Parliament House. Nothing, however, could break the iron spirit of Fawkes. He was executed last of all—probably last by a refinement of cruelty, that he might, to use the words of the French Revolutionists, drink long of death. He was so weak with torture and illness that he could hardly walk up the steps of the scaffold. There he muttered a few words, crossed himself, and flung himself defiantly from the ladder.[1]

Thus ended this terrible conspiracy, which sent a thrill of horror throughout the whole country, and is thus alluded to in a quaint treatise published in 1606, entitled "A comparative Discourse of the Bodies natural and politique." "The verie relating or mentioning thereof dawnteth my hart with horror, even shaking the verie pen in my hand, whilst I think what a shake, what a blast, or what a storme (as they termed it), they ment so suddenly to have raised for the blowing up, shivering into pieces, and whirling about of those honourable, anointed and sacred bodies, which the Lord would not have to be so much as touched."[2]

Oldcorne and Garnett,—the superior of the order of the Jesuits, then recently introduced into England,—who were supposed to be deeply implicated in the conspiracy, were captured at Hendlip Hall, near Worcester, a quaint mansion, full of

> " Rich windows that exclude the light,
> And passages that lead to nothing,"

—which, with its many nooks and secret chambers, seemed, it has been said, to have been constructed to harbour recusants. It required many days to discover their actual lurking place, as

---

[1] For an account of the conduct of Fawkes, see a pamphlet entitled, "Gunpowder Plot: Arraingement and Execution of the late Traytors, the 27th January last past." This exceedingly rare production is quoted in *Notes and Queries*, 5th series, ii. p. 361 : "Last of all came the great Devil of all, Fawkes, alias Johnson, who should have put fire to the powder. His body being weak with torture and sickness, he was scarce able to go up the ladder, but with much ado, by the help of the hangman, went high enough to break his neck with the fall: who made no long speech, but, after a sort, seeming to be sorry for his offence, asked a kind of forgiveness of the King and the State for his bloody intent, and with his crosses and idle ceremonies, made his end upon the gallows and the block, to the great joy of the beholders, that the land was ended of so wicked a villany."

[2] Quoted by Jardine, "Criminal Trials."

they had been concealed in a curious recess, the exterior of which was made to resemble part of a chimney. Here they had been fed for some time by means of soup and other liquids administered through a quill. Owen, the servant of Garnett, who was committed to prison with him, having already undergone the torture, and expecting forthwith to undergo it again, ripped himself up with a small dinner-knife allowed him for his meat.

The character of Garnett has been drawn very severely by Mr. Hepworth Dixon in his amusing book, "Her Majesty's Tower." He accuses the Jesuits of drunkenness and loose living, but it appears difficult as we rake among these popular scandals to get at the exact truth. There is certainly no direct evidence on the point, nor are we sure of any safe inferences from the fact that, as a Jesuit, his life was "a daily lie," as the author terms it. He was brought before Coke, who exhibited the usual spectacle of fulsome adulation of James and childish pedantry. He again asserted that the King in the whole matter of the Gunpowder Plot had been directed by a miracle. "God put it into His Majesty's head to prorogue the Parliament; and, further, to open and enlighten his understanding out of a mystical and dark letter, like an angel of God, to point to the cellar and command that it be searched; so that it was discovered thus miraculously but even a few hours before the design should have been executed." The insufferable pedant then wound up with a series of puns, ingenious alliterations, and all the euphuistic arts of which he was so great a master.

Nothing, however, could be proved against the prisoner, except that he had been guilty of misprision of treason, *i.e.* had not revealed the conspiracy when it had been communicated to him in confession. So brutally did Coke interrupt the unhappy man, that James, who was himself a witness of the trial, declared that the Jesuit had not had fair play. He was, however, found guilty; but so ill-satisfied was the court with the evidence against him, that a trap was laid to draw from his own mouth some admissions which would be sufficient to condemn him. Garnett and Oldcorne were allowed to associate in prison; and a certain Forsett, and Lockerson, Lord Salisbury's secretary, were placed in ambush to hear their conversation. An account of this was published in a curious tract, called, "The Interlocution between Garnet and Hall, the Jesuit, in prison, overheard by two worthy Gentlemen that were in insidiis."[1] It was chiefly on the evidence of these spies that the unfortunate Jesuit was led to the scaffold. The 1st of May had been originally fixed for his execution. "It was looked yesterday," says Sir D. Carleton, in a letter in the State Paper Office, dated 2nd of May, 1606, "that Garnet should have *come a-maying* to the gallows, which was set up for him in St. Paul's Churchyard on Wednesday, but upon better advice his execution is put off till to-morrow, for fear of disorder among prentices and others in a day of such misrule. The news of his death was sent to him upon Monday by Dr. Abbott, which he could hardly be persuaded to believe, having conceived great hope of grace by some good words and promises he said were made him, and by the Spanish ambassador's mediation, who he thought would have spoken to the King for him." On the 3rd of May, however, Garnett was drawn on a hurdle to the place of execution. By the express command of the King he remained hanging on the gallows till quite dead. Many miracles were reported to have occurred at his death. At Hendlip, where he was apprehended, an entirely new species of grass grew up, and was neither trodden by passengers nor nibbled by cattle. A spring of oil burst out on the place of his execution. An ear of straw, which had been put in a basket with the Jesuit's mangled and bleeding quarters, was found to have his likeness upon it, and became an object of Roman Catholic veneration.

The effect of the Gunpowder Plot upon the position of the recusants in England may be easily imagined. In the next Parliament that met (Jan. 21, 1606), an Act was passed

---

[1] Quoted by Jardine, "Criminal Trials."

requiring them to take the sacrament once a year at least; their absence from church was punishable by heavy fines; an oath of allegiance, renouncing the Pope's authority in the most offensive terms, was imposed; persons harbouring recusants, or keeping servants who did not attend church, were to forfeit £10 per month. Another statute banished all recusants from court, and declared them incapable of holding any public office—of being executors, or guardians, or practising any of the liberal professions.

Such was the condition of the Roman Catholics in the reign of James I., and in this state they remained till his successor, wanting money and afraid to call a parliament, was willing to allow them to compound for their recusancy.

It remains for me in conclusion to say a few words about Williams's ballad. I am afraid it cannot be asserted either to possess much literary merit or to furnish us with any new and curious facts. In the true spirit of the age, with its puns and anagrams, he treats us to a variety of quibbles on the names of the conspirators.

> "Bates might in this poynte haue bated an ace." (p. 46.)
> "Nexte, Catesbye: thou didst playe the wilye catt." (p. 44.)

He tells us that when Fawkes—or Guido Vaux, as he calls him—was apprehended, many reliques were found upon him.

> "And when hee was tane, the rellicks weare founde,
> As a hayric shurte, with other popishe trashe." (p. 49.)

His loyalty is of an oppressive kind, and such as would satisfy the requirements of the most enthusiastic gold-stick. He laments that the "Lord's anointed" was so near being removed from the earth;—

> "For greate is the maiestie of Roiall kinges,
>   that here vppon earthe gods vicegerents bee!
> There lookes to trechorye are fearfull stinges;
>   There eyes, like Argus, to beholde and see,
>   even to there myndes that good subiects bee.
>   From those that seke maiestie to betraye,
>   Hee treason can fynde, and the same bewraye." (p. 55.)

He also re-echoes the tedious commonplaces about the discovery of the letter by the British Solomon. We must remember, however, that Williams,—a fact which Mr. Furnivall has also noticed,—in these grovelling adulations, was sinning in excellent company. There is something very choice about the following anecdote related in the Life of Waller: "That Parliament[1] being some time after dissolved, on the day of its dissolution, he (Waller), out of curiosity or respect, went to see the King at dinner, with whom were Dr. Andrews, Bishop of Winchester, and Dr. Neal, Bishop of Durham, standing behind His Majesty's Chair. There happened something very extraordinary in the Conversation those Prelates had with the King, on which Mr. Waller did often reflect. His Majesty asked the Bishops, 'My Lords, cannot I take my subjects' money when I want it, without all this formality in Parliament?' The Bishop of Durham readily answered, 'God forbid, Sir, but you should, you are the breath of our nostrils.' Whereupon the King turned, and said to the Bishop of Winchester, 'Well, my Lord, what say you?' 'Sir,' replied the Bishop, 'I have no skill to judge of parliamentary cases.' The King answered, 'No Put-offs, my Lord, answer me presently.' 'Then, Sir,' said he, 'I think it's lawful for you to take my Brother Neal's money, for he offers it.'"

Williams had previously tried to force himself upon royal notice : "And one of them I Did presente to your famouse Sonne, Prince Henrie, when your maiestie was in your progresse in Nottingham-shere, at the Howse of one Sir Iohn Byron, a knight, that Dwelleth in the forrest of mansfilde. *But I never harde anye awnswer of it.*" (p. 39.) This occurrence must have taken place either in 1612 or in 1614—probably the former year. Nicholls, in his "Progresses, etc., of James the First" (vol. ii. pp. 460, 461) tells us, "On the 14th of August, [1612], the King left Rufford, but not Sherwood Forest. He took up his lodging at Sir John Byron's, Newstead Abbey, about ten miles

---

[1] The last Parliament of James I. See "Life of Waller," p. v. (ed. 1722).

distant across the Forest, and for three days longer explored the haunts of Robin Hood and his merry men all." This Sir John Byron—the ancestor of the poet, who has made the name for ever celebrated—entertained James in one of his progresses at Newstead Abbey. He had previously been knighted at Worksop, in 1603, when he met the King. At this time the mansion was celebrated for its splendour, and the park for its rural beauties ; but the latter was afterwards divided into farms, and the whole property had suffered great deterioration before it came into the hands of the noble poet. The estate, which originally belonged to some Black Canons, was granted at the Dissolution of the Abbeys to the Sir John Byron then living, who was the Lieutenant of Sherwood Forest. Since the poet's time it has changed hands more than once. It has formed the subject of one of the most delightful papers of Washington Irving.[1]

As regards Richard Williams, the author of the first three poems, no information which can be relied upon seems forthcoming. The name, to begin with, is a very common one. There are no published productions by an author so styled in any catalogues of seventeenth century literature. In the preface to "The Complaynte of Anthonye Babington " he speaks of his "old eyes," and tells us that the pieces on Babington and the Gunpowder Plot were written just after the occurrence of these events. A writer in the *Athenæum* (May 22, 1869) doubts these two last statements, and considers that the poem on Essex was written after the arrival of James I. in London. This opinion seems especially borne out by the 54th and 55th verses :

---

[1] A good description of Sherwood Forest, printed by Major Rooke for private circulation, was copied in Harrod's "History of Mansfield," pp. 18 *et seq*. At the time of King James's visit it had been recently surveyed; and then contained,—arable land, 44,839 acres ; woods, 9,486 ; waste, 35,080 ; Clipstone Park, 1,583 ; Beskwood Park, 3,672 ; Bulwell Park, 326 ; Nottingham Park, 129 ; total, 95,117 acres.

> "And daylie more his fame is raysde,
> Synce our kinge came to swaye this lande.
>
> .   .   .   .
>
> Oure kinge dothe countenance his frends,
> Suche as in life tyme helde hym dere;
> On them Riche Honors daylie spends,
> for love to them and this greate peere;
> His Sonne attendante on the prince,
> Which envyes spite maye well convyuce." (pp. 34, 34.)

In the Calendar of State Papers for reigns of Elizabeth and James I. we find here and there a Richard Williams, but no one that can be satisfactorily identified with our author. There is a man of the name who appears to have acted as a kind of general agent and steward to Lord Cobham; but since that nobleman was one of the most inveterate enemies of Essex, it is hardly probable that a retainer would be found singing the praises of the ruined Earl.

In 1624 (March 30) we find a grant to Rich. Williams of a lease of lands in the counties of York, Northumberland, Cumberland, Huntingdon, and Cambridge, value £49 16s. 10d., at request of Robert May of the bedchamber, and in consideration of his faithful service. Perhaps this may be the man, and if so, it is probable that it is all we shall ever discover concerning him. At such a period of history men of humble station and poor ability followed the fate of the common herd of humanity: they "died and made no sign."

In 1627 (reign of Charles I.) a Richard Williams is recorded as presenting a petition for increase of pay. Perhaps this may have been our author, grown grey in service about the Court.

W. R. MORFILL.

A Poore Mans Pittance.

THE BOOKE TO YOUR MAIESTIE.

Althoughe I bee not cladd in golde,
Nor withe a cover gorgeouse fyne,
Perhaps in mee you maye beholde
Thinges that to vertue doe Incline,
Passinge some glittringe giftes *that* shyne.

If mee to reade youle take the payne,
Your grace—I hope—shall reape *the* gayne.

2

This booke contaynes three severall subiects, as appeers in my peticion to your Roiall maiestie.

A POORE MANS PITTANCE,

Contayninge three severall subiects:—

1. The firste, the fall and complaynte of Anthonie Babington, whoe, with others, weare executed for highe treason in the feildes nere lyncolns Inne, in the yeare of our lorde 1586

2. The seconde contaynes the life and Deathe of Roberte, lorde Deverox, Earle of Essex, whoe was beheaded in the towre of london on ashwensdaye mornynge, Anno 1601

3. The laste, Intituled "acclamatio patrie," contayninge the horrib[l]e treason that weare pretended agaynste your Maiestie, to be donne on the parliament howse The seconde yeare of your Maiestis Raygne . . . . [1604]

[leaf 3.]

To the kinges moste Excellent Maiestie, with all other kinglie Titells and Dignities what soever, To whome *your* poore humble subiecte, Richarde Williams, wisheth healthe, longe life, and Manye happie years to Raygne over vs, to the glorye of god, and *your* maiesties comforte.

My Dreade and Roiall Soveraygne,

This Anthonie Babington was borne at a mansion howse of his fathers, called Dethicke, in the Countie of Darbye, in the parrishe of Crietche ; whose father was a man of good accompte, and lived well and orderlie in his contrie, kepte a good howse, and releived the poore; But he was Inclined to papistrie, as the tymes then requyred; whoe had a brother that was a Doctor of Divinitie in Quene Maryes dayes, of whome some mention is made in this storye. This Authonye the Sonne was a yonge man, [leaf 3, back.] well featured, and of good proportion in all the lyniaments of his bodie ; of a moste pregnante fyne witt, and greate capacitie; had a reatchinge head, and a moste prowde aspiringe mynde; and by nature a papiste, where-in hee was borne and brought vpp ; where[as], if hee had bene trayned otherwise, he might haue proved a good member of the common wealthe, where nowe hee became a reproche and scandall to the same.

In whose course of life manye accidents hapned,

even from his birthe to his deathe, as appeares in
this his complaynte; wherein I haue followed the
methode of a booke Intituled " the mirror of maiestrates[1]," wherein everye man semes to complayne of
his owne mysfortunes: humblie besechinge your
royall maiestie to pardon all Defectes, aswell in my
writinge as in the basenes of the verse.   In the one,
I haue donne aswell as my learninge did serve me;
for the other, aswell as my olde eyes woulde permitt
mee, whiche I beseche your roiall maiestie to censure[2] withe clemencye, and I will trulie praye to the
almightie for the longe continuance of youre healthe
and happie estate, bothe to gods glorye and your
maiesties comforte,

Your poore Distressed subiecte,

Richarde Williams.

---

[1] A Myrrovre for Magistrates.   Wherein may be seen by example of other,
with howe greuous plages vices are punished: and howe frayle and vn-
stable worldly prosperitie is founde, even of those whom Fortune seemeth
most highly to fauour.   Imprinted at London in Flete-strete nero to Saynct
Dunstones Church by Thomas Marshe.   1559, 4to, 81 leaves, black letter.
(Other editions in 1563, 1571, etc. etc.)—*Hazlitt's Hand-Book.*

[2] judge, criticize; *not* blame.

5

The Complaynte of Anthonye Babington, [leaf 4.]

sometyme of lyncolnes Inne, Esquier, whoe, with others,
weare executed for highe treason In the feildes nere
lyncolns Inne, the xix[th] of September, Anno   . . 1586:

A Dreame or Induction.

Late, wearied withe my daylie toyle,
  to bedd my selfe I dreste,
Whereas[1] a slomber caught mee sone,
  yet coulde I take no reste;   4

But fallinge in a fearfull dreame,
  me thought there did appeare
One cladd in roabes more white then snowe,
  whose face did shyne moste clere,   8

Whose gorgeouse garments weare bedeckt
  withe moneths, dayes, and howres;
vppon his head hee likewise ware
  a crowne of fragrante flowres.   12

Celestiall signes did hym attende,
  and compaste hym like case[2];
The mone and starrs attendante weare
  vppon his princelie grace.   16

Whiche, when I veiwde with mortall eyes,
  I freighted was withe feare;
But hee, to comforte me, beganne,
  and spake as you shall heare :—   20

"Williams! shake of this sluggishe slepe!
  prepare to followe mee;
ffor strange thinges I haue to reveale,
  whiche I will showe to thee."   24

"O soveraygne god, I thee bespeke,   [leaf 4, back.]
  what god so ere thou bee,
Whiche doest not daigne in deitie[3]
  to showe thie selfe to mee.   28

"If symple I maye bee so bolde,
  of thee I fayne woulde knowe,
What god thou arte, what sacred wight,
  to me declare and showe!"   32

---

[1] Wherein.   [2] likewise.   [3] MS. dietie.

" I morpheus hight, ruler of night,
    thus poetts of mee doe fayne:
Arise," quothe hee, " and followe mee !
    I bidd thee once agayne.   36

" Reiecte all care; caste of all feare;
    to ludd's towne Ile thee bringe,
That is renowned throughe the wordle[1];
    there shalte thou vewe a thinge."   40

Wherewith I rowsed vpp my selfe,
    and quicklie was I dreste;
And vncouthe wayes I followed hym,
    and did but seldome reste.   44

At laste hee thus spake vnto mee,
    thatte[2] wearye shoulde appeare,
" Thie Iorneye drawes vnto an ende,
    wee shall anon bee there."   48

Thus as wee paste by dale and hill,
    appeares vnto oure vewe—
Withe brave prospecte,—a cittie fayre,
    whose cituation well I knewe.   52

So longe wee paste, till at the laste   [leaf 5.]
    to a famose bridge wee came,
Where olde Thameyse, with surges greate
    still beateth on the same.   56

It was aboute the howres of twelue,
    when chymes did swetelie ringe,
And nature then due reste did yeilde
    to everye livinge thinge;   60

And all was hushte in quyett sorte,
    the starrs did shyne moste clere,
When on a sodden (as mee thought,)
    a voyce soundes in myne eare,   64

Wherewith I sore affrighted was,
    my bodye gan with feare to quake;
Morpheus than to comforte me began,
    and theise wordes in effecte hee spake: 68

" Shake of all tymrose feare !" quothe hee,
    " amased so, whie doest thou stande ?
ffor this cause haue I brought thee here,
    to take theise thinges in hande.   72

---

         [1] world.   [2] MS. thacte.

Caste vpp thie head, lifte vpp thyne eyes !
  what doest thou there beholde ?"
Where suche a spectakle I did vewe,
  as made my harte full colde.   76

There might I perceive manye mens hedd*es*
  on toppes of poales to stande,
Whiche did to suche parsons belonge,
  as weare traytors to this lande.   80

ffourtene of them above the reste   [leaf 5, back.]
  in a higher degree weare placeste,[1]
Whiche morpheus sayde weare hedds of those
  ther[e] executed laste.   84

And one of them in highest degree
  Did stande in open vewe,
Where sounded suche a harrishe[2] voice
  as did my feares renewe :   88

" Good contrie man ! I doe thee praye,
  vouchsafe some paynes to take ;
And thats the cause I haue sente for thee,
  my tragedie to make.   92

" Thoughe thou symple and vnlearned bee,
  doe not refuse this payne ;
Wishe Gentelmen all, by me take heede,
  so good will thou shalte gayne   96

" of all suche as good subiects bee :
  for the reste, take thou no care ;
But penne my tragedie in suche sorte
  as memorye shall to thee declare ;   100

" And tell them, thoughe I weare no pere,
  I presumed with the beste ;
Therefore as worthie to be harde
  as anye of the reste.   104

" Iacke cade, and Iacke strawe, they bothe
  haue tolde there ruthles tale ;
Cardinall wolsey and shores wife
  Haue rewde there bitter bale ;   108

---

[1] Pronounce *plast :* see p. 30, l. 188, note (²).   [2] harsh.

" And late, fayre rosamonde hathe complaynde, [leaf 6.]
  that longe synce was forgott;
Wherefore, to presse amongst the presse,
  I truste twilbe my lott.   112

" My worshipfull frends, they still doe live
  in credditt, love and fame :
The worse my happe, I shoulde begynne
  my kynne or stocke to shame !   116

" But thou, my frende, pleade thou my cause !
  at large, penne downe my case,
That I to all example maye bee,
  that fall for wante of grace."   120

Whereto I fayne woulde haue replide,
  myne Ignorance to excuse,
But morpheus wilde me scilence kepe,
  no talke hee wishte me vse.   124

" Come on," quothe hee, " lett vs bee gone,
  the tyme for anye man dothe not staye."
So in haste I wente, and home I came,
  I knowe not well whiche waye ;   128

But at the laste, when I wakened was,
  and sawe it was a dreame ;
" O god !" quothe I, " nowe comforte me !
  what maye this nights[1] worke meane ?" 132

And sondrie cogitations in mased mynde [leaf 6, back.]
  did daylie mee moleste,
And till I had sett downe the same,
  I never coulde take reste ;   136

Whiche, thoughe it bee but rudelie donne ;
  yet take it in good parte,
Whiche presente the same to yo*u*r highnes vewe
  withe a frendlie willinge harte.   140

finis.

---

[1] MS. mights.

ANTHONIE BABINGTON HIS COMPLAINT.

I.

What will it avayle, on fortune to exclame,
  when as due desarte is cheifest cause of all?
my selfe, and none but my selfe, Iustlie can I blame,
  That thus haue procured myne vntymelie fall,   144
  and turned haue my honnye swet vnto bitter gall.
    wherefore, good ffrende, take thie penne and write,
    and in mournfull verse my Tragedie recite.   147

II.

Longe might I haue lived a contented happie state,
  and haue borne a porte and countnance with the beste;
If fortune shoulde me checke, I coulde her mate;
  Thus none, like me, more happie was and bleste,   151
  Till that discontente procured myne vnreste,
    And the pompe of pride so glared in myne eyen,
    That I reiected vertue moste Devyne.   154

III.

But firste, I will tell thee myne estate and name,
  and contrie soile where I was bredd and borne:
Anthonie Babington I hight; of a worthie howse I came,
  Till my mysdemeanors made me forlorne,   158
  givinge cause to my foes to laughe me to skorne,
    whoe haue stayned my state, and blemisht my name:
    In clymbinge by follie, [I] haue falne to my shame. 161

IV.

At Dethwicke in darbye-shere I was bothe borne and bredd,
  my father was an Esquier of good reputation,
A good howse hee kepte, a vertuose life hee ledd;
  my selfe, beinge a childe, was holde in estimation,   165
But havinge gott the rayne, I changed my facion;
    Then privatlie I sought myne owne will and pleasure,
    livinge to my likinge, but never kepte a measure.   168

v.

Doctor Babington, myne Eame[1], did pronosticate [leaf 7, back.]
 that harde was the happe whereto I was borne:
Hee sayde, that 'pride my glorye shoulde abate,
 and destenye had decreede I shoulde bee forlorne;' 172
Whose wordes my father then helde in scorne.
  "O trayne hym vpp well!" myne vnkell did saye,
  "vnlesse[2] hee repente the same another daye. 175

vi.

"Give hym not, brother, his libertie in youthe,
 for then olde dayes hee never shall see;
Hee is my nephewe, the more is my rewthe
 to thincke of his happe and harde destinye! 179
If skill beguyle me not, hanged hee shalbe."
  This was the foresight of my fathers brother,
  ffor whiche love of his hee was hated of my mother. 182

vii.

I knowe not where[3] hee spake by hassarde or skill,
 for suche Divinations I doe not commende;
yet his counsell was good, to flie future ill;
 for whoe-so in vertue there dayes doe not spende, 186
shalbe sure, with me, repente them in thende.
  The proofe of myne vnkells worde I founde to trewe,
  as by the sequell Hereafter you maye veiwe. 189

viii.

Not longe after, my father resyned vpp his breathe,
 and lefte my wofull mother with a greate charge,
Whiche proved for vs all to tymelie[4] a deathe,
 ffor then, good gentelwoman, her purse ranne at large, 193
 Havinge of debts and legacies greate somes to discharge.
  But in the state of widowhode not longe shee tarried,
  ffor with that good gentelman, Henrye foliambe she
   married. 196

---

[1] A. Sax. *eám*, an uncle. [2] lest. [3] whether. [4] early.

IX.

Whoe loved vs all tenderlie as wee had bene his owne, [leaf 8.]
  and was verye carefull of oure education;
Whose love to mee was diverse wayes showne,
  and I of the same had daylie probation,[1]   200
  As by this maye appeare of whiche I make narration:
    Withe his owne chayne of golde hee woulde me often decke,
    Whiche made me a prowde boye, to weare aboute my necke.   203

X.

As on a tyme this chayne aboute my necke I did weare,
  and goinge to an orcharde some aples to gett,
Where clymbinge a highe tree, as one without feare,
  the boughe then brake whereon my foote I sett,   207
  and downwarde I slipt, but was caught in a nett;
    In the tree I was hanged faste by the chayne;
    So desyre of my pride was cause of my payne.   210

XI.

But [I] was not suffred there longe to hange,
  but was nere strangled or I was taken downe,
ffor there I strugled with suche a deadlie pange,
  my mother, shee freighted, and fell in a sowne,[2]   214
  and greife made my father likewise to frowne;
    But my revivinge there sorrowes over-caste;
    Then they reioyeste, sayinge my destenye was paste. 217

XII.

Thus carelesse a tyme with them I liude at pleasure,
  surfetted with selfwill and with fonde delite;
I knewe no golden meane, nor never kepte a measure,
  but like a kyndlie[3] beare gan tymelie to byte;   221
  Even then I harborde envye, and sucked despite,
    And pride at that Instante tooke so depe a roote
    That humillitie for ever was troden vnder foote.   224

---

[1] proof.   [2] swoon.   [3] natural.

XIII.

In myne none-age I was when my father dyde.   [leaf 8, back.]
 phillip draycott of paynslie, hee did me obtayne,
Whoe had appoynted me his doughter for my bryde,
 and in whose howse a space I did remayne :   228
There suckte I pleasure that proved to my payne,
  There was I misled in papistrie my soule to wounde,
  There was I corrupted, made rotten and vnsounde.   231

XIV.

There, even there, a while I spente my youthfull tyme ;
 there was I lulled in securitie faste a-sleepe ;
The[r]e was I frollicke, there was I in my pryme,
 In Iollitie then I laught, but never thought to weepe,   235
 my witts weare moste fyne, & conceits verye depe.
  But oh, paynslie, paynslie, I maye thee curse !
  where nature made me ill, education made me worse ; 238

XV.

ffor by nature I was withe papistrie infected,
 but might haue bene restrayned, had it pleased god.
My father and myne Eame, they weare suspected ;
 theye lived with there conscience, wherein I was odd,   242
 Therefore was beaten with a more sharper rodd.
  There conscience they kepte, & ruled it by reason,
  livinge like subiects, and still detested treason.   245

XVI.

My fatherinlawe still ledd me to what I was Inclynd[e],
 I meane, for my conscience, no farther hee woude deale ;
my mayntuance [was] sufficiant to contente my mynde,
 so that all this while I tasted nought but weale,   249
 but coulde not bee contente, w*h*ich I muste nedes reveale ;
  my fyne head was desyrouse to studye the lawe,
  In attayninge whereof I proude[1] my selfe a daw[2].   252

XVII.

And for that cause forthwith I to london wente,   [leaf 9.]
 where in lyncolns Inne a student I became,

---

[1] proved.   [2] a foolish fellow.—*Nares.*

and there some parte of my flittinge tyme I spente;
  but to bee a good lawier, my mynde woulde not frame; 256
I addicted was to pleasure, and given so to game;
    But to the Theatre and Curtayne[1] woulde often resorte,
    where I mett companyons fittinge my disporte.   259

XVIII.

Companyons, quothe you? I had companyons in deede,
  suche as in yoake with me weare well contente to drawe,
lyncked so in myscheife, wherein wee did exceede,
  wee cared not for order, nor paste[2] of reasons lawe;   263
  of god nor of good man wee stoode in litle awe;
    wee paste the bounds of modestie, and lived without shame,
    wee spotted *our* conscience, and spoiled *our* good name. 266

XIX.

Wee carde not for the churche; that place we not frequented;
  the taverns weare better oure humors to fitt;
The companye of dayntie dames wee cheiflie Invented,[3]
  withe whome in dalliance wee desyred ofte to sitt: 270
  Theise weare the fruytes of *our* yonge hedds and witt.
    Thus in lustie libertie I ledd a loose life,
    and thoughe I weare married, I carde not for my wife. 273

XX.

Yett to the sermons wee woulde often resorte,
  not in hope edification by them to obtayne,
But rather to Ieste, and make of them a sporte,
  whiche nowe I feele, to my sorrowe, greife, and payne: 277
  Theise bee the fruytes that sichophants doe gayne,
    Cheiflie when theye mocke and skorne gods worde,
    Disdayninge the servants and prophetts of the lorde. 280

---

[1] *Curtain.* A theatre which appears to have stood in Moorfields, and to have been celebrated for the performance of humorous and satirical pieces. See Collier's Annals of the Stage, iii. 268, and the quotations in *Nares*.

[2] *Pass*, to care for or regard: 'As for these silken-coaten slaves, I *pass* not,' 2 Hen. IV, iv. 2. 'Men do not *passe* for their sinnes, doe lightly regard them.' *Latimer, Ser. Ded.*—Nares.

[3] Or Bacchus merry fruit they did *invent*. Spencer, F. Q. i. iv. 15.
        And vowed never to returne againe,
      Till him alive or dead she did *invent*.
                    Ibid. iii. v. 10.—Nares.

XXI.

With Catholicks still conversante I coveted to be,   [leaf 9, back.]
  that weare alwayes in hope, and looked for a daye,
Gapinge for a change which wee trusted to see.
  Ambition so stonge me, my selfe I coulde not staye,   284
  Whiche makes mee sighes to sighe well-a-waye;
    Then I had my will, and playde with pleasures ball,
    Then I was alofte, and feared not this fall.   287

XXII.

Yett so covertlie all this tyme I did my selfe behave,
  and so closelie wrought in subtell synons frame,
What so ere I thought, my selfe I sought to save,
  livinge all this while without suspecte or blame;   291
  and more to wynne me credditt, a courtier I became,
    Where the syrens songe so swetelie I did synge,
    I never was suspected to worke suche a thinge.   294

XXIII.

The nobles of the courte of me thought so well,
  that often to there tables they woulde me Invite,
Where in gesture and talke I did the common sorte ex-
    cell,
  Thereby wynninge favor in my companye to delite;   298
  Whiche with a Iudas kisse I sought to requyte,
    As in sequell of my storye shall after appeare,
    Whiche I shame to tell, it toucheth me so nere.   301

XXIV.

And daylie more and more my credditt did increase,
  and so in like manner did pride still abounde;
Beloved I was bothe of more and lesse.
  when my Inwarde motions weare all vnsounde,   305
  my parsonage was comelie which favor eache where founde;
    But pryde had so blynded me, I could not see
    That with Icarus alofte I mynded was to flee.   308

XXV.

The grounde that I troade on, my feete coulde not holde, [leaf 10.]
  nor I bee contente in a happie state to reste,
lyke Bayarde that blushed not, then was I more bolde
  when Rancor Inwardlie still boyled in my breste,   312
  That like an vnnaturall birde I filed my neste,
    In parlinge with parasites that looked for a daye;
    By the counsell of Caterpillers I wrought my decaye. 315

XXVI.

Then I beganne to prie in-to matters of the state;
  and with what I liked not, I secrett faulte did fynde;
Where I fawned openlie, I inwardlie did hate,
  and to my confederates woulde closelie breake my mynde, 319
  I meane, to suche as to my lore weare Inclynde,
    Betwene whome and me suche myscheife wee Invented,
    That wee thought to haue made all Englande repented. 322

XXVII.

Where-vppon in-to france a Iorney I did frame,
  to parle with padgett, Morgan, and others of that crewe.
What wee had but decreede, they resolved on the same;
  Whose pretended purpose, at large when I knewe,   326
  I willinglie consented too,—which makes me nowe to
    rewe,—
    and to sett the same forwarde, a sollemne oathe did
    take.
    o cursed conscience, that a traytor didst me make!   329

XXVIII.

Then Into Englande I retornde agayne with spede,
  and gott conferrence hereof with some of greate fame.
Manye weare the plotts whereon wee agreed,
  and greate the attempts whereat we did ame,   333
  which afterwarde proved oure ruynose shame;
    and aspiringe pride so fyred my harte,
    I was contente to playe a traytors parte.   336

his artickles of arraygnmente. [leaf 10, back.]

XXIX.

Yee, to bee a moste savage monster agaynste all kynde,
  In sekinge the deathe of my Quene, the lords anoynted;
Ambition so stonge me, that I was starke blynde
  in pluckinge her downe that god had appoynted,   340
  and the vnitie of the realme in sonder to haue ioynted,
    To haue made kings and rulers at *our* owne pleasure,
    To haue exceeded in vyllanye without rule or measure. 343

XXX.

To haue made suche lawes as wee thought beste,
  to haue turned the state quyte vpsyde downe,
The nobles to haue slayne, and clene dispossest,
  and on a strangers hedd haue placed the crowne :   347
  Herein wee weare resolute, but fortune did frowne :
    no ! twas god woulde not suffer *our* villanyes take
      place,
    But vnlookte for, revealde them, to *our* shamefull dis-
    grace.   350

XXXI.

ffarther, *our* Intente was to poyson the ordinance of the
    realme,
  a moste haynouse matter as ever was Invented :
Whoe ever hathe harde of trecheries so extreame,
  concluded, agreed vppon, and fullye consented ?   354
  an wofull matter, of all to bee lamented !
    all courtrolls and records wee wente[1] to haue raced,
    and them to haue burned, spoyled and defaced.   357

XXXII.

The fayre cittie of london wee also mente to rifell,
  to haue robde the riche, and killed eke the poore ;—
Theise thinges in effecte wee counted but a trifell,—
  In all places of the lande [to] haue sett an vprore,   361
  The wealthie to haue bereaude bothe of life & store ;
    no state nor degree wee never mente to spare ;
    But if hee woulde resyste, deathe shoulde bee his share. 364

---

[1] weened, thought, *not* went-in.

XXXIII.

Theise weare *our* intents,with mischeifs manye more, [leaf 11.]
even confusion to the whole realme to haue brought.
Confederates wee had, and that no small store,
  Whiche ruyne and destruction weare redie to haue wrought;
  wee either mente to make or bringe all to nought;   369
    nought! yee, nought in deede! for nought weare *our*
      happs,
    ffor desperate myndes doe feare no after-clapps.   371

XXXIV.

So forwarde wee [we] are, that the verye daye was sett
  to murther *our* good Quene that god had preserved:
Barnewell and savage shoulde haue donne the feate,
  but Iustice rewarded them as they well desarved,   375
  beinge twoe monstrose traytors *that* from dutie swarved.
    The Daggs[1] and all things weare redye preparde;
    But in the nett they layde, they them selves weare snarde.

XXXV.

And ballarde that beaste, hee into Englande was come, 379
  a Iesuite, a preeste, and a Semynarie vilde,[2]
Hee brought with hym *our* absolution from roome,
  promysinge good successe,—wherein he was beguylde,— 382
  So that from *our* hartes all pittie hee exilde;
    and still hee incoraged vs in myscheifs to proceede,
    Egginge vs forwarde, wherein there was no neede. 385

XXXVI.

But god woulde not suffer vs so closelie to worke,
  but that all *our* doyngs laye open in his sight,
revealinge those myscheifs that in *our* hartes did lurke.
  when wee suspected not, hee brought the same to light; 389
  Then muste wee hyde *our* hedds, or scape awaye by
    flight;
    But when wee had Incklinge *our* treasons weare de-
    scryde,
    Awaye, awaye in haste! twas then no tyme to byde. 392

---

[1] Dag, a pistol.—Halliwell.   [2] vile.

III.   C

XXXVII.

Then watche and warde was made in everye coaste, [leaf 11, back.]
  then weare wee taken eache howre of the daye;
My selfe was once taken : but whie shoulde I boaste
  Howe that I made a scape, and so gott awaye,   396
  not knowinge where to goe, nor haue perfitt staye?
    But to harrowe-on-the-hill my selfe I convayde;
    There in Bellamyes howse a litle tyme I stayde.   399

XXXVIII.

But there was made for me suche previe watche & warde,
  and the contrie so besett, I no where coulde flie;
all hope of my escape was vtterlie debarde,
  and searche in eache corner was made so nye   403
That I was compelde this polecye to trye,
    To forsake the howse, and my selfe disguyse
    lyke an Inkeper of london, to bleare the peoples eyes. 406

XXXIX.

But a rewarde was promyste hym that coulde me take,
  whiche made the people looke so muche the nere[1];
And beinge constrayned the howse to forsake,
  [We] walked throughe the pastures as men without
    feare;
my man like an hostler was cladd in symple geare;   411
    But this woulde not serve, if truthe I shall tell,
    my favor I coulde not change, my face was knowne
    well.   413

XL.

There was a poore man, a weaver, was one of the watche,
  by whome the gate[2] laye as of force I muste walke;
Hee came to me boldlie, by the arme did me catche,
  "Staye, good frende!" quothe hee, "with you I muste
    talke."   417
my conscience beinge guyltie, my tonge gan to balke:
    "wee are not those you looke for," I foltringlie did saye;
    "our commyssion," quothe hee, "is all passengers to
    staye."   420

---

[1] nearer, closer.   [2] road, way.

XLI.

Then the people gan flocke aboute me a-pace,   [leaf 12.]
  and before the master of the rolls I forthwith was brought.
when I came there, I was knowne by my face
  To bee the same man that theye so longe had sought,   424
  and cheifest of the crewe that all the sturr had wrought.
    Sir Gilberte Gerrarde Examynde, and sente me to the
      towre,
    and stronglie was I guarded with a mightie greate powre.
                                427

XLII.

Then the londiners reioyced, and merrye did make
  with ringinge of bells, givinge god the prayse.
All my olde common frends did me clene forsake,
  That before had flattred me dyverse & sondrye wayes; 431
  But favor, frendshipp, and faithe, by treason Decayes,
    as appears by me, whose fame, credditt, and renowne,
    my traytrose attempts had sone plucked downe.   434

XLIII.

Then shortlie after to the kings benche wee weare brought,
  and a nomber of others, confederates like case,
There to make awnswer to the deedes wee had wrought;
  but then my glorye gan declyne a-pace;   438
  yet with a countnauce I sett thereon a face;
    where beinge arraygned, I guyltie was founde
    of highe treason agaynste my kinge and crowne.   441

XLIV.

Barnewell and savage had confest the same before;
  then bootelesse twas for vs anye poynte to denaye,—
our conscience beinge guiltie, it Irkte vs the more,—
  So that fourtene of vs weare condemned that daye. 445
  Wee carde not for deathe, wee stowtlie did saye;
    our Iudgment was to be hangde, and quartred like
      case,
    of whiche wee made no accounnte; deathe coulde vs not
      disgrace.   448

XLV.

And nowe the daye of *our* execution drewe nere, [leaf 12, back.]
  In whiche woe did playe *our* laste tragicke partes,
when seven of vs on hurdells from the towre dra[w]ne
    weare,
  Whiche was no small corsive[1] to *our* heavie hartes,   452
yet a luste rewarde for *our* wicked desartes.
    The people flockte aboute vs *with* this heavye sounde,
    " God save the Quene ! and all traytors confounde !" 455

XLVI.

In the feilds nere lyncolns Inne a stage was sett vpp,
  and a mightie highe gallose was raysed on the same,
Whiche was the verye Instrument, & *our* deadlie cuppe,
  of whiche to taste *our* selues wee muste frame;   459
and beastlie Ballarde, twas hee beganne the game,
    Whoe was hangde and quartred in all the peoples sight,
    and his head on a poale on the gallose sett vpright. 462

XLVII.

Nexte muste I make redye to treade the same dance,
  whereto I preparde my selfe as a man *without* feare :
Thousands lamented I had so harde a chance,
  and for me there was shedd manye a salte teare.   466
They lookte for confession, but weare never the nere ;
    Si*r* ffrancis knolls, *with* others, offerde *with* me to
      praye :
    " none but Catholicks prayers will proffitt," thus did I
    saye.   469

XLVIII.

Thus Died I stoutlie, and did not trulie repente
  my wicked life paste, and moste haynouse treason.
If in a good cause my life had bene spente,
  To haue avoucht the same there had bene some reason ; 473
But wickedlie I lived and dyed at that season :
    Havinge hanged a while, and my head cutt of in haste,
    on the right Hande of Ballards it was placest.   476

---

[1] corrosive.

XLIX.

Then Died Bar[n]well, Savage, and yonge Tushborne also,
 withe Tilnie and Abington, in order as they came.
But o, Tuchborne, Tuchborne! thou makest me full woe!
· ffor I was the firste that allurde thee to the same,   480
 Thie witts beinge yonge, likewaye I did frame;
   Thou beinge well Inclinde, throughe me didst consente
   To conceale the thinge that made vs all repente.   483

L.

The nexte daye dyed Salsburye, Henrye Dune, and Iones,
 with Iohn Travice of prescott, w*hi*ch is in lancashere;
So did Iohn Charnocke, a traytor for the nonce.
 Roberte Gage of Croyden muste then on stage appeare, 487
 and lastlie Bellamye, *our* hoste, that made vs all the
     chere:
   Theise seven weare executed on saynte matheues daye,
   The twentithe of September there partes they did playe.
     490

LI.

Oure quarters weare boyled like the fleshe of swyne,
 and on the cittie gates in open vewe doe stande;
oure conceited hedds, that once wee thought so fyne,
 on london bridge bee spectakles to subiects of the lande, 494
 Warninge them to shunne to take like things in hande.
   Our soules in the censure of gods Iudgments doe reste:
   This was the rewarde for the treasons wee profeste.   497

LII.

Thus haue I tolde thee my tragedie at large,
 in everye particular as the same was wrought;
reporte it to my contrie-men, I thee straytlie. charge,
 to shune those things that my destruction brought;   501
 ffor traytrose attempts at all tyme prove nought:
   Serche *our* Englishe Chronikels, & thou shalte fynde the
     same.
   That " whoe begyns in trecherie, hee endeth still in
     shame.   504

LIII.

[leaf 13, back.]

At my requeste, therefore, admonyshe then all men
  to spende well the tallente that god hathe them lente;
and hee that hathe but one, lett hym not toyle for tenue,
  ffor one is to muche vnlesse it bee well spente,   508
I meane by ambition, leaste hee to sone repente.
    To conclude, happie is the man, and threefolde bleste is
      hee,
    That can bee contente to live with his degree.   511
              felix, quem[1] faciunt aliena
                  pericula cautum.
                        finis.

---

quam.

The Life and Death of Essex.

[Arundel MS. 418, leaf 14.]

To oure Roiall kinges moste
Excellente maiestie

This booke—my gratiouse Soveraygne—of the life and
deathe of my lorde of Essex, I did write presentlie vppon
his deathe, and did bestowe the same on some of my honorable and worshipfull frends, whoe thought well of the same,
In regarde that I had written the truthe bothe of his life
and manner of his deathe; and nowe [I] haue revived the
same, and make presente of it to your princelie maiestie,
which I beseche you accepte, as a poore pittance of my zeale
and Dutie to your highnes, and that it woulde please you to
pardon all defectes of the same, wherein you bynde me for
ever to praye for your Roiall maiestie longe to raynge
over vs //

your maiesties poore distressed
Subiecte, Richarde Williams

[leaf 15.]

A lamentable Motion or mour[n]full remembrance for the
Deathe of Roberte Lorde Deverox, Late Earle of Essex,
whoe was beheaded in the Towre of london on ashwensdaye
mornynge in the yeare of oure lorde—1601—

I.

Englande! thou haste cause to complayne,
  to thincke vppon hym that is gone,
Whose face thou nere shalte see agayne,   3
  Whiche is the cause of this thie mone,
    Doughtie Deverox, that famose Earle,
    That Iewell rare, that princes pearle.   6

II.

And is hee gone, and gone in-deede?
  a corsive[1] greate, a gallinge greife,
The whiche makes manye a harte to bleede;   9
  but all in vayne, without releife,
    To thincke this worthie peere shoulde die,
    Whose harte was fraught with pietie.   12

III.

Thoughe hee bee gone, hees not forgott;
  nor will not bee this manye a yeare,
Thoughe sorrowe fall vnto oure lott   15
  for losse of this moste gallante peere.
    Essex! Essex! (manye doe saye,)
    By envies spite was made awaye: 18

IV.

Whose vertues, If I coulde recounte,   [leaf 15, back.]
  on whiche to thincke dothe passe my skill,
Leaste Muses of parnassus mounte   21
  Herein shoulde guyde my symple quill:
    But tushe! I can them not rehearse
    In suche base stile and symple verse.   24

---

[1] corrosive.

V.

Yet will I doe the beste I can :
　His frends will take it in good parte,
Thoughe I Decipher not the man　　　　　27
　　accordinge to his highe desarte,
　　　whose vertues aymde at higher things
　　　Then pan can pipe on oaten strings.　　30

VI.

ffirste, for his birthe and highe discente,
　tis knowne hee came of noble blood ;
Trewe Honor was his whole intente,　　　33
　　To Doe his Quene and contrie good ;
　　　But cheiflie, gods truthe to mayntayne,
　　　ffor whiche hee sparde no toyle nor payne.　36

VII.

Lett his greatest enemyes saye,
　what toyle it was hee did forsake,
If maiestie wilde, hee then strayght-waye　39
　　moste willinglie woulde vndertake ;
　　　Earle Essex was ever preste
　　　To see his contries wrongs redreste.　　42

VIII.

That Portingale can witnesse well,　　　[leaf 16.]
　and Don anthonie, then there kinge ;
Where haughtie valor did excell,　　　　45
　　That man in his estate to bringe.
　　　At lisborne gates this challenged hee,
　　　" The prowdest within, come forthe to me !"　48

IX.

But when hee sawe it was [in] vayne,
　He stucke his Dagger on the gate,
Whereon hee honge his golden chayne,　　51
　　as skornynge there the prowdest made :
　　　" This shalbe[1] token that I bringe
　　　To you your trewe anoynted kinge."　　54

---

[1] MS shalle.

X.

Seinge hee coulde not there prevayle,
  withe Honor [he] marched thence awaye.
The spanyards pride hee ofte did quayle,   57
  and wrought there ruyne night and dayé,
    And so came home with threefolde fame;
    Then Honored was brave Essex name.   60

XI.

Then Into ffrance this lorde was sente,
  And Walter Deverox, his brother dere;
Ten thousande men with hym there wente   63
  Taccompanye this gallante peere.
    At Gurnaye hee greate fame did wynne;
    That towne by valor hee tooke in.[1]   66

XII.

To-wardes brave [Rouen] then marched hee,   [leaf 16,
  His brother leadinge his brave trayne,   back.]
Whoe was shott by the enemye   69
  So cruellye, that hee there was slayne;
    whoe, to revenge his brothers deathe,
    vowed there to spende his latest breathe.   72

XIII.

The frenche kinge Did his furye staye,
  whoe with greate multitudes came there;
But withe Honor Hee marcht awaye,   75
  ffor hee there forches did not feare.
    Then Deverox in esteme was heilde,
    whoe gott renowne in Towne and feilde.   78

XIV.

But nexte Cales commeth to my mynde,
  where, in despight of Spannyshe pride,
A goodlie Towne hee there did fynde,   81
  well Rampyrde, mande, and fortified:
    His foes agaynste hym there did stande
    moste stronglie, bothe by sea and lande.   84

---

[1] took, captured.

XV.

But brave Honor did there prevayle,
  and valor Ioyned to the same;
when foes did freshlie hym assayle,   87
  " Saynt George and Essex:" at w*hi*ch name
    It Ioyed so eache Englishe Harte,
    The spanyards felte bothe woe and smarte.   90

XVI.

And so that Towne hee bravelie entred,   [leaf 17.]
  Sir Iohn Wingfilde beinge nere hym,
That, withe brave Essex boldlie ventred,   93
  and as a faithfull fre[n]de did chere hym;
    But cruell Deathe, with deadlie darte,
    Then strooke[1] this gallante to the harte.   96

XVII.

ffor nexte before hym hee was slayne
  withe shott that came from of the wall;
whiche was to hym a threefolde payne,   99
  to see his frende so nere hym fall;
    But greefe coulde doe his frende no good;
    withe furyé hee revengde his blood,   102

XVIII.

And in despite hee wanne the towne
  of all that semde hym to resiste.
Then firste, good lawes hee did sett downe,   105
  His souldiers furye so Dismyste,
    and charged them vppon there lives
    not to deflowre maydes nor wives.   108

XIX.

A leiftenant brake his commande,
  whoe deflowred there a mayde;
But hee was hanged out of hande,   111
  to make the reste by hym affrayde;
    Three howres on markett crosse honge hee,
    That all his Iustice there might see.   114

---

[1] MS. stroote.

XX.

Greate mercye hee did likewise showe,   [leaf 17, back.]
  not Ioyinge in sheedinge guyltlesse blood,
nor Tryvmpht in the yeildinge foe,   117
  nor suche as at his mercye stood :
    Whiche clemencye his foes did prayse
    To his greate fame, even sondrye wayes.   120

XXI.

His warrs by seas weare of like force :
  The spannyshe shipps weare stronglie mande,
where was made manye a lowlie corse   123
  That stoutlie at defence did stande;
    But *our* shipps fought with suche greate yre,
    That twoe of them they sett on fyer,   126

XXII.

And twoe of them they brought awaye
  Home Into Englande for a price;
Ransackte the towne; then woulde not staye,   129
  But marcht from thence with good advice.
    Then Essex name was in accounte :
    whoe but Deverox did then surmounte ?   132

XXIII.

Yet er hee wente from thence awaye,
  The Spanyards for the Towne agreede,
And certen somes to hym did paye;   135
  So then they marcht awaye with speede,
    And paste the seas, with sayles on hie,
    As men resolude[1] to fight, not flie.   138

XXIV.

To the Ilands Hee marched then,   [leaf 18.]
  where of treasure hee gott good store,
withe all oure gallante Englishmen;   141
  all had Inoughe, what woulde you more ?
    yet more they had gotten that daye,
    But that ill lucke did crosse there waye.   144

---

[1] resolved.

XXV.

Then came hee home with honored fame;
  then was hee loude[1] of prince and peere;
Admyred then was Essex name,   147
  and as there lives they helde hym dere.
    Yet envie might repyne as then,
    That alwayes lurckes in enviose men.   150

XXVI.

Then Generall hee was elected,
  In Irlande for to beare the swaye,—
A Trayne[2] whiche hee not suspected,   153
  To worke his ruyne and decaye;
    Greate promyses to hym weare made,
    But in performance they did fade,—   156

XXVII.

And gallantlie hym selfe preparde
  with a moste brave and warlike trayne,
(no coste to furnishe hym was sparde;)   159
    whoe might hym serve, was gladd & fayne,
      moste voluntaryes; fewe weare preste
      That wente with hym, some of the beste. 162

XXVIII.

Hee there did spende bothe toyle and payne   [leaf 18,
  to doe His Quene and contrie good;   back.]
Hee Honor and good fame did gayne,   165
  the whiche did coste his derest blood;
    ffor there a plott for hym was layde,
    Whiche withe his honored hedd hee payde.   168

XXIX.

But treason was layde to his charge,
  and manye artikles obiected;
whoe rowed not so in follies barge,   171
  and thinges propounded not suspected;
    and suche at that tyme bare the swaye,
    as sought his ruyne and decaye;   174

---

[1] loved.   [2] artifice, stratagem: *Macb.* iii. 4, *Spencer*, F. Q. i. iii. 24.—Nares.

XXX.

And so hee was condem*n*de to dye,
  the whiche hee tooke in quiett parte,
and to the lorde his god on hie.   177
  Hee yeilded hym with all his harte.
    Deathe coulde not Daunte his noble mynde;
    Vnto His Quene hee was moste kynde.   180

XXXI.

And so hee ever did proteste
  Hee mente her maiestie no harme;
no one thought in his harte did reste,   183
  Thoughe synon[1] subtellie did charme
    In secrett sorte his blood to spill:
    Hee was contente, they had there will.   186

XXXII.

Yet mai[e]stie woulde hym discharge,   [leaf 19.]
  and haue releaceste[2] hym from his thrall;
But Rawe-bones layde on lies at large,   189
  and howrelie sought to see his fall;
    whoe never stayde, till they gott synde[3]
    His doome of deathe, to please there mynde. 192

XXXIII.

And then in all post haste withe speede
  Theye to the Towres leiftenna[n]t came,
withe strickte com*m*ande to doe the deede,   195
  as hee woulde awnswer to the same
    If hee made staye, or once delayde
    The prescript howre; w*hi*ch hee obayde.   198

XXXIV.

Yet greiude in mynde, hee loude[4] hym dere,
  But muste her highe com*m*ande fulfill.
when this good man of this did heare,   201
  Hee sayde "good lorde, bleste be thie will!
    I thancke my god and my good Quene
    That thus myndefull of me haue bene.   204

---

[1] Cecil or Cobham.
[2] Pronounce *releast*: compare *disgraceste* for *disgraced*, l. 331; and *placeste* for *placed*, l. 333, below; p. 7, l. 82, above.   [3] signed.   [4] loved.

XXXV.

" To-morrowe morninge I shall paye
  the debte that I doe owe her grace.
my life to her I downe will laye
  moste willinglie, within this place;
    Then my frends, that my Gardiants bee,
    Shall see my god moste stronge in mee."

207

210

XXXVI.

That night in prayer hee did passe,   [leaf 19, back.]
  moste ferventlie, vnto the lorde;
no feare of deathe his troble was;
  His mynde was fixte on gods pure worde;
    His care was cheife for his greate synne
    and loathed luste hee had liude in.

213

216

XXXVII.

And godlie men withe hym did praye,
  coufirmde his faithe on christe a-bove,
Howe hee[1] had washte his synns awaye,
  of his mere mercye and greate love,
    nowe home from strayinge did hym call;
    Hee on his shoulders woulde beare all.

219

222

XXXVIII.

Moste of the night that waye hee spente,
  and ofte woulde comforte his dere frends
That semed for hym to lamente:
  " wepe not for mee ! men haue there ends.
    all that [be] borne, nedes muste dye;
    To-morrowe mornynge so muste I.

228

XXXIX.

Ashwensdaye mornynge nowe was come;
  His deadlie foes as earlie there,
And yet that loude [him] there weare some,
  That came to see with greife and feare.
    All thinges in haste prepared was,
    That this peere to his deathe might passe.

231

234

---

[1] he who.

XL.

A place appoynted in the towre,   [leaf 20.]
  withe stage and blocke, and all things fitt,
Made redye agaynste the verye howre,   237
  with seates for suche nobles to sitt
    That came to see hym loose his head,
      where manye brinishe teares weare spredd. 240

XLI.

Then came this peere with countnance mylde,
  as Lambe vnto his slaughter ledd :
His foes, whiche pittie had exilde,   243
  ffor verye shame helde downe there head,
    To thincke in mynde what they had donne,
      Thus to ekclipse bright Honors sonne.   246

XLII.

Then kneelinge downe, his prayer did make
  vnto his god in Heaven above ;
all wordlie[1] motions did forsake,   249
  forgave his enemyes with love,
    " Lorde, laye not this vnto their[2] charge !
      my Deathe I haue deserude at large."   252

XLIII.

His greatest wordlie care was this,
  Hee had some frends that loude hym well,
That never knewe secrett of his,   255
  nor previe weare to his counsell,
    yet weare in troble for his sake ;
      But hoapte his Quene woulde mer[c]ye take. 258

XLIV.

The Headsman kneeled on his knee,   [leaf 20, back.]
  and sayde, " my lorde, forgive your deathe !"
" Withe all my harto I forgive thee ;   261
  Dispatche at once ! come, stoppe my breathe !
    Thou, Iustice mynister arte here ;
      Come, doe thie office, and haue no feare !   264

---

[1] worldly.   [2] MS. my.

XLV.

" Come nowe," quothe hee, " whats to bee donne ?
   wee maye dispatche the same with spede ;
my glasse on earthe (I see) is ronne,   267
   And lachesis will cutt the threede,
      whoe prepared hathe His sharpned knife
      To reave me of my vitall life."   270

XLVI.

Then layde his bodye flatt alonge,
   His head likewise vppon the blocke ;
But Headsman did threfolde wronge,   273
   whoe tooke at hym three severall stroakes
      Er head from bodye wente a-waye ;
      yet as a lambe hee quyett laye.   276

XLVII.

Thus this greate peere ended his life,
   and brought his soule to quyett reste,
ffree from the cares of wordlie strife,   279
   whiche daylie did his mynde moleste ;
      And nowe with god in glorye dwells,
      whereas his ioye earthes ioye excells.   282

XLVIII.

As Hee with god, a-bove dothe reste,   [leaf 21.]
   Hee hathe lefte vs here to complayne ;
oure hartes withe sorrowe are distreste,   285
   and comfortles wee still remayne
      ffor wante of hym that so is gone,
      whiche is the subiecte of our mone.   288

XLIX.

The noble men, they wante a peere,
   withe them in counsell that did sitt ;
Captaynes, a leader they helde dere,   291
   a seconde sallomon for witt,
      a Iosias stronge, grave and wise,
      affable, kynde, but not precyse.   294

L.

Souldiers doe there Generall wante,
  that still was wonte to see them payde
Thoughe Captaynes woulde the same supplante,   297
  and they longe tyme shoulde bee delayde ;
    whiche, when Essex of that did here,
    Hee turnde to ioye there mournfull chere.   300

LI.

whoe cassirde[1] suche as delte not well ?
  ffrom his bandes bannysht them awaye ?
Wherein his Honor did excell ;   303
  Then souldiers trulie had there paye :
    Here was trewe fame wonne by desarte ;
    This showde the Honor of his harte.   306

LII.

Widowes doe wayle, and children crye,   [leaf 21, back.]
  and manye fatherlesse lamente ;
Maydes at there distafes showe cause whie   309
  wee moved are withe discontente ;
    ffor there, in dolefull tunes theye singe,
    " Essex, Essex, did comforte bringe."   312

LIII.

The poore that begge at everye dore,
  In heavie notes recorde his fame ;
Hee alwayes loude the needye poore,   315
  and they admyrde good Essex name ;
    no whippinge stockes hee did Invente,
    Theye weare not made by his consente.   318

LIV.

And daylie more his fame is raysde,
  Synce *our* kinge came to swaye this lande ;
nowe is hee myste, nowe is hee praysde,   321
  Whiche *our* good kinge well vnderstands ;
    His maiestie hym selfe is sadd,
    Whereat his foes are nothinge gladd.   324

---

[1] cashiered.

LV.

Oure kinge dothe countenance his frends,
  suche as in life tyme helde hym dere;
on them Riche Honors daylie spends,   327
  for love to them and this greate peere;
    His Sonne attendante on the prince,
    Whiche envyes spite maye well convynce.   330

LVI.

Whereas his foes, they are disgraceste,[1]   [leaf 22.]
  but Iustlie, throughe there owne desarte;
In lymbo patrum some are placeste,[2]   333
  whiche is a terror to there hartes;
    yett this maye well putt them in mynde,
    To Essex they haue bene vnkynde.   336

LVII.

God grante theye maye thincke of the same,
  and trewe teares of repentance bringe;
They nowe are scandalde with defame   339
  for treason agaynste oure good kinge.
    But if truthe bringe treason to light,
    God sende them there desartes by right.   342

LVIII.

And suche measure as they haue mett[3]
  To worthie Deverox, whiche wee mysse,
Iustice the like on them maye sett;   345
  Theye maye withe truthe acknowledge this,
    "That noble pere whiche wee betrayde,
    His blood on vs is Iustlie layde."   348

LIX.

God sende all greate men to take heede,
  and withe there state to bee contente,
leaste that ambition chance to breede   351
  Suche thoughts as maye make them repente
    To hassarde state and noble name,
    To bee Impeached withe defame.   354

---

[1] Cp. *defaceste* for *defaced*, p. 48, l. 294, etc.
[2] Cp. p. 7, l. 82.   [3] meted.

LX.

Noble Essex was beloved well   [leaf 22, back.]
 of riche and poore of eache degree;
Hee loved was, as fame dothe tell,   357
 of suche as never did hym see.
  Tushe! that was hitt the commons love!
  His Honors periode did prove.   360

LXI.

Oh that pure love shoulde turne to spite,
 or honye swete converte to gall!
Oh that trewe Honors cheife delite, 363
 By envye shoulde gett suche a fall!
  Oh that theise wordes I doe rehearse,
  Might withe remorse there malice peirce! 366

LXII.

Well! hee is gone! that is to trewe!
 yet ins[1] posteritie dothe live;
Twoe gallante Impes, that doe renewe 369
 the fame that Essex dothe vs give;
  Twoe gallante sonnes of Deverox race,
  Whiche hardlie can broke[2] his disgrace. 372

LXIII.

ffor nature gynnes to beare a swaye
 alredye in there youthfull pryme:
To perfection come it maye,   375
 when leaste tis thought in after tyme,
  perhaps to bee revengde on those
  Haue bene there fathers greatest foes. 378

LXIV.

I wishe it not: gods will bee donne! [leaf 23.]
 But guyltlesse blood will vengance crave;
The father crye[s] vnto the Sonne · 381
 from his Horried tymeles grave.
  Thus writers write, thus poetts fayne;
  manye forgotten, a-newe complayne. 384

---

[1] in his.   [2] brook.

LXV.

But farewell Essex, noble peere !
  farewell, trewe Honor, that did shyne !
Thie beames weare splendante, pure, and clere,   387
  and thou the prospecte of *our* tyme !
    Thou throughe the pikes didst boldlie ronne ;
    Deserved fame hasto trulie wonne.   390

LXVI.

All that loves thee bidds thee farewell,
  ffrom Highest to the lowest degree ;
But sure, thie fare dothe farr excell   393
  The greatest peeres on earthe that bee.
    Gods presence is thyne onelie foode,
    That bought thee with his derest blood.   896

vivit post funera virtus.

finis. R. W.

[Arundel MS. 418, leaf 24.]

Acclamatio Patrie,

or

The comp[l]aynte of the good subiects of Englande for the
myserie of these Tymes,
Or the powder Treasons:
otherwise
a pulpitt for papistes, and a trappe for Traytors.

To our Roiall kinges moste excellente
maiestie.

Moste dreade and gratiouse Soveraygne, this booke I did
write presentlie vppon the Dangers paste of this horrible
pretended[1] treason; and seynge no other had written thereof,
I did pretende[2] to haue put the same in printe, and had
gotten it lycenced accordinge to order.   But a printer asked
me a some of moneye for the Impression, whiche I was not
able to paye; and so I kepte it privatt, But that I presented
[leaf 24, back.] Some of them to my Honorable and worshipfull
frendes; and one of them I Did presente to your famouse
Sonne, Prince Henrie, when your maiestie was in your progresse in Nottingham-shere, at the Howse of one, Sir Iohn
Byron, a knight, that Dwelleth in the forrest of mansfilde. But
I never harde anye awnswer of it; and nowe haue thought it
good to presente it your Highnes, amongst the reste of my
labors : not that the particulars are vnknone to your maiestie,
but that thereby you maye see my love and dutifull zeale
to you my kinge, and contrie.   Moste humblie besechinge
your Highnes to pardon myne attempte, and to accepte of
the same, whoe will and doe, Daylie praye to the almightie
to kepe and defende you from all traytrose attempts, and
that you maye live manye yeares to rule and Raygne over
vs.

Your maiesties poore Distressed
Subiecte, Richarde williams.

---

[1] intended.   [2] intend.

Aclamatio patrie, or   `   [leaf 25.]
The complaynte of the good subiects
of Englande for the myseryes of theise
Tymes;
Withe a trappe for Traytors,
and a pulpitt for papistes.

I.

What cause haue al good subiects to complayne
  for *our* dere contrie, spotted *with* defame,
The whiche, trecherie dothe polute and stayne,
    and woulde ecklipse the glorie of the same,—   4
    But, to there ruyne and endlesse shame,
      our roiall kinges maiestie to surprise,
      and ore his progenye woulde Tyranise.   7

II.

Oh Englande, Englande! a moste happie soile,   ˏ
  that hathe bene the nurse of roiall kinges!
o vilde[1] viprose broode, that seke the spoile
    of *your* dere mother! that *with* payne forthe brings   11
    bothe wholesome flowers, and netles that stings!
      vnnaturall children, and bastards broode,
      That woulde glutt *your* selfe *with* her dereste blood! 14

III.

What did you Imagyn, when you began
  this dangerose attempte and moste wicked[2] treason,
Hatefull to god, odiouse to man,
    wherein you had nor grace, nor reason?   18
    all pittie bannysht, *your* fruytes that season,
      you that in an Instante woulde all destroye,
      abridginge all hope of *our* contries ioye.   21

IV.

If his maiestie, Tyranouse had bynne,   [leaf 25, back.]
  and had ruled *with* rigor this fertile lande,
and that god had sente hym to plauge[3] *our* synne,
    wee ought not his holie decrees withstande,   25
    nor agaynste his highnes once lifte *our* hande.
      whie? because hee is the lordes anoynted,
      over vs to Raygne, by hym appoynted.   28

---

     [1] vile.   [2] MS. wicted.   [3] plague.

V.

But hee is mercyfull; you knowe it well !
  Hee makes good lawes, and dailie sekes for peace !
Reporte in eache contrie his fame dothe tell,
  althoughe vntrustie traytors never ceasse   32
    To augmente his feares, and greives increase ;
      But hee, resolude, in god putteth truste,
      whoe is a rocke and safegarde to the iuste.   35

VI.

Doe what you can, not one heare shall fall
  nor be dyminisht from his highnes head !
Thoughe you practise, frett, fume, splitt your gall,
  your attempts are vayne ! you sonder but the thredd 39
    whiche destruction for your selues hathe bredd !
      wee good subiectes Ioye at your Illusion,
      To see your ruyne and sole confusion !   42

VII.

Consider what twas you woulde haue donne :
  the moste odiouse thinge that ever was Invented !
To ecklipse the glorye of Englands sunne,
  withe the devill and hell you had Indented,[1]   46
your owne damnation had consented !
    The like nere harde synce the wordle began !
    Murther, ruyne, and wracke of manye man !   49

VIII.

you threwe at all, but haue loste your firste mayne : [leaf 26.]
  you aymde at fayrest kinge, Quene, prince, and all,
and the whole nobillitie to haue slayne,
    The learned Bishopps to haue brought to thrall,   53
    and of wise Burgeses haue wrought the fall ;
      To haue blowne them vpp without all pittie,
      Haue burnde the kings howse, and fyred *the* cittie !

IX.

Yee ! at an Instante this shoulde haue bene wrought,
  when they weare busied to make good lawes !
In whose trewe hartes no trechery was thought,
  But there contries good was the onelie cause,   60
  when you—worse then[2] ravens or chatringe dawes—
    There vtter subvertion had devisde
    By treason, which god hathe ever despisde,   63

---

[1] Covenanted by an indenture or indented deed.   [2] MS. then then.

x.

Tyrranye, crueltie, and moste wicked hate,
to Dinge[1] them downe with myndes variable,
of there soules as then not myndinge the state ;
   Some weake in faithe, in conscience not stable !   67
   But that gods mercyes are ever able
     To save synfull soules at his good pleasure,
     you might haue robde them of heavens treasure.   70

xi.

you respected neither bodie nor soule !
ambition kepes no lymmitts nor boundes :
your aspiringe myndes had dared[2] controule,
   your conscience, spotted and full of woundes.   74
   like men not sicke, yet sodenlie swounndes,
     So you felte no greefe, yet sodenlie fell
     Without gods mercyes to the depest hell.   77

xii.

What Had ensued if you had prevaylde ?   [leaf 26, back.]
woes, ruyne, and vtter confusion !
Gods holie truthe by your means had quaylde,
   and poperye agayne had made Intrusion,   81
   and light darkned with your Illusion !
     Then to puritanes and protestants woe !
     There wives, children, and there lives, to forgoe !   84

xiii.

A thousandes mysecheifes more had attended :
all vyllanyes then had bene sett abroache ;
Howe [could] Innocence, haue Rigor defended,[3]
   when truthe to bee tryed durste not approche ?   88
   But crueltie over hym woulde Incroche,
     Tyranisinge too, and laughe at his fall :
     The tyme nowe is come thou shalte paye for all !   91

xiv.

Then, woe to the riche that had purste vp golde !
and woe to anye that had gotten treasure !
ffor then base Rascalls woulde haue bene bolde,
   Haue robde and trivmpht at there pleasure ;—   95
   for vyllanye never kepes a measure ;—
     yee woe to all that did houestlie meane !   97
     yer the harvest weare come, the slaves woulde glean [e].

---

[1] strike, smite.   [2] ? MS.   [3] warded off.

XV.

Havocke they woulde haue cryed :
 "the tyme is nowe come, lets rifell for all !
of theise cormorants weele abate the pride,
    and of greasie churles weele splitt the gall !   102
    Better theise lacke, then good fellowes fall :
      ffor what they haue gott by vnlawfull gayne,
      To spende for there sakes weele take the payne.   105

XVI.

" This is the daye wee haue longe looked for,   [leaf 27.]
    and nowe tis come, weele sett cocke on hoope.
Tushe ! feare not, hostice ! weele paye thee the score !
    Be merrye, my wenche, doe no longer droope !   109
    ffor this, manye a carle wee haue made to stoope."
      Thus villanye woulde vaunte, more then I write,
      or my skilles[1] penne is able to recyte.   112

XVII.

This, *our* generall ruyne woulde haue bene !
    If treason had brought his purpose to passe,
wee dolefull dayes in Englande shoulde haue sene,
    withe moste greivose grones cryinge 'alas,   116
    That ere suche crueltie Invented was !
      That wee lived to see these dolefull dayes,
      where wronge abuseth right so manye wayes !'   119

XVIII.

But god in mercye did beholde *our* estate,
    and in his goodnes hathe looked vppon vs
when wee weare cyrcumvented with deadlie hate,
    all hope of remorse had quyte forgon vs,   123
    and that destruction was nerest on vs,
      Confusion preste[2] with his bloodye hande
      To overthrowe the state of this *our* lande.   126

XIX.

Nowe particularlie Ile touche there names
    that thus had plotted oure generall fall,—
I proteste to my greefe, but to there shames,—
    That mente to haue made havoke of all,   130
    and turnde oure honye to moste bitter gall,
      Infectinge the swete and moste pretiose springs
      ffrom whence came the nectar of roiall kinges !   133

---

[1] skill-less.   [2] ready.

XX.

Percye ! thie honor of valor firste begane   [leaf 27, back.]
　　when Haughtie Hott-spurr did firste wynne that name
By peircinge the eye of a moste brave man
　　　In a famose combatt; but nowe the same   137
　　　Treason hathe stayned, to thie[1] endlesse shame
　　　　Of thee and all that honorable race,
　　　　of whiche thie trecheries haue sought disgrace.   140

XXI.

Didst thou not sarve thie dreade roiall kinge ?
　　and nere[2] his person in accounte helde dere.
Oh vilde cursed viper ! whye wouldst thou stinge
　　　or poyson the fountayne that ranne so clere ?   144
　　　contente coulde not please thee, it dothe appeare ;
　　　　But thyne aspiringe ambitiouse pride
　　　　Bothe wise men doe hate, yee, and fooles deryde ! 147

XXII.

And nowe thie prowde head orepries that place
　　where monstrose treason shoulde haue bene effected !
pittie, so brave a man shoulde wante the grace
　　　of god and man to bee so reiected,   151
　　　plottinge cruelties nere before suspected :
　　　　I meane, the horror thou mentst to bringe
　　　　vppon thie contrie and thie roiall kinge.   154

XXIII.

Thie selfe weare caught in the trappe thou didst laye,
　　tane in the snare thou thie selfe devisde.
Thie quarters doe stande for foules as a praye,
　　　thie life thou didst leese[3] as a traytor surprisde,   158
　　　Thie conceytes all dasht, that thou hadst devisde ;
　　　　Thie head and quarters farr severed doe stande,
　　　　Devided in sondrye places of the lande.   161

XXIV.

Nexte, Catesbye : thou didst playe the wilye catt,   [leaf 28.]
　　and wearte cheife agente in this wicked treason,
Not, naturallie, to spoile the noysome Ratt,
　　　But moste agaynste kynde, at that Instant season   165
　　　Hadst plotted, bothe agaynste pittie and reason,
　　　　Thie kinges confusion and wracke at the leaste ;   167
　　　　whiche showes thou wearte a filthie scratchinge beaste,

---

[1] the.　　　[2] never.　　　[3] lose.

XXV.

And wouldst scratche downe the parlament howse
  and all the nobles assembled that tyme:
Here was a cruell catt to catche a mouse!
  Here was the scomme of filthie mudd and slime! 172
  Here treason shoulde haue bene broacht in the pryme!
    But it pleasde god this catt was caught ithe snare,
    And tangled in the grynne[1] or hee was aware; 175

XXVI.

And his head likewise elevate dothe stande
  over that place hee woulde haue destroyde,
a prospecte to good subiects of the lande
  whome his villanyes woulde fayne haue anoyde; 179
  But horror his stomake had so overcloyde
    That it vomyted forthe his skandalouse shame,
    To the sole discreditt of Catesbyes name. 182

XXVII.

O sir Everarde Digbye! thou wearte a knight,
  a man whose wisedome shoulde haue tane heede,
And wayed howe god dothe defende the right,
  and howe traytors in thende did ever speede, 186
  Desarte had alwayes his desarved meede;
    Experience whereof thou longe hadst sene
    In treasons plotted agaynste our late Quene. 189

XXVIII.

Howe god was still her maiesties defence   [leaf 28, back.]
  when traytors sondrye wayes sought her fall,
Howe, vnsuspected, hee bewrayde there pretence,[2]
  Parrye maye stande an example for all, 193
  His owne feare frettinge so at gall,
    That when hee quiveringe nere her grace did stande,
    The Dagge[3] was redye to fall forthe his hande. 196

XXIX.

Digbye! this might haue bene a warninge for thee,
  and to all others of that cursed crewe!
But weale his good happe in tyme coulde not see,
  and discontente makes manye one to rewe, 200
  so become trustles, to there prince vntrewe.
    Digbye in like predicamente hathe bynne;
    Digged a pitt, and hym selfe fell in. 203

---

[1] snare, gin.   [2] intention.   [3] Pistol.—*Halliwell.*

XXX.

Nexte, Roberte wynter, Ithe cath[a]loge I fynde ;
  a man whose name Destruction woulde bringe,
whoe in this action bare a traytrose mynde,
    and woulde destroye the glorye of *our* springe,   207
    consentinge to the Deathe of *our* roiall kinge ;
      whose boystrose gale shoulde haue blowne suche a blaste,
      To haue made all Englande othe sodden agaste,   210

XXXI.

yee, to haue blowne vpp all w*i*thout remorse,
  The kinge, Quene, prince, and nobles together,
Turnde manye good man vnto a dead corse
    w*i*th mangled lymbes. was not this foule weather   214
    when furye shoulde haue hoysted vpp altogether ?
      This was wynters love and holye zeale !
      Suche blastes, lorde, cutt of from this c*om*mon weale ! 217

XXXII.

The nexte is Iohn Grante, whoe might grante in-deede [leaf
  Hee was a traytor in the highest degree,   29.]
Grantinge in this action his overmuche spede,
    That his good estate in tyme coulde not see :   · 221
    ambitiouse myndes nere contented bee,
      as appearde in actions of this Grante,
      In whose will to treason there was no wante.   224

XXXIII.

And all muste grante that hee deserved deathe
  ffor his attempts in that moste wicked deede,
That cruellie woulde haue abridged the breathe
    of manye thousandes, if treason coulde spede,   228
    and manye a mothers childe haue made to bleede :
      Tis generallie granted hee was vniuste,
      a vyllayne, a traytor, not worthie of truste.   231

XXXIV.

Bates might in this poynte haue bated an ace,
  that was (as tis sayde) Traytor Catesbies man :
Swashbucklers ronne on to there myscheifs apace,
    and forwarde the same asmuche as they can ;   235
    There orehastie spede they afterwards ban,
      To the overthrowe of them and there states,
      as well appearde by this fellowe Bates.   238

XXXV.

Thoughe men there masters ought trulie to sarve,
   as in dutie theye thereunto are bounde,
[*Yet should they not plot their king's head off to carve,*[1]]
    By treason sekinge there states to confounde,   242
    There kinge and contrie with horror to wounde ;
      no servante in this ought take his masters parte,
      leaste Gwerdonde as bates, for his Iuste desarte. 245

XXXVI.

nowe another wynter came in the thronge,   [leaf 29, back.]
   that blewe his blustringe blastes in this realme,
for hee at roome had bene resident longe,
    But came to Infecte this moste sacred stream,   249
    Makinge his brother blowe suche a gleame
      of treason as never was harde of before :
      a cruell wynters blaste, that vexte vs sore !   252

XXXVII.

Weare theise, wynter, the beste fruyts thou couldst bringe,
   I muste nedes confesse thie comfortes weare colde,
with thie whirlinge wyndes to wither *the* springe
  so sone : but that it hathe bene oftymes tolde,   256
    'Myscheife is ever in all things to bolde.'
      proofe in thee, for the broyles thou haste bredd
      Hathe severde thie quarters farr from thie head. 259

XXXVIII.

Thou mightst well haue exclamed on roome,
   as of thie myserye the fynall cause,
where princes are censurde with heavie doome,
    that resiste agaynste there catholicke lawes,   263
    makinge subiects rebell, not takinge pawse,
      nor wayinge what god *commandes* in his worde, 265
      "ffeare god, love the kinge," thus scriptures recorde.

XXXIX.

Then Rockwood hathe rocked hym selfe faste a-slepe,
   lulled by treason to swete securitie,
whose witts weare fyne, and conceites verye depe,
    But blotted and stayned with all Impuritie ;   270
    whose harte was fraughted[2] with obduritie,
      That hee those vyllanyes putt in vre,[3]
      Contries ruyne by treason to procure.   273

---

[1] A line left blank in the MS.   [2] freighted, fraught.   [3] use, practice.

XL.

Rockwood was namde to bee an Esquier,   [leaf 30.]
  and one that might haue lived in good sorte :
and Rockinge ambition blewe the fyer
    That kindled the scandall of ill reporte,   277
  and of trewe allegiance batterde the forte :
      Poperye so pufte hym with discontente,
      That his posteritie shall ever repente.   280

XLI.

Then came keyes, a gentelman by discente,
  a notable papiste, so longe tyme knowne :
Subversion of the state was his intente,
    as by the seedes appeare, which hee hathe sowne ; 284
  whoe mente at randome all downe haue mowne,
      Govermente and state, thus they had decreede :
      keyes was an agente, and forwarde in the deede. 287

XLII.

This keyes, of treason opened the locke
  whiche keyes of Iustice shoulde haue kepte shutt,
In sekinge to remove the surest rocke,
    To whose hande the sworde of auctoritie is putt, 291
  at whose life this traytor made his butt :
      But in theise demeans hee made suche greate haste,
      The keyes of Iustice haue his life defaceste. 294

XLIII.

Nowe laste, thoughe firste of Balams broode,
  Came Gwido vaux, the moste tyranose man,
and one whose glorye was spillinge of blood,
    and the onelie agente this mischeife beganne, 298
  And verye Instr[u]ment whome all men maye banne.
      Hee, to all of this storye shalbe teller,
      Maye well be calde the Devill in the celler. 301

XLIV.

Hee in His celler a trappe had planted,   [leaf 30, back.]
  Herewith to haue spoilde the moste noble blood,
In whome nor prudence nor mercye wanted,
    whoe is sole defendor of brittaynes good, 305
  agaynste whome this furye raysde the flood,
      Worse then Cateline raysde at roome ;
      But sone confounded by gods mightie doome. 308

XLV.

O traytrose Iudas! or farr worse then hee,
  whoe for love of pelfe did his master betraye!
aux, so blynded withe poperie, coulde not see
    Immynent dangers of that dreudfull daye,   312
    where manye thousands shoulde sighe well-awaye!
      Hee was pardonde, destruction to bringe
      vppon his contrie and his roiall kinge.   315

XLVI.

And when hee was tane, the rellicks weare founde,—
  as a hayrie shurte, with other popishe trashe,—
and hee in wordes as a traytor vnsounde,
    whiche caused Iustice whipp sorer with his lashe;   319
    The Horror of his actes did good stomakes abashe,
      But at laste, when popishe helpes had no hope,
      Hee made his laste ende in a hempen rope.   322

XLVII.

Was ever suche trecherie harde of before?
  yet Englande, traytors at all tymes hathe bredd;
But of this consorte there weare suche greate store,
    whoe in confusion had gatherde to a hedd,   326
    Beinge all perswaded they shoulde hane spedd.
      But see the mercye and love of *our* god!
      ffor mercye and mallice are things farr odd.   329

XLVIII.

When thinges weare sorted to a full effecte,   [leaf 31.]
  and the tyme nowe come that was appoynted,
and all thinges planted *without* suspecte,
    To haue made awaye the lordes anoynted,   333
    and all vnion in sonder haue ioynted,
      Even then, a letter contayninge fewe lynes,
      By one of them written, all vndermynes!   336

XLIX.

O happie hande that did write the same,
  thoughe theffecte proved agaynste his mynde!
yet glorified bee gods sacred name!
    for thereby wee did preservation fynde,   340
    owre[1] lives preserved from these cormorants kynde,
      That withe fyer and powder woulde [have] vs anoyde,
      and in an Instante haue Englande destroyde. 343

---

[1] ? MS.

III.   E

L.

Then had approachte oure desolation !
  ruyne and murther had bene redye preste !
Then Roome, withe all her abhomynation,[1]
    woulde once agayne on highe avance her creste,   347
    and all godlie lawes shoulde haue bene depreste !
      In amplest sorte, without condition,
      Cruellye executed there commyssion !   350

LI.

Then widowes shoulde haue waylde there husbands wante,
  and children haue wayled for there fathers dead,
Mothers for children w*h*ich theye woulde supplante,
    Sisters for brothers manye a teare haue shedd,   354
    Manye fathers haue gone with greife to there bedd
      ffor losse of there sonnes, whome crueltie kilde ! 356
      muche Innocent blood shoulde then haue bene spïlde,

LII.

All recordes of lawes as then defaced,   [leaf 31, back.]
  all precedents likewise shoulde haue bene burned,
Counselers Iudges and clarkes disgraced,
    and there former hopes to sorrowe turned ;   361
    yee, all good men with greife haue mourned
      To see the desolation of theise dayes,
      where myscheife had Tryvmphed so manye wayes ! 364

LIII.

Then haue wee not cause to prayse *our* god,
  whoe from theise dangers hathe vs preserved,
and fre[e]d vs from this heavie smartinge rodd
    of suche traytors as from dutie swarved ?   368
    and like sawcye mates they woulde haue carved
      of manye good men bothe there goods & life :
      yee, one small letter hathe barde this strife.   371

LIV.

Here was the wisedome of *our* god to bee sene !
  Here mans owne wisedome was proved but vayne !
Here, where so manye consultations had bene,
    Here to plott and practise there witts they strayne, 375
    Here, marke by there vyllanyes what they gayne !
      a trappe they had layde, and bayted a gynne,
      Thee hooke they swallowed, and pitt they fell in ! 378

---

[1] Cp. *The Fal of the Romish Church, with al the abhominations*, black letter,
in Lambeth Library.

LV.

And so by Iustice haue repte there desartes,
  and gwerdon due to suche mercyles men :
Hanged and quartred, and there traytrose hartes
    Withe bowells and members burned, and then   382
    There bodyes butcherde in sight of manye men,
      That greatlie did lamente there lacke of grace,
      That by treason woulde there glorye deface.   385

LVI.

The treasons that Babington once Invented,   [leaf 32.]
  withe yours in no sorte might bee comparde !
Theye to the Deathe of there Quene consented ;
    you aymde at all—a crueltie never harde !   389
    all sparkes of christianytie debarde,
      The kinge, Quene, prince, and nobles fynall doome !
      Suche bee the fruytes that bee plotted at roome, 392

LVII.

And hither are sente to bee Ingrafted
  By Iesuytes ithe hartes of good mens mynde !
an1 manye other dreggs are hether wafted
    of superstition, mens hartes to blynde,   396
    Causinge them to poperye [to] bee Inclinde :
      So, by wicked Bellamytes'[1] perswation,
      They Hassarde the Danger of there salvation, 399

LVIII.

And are Egged on to treason like case,
  bothe agaynste kinge and contrie to rebell,
Sekinge the Image of god to deface :
    what is donne agaynste hym, all is well !   403
    loe, theise bee the fruytes of that romyshe hell !
      and when [their] soules are secluded[2] gods glorye,
      Then will they fishe for them in purgatorye.   406

LIX.

But that rotten staffe is disfavorde quite,
  and hope of purgatorye out of requeste ;
no wise men in suche things will take delite ;
    with suche heavie burthens theyele not bee prest ; 410
    There hope is ' oure god hathe purchacste the reste
      of repentante synfull soules after deathe,'
      Purgatorye longe synce hunted out of breathe.   413

---

[1] f Bedlamites or Balaamites : the Jesuits, Garnet, Oldcorne, etc.   [2] shut out of.

LX.

Saynte ffrancis maye faste, firste auchtor of *the* same, [leaf 32,
   of whiche hee ever hathe bene the cheife proppe,   back.]
But nowe waxte olde, decripitt and lame,
   His requiem masses downe are lopte,   417
   The zeale of gods truthe that streame hathe stopte ;
      That scarbugge[1] w*hic*h did so manye affright,
      By triall of truthe is quyte put to flight ;   420

LXI.

And, good bee praysde, all *your* popishe trashe
   accounted as thinges frivolose and vayne ;
your eare-confession, and suche myshe-mashe
   of filthie vilde dreggs, gods glorye to stayne,   424
   By whiche to *your* state you horded vpp gayne,
      Is quite from brittayne banyshed awaye,
      ffrustrate *your* hopes, and you haue loste the daye, 427

LXII.

Yee, the greate daye of *your* expectation !
   and *your* hopes all turned to darkest night,
Wherein shoulde haue bene suche Innovation
   agaynste nature, agaynste equitie and right,   431
   If *your* devises haue prevayled might,
      when one of *your* crewe, and with you accurste,
      Thoughe agaynste his will, revealde it at firste, 434

LXIII.

And by his written letter hathe taught you to preache,
   what doctryne, the whole wordle knoweth to well,
veryfyinge what you before did teache,
   In catholicke errors to make men dwell,   438
   Teachinge the waye that leadeth to hell :
      your pulpitt was a Gibbett raysed on hie,
      whereon for treason you weare Iudged to dye,   441

LXIV.

A pulpitt where manye haue preached before,   [leaf 33.]
   that haue bene traytors agaynst kinge and state.
God grante, I praye, there never bee more,
   withe you so puffed withe wordlie hate,   445
   But that there Rigor maye in some sorte bate,[2]
      or like sicke Horses, to cure the fallose,[3]
      God sende you all maye preache on the gallose,   448

---

[1] Scare-goblin, or -bugbear ; like scare-crow.   [2] Abate.
[3] *Fellon*, a disease in cows : *felone*, a sore or whitlow.—*Halliwell.*

LXV.

As some of them of late weare forced to preache
 In pawles churchyarde, weste parte of the same,
Where a Highe Gibbett farr above *our* retche
  was there elevated on a wooden frame, 452
  and to see them there manye thousands came :
   Sir Everarde Digbye, hee repentant dyde,
   But on the Catholyke faithe hee still relyde. 455

LXVI.

Then preacht wynter, Grante, and Bates like case ;
 But one selfe doctryne they agreede vppon,
There pulpitt to papistes a foule disgrace,
  that weare there in place spectators on ; 459
  There wante of grace bewaylde of manye one,
   I meane, good subiects of Towne and cittie
   That shedd brynishe teares for there soules pittie. 462

LXVII.

Thexecutioners playde there butchringe partes
 as Iustice had doomde, and Iudgment had paste,
and traytors gwerdonde for there desarte,
  The rewarde of trecherye payde at laste ; 466
  for they muste nedes fall that ronne in suche haste
   Into the gulphe of Iminent Dangers,
   That to allegiance become suche strangers 469

LXVIII.

As did theise foure herebefore recited,   [leaf 33, back.]
 and all the reste of that vilde faction :
at there fall I knowe papistes are spited,
  ffor manye weare prevye to the action 473
  whose lives haue not yet made satisfaction ;
   leaste[1] theye repente there purpose in this case,
   God sende them preache on some suche like place. 476

LXIX.

Then to westmynster other foure weare drawne
 on Hurdells throughe london, to there disgrace,
To the olde pallace where treason was sowne ;
  there was elevated there preachinge place, 480
  where wynter, firste of that rebelliose race,
   preacht popishe doctryne to confirme his faith[e] ;
   But the Hangman quicklie stopped his breathe. 483

---

[1] unless.

LXX.

Then Died Rockwoode, Vaux, and keyes the laste,
  all on the same pulpitt made there endes;
But with hangmans helpe there paynes weare sone paste;
    There deathes a corsyve to there popishe frends,   487
    and a comforte to suche as the welfare intends,
      And to kinge and contrie wishe all good,
      livinge in dutie, not thirstinge for blood,   490

LXXI.

All theise traytors that before are named,
  with others by Iustice doomde in like cases,
whose aspiringe mynde the gallose hathe tamde,
    In worcester, stafforde-shere, and suche like places, 494
    where theise traytors lurkinge hydd there faces,
      Thoughe covertlie hyd, yet founde out at laste,
      And with theise in rancke deserve to be placeste. 497

LXXII.

Stephen litleton, thou hadst cause to repente !   [leaf 34.]
  thie howse was receptakle of the reste.
God grante thie trecherie thou didst lamente,
  and that contrition harborde in thie breste;   501
ffor in theise actions thou weare to preste ;[1]
    ffor in Holbage howse thou didst receve them,
    and ronnynge awaye, as a praye didst leave them. 504

LXXIII.

And percye and Catesbye bothe there weare kilde,
  Withe twoe of the Wrights, and others I not name;
Muche traytrose blood that tyme there was spilde,
    That never to triall of Iustice came;   508
    The Desperate vyllaynes had vowed the same,
      never to bee tane, and by Iustice tryde,
      what hassarde so ere there fortunes did byde.   511

LXXIV.

But tis thought there bee some of greater states
  that haue bene agents and Dealers therein :
Tis pittie that ever by suche base mates
    they shoulde bee counselde[2] to suche deadlie synne, 515
    Or that anye peere shoulde bee sene therein,
      To ecklipse the glorye of Honored fame,
      and bee scandalizde with touche of the same; 518

---

[1] Ready.   [2] MS. comselde.

LXXV.

ffor greate is the maiestie of Roiall kinges,
    that here vppon earthe gods vicegerents bee!
There lookes to trecheryè are fearfull stinges;
    There eyes, like Argus, to beholde and see,   522
    even to there myndes that good subiects bee.
      ffrom those that seke maiestie to betraye,
      Hee treason can fynde, and the same bewraye.   525

LXXVI.

God grante all [these] subiects example maye bee [leaf 34,
    to all others, hereafter to beware,   back.]
The saftie of there states to beholde and see,
    and of allegiance haue a speciall care,   529
    leaste the like gwerdon fall to there share;
      So generallie wishinge all to take hede,
      Theye in aftertymes the better maye spedc.   532

LXXVII.

The guylte of the harte is knowne by the eye:
    althoughe traytors connynglie dissemble,
The wisedome of princes can sone aspie
    out those secrett; for feare makes them trcmble,   536
    and there guyltie consciences to wemble.[1]
      There outwarde countnances then bewraye[2]
      What theye[3] haue thought, or tonges can saye.   539

LXXVIII.

A conscience clere, no prerogative needs,—
    loe, here is the wisedome of *our* good god!—
when corrupted myndes with there horror bleedes.
    Thus truthe and villanye are things farr odd,   543
    The one withe love, the other with Iustice rodd;
      Thus bothe are gwerdonde in thende, wee see:
      Then whoe woulde venter a traytor to bee?   546

LXXIX.

Whie, none but fooles that haue loste there witts,
    and wasted out the same on foolishe toyes,

---

[1] *Wcmble*, to turn a cup upside down in token of having had enough tea, (Northern;) *Wamble*, to roll, to rumble, (*Halliwell;*) to move in an undulating manner, (*Jamieson;*) to rise up as seething water does, to wriggle like an Arrow in the Air. (*Kersey's Philipps.*)

[2] MS. bewaraye.   [3] MS. there.

So then will venter on suche franticke fitts,
 and woulde thereby abridge other mens ioyes. 550
 See here, the sequell proves there owne anoyes !
  This tale of treason and her sadd storye,
  of manye a man hathe dym*m*de the glorye, 553

LXXX.

And alwayes hathe, synce the wordle beganne, [leaf 35.]
 that eve in parradise did Adam betraye,
whiche was the ruyne of the state of man,
 To all posterities the sole decaye 557
 till god in mercye washte the same awaye :
  onelie by the deathe of his beloved sonne
  Brusinge the Serpents head, *our* ioyes begonne. 560

LXXXI.

So that the Devill the firste traytor was,
 thoughe transformed into an angell bright,[1]
Intendinge subtellie to bringe to passe,
 By polecye turninge darknes to light, 564
 That for Imitac*i*on all others might
  Slilye goe aboute when they tyranise,
  or w*i*th an Intente myscheife to devise. 567

LXXXII.

So when anye man to myscheife is bente,
 withe full resolve to prosecute the same,
His master is preste[2] to forwarde his Intente,
 Ats[3] elbowe egginge hym, devoyde of shame, 571
 Makinge hym worke in destructions frame
  The webbe[4] of woe, to overthrowe his state
  By murther and treason, w*h*ich god dothe hate. 574

LXXXIII.

But now, you sacred muses, guyde my penne !
 Devyne Minerva, rule my artlesse[5] quill,
That I maye sett forthe to the vewe of all men
 His worthe, whoe farr surpasseth my small skill, 578
 yet will expresse a loiall subiects will
  To eternyze here his deserved fame,
  Terrifyinge traytors at sounde of the same ! 581

---

[1] *Originally* of light.   [2] Ready.   [3] At his.
[4] MS. woble.   [5] Unskilful.

LXXXIV.

ffirste, hees religiouse : thats knowne well :   [leaf 35, back.]
  to sett forthe gods glorye, his speciall care,
what paynes hee takes therein, the wordle can tell ;
  what metings and assemblies hee did prepare,   585
  To haue things reformed, thought out of square,
    Where his maiestie in presence did sytt
    Hearinge controversies, for a kinge moste fitt.   588

LXXXV.

Then hees mercifull, and no rigor showes,
  all crueltie Bannyshed from his harte :
His bountie and love, whoe is it but knowes ?
  In amplest wise gwerdonynge trewe desarte,   592
  and vnto subiectes dothe eache waye Imparte ;
    yee, of stubborne papistes hathe stayde the leasure ;
    But theyle bee reformed at there owne pleasure,   595

LXXXVI.

Or els by treason will cutt out there waye,
  and so Intrude on his highnes favor,
of hym and his sekinge the sole decaye.
  Dothe this of good religion savor ?   599
  no ! obstinate men ! you doe but glavor[1] !
    where his highnes seekes *your* quiett and peace,
    you onelie seeke his sorrowes to Increase !   602

LXXXVII.

Hee is also called the prince of peace,
  ffor whiche all nations to hym haue sente.
In leauge[2] with all princes, olde quarrells ceasse ;
  Quyet of his contrie hathe eache waye mente.   606
  But aspiringe myndes are never contente,
    If an angell from heaven hither came downe   608
    To rule here in earthe, and weare Brittaynes crowne.

LXXXVIII.

What vertues in anye kinge hathe ever bene,   [leaf 36.]
  but in his maiestie wee maye fynde them ?
Takinge patrone from *our* late blessed Quene,

---

[1] to sooth up, or fawn upon.—*Kersey's Phillips ;* to flatter.—*Nares.*   [2] league.
III.   F

vnto whose love hee ever combynde hym,   613
and shee in like love did ever mynde hym,
  as boinge trewe heire of her roiall race,
  Endowed bothe with her vertues and gra[ce].   616

LXXXIX.

Hee is also wise, hee is Iuste and learned,
  provident and carefull for subiects [g]ood;
whose wisedome, withe sallomon, hathe [disce]rned
  whoe is the right childe of Harlotts b[lood];   620
  whose learnynge, the truthe sone vnderstoode
    without devydinge the same a-sonder,
    To gods glorye and oure greate wonder.   623

XC.

Hee is likewise provident for the poore,
  restrayninge the canckers of his common-wealthe
That vagarantlie begg from dore to dore,
  thoughe still they wander vpp and downe by stealthe; 627
  and for maymed souldiers provided healthe,
    and stipens[1] in places for them to live,
    In all sheres[2] the contries doe pentious give.   630

XCI.

Hee mayntaynes Hospitalls for the disseasde,
  where the sicke are healde, the lame are cured;
But mall-contented myndes are never pleasde,
  when withe ambition theye bee in-vred,   634
  a Dissease that never can bee cured,
    Tis so puffed with hate, and [with] furye dothe swell,
    It often drawes downe tho sicke soule to hell.   637

XCII.

Nowe to conclude, or[3] I haue well begonne   [leaf 36, back.]
  to prayse his vertue that dothe prayse surmounte,
leaste I shoulde darken the glorye of the sonne,
  whose fame is boundlesse, passinge my accounte,   641
  vnlesse withe phaeton I presume to mounte,
    To rule don phebus steedes and fyrye carr,
    That where I shoulde make I shalbe[4] sure to marre. 644

---

[1] stipends.   [2] shires.
[3] before.   [4] MS. shalle.

XCIII.

[G]od blesse and preserve this our roiall kinge !
   [And fro]m traytrose practises defende hym,
[In wh]ose harte trewe contente maye daylie springe ;
   [A lo]nge and happie raygne ore vs god sende hym ! 648
confounde all suche as evill pretende[1] hym !
   God blesse our Quene, prince, and nobles of the lande !
protecte them, swete Iesus, with thie mightie hande !
                          Amen !   652

Lorde, I am bolde on thie mercyes to persever :
poore williams thus dothe praye, and will doe ever.

                         finis—R. W.

---

[1] Fr. *pretendre,* aime at . . lay or put in for; also, to meane; intend.—*Cotgrave.*

[If any readers feel that *"poore williams's"* flunkeyism is as bad as his verse, let them remember how much of that quality there was in England in James's time ; let them compare *A Prophecye* in the Percy Folio *Ballads and Romances*, iii. 372–3, and think that, as Williams was evidently begging for relief, he may be excused for laying on the praise and glory thick enough to suit James's taste.   R. W. was no worse than hundreds of divines and statesmen of his day.—F. J. F.]

Of Edward, Duke of Bokyngam.

In these verses we have the threnody of the unfortunate Duke of Buckingham, put to death at the beginning of the reign of Henry VIII. The charges upon which he suffered appear to have been absolutely devoid of proof. Among others, he was accused of aspiring to the crown in 1511, and with consulting a certain Nicholas Hopkins (a Carthusian monk, who pretended to be a necromancer) on the subject of the King's death. He was executed May 17, 1521.

The account of his trial as given by Holinshed is very fresh and graphic, and was evidently familiar to Shakspere when he wrote the scene so well known to the readers of Henry VIII.

"Thus was this prince duke of Buckingham found giltie of high treason, by a duke, a marques, seven earles, and twelve barons. The duke was brought to the barre sore chafing, and swet marvellouslie; and after he had made his reverence he paused a while. The duke of Norffolke, as judge, said: 'Sir Edward, you have heard how you be indicted of high treason; you pleaded thereto not giltie, putting your selfe to the peeres of the realme, which have found you giltie.' Then the duke of Norffolke wept and said: 'You shall be led to the king's prison, and there laid on a hardle, and so drawne to the place of execution, and there be hanged, cut downe alive, your members cut off and cast into the fire, your bowels burnt before you, your head smitten off, and your bodie quartered and divided at the king's will, and God have mercie on your soule. Amen.'

"The duke of Buckingham said: 'My lord of Norffolke, you have said as a traitor should be said unto, but I was never anie: but, my lords, I nothing maligne for that you have doone to me, but the eternall God forgive you my death, and I doo: I shall never sue to the king for life, howbeit he is a gratious prince, and more grace may come from him than I desire. I desire you, my lords, and all my fellows, to pray for me.' Then was the edge of the axe turned towards him, and he led into a barge. Sir Thomas Lovell desired him to sit on the cushins and carpet ordeined for him. He said: 'Nay; for when I went to Westminster I was duke of Buckingham, now I am but Edward Bohune, the most caitife of the world.' Thus they landed at the Temple, where received him Sir Nicholas Vawse and Sir William Sands, baronets,[1] and led him through the citie, who desired ever

---

[1] *sic* in the original. *Query* " bannerets."

the people to pray for him, of whome some wept and lamented, and said: 'This is the end of evill life, God forgive him; he was a proud prince, it is pitie that he behaved him so against his king and liege lord, whome God preserve.' Thus about foure of the clocke he was brought as a cast man to the Tower."

Such was the end of this unfortunate man, the head of whose family had been sent for generations to the shambles. See Shakspere's Henry VIII., Act II. Scene 1.

Of the twenty-two stanzas of the ballad, nineteen ryme the second and fourth lines in *-ess*.

[Harl. MS. 2252, leaf 2, back.]

I.

Alas! to whom shuld I complayne,[1]
   or shewe my wofull heyvynes,
Sythe fortune hathe me in dysdayne,
   & am exiled, Remedyles?

II.

o flateryng fortune! I May the Call;
   thy Chaungebyll chance I can expres;
moste lykeste A wreche vnnaturall,
   þou haste exiled, Remediles.

III.

Alas! Alas! remediles!
   put am I to mortall dystres!
exilyd for evyr, Remedyles,
   by Cawtellment, & remediles!

IV.

Art thow A god? or by whose lawus
   doste take on þe suche enterprise,
to take on the with-owte A Cawse,
   whyche yet dyd never preiudyse?

V.

Leve of þⁱ woe to wreke on me,
   To leve A lady all Comfortles;
hyt ys no poynte of chevalry,
   nor yet no Towche of Icntylnes.

---

[1] In the MS., several of the final letters, as s, m, n, f, d, have a curl or tag, but they appear to belong to the flourish of the hand.

VI.

I say Adew! but not farweti!
  False, flateryng, fortune, with dobylnes
Thow haste exilyd, whych dyd exseti,
  The Chefe refuge of my dystres.

VII.

o god, þat ati þis world hathe wrowghte!
  whom shuld I tryste? whych be perforce,
That I Browght vppe & made of nowghte
  haþe me Acusyd, Remedyles.

VIII.

ensampyti by me All lordes may Take,
  to whom þer myndes they do exprese;
on, of my Counceti þat I dyd make,
  haþe me Acusyd, remedyles.

IX.

defawte in my prynce can I none fynde,
  hys lawys to vse with Ryghtwysenes;
In them þat contrary he doþe fynde,
  To correcte them, remedyles.

X.

for, no dowte, dethe haue I deseruyd;
  good lord, to þe I me confesse;
thy grace in me was not Regardyd,
  Therfor I dye now remedyles.

XI.

Sumtyme my name was famuslye sprede,
  A duke Ryati, in þis land pereles;
& nowe, Alas! lost ys my hede,
  exilyd for evyr, Remedyles!

XII.

Now take I my dethe here paciently;
  hyt bothyth [1] me not to make no stryffe.
Was I never false to the kyng nor þe Crowne,
  but only to myn owne lady & wyffe.

---

[1] booteth, advantages.

XIII.

for-gyve me, lady, as þou wold forgevy*n* be!
  my payn*us* here they be fułł thycke.
pray ye for me! and I wyll pray for yow Agayne,
  & yf þ^e dede may pray for þ^e quykc[ke].

XIV.

And nowe, farwełł myne owne lady swete!
  my payn*us* styll they do Increse;
I truste ons Agayne yow & I shall mete,
  & nev*er* to be exilyd, Remedyles.

XV.

Adew, my lady & wyfe!
  And C*om*forte yo*ur* selfe in hevynes;
for to beweyle the losse of my lyfe,
  To me hyt ys remedyles.

XVI.

o ye nobyll lord*es* & ladys fayre!
  pray to ow*er* kyng, In my dystresse
To be graci*us* to my wyfe, chy*l*d*er*, & myne Ayre,
  þ*at* he exile the*m* not Remedyles.

XVII.

for, of my fawte no thynge they knowe;
  ow*er* lord god take I to wytnesse!
vnto þ*er* kyng bothe faythfułł & Trew:
  Exile them not Remedyles.

XVIII.

Therfor, Adew, my lord*es* ałł!
  The darte of deþ^e me [dothe] oppresse,
for to c*om*playne of my mortałł fałł,
  To me hyt ys remedyles.

XIX.

Farwełł, my good frend*es*, & *seruantes* trewe!
  I pray yow all of Ientylnes.
To pray to ow*er* lord Cryste I*es*u,
  to haue m*er*cy of my wrechydnes.

XX.

Now where ys he Thys dede do shatt ?—
    geve me leve to speke whyle I haue brethe ;—
here, before *þis* lord*es* att,
    hertely here I forgeve þ^e my dethe.

XXI.

In Man*us* tuas, I com*m*en*d* me to the, I*e*su !
    my body ys here in *þis* dystresse.
now, good lord, as þou arte A Iust*es* trewe,
    exile not my pore sowle, remedyles !

XXII.

I*e*su ! Reward them bothe bodely & goostlye,
    from all*e* adu*er*syte & grete dystresse,
þ*at* wyll pray for the sowle of the dwke of bokyngam,
    þ*at* late was exiled remedyles.

POEMS RELATING TO QUEEN ELIZABETH.

In the following poems, although perhaps few of them can boast of any considerable literary merit, we have a lively picture presented to us of the Maiden Queen, and the estimation in which she was held by her contemporaries. Despite many personal foibles, and a Tudor-like tendency to rule with the strong hand, there can be no doubt that Elizabeth was popular among her subjects: her natural good sense taught her when to stop in her efforts to enforce any of her arbitrary measures: she calculated the pulse of the nation, and kept its beatings regular. If we were to trust the panegyrics written during her reign, she was a paragon of every excellence—intellectual and moral; and mercenary poets were not unwilling to see all conceivable beauties in a woman of seventy, whose cheeks were resplendent with paint, and whose head was bedecked with a red wig.

Such was the Britomart and Gloriana of Spenser: the heroine of whom Raleigh and Essex were knight-errants. The anonymous versifiers, some of whose productions are here for the first time printed, spoke of her as a Venus and Minerva: in her youth she may have had some remote claims to the former appellation; throughout her whole life she might have assumed the latter title with no great inconsistency. With considerable penetration, a ready wit, and a wonderful power of selecting able and suitable agents for her purposes,—witness the brilliant men who composed her court,—she was also a woman of considerable reading, and the mistress of many languages. Elizabeth affected a taste for philological pursuits. Jerome Horsey, the celebrated ambassador to Russia, tells us that when he came back to England, and showed Her Majesty the letter received from the terrible Ivan Vasilievitch, —the annals of whose reign in the bloody fasti of Muscovy seem more than usually besmirched,—the Queen looked with great curiosity at the words in the Slavonic tongue, adding, "I could quicklie lern it." He also tells us that she asked "if such and such letters and asseveracions had not this signification," etc. The poets who praised her linguistic acquirements had probably some good ground for their representations. We know that female education in those days was a solid affair, and had little in common with the mincing elegancies held sufficient by modern society. Camden tells us that "before she was seventeen years of age, she understood well the Latin, French, and Italian tongues, and had an indifferent knowledge of the Greek."

Roger Ascham has recorded her proficiency in the latter language ("Epistolarum Libri Quatuor Oxoniæ," MDCCIII., p. 52, Letter to Joannes Sturmius)—

"Si aves scire, quidnam rerum ago in Aula, jntelligas nunquam mihi magis optatum otium concessum fuisse in Academia; quam nunc est in Regia D. Elizabetha et ego una legimus Græce orationes Æschinis et Demosthenis περὶ Στεφάνου. Illa prælegit mihi et primo aspectu tam scienter intelligit, non solum proprietatem linguæ, et oratoris sensum: sed totam caussæ contentionem, populi scita, consuetudinem, et mores illius urbis, ut summopere admirareis."

This is a large measure of praise, unless, as is perhaps too often the case, the schoolmaster is wholly lost in the courtier. The story of the arrival of the Polish ambassador, Paul Dzialinski, who was sent by Sigismund II. in 1597, is well known. He was a man of stately presence, and appeared in an elaborate suit of black velvet; on being introduced before the Queen, he made a long oration in Latin, complaining of the wars between the English and Spaniards, whereby he asserted that the commerce of Poland was seriously injured. In reply, Elizabeth broke out into a vehement tirade in excellent Latin, in which, as Speed says, "lionlike, rising, she danted the malapert orator no less with her stately port and majestical deporture, than with the tartness of her princely checks."

Of her poetical talents Master George Puttenham speaks with no little praise, although perhaps his critical powers are somewhat blunted by a courtier's adulation: "I finde none example that euer I could see, so well maintayning this figure in English meetre as that ditty of her Maiesties owne making, passing sweete and harmonicall, which figure begins as his very originall name purporteth the most bewtifull and gorgious of all others, it asketh in reason to be reserued for a last complement, and desciphred by the arte of a ladies penne, her selfe beyng the most gorgious and bewtifull, or rather bewtie of Queenes."

Some of the poems have reference to the suit of Anjou, the brother of Henry III. of France, whose visit to England in 1581 had almost resulted in the loss of the Queen's heart. She was then in her forty-seventh year, and before the whole assembled court was seen to take a ring from her finger and place it upon his, as that of her affianced lover. On the following morning, however, her suitor found her anxious and weeping, and she then told him that on advising with her council, she had again made up her mind never to marry. On returning to his apartments the Duke, mortified and stung to the quick, is said to have uttered many sententious speeches on the wayward wills of women, and to have flung the ring of betrothal to the winds. He returned to France, and soon afterwards died.

Elizabeth, who, as we have before mentioned, occasionally ventured upon composition, did not allow Anjou to depart without a poetic lamentation. In the following verses, preserved in the Ashmolean Collection, her feelings found vent:—

[Ash. MS. 781, p. 142.]

"I greive, and dare not shewe my discontent;
 I love, and yet am forst to seeme to hate;
I do, yet dare not say I ever meant;
 I seem starke mute, but inwardly do prate;
I am, and not; I freese, and yet am burn'd,
Since from myself, my other self I turn'd.

"My care is like my shaddowe in the sunne,
 Followes me fliinge, flies when I pursue it;
Standes and lies by me, doth what I have don;
 His too familiar care doth make me rue it:
No meanes I finde to rid him from my brest,
Till by the end of thinges it be supprest.

"Some gentler passions slide into my minde,
 For I am softe, and made of melting snowe;
Or be more cruell, Love, and soe be kynd,
 Let me or flote, or sinke, be high or lowe:
Or let me live with some more sweete content;
Or dye, and soe forget what love ere meant.

"Eliza Regina, upon Mounzeur's departure."

It was well for the country in every way that the marriage never took place. The Duke, an unamiable and selfish man, the degraded scion of the most infamous line of kings which has ever occupied the French throne, was only known to be hated, and the English viewed the proposed alliance with great dislike. Such a union must also have involved us in many political complications, as that of Mary with Philip of Spain had done. A vehement diatribe against the marriage, entitled "The Gaping Gulfe," was written by one John Stubbs, who afterwards suffered severely for his freedom. The following curious account of his punishment is taken from Camden's "History of Elizabeth," book iii. p. 270:—

"Hereupon Stubbs & Page had their Right hands cut off with a cleaver, driven through the Wrist by the force of a Mallet, upon a Scaffold in the Market-place at Westminster. The Printer (Singleton) was pardoned. I remember (being there present) that when Stubbs, after his Right hand was cut off, put off his Hat with his Left, and said with a loud voice, 'God save the Queen!' the Multitude standing about was deeply silent: either out of an Horrour at this new and unwonted kind of Punishment; or else out of Commiseration towards the man, as being of an honest and unblamable Repute; or else out of Hatred of the Marriage which most men presaged would be the Overthrow of Religion."[1]

---

[1] Camden describes Stubbs as "John Stubbs, of Lincoln's-Inne, a fervent hot-headed Professor of Religion," and states that the crown lawyers questioned the legality of the Act of Philip & Mary "against the Authours and Publishers of Seditious Writings."

It will be observed that these poets have a somewhat uniform note—the virtues, beauty, and intellect of their mistress. To them she was

"The fair vestal thronèd in the west,"—

the lady with

"————————awe commanding face
Attempered sweet to virgin grace,"

as Gray has it. Those who spoke more plainly, either as foreigners, or trusting their private opinions to the secrecy of a diary, could give a portrait of our heroine from a somewhat different point of view. Let us hear the account of Paul Hentzner, a German, who visited the country in 1598. The original is in Latin, but has been translated by Horace Walpole: "Next came the Queen, in the sixty-fifth year of her age, we are told, *very majestic;* her face oblong, fair, but wrinkled; her eyes small, yet black and pleasant; her nose a little hooked, her lips narrow, and her teeth black (a defect the English seem subject to, from their too great use of sugar); she had in her ears two pearls, with very rich drops; she wore false hair, and that red; upon her head she had a small crown, ... and she had on a necklace of exceeding fine jewels; her hands were small, her fingers long, and her stature neither tall nor low; her air was stately, her manner of speaking mild and obliging. That day she was dressed in white silk, bordered with pearls of the size of beans, and over it a mantle of black silk, shot with silver threads; her train was very long, the end of it borne by a marchioness; instead of a chain she had an oblong collar of gold and jewels. As she went along in all this state and magnificence, she spoke very graciously, first to one, then to another, whether foreign ministers, or those who attended for different reasons, in English, French, and Italian; for besides being well skilled in Greek, Latin, and the languages I have mentioned, she is mistress of Spanish, Scotch (*sic*), and Dutch; whoever speaks to her, it is kneeling; now and then she raises some with her hand. While we were there, W. Slawata, a Bohemian baron, had letters to present to her; and she, after pulling off her glove, gave him her right hand to kiss, sparkling with rings and jewels—a mark of particular favour; wherever she turned her face, as she was going along, everybody fell down on their knees. The ladies of the court followed next to her, very handsome and well-shaped, and for the most part dressed in white. She was guarded on each side by the gentle-men-pensioners, fifty in number, with gilt battle-axes. In the ante-chapel next the hall where we were, petitions were presented to her, and she received them most graciously, which occasioned the exclamation of 'Long live Queen Elizabeth!' She answered it with, 'I thank you, my good people.'"

No one can deny that the foreigner has left us a very vigorous picture of the "Great Eliza."

The following curious memoranda, compiled by Dr. Simon Forman, are to be found among the Ashmolean MSS. preserved in the Bodleian. In them the Queen appears in a very homely light.[1]

[Ash. MS. 226, fol. 44.]

"Anno 1597, the 23 Januaria, about 3 A.M., I dreampte that I was with the Queene, and that she was a lyttle elderly woman in a Corse whit peticote all vnredy, & she & I walked vp and downe thorowe Lanes & closes talkinge & reasoning of many matters; at Last we came over a thicket close wher were many people, and ther were too men at hard words, and on of them was a weauer, a talle man with a raddish herd distracte of his wits, and she talked to him, and he spak very merily vnto her, & at Laste did take her and kyst'her. Soe I tok her by the Arme & puld her away, & told her the fellowe was franticke, and soe we went from him, & I led her by the Arme still, and then we wente thorowe a durty lane. And she had a long whit smok, very clene and faire, and yt drailled in the durte & her cote behind, and I toke her cote & did carry'yt vp a good waie, and then yt hunge to lowe before. And I towld her in talk she should do me a fauour to let me waight on her, & she said I should. . . . . And soe we talked meryly, & then she began to lean vpon me when we were paste the durte, & to be veri familiar with me, and me thoughte she began to Loue me. And when we were Alone out of sighte me thought she wold haue kissed me. And with that I waked. That morninge soe sone As I was vp, came

---

[1] "Lilly tells us in his autobiography that Dr. Simon Forman 'travelled into Holland for a month in 1580, purposely to be instructed in astrology, and other more occult sciences, as also in physic, taking his degree of doctor beyond seas,' and afterwards lived in Lambeth, with a very good report of the neighbourhood, especially of the poor, unto whom he was very charitable. Lilly says further, 'he was a person that in horary questions (especially thefts) was very judicious and fortunate; as also in sickness, which indeed was his master-piece.' If this means that he was a master in the art of secretly destroying health and life, a subtle practitioner in poisons, the infamous story of Lord and Lady Essex, and the tragedy of Sir Thomas Overbury, will sufficiently bear out the statement. 'In resolving questions about marriage,' Lilley adds, 'he had good success; in other questions very moderate.' As for a remarkable memorandum which the doctor left behind him—'This I made the Devil write with his own hand in Lambeth Fields, 1596, in June or July, as I now remember'—we must be excused from believing the affirmation till some unexceptionable witness is brought forward who will swear to his infernal majesty's handwriting."—Knight's "London," vol. iii. p. 251.—In the paper from which this passage is extracted, we have a very interesting sketch of the life of Forman and other mountebanks of the period, notably Dee, Kelly, and Lilly—the adventures of the first of the three being of a highly romantic character. There are many MSS. in the Ashmolean Collection entirely written by Forman, one of them giving an account of his early life.

Mr. Sefton vnto me, to entrete me to forgive him, and soe end his matter; but he wold not pay my charge, nor mak me Any recompense, nor haue Any man to heare the matter, & after moch talk I told him no, & soe with moch a doe we departed: ther was nothing ells fell out that Dai, but at afternone Jone mi sister cam to me, and I went to Δλχ (Dulwich?) to the (cypher), and helth (cypher), quia Dominus egrotabit diu ex. mightily."

[Fol. 45.] "Then the 22 of Feb. I dreamt of the quene that she came to me all in black & a french hode; that dai I had Anger by Doryty and Mrs. Pennington, that came to me About words my man spake."[1]

Ben Jonson twice mentions this celebrated quack :

"*Dauphiné.*—I would say thou hadst the best philter in the world, and couldst do more than madam Medea or doctor Foreman."—*Silent Woman*, act iv.

"Ay, they do now name Bretnor, as before they talked of Gresham, and of Doctor Foreman."—*The Devil is an Ass*, act i. scene 2.

---

[1] Ash. MS. 226 is a volume consisting of several quires of paper bound together, thus entitled by Ashmole, "Figures set upon Horary questions, by Mr. Simon Forman, 1597, vol. 2, being his medical and astrological Practice from 20th January, 1597, to 20 February, 1598. Forman born 1552, died 1611."— Ash. MS. 219 is a volume by Forman of the same description as the foregoing. He has recorded (fol. 53), "The words that Peter Sefton of the ston house, Clarke, uttered againste Simon Forman the 9th of May, 1599, with the names of the witnesses, and a note that he was arrested for the same;" and in Ash. MS. 236, another MS. of Forman's, Sefton's "matter" is brought to a close by a "copy of a certificate of oath made by Thomas Grene, serjeant, of the delivery of a bond by S. Forman, for settling the dispute between him and Peter Sefton (23 May, 1599)." Occasionally he applies his astrological knowledge to very practical questions, as when he seeks to find out "whe[the]r Danson will pay me my money the next court day" (24 Jan. 1610).

The Partheniades of George Puttenham.

OF George Puttenham, the author of the "Arte of English Poesie," 1589, our records are very meagre. He was born about 1532, and probably died somewhere near the close of the same century. The poem is here printed from a Cottonian MS. If we had any doubts about the writer, they would certainly be removed by the following allusion in the above-cited work:

"This considered, I will let one figure enioy his best beknowen name, and call him stil, in all ordinarie cases, the figure of comparison, ... as when we sang of our Soueraigne Lady thus, in the twentieth Partheniade—

As faulcon fares to bussardes flight," etc.

The authorship of Puttenham was known to his contemporaries. Sir John Harington, in the preface to his translation of "Orlando Furioso" (London, 1591), alludes sarcastically to his slender poetical merits: "Neither do I suppose it to be greatly behoofull for this purpose, to trouble you with the curious definitions of a Poet and Poesie, and with the subtill distinctions of their sundry kinds; nor to dispute how high and supernatural the name of a maker is, so christened in English by that vnknowne godfather, that this last year save one, viz. 1589, set forth a booke called the Arte of English Poetrie. . . . . . . For though the poore gentleman laboreth greatly to proue, or rather to make Poetrie an art, and reciteth as you may see in the plural number, some pluralities of patterns, and parcels of his owne Poetrie, with divers pieces of Partheniads and hymnes in praise of the most praiseworthy: yet whatsoeuer he would proue by all these, sure in my poore opinion he doth proue nothing more plainly, than that which M. Sidney and all the learneder sort that have written of it do pronounce, namely, that it is a gift, and not an art. I say he proueth it, because making himselfe and so manie others so cunning in the art, yet he sheweth himself so slender a gift in it."

In a list of works written by Puttenham, copied by Ritson from a memorandum made by George Steevens out of a paper in the handwriting of Ben Jonson, the name Partheniades also occurs (see Carew Hazlitt's "Handbook of Elizabethan Literature," p. 488). Besides these mentions, I may notice that a part of the poem was printed in Nichols' "Progresses of Queen

Elizabeth," 1823, and again in "Ancient Critical Essays," edited by Joseph Haslewood, 1811. It will be observed that the copy of the piece is not complete: at least three of the divisions being omitted. It was probably presented to the Queen on New Year's Day, 1579. In his reprint, Haslewood has not attempted to explain any of the difficulties which the poem contains.

[MS. Cott. Vesp. E. viii. leaf 169.]

The principall addresse in nature of a New yeares gifte, seeminge therebye the Author intended not to have his name knowne.

Parthe: 1. Gracious Princesse, Where princes are in place
Thaleia.
To geue you gold, and plate, and perles of price,
It seemeth this day, saue your royaꝇ advice,
Paper præsentes should haue but little grace.
But sithe the tyme so aptly serues the case,   5
And, as some thinke, youre highnes takes delighte
Oft to pervse the styles of other men,
And oft youre self, with Ladye Sapphoes pen,
In sweet measures, of poesye t'endite
The rare affectes of your hevenly sprighte,   10
Well hopes my Muse to skape all manner blame,
Vttringe your honours, to hyde her owners name.

The author choosinge by his verse to honour the Queenes Maiestie of England Ladye Elizabeth, bodily preferreth his choise *and* the excellencye of the subiect before all others of anye Poet, auncient or moderne.

Parthe. 2: Greeke Achilles and his peeres did enioye
Clio: 2.
Greate Homers troompe, for theyr high valiaunce,
And Maro woulde in stately stile advaunce   15
Æneas, and that noble reste of Troye.
In martial moodes Lucane did singe the chaunce,
Ende and pursute of that lamented warre
Of proude allyes, whose envy spredd so farre,
As exilde Roome all egall governaunce.   20

Horace honourd August, the highest of names,
And yet his harte from Mecene neuer swerude.

Ovide helde trayne in Venus courte, and serude
Cheife secretarye to all those noble Dames,
Martyres of loue, who so broylde in his flames   25
As both theyr trauth *and* penance well deserude
All in fine gold to haue theyr image kerude,
For cleere recorde of theyr most woorthy fames.

By the brighte beames of Cynthia, the sheene, [If. 169. bk.]
Cupide kendled the fyres of properse,[1]   30
Tibullus teares bayned[2] Neæras herse,
And ladye Laura, her graces that grow greene,
By Dan Petrarche, of Tuskan poets prince.
Anacreon sange all in his wanton spleene;
But proude Pindare, he spilde the praises cleene   35
Of all Liricques that were before or since.

I singe noe bloodd, nor battayles in my verse,
Amorous odes, or elegies in teene,[3]
Churlishe satire, as Juvenall and Perse;[4]
But in chast style am borne, as I weene,   40
To blazon foorthe the briton mayden Queene,[5]
Whose woorthes surmount them all that they reherse.

    That her Ma*ie*stie (twoo thing*es* except) hath all
the partes that iustly make to be sayd a most happy
·creature in this world.

Parthe: 3.
Erato.   Youthfull bewtye, in body well disposed;
Louelye fauoure, that age cannot deface;
A noble harte, where nature hath inclosed   45
The fruitfull seedes of all vertue and grace;
Regall estate, coucht in the treble crowne,
Ancestrell all, by linage and by right;
Store of treasures, honour and iust renowne;
In quiet raigne, a sure redouted mig[h]t;   50
Fast frindes, foes few or faint, or overthrowen;
The stranger toonges, and the harts of her owne:

---

[1] Propertius.   [2] Bathed, Fr. *baigner*.
[3] Grief, spito.   [4] Persius.
[5] A favourite epithet of Elizabeth among the poets of the period.

Breife ; both nature and nourriture haue doone,
With fortunes helpe, what in their cunning is
To yelde the erth, a Princelye paragon.   55
But had shee, oh ! the two ioys shee doth misse—
A Cesar to her husband, a Kinge to her soone—.
What lackt her highnes then to all erthly blisse?

[ll. 170.]   That her Maiestie surmounteth all the Princesses
                  of our tyme in wisedome, bewtye, and magnanimitye,
                  and ys a thinge verye admirable in nature.

Parthe: 4: Whome Princes serve, and Realmes obay,
Thulia.
            And greatest of Bryton kinges begott,   60
            Shee came abroade even yesterday,
            When such as saw her knew her not ;
            For one woold ween that stoode a farre
            She were as other weemen arre.

            In trauthe it fares much otherwise :   65
            For whilest they thinke they see a Queene,
            It comes to passe ye can devise
            No stranger sight for to bee seene ;
            Suche erroure falls in feble eye
            That cannot view her stedfastlye.   ·   70

            How so ? alas ! forsooth it is,
            Nature, that seldome woorkes amis,
            In woman's brest by passinge arte
            Hath harbourd safe the Lyons harte,
            And featlye fixt, with all good grace,   75
            The serpentes hedd and angells face.

           That wisedome in a princesse is to be preferred
           before bewtye, riches, honour, or puissaunce ; but
           where all the partes concure in one person, as they
           doe moste evidently in her Maiestie, the same is not
           to be reputed an humane, but rather a diuine per-
           fection.

Parthe: 5 The Phrigian youth, full ill advised,
Melpo-
mene.   To iudge betweene goddesses thre,

All worldly wealth and witt despised,
And gaue the price to cleere beawtee :   80
His meede therfore was to win grace   [lf. 170 bk.]
Of Venus, and her louinge race.
The wandring prime and Knightes of Troye,
Who first broughte bale to Tyrian towne,
Coulde never finde comforte or ioye   85
While Juno did vppon them frowne :
Hir wrathe appeased, they purchaste reste,
An Lavine lande theire owne beheste.
I am not rapte in Junoes spheare,
Nor with dame Venus louelye hewe ;   90
But here one earthe I serue and feare,
O mayde Minerue, thine ydoll true,
W[h]ose power preuayles in warr and peace,
So as thy raigne can no tyme cease.

The addresse.

Princesse, yee haue the doome[1] that I can giue,
But seldome sitts the iudge that may not erre ;
Whence, to be sure, I haue vowed while I liue,
T' addore all three godheads in your own starre.

 That vertue ys alwayes subiect to envy and many
times to perill; and yf her Ma*ie*sties most notable
prosperities haue ever beene maligned, the same
hath beene for her only vertues sake.

Partbe : 6
Melpo-
mene.
 Fayre Britton maye,[2]   95
Wary and wise in all thy wayes,
Never seekinge nor finding peere,
When ere thy happe shalbe to heere
My mouth be muet in thy prayse
But one whole daye,   100

Sweare by thine head,   [lf. 171.]
And thy three crownes, it must needes bee
Whilest I admire thy rare bewtye
I am forspoke, in spite of thee,
By some disdaynefull curst feyrye,   105
Or sicke, or dead.

------

[1] Judgment.   [2] Maid.

But while thy mighte
Can keepe my harte queavinge[1] or quicke,
Trust me my lippes shall neuer lenne[2]
To power thye prayses to my penne,   110
Till all thy foes be sorrowe sicke
Or dead out right.

They saye not soothe
Of grace and goodnes that mainetayne
Them to be thinges so safe, so louelye;   115
I see nothinge vnder the skie
Abide suche daunger and disdaine
As vertue doothe.

Then, if theyr bee
Any so canckred harte to grutche[3]   120
At your gloryes, my Queene, in vayne,
Repininge at your fatall raigne,
It is for that they feele to muche
Of your bountee.

Parthe: 7
Euterpe.

A ryddle of the Princesse Paragon.[4]

I saw marche in a meadowe greene   125
A fayrer wight then feirye Queene;
And as I woulde approche her neere,
Her head ys shone like Christall cleere;
Of silver was her forehead hye,
Her browes two bowes of Henevye;[5]   130
Her tresses troust were to beholde,
Frizeld and fine as frenge of gold;
Her eyes, god wott what stuffe they arre,
I durst be sworne eche ys a starre,
As cleere and brighte as to guide   135
The pilot in his winter tide;
Twoo lippes wroughte out of rubye rocke,
Like leaues to shutt and to vnlocke,

---

[1] Quaving, shaking. Cf. quaver.   [2] Lend, A.S. *lene.*
[3] Grieve, envy, grumble.
[4] "Specially of faire women whose excellencie is discouered by paragonizing, or setting one to another, which moued the zealous Poet, speaking of the mayden Queene, to call her the paragon of Queenes."—Puttenham's *Art of Eng. Poesie.* Of Ornament, Lit. III.   [5] Ebony.

As portall doore in princes chamber ;
A golden toonge in mouth of amber,   140
That oft ys hard, but none yt seethe ;
Without a garde of yvorye teethe,
Even arrayed, and richelye, all
In skarlett, or in fine corrall ;
Her cheeke, her chinne, her neck, her nose,   145
This was a lillye, that was a rose ;
Her hande so white as whales bone,
Her finger tipt with Cassidone ; [1]
Her bosome, sleeke as Paris plaster,
Held vpp twoo bowles of Alabaster ;   150
Ech byas was a little cherrye,
Or as I thinke a strawberrye ;
A slender greve,[2] swifter then Roe,
A pretye foote to trippe and goe,
But of a solemne pace perdye,   155
And marchinge with a maiestye ;
Her body shapte as strayghte as shafte,
Disclosed eche limbe with-outen craft,
Saue shadowed all, as I could gesse,
Vnder a vayle of silke Cypresse,   160
From toppe to toe yee mighte her see
Timberd and tall as Cedar tree,
Whose statelye turfe exceedeth farre
All that in frithe [3] and forrest arre.
This markt I well, but loe anone,   [lf. 172.] 165
Me thought all like a lumpe of stone—
The stone that doth the steele enchaunte
The dreadfull rocke of Adamante,
And woorkes the shippe, as authors speake,
In salt sea manye a wofull wreake—   170
Her hart was hidd, none might yt see,
Marble or flinte folke weene yt bee ;
Not flint I trowe, I am a lyer,
But Syderite [4] that feeles noe fier.
Now reed aright, and do not mis,   175
What iolly [5] dame this ladye is.

---

[1] Cassidony, a kind of precious stone.   [2] Old French grève, the shin.
[3] A wood : the word occurs in Chaucer.   [4] The loadstone.
[5] The old Spenserian use of the word—
    " Full iolly knight he seemd, and faire did sitt,
      As one for knightly giusts and fieree encounters fitt."
            —Faerie Queene, book i. canto 1.

The assoile.[1]

This fleshe and bloode, this head, members and harte,
These lively lookes, graces, and bewty sheene,
Make but one masse, by nature and by arte
Rare to the earth, rathe to the worlde seene :   180
Would yee faine knowe her name and see your parte ?
Hye, and beholde a while the mayden Queene !

The assoile at large, moralized in three Dizaynes.

Parthe: & Thalia.   A hed harbroughe[2] of all counsayle *and* witt,
Where science dwells makinge a liuely sprighte,
And dame discourse, as in her castell sitt,   185
Scanninge causes by minde and by forsighte ;
A cheere Where Looue and maiestye doe raigne
Both mild and sterne, having some secret mighte ;
Twixte hope and dreede, in woe, and with delighte,
Mans harte in holde, and eye for to detayne ;   190
Feedinge the one with sighte in sweete desyre,
Dauntinge thother, by daunger to aspire.

Affable grace, speeche eloquent and wise,
Stately præsence, suche as becometh one
Whoe seemes to rule realmes by her lookes alone, [172 bk.]
And hathe what ells dame Nature coolde devise   196
To frame a face and corsage paragon,
Suche as these blessed sprightes of paradise
Are woonte to assume, or suche as lovers weene
They see sometimes in sleepe and dainty dreame,   200
In femall forme a goddesse, and noe Queene,
Fitter to rule a worlde then a realme.

A constante mynde, a courage chaste and colde,
Where loue logget[3] not, nor loue hathe any powres ;
Not Venus brandes, nor Cupide can take holde,   205
Nor speeche prevayle, teares, plainte purple or golde,
Honoure, nempire, nor youthe in all his flowers,
This wott ye all full well yf I do lye :

---

[1] "The assoile," absolution, *i.e.* as we now say of a riddle, the solution ; a favourite word with Puttenham.

[2] A head ; the harbour or lodging.   [3] Lodgeth.

> Kinges and kinges peeres, who haue soughte farre
>   and nye,
> But all in vayne, to bee her paramoures,   210
> Since twoo Capetts,[1] three Cezaimes[2] assayde,
> And bidd[3] repulse of the great Britton Mayde.

> A verye strange and rufull vision presented to
> the authoure, the interpretation wherof was left to
> her Maiestie till by the purpose discovered.

(Parthe: 9.)
> In fruitfull soyle beholde a flower sproonge,
> Distayninge golde, rubyes, and yvorye;
> Three buddes yt bare, three stalkes, tender and younge,
> One moare middle earthe, one toppe that touche the
>   skye,   216
> Under the leaues, one branches brade and hye,
> Millions of birds sange shrowded in the shade;
> I came anone, and sawe with weepinge eye
> Twoo blossoms falne, the thirde began to fade, 220
> So as, within the compas of an houre,
> Sore withered was this noble deintye flowre,
> That noe soyle bredd, nor lande shall loose the like,
> Ne no seazon or soone or sokinge showre [lf. 173.]
> Can reare agayne for prayer ne for meede. 225
> "Woe and alas!" the people crye and shrike,[4]
> "Why fades this flower, and leaues noe fruit nor seede?"

Perthe: 10.
Culliope.
> Another vision happned to the same authoure
> as Comfortable *and* recreatyve as the former was
> dolorous.

> A royall shippe I sawe by tyde and by winde,
> Single and sayle in sea as sweet as milke;

---

[1] "Since twoo Capetts." Lingard, vol. vi. p. 31, has given us a list of the suitors for the hand of Elizabeth. The two Capets were the Duke of Anjou and his younger brother, the Duke of Alençon.

[2] Probably a slip of the pen for Cezarins. Perhaps the allusion is to Philip I. of Spain, who had previously married her sister Mary. His son, the mad Don Carlos, who seems to have been proposed as her husband; John Emmanuel Philibert, Duke of Savoy, who was a scion of the Imperial House; or perhaps the Archduke Charles, the third and youngest son of the Emperor Ferdinand I.; may be meant. Of the last Coxe says (History of the House of Austria, ed. 1810, vol. ii.): "He was also a candidate for the hand of Elizabeth of England, and like other princes was disappointed by her maiden coyness, or independent spirit." He certainly did not make his appearance in England, like Anjou, only to undergo the indignity of a public rejection.

[3] Invited.

[4] Shriek.

Her Cedar keele, her mast of gold refined,   230
Her takle and sayles as silver and silke,
Her fraughte more woorthe then all the wares of Iude;
Cleere was the coaste, the waues were smooth and still,
The skyes al calme, Phœbus so brighte he shined ;
Æolus in poope gaue her wether at will ;   235
Dan Neptune stered, while Proteus playde his sporte,
And Neræus deinty dauters sange full shrill,
To slise her sayles, that they mighte swell theyr fill ;
Jove from aboue his pleasant showers powrde ;
Her flagge, it beares the flowers of mans comforte : 240
Noue but a kinge or more maye her abourde ;
O gallant peece, well will the Lillye afoorde
Thow strike mizzen and anker in his porte !

That her Ma*ie*sties most woorthye renowne can
not perishe while the worlde shall laste, with certayne philosophicall opinions touchinge the beginninge and durabilitye of the worlde.

Parthe: 11.
Vrania. O mightye Muse !
The *mignionst*[1] mayde of mounte Parnasse,   245
Ever verdurde with flowre and grasse
Of sundrye hews,
Saye, and not misse,
How longe agone and whence yt was
The fayre rounde worlde first came to passe   250
As yt now ys ?

There be that saye   [173 bk.]
How yt was never otherwise
Then as wee see it with our eyes
This very daye ;   255
There bee agayne
A secte of men, somewhat precise,
Beleeue a godd did yt devise,
And not in vayne,

Nor longe agone,   260
Onely to serue Adam's linage
Some little while as for a stage
To playe vpon ;

---

[1] Fr. mignon.

And by despighte
One daye agayne will in his rage   265
Crushe it all as a kicson cage[1]
And spill it quite.

Some weene it must[2]
Come by recourse of praty moates,
Farr finer then the smallest groates   270
Of sand or dust
That swarme in sonne,
Clinginge as faste as little clotes[3]
Or burres vppon younge children's cotes
That slise and runne.   275

Other suppose
A *νοῦς* approcht, and by reason
Brought it to shape and to season
From a Chaos;
But some tech vs,   280
By playne proofes, whye yt were begone;
Nor never more shalbe vndone,
But byde even thus,

Whoorlinge his whott[4]   [lf. 174.]
And endlesse roundell[5] *with* a throwe,   285
Swifter then shaft out of a bowe,
Or cannon shott.
O bootlesse carke
Of mortall men searchinge to knowe,
Or this or that, since he must rowe   290
The dolefull barke

---

[1] *Query* kecky, hollow. See Halliwell's Dictionary.

[2] Puttenham is here displaying to some advantage his attainments in philosophy. It was Anaxagoras who considered *νοῦς* to be the primary cause of all things, and in order to explain the creation of all existing things, Democritus maintained that there were in infinite space an infinite number of atoms or elementary particles, homogeneous in quality, but heterogeneous in form. He further taught that these atoms combine with one another, and that all things arise from the infinite variety of the form, order and position of the atoms in forming combinations. The cause of these combinations he called chance (τυχη), in opposition to the *νοῦς* of Anaxagoras.—Dr. Smith's " Classical Dictionary."

[3] A.S. *clate*, a bur sticking to man's clotbes, the cloth bur (Somner in Bosworth). " *Clote*, herbe. Lappa bardana, C. F. *lappa rotunda* (glis, P.)."—Promptorium. See Dr. Prior's " Popular Names of British Plants:" " *Clot-bur*, the bur-dock."

[4] Whirling his ?

[5] " *Rundle* or *roundel* (in heraldry), the figure of a round ball or bullet."—Phillipps.

Which Charon guydes,
Fraught ful of shadows colde and starke,
That ferrye to the coontryes darke,
Tendinge theyr tydes !   295
Since stoute nor stronge
Metall, nor moulde of worldlye warke,
Nor writt of any cunninge clarke,
Can last soe longe

To outlast the skye.   300
Honour, empire, nor erthly name,
Save my princesse most woorthye fame,
Which cannot dye !

Purpose.   Howe twoo principall exploytes of her Ma*ie*stie
since shee came to the crowne—to weete, establishment of religion and peace—doe assuredly promise
her in this life a most prosperous raigne and after
her death a woorthye and longe lastinge name.

What causes mooved so many forreinge Princes
to bee sutours to her Ma*ie*stie for mariage, and
what by coniecture hath hitherto mooved her to
refuse them all.

Parthe: 12.
Vrania.   Not youre bewty, most gratious soveraigne,   [174 bk.]
Nor maydenly lookes, mayntaynde with Maiestye, 305
Your stately porte, w*h*ich dothe not matche but stayne ;
For your Pallas, your presence, and your trayne,
All Princes courtes, myne eye coulde ever see.
Not your quicke witts, your sober governance,
Your cleer forsighte, your fayt[h]full memorye,   310
So sweete features in soe stayed countenance ;
Nor languages w*it*h plenteous vtterance,
So able to discourse and entertayne.

Not noble race, farre beyonde Cesars raigne
Runne in right line, and bloode of noynted Kinges ; 315
Not large empire, armyes, treasures, domayne,
Lustye liuries, of fortunes deerst derlinges ;
Not all the skills fitt for a princelye dame,
Your lerned Muse with youth and studye bringes ;

Not true honoure, ne that *im*mortall fame   320
Of mayden raigne, your onelye owne renowne,
And noe Queenes ells, yet suche as yeeldes youre name
Greater glorye then dooth your treble crowne.

Not any one of all these honourde partes,
Youre princely happs and habites that doe move,   325
Or, as it were, enforced all the hartes
Of Christen Kinges to quarrell for your love;
But to possesse at once and all the goode
Arte and engyn,[1] and every starre above
Fortune or kinde coolde farce[2] in fleshe and bloode, 330
Was force ynoughe to make so many strive
For your person, Who in our worlde stoode
By all consents the mignonst mayde to wiue.

But now (saye they) what crueltye coold dryue   [lf. 175.]
By such repulse your harte harder then stone   335
So many hopes of princes to depriue?
Forsoothe, what guyftes God from his regall throne
Was woont to deale by righte distributyue;
Share meale to eche, not all to anye one;
O peerles yow! or ells no one alive,   340
Your pride serves you to seize them all alone;
Not pride, Madame, but prayse of your lyon
To conquer all, an[d] be conquerd by none.

Conteininge a resolution politique touchinge the
feminyne gover[n]ment in Monarchye with a de-
fensive of her Ma*ie*sties honoure and constancye for
not enclininge her courage (after the example of
other ordinarye weemen), nor yet to the appetite of
most greate princes, eyther in the affayre of her
Mariage or of her manner of regyment.

What thinges in nature, co*m*mon reason, and
cyvill pollicye goe so faste linked together as
they maye not easilye bee soonedred without
pre*i*udice to the politike bodye, whatsoever evill or
absurditye seeme in them.

----

[1] Skill, cunning.   [2] Stuff.

Parthe. 13.
Thalia. Princesse, my Muse thought not amys
To enforme your noble mynde of this ;   345
Sythens yee see all wordlye men,
How they runn ryott now and then,
By mistakinge and want of sence
In thinges of little consequence,
Truly discerned as they maye bee   350
By one of royall Maiestie,
And deepe discourse and earnest zeale,
As yours is for all our weale,
Or ells it maye full oft befall,
For thinges of no moment at all,   355
Discorde maye grow by braule and iarre,
Thence faction, thence cyvile warre,
Which, when the popular brayne ys woodd,[1] [f. 175 bk.]
Coold not be stauncht with-outen bloodd ;
And now betymes ye may prevente,   360
By this humble advertismente,
Shewinge the soomme and points in cheefe,
That wholly make and marre this greefe ;
Remove misterye from religion,
From godly feare all superstition,   365
Idolatrye from deepe devotion,
Vulgare woorshippe from worldes promotion,
Take me from hallows ceremonye,
From sects errours, from Sayntes hyppocrisye,
Orders and habites from graduates and clerkes, 370
Penaunce from sinne, and merite from goode werkes ;
Pull people and theyr prince asoonder,
From games to gaze at and miracle to woonder ;
Forbidde pesauntes theyr countrye sporte,
Preache all trothe to the raskall sorte,[2]   375
Pull prophane powles out of all yoke ;[3]

---

[1] Mad.

[2] Rascals, low people, the refuse.

[3] St. Paul's was the great preaching place of London, and yet was made the
resort of gallants and vicious characters. See in Dekker's *Gull's Hornbook* the
chapter "How a gallant should behave himself in Paul's Walks," and *The
Meeting of Gallants at an Ordinarie; or, The Walkes in Powles*, 1604 (Percy
Society, 1841), etc., etc. The "out of all yoke" doubtless refers to Elizabeth's
only allowing "Established" ministers to preach. Dekker says: "He that
would strive to fashion his legs to his silk stockings, and his proud gait to his
broad garters, let him whiff down these observations; for if he once get to walk
by the book, and I see no reason but he may, as well as fight by the book,
Pauls may be proud of him."

Let popular preachers beare a stroke ;
Remoue rigour from humane laws,
Credulitye from prophetts saws ;
Let reason range beyonde his creede,   380
Mans faythe languishe nor conscien[c]e bleede ;
Make from olde reliques reverence,
From publique shews magnificence ;
Take solemne vows from Princes leagues,
From sanctuary privileage ;   385
Take me from publique testimonye,
Book oathe by trouthe or periurye ;
Take pompe from prelates, and maiestie from Kinges,
Solemne circumstance from all these wordly thinges,
We walke awrye and wander *without* lighte,   390
Confoundinge all to make a Chaos quite.

Purpose.

    Conteinynge an invective agaynste the puritanes,
w*i*th singular *commendacion* of her M*aie*sties con-
syderate iudgment *and* manner of proceedinge in
the cause of religion.   The daunger of innovations
in a *com*mon welth, the poison of sectaryes, and
perillous yt ys to shake religion at ye roote by
licentious disputes and doctrines.

[lf. 176.]

    That amonge men many thinges be allowed
of necessitye, many for ornam*ent*, w*hi*ch ca*n*not
be misliked, nor well spared w*i*thout blemishe to
the cyvile life.

Parthe: 14
Calliope.   Deny honoure to dignitye,
And triumphe to iust victorye ;
Pull puisance fro*m* soverayntee,
And creditt from authoritee ;   395
Set magistrate fro countena*n*ce,
Part veritye and false se*m*blance,
Wronge and force from invasion,
Fayned speeches from persuasion ;
Take hartye love from ielosye,   400
And fraude from cyvile pollicye ;
Moorninge and doles from buryalls,
And obsequies from funeralls ;
From holy dayes, and fro weddinges,

405

Minstrells and feasts and robes and ringes;
Take fro Kinges Courtes intertaynmentes,
From Ladyes riche habillimentes,
From cour[t]ly girles gorgious geare,
From banquetts mirthe and wanton cheare;
Pull out of clothe and comelye weede   410
The nakt carcas of Adames seede;
From worldlye thinges take vanitee,
Sleit, semblant, course, order and degree:
Princesse, yt ys as if one take awaye
Greene wooddes from forrests, and sunne-shine fro the
  daye.   415

Purpose.   Agaynste the same Puritantes a desive[1] of Courtiers and all auncyent Courtly vsages, devised as
well for the publique intertaynements as for other
private solaces and disportes not scandalously evill
or vicious.

      That her Ma*ies*tie is the onlye paragon of princes
in this oure age.

Builde me of bowghes a little bower,
And sett it by a statelye tower;
Set me a new robe by an olde,
And eourse coppar by duckate golde;
An ape vnto an elephante,   420
Bruckle bryall to diamante;[2]
Set Naples courser to an asse,[3]   [176 bk.]
Fine emerawde vnto greene glasse;
Set rich rubye to redd emayle,
The ravans plume to peacockes tayle;   425
Laye me the larkes to the lysardes eye,
The duskye clowde to azure skye;
Sett shallow brookes to surginge seas,
An orient pearle to a white pease;
Matche Camells hayre to satten silke,   430
And alloes with almounde milke;

---

[1] *sic.* *Query* an error for *device*.
[2] Brittle beryl to diamond.
[3] The Neapolitan horses must have been choice ones.

Compare perrye to Nectar wyne,
Juniper bush to lofty pine :
There shall no less an oddes be seene
In myne from everye other Queene.   435

Purpose.   By the generall commendacion of her Maiestie in
the hihest degree of prayse, The author sheweth
the vertue and envyous nature of a paragon, and
how excellencye cannot appeere but by comparison.

A comparison shewinge her Maiesties super-
excellencye in all regall vertues.

Parthe:16
Euterpe. As faulcon fares to bussardes flighte,
As egles eyes to owlatts sighte,
As fierc saker[1] to kowarde kighte,
As britest noone to darkest nighte,
As amerike is farre from easte,   440
As lyons lookes fears everye beaste,
As soommer soonne exceedeth farre
The moone and everye other starre :
So farre my princes prayse doth passe
The famoust Queene that ever was.   445

Purpose.   All prayse by resemblance ys voyde of offence;
that by comparison odious be in the superlative (be
it never soe true), it savoureth a certayne grosse
adulation which being to her Maiesties naturall
modestye nothinge agreeable, the authoure seeketh
to salve the sore of her opinion and his suspected
sentence by tempringe the excesse with a pretye
difference made betweene a bare resemblance and a
*[*If. 177.]* comparison *drawne out of the priuciples of iustice,
as yf one should saye the prayse that ys iustlye given
ys well given, and ought not to be misliked, thoughe
yt surmounte the common credite and opinion.

An hymne or divine prayse, vnder the title of
the goddesse Pallas, settinge foorthe hir maiesties
commendacion for hir wisedome *and* glorious
governement in the single lief.

---

[1] The peregrine falcon.

O *Pallas*, Goddesse soverayne,
Bredd out of great *Jupiters* brayne,
That thoughe thou be no man mervells,
All honoure and witt and nothinge ells ;
Thow that ner was widowe ne wife,   450
But a true virgin all thy life,
Be it for some rare presidente
Of all feminyne gover[n]mente,
Or that thow trowe no godd above
Was ever woorthye of thye love ;   455
Thou that rangest battayles in fielde,
And bearest harnesse, speare, and shielde,
And in thine vniversitye,   ·
The peacefull branche of Olyve tree,
Lendinge out of thyne endlesse store   460
All mortall men both law and lore :
Goddesse, as we poore pilgrimes weene,
Of spinsters, *and* of Poets Queene,
And therfore hast in solempne wise
Thy temples and thy sacrifise,   465
Thine himnes, thy vowes, thy noones, thy clerk*es*,
And all that longes to holye werk*es*,
The whole wide worlde for them to dwell,
And Athens for thye chief chappell ;
But O now twentye yeare agon,   470
Forsakinge Greece for Albion,[1]
Where thow alone doost rule and raygne,
Empresse and Queene of great brittrayne,
Leavinge thye lande, thye Bellsire[2] wan,
Too the barbarous Ottoman,   475
And for grief chaunged thy holy hawnte   [177 bk.]
Of mount Parnasse to Troynovaunte ;[3]
All Atticke showres for tems to sydes,[4]
Tems easy for hys easye tydes,
Built all alonge with mannours riche,   480
Quinborow[5] salt sea, brackish Greenewich ;

---

[1] This, probably, marks the date of the poem, viz. 1578, as Elizabeth came
to the throne in 1558.

[2] Beau sire, probably Jupiter.

[3] The old mythical name of London. See Geoffrey of Monmouth.

[4] Thames's two sides or shores.

[5] Quinborough = Queenborough, an ancient but poor town of Kent, in the
Isle of Sheppey, situated at the mouth of the river Medway. . . . . . It is fifteen

Then that where Britton raygne begone,
The Tower of louely Londone,
Westminster old and new Pallace,
Richemounte not great but gorgias ;   485
Huge Hampton court, y^t hath no peere
For stately roomes and turretts cleere,
Save Windsor sett on Barock*es* border,[1]
That temple of thye noble order,
The garter of a lovely dame,   490
W*h*ich gave yt first device and name :—
O ladye, hence to hethennesse,
Only vmpire of warre and peace,
When cityes, states, countryes, and kinges
Creepe to ye covert of thye winges ;   495
Thow y^t canst dawnt thye forren foes,
To ridde thye realme of warre and woes,
Purchasing peace w*i*thout battayle,
So firme an one as cannot fayle ;
Thy tyme not yet in tyme to bee,   500
By any signe that man may see ;—
Thow that besydes forreyne affayres
Canst tend to make yerely repayres,
By so*m*mer progresse[2] *and* by sporte
To shire, and towne, Citye, and porte,   505
To view and compasse all thye lande,
And take the bills w*i*th thine owne hande
Of clowne and carle, of knight and swayne,
Who list to thee for right complayne,
And therin dost such iustice yeelde,   510
As in thye sexe folke see but seelde,
And thus to doe arte lesse afrayde
W*i*th houshould trayne, a syllye mayde,
Then thyne auncetours one of tenne
Durst do w*i*th troopes of armed men ;—   515
Thow that canst tende to reade and write,   [If. 178.]
Dispute, declame, Argewe, endyte
In schoole and vniversitye,

---

miles N.W. of Canterbury and forty-three E. of London.—*Gazetteer*, 1801. Here
a castle was originally built by Edward III. in honour of his wife Philippa.
  [1] Barockes border, *i.e.* Berkshire.
  [2] See Nichols's " Progresses and Public Processions of Queen Elizabeth,"
1st ed. 1788–1807, or 2nd ed. 1823, 3 vols., 4to.; and Laneham's Letter, 1575,
edited by F. J. Furnivall, Esq., for the Ballad Society.

In prose, and eke in poesye,
In greek, latine, *and* fine tuskan, 520
In frenche, and in Castillian,
So kindlye and quicke as old and younge[1]
May doubte w*hi*ch ys the mother tounge :—
O thow, the lovely mayde above,
Who hast conquerd the god of love, 525
And skapte his mother suttle gynne,
Triumphed one him and all his kinne ;—
Yf thou be all ys sayde afore,
Or yf thou be a great deale more
Then I can vtter any wayes, 530
Not schiphringe[2] thee of thye iust prayse ;
How longe ys yt ere we forgett
Thyne erthly name *ELIZABET*,
And dresse the as thou dost deserve,
The titles of *Britton Minerve ?* 535
In skye why stall we not thye starre
Fast by the syde of great *Cesar ?*
Or ells apoynt thy plannett where
Shines *Berenices* golden heare ?
For we suppose thou hast forswore 540
To matche w*ith* man for evermore.
Whye build we not thye temples hye,
Steples and towers to touch the skye,
Bestrewe thine altars w*ith* flowers thicke,
Sence them w*ith* odours arrabicque, 545
Perfuminge all the revestryes[3]
W*ith* muske, Cyvett, and Ambergries,
In thy feast dayes to singe and dawnce
W*ith* lively leps and countenance,
And twise stoope downe at everye leape 550
To kisse the shadow of thy foot-stepe,
Thy lyvinge Ymage to adore,
Yealding the all earthly honour :
Not earthlye, no, but all divyne,
Takinge for me thys hymne of myne ! 555

---

[1] See Paul Hentzner's account of the Queen's linguistic studies, which (all flattery deducted) appear to have been considerable.

[2] *Query* A.S. *scyp*, a shred; or the Promptoiium "Schyvere (slice) of brede or oþer lyke. *Lesca, scinda*, Schyveryn or ryvyn a-sundyr. *Crepo*."

[3] The place in a church where the priest revested himself, or put on the sacred garments. It has been contracted into vestry.

Elizabeth Lord Saue.

[Rawl. MS. 185, fol. 13.]

A proper new ballade, wherein is plaine to be seene how god blesseth england for loue of o^r Queene.

SOUNG TO Y^E TUNE OF *tarletons caroll.*[1]

London, london, singe and praise thy lord!
   let englands Ioy be seene;
Trew subiects, quickly shew, w^{t}h one accorde,
   yor loue vnto yor queene
    Elizabeth so braue,

---

[1] Richard Tarleton, the well-known jester and mountebank of the times of Elizabeth. The reputation of Tarleton is shown by the following lines in the Moral Play of the Marriage of Wit and Science: "One of the allegorical characters, Will, afterwards takes a 'picture' out of the Clown's basket, and asks whom it represents. Simplicity replies that it is Tarlton, which is followed by the question, 'What, was that Tarlton?' Simplicity then informs him that Tarlton was originally a water-bearer, adding—

'O, it was a fine fellow as ere was borne!
There never will come his like while the earth can corne.
O, passing fine Tarlton! I would thou hadst lived yet . . .
But it was the merrriest fellow, that had such jestes in store,
That if thou hadst seene him thou wouldst have laughed thy hart sore.'

His death occurred on the 3rd of September, 1588." (See Collier's "History of the Stage," ii. 351. London, 1851.)

The reader will find a woodcut of Tarlton (the orthography of the name seems uncertain) playing upon his pipe and drum in the "Book of Roxburghe Ballads" edited by Mr. Collier (1847). The entry of his burial may be found in the register of St. Leonard's, Shoreditch. It is conjectured that he died of the plague. His "Jests" appear to have been frequently reprinted, and entitle him to the reputation of the Joe Miller of his time. Thus we have "Tarlton's Iests, drawne into these three parts—

1. His Court-witty Iests.
2. His Sound-city Iests.
3. His Countrey-pretty Iests.

Full of Delight, Wit, and Honest Mirth. London, printed by I. H., 1611." This book has been reprinted for the Shakspere Society (see Carew Hazlitt's "Handbook"). Also "A newe booke in English verse, entitled Tarlton's Toyes. Licensed to Richard Jones, Dec. 10, 1576." And lastly, to close the scene, "A Sorrowful newe Sonnette, Intituled Tarlton's Recantation uppon this theame gyven him by a Gent. at the Belsavage without Ludgate (nowe or ells never) beinge the last theame he songe. Licensed to Henrie Kyrkham, ij die Auguste, 1589," and "A pleasant Dyttye Dialogue wise betweene Tarlton's Ghost and Robyn Good Fellowe. Licensed to Heny. Carre, xx° die Auguste, 1590."

Whose vertues rare beseeme her well,   6
from all y world she beares y bell;
her dew deserts no toung can tell,
   Her selfe she doth behaue,
That all y world doth marvell much
How nature should frame anie such,
of vice none lyving can her tuch.[1]   12

For Iustice Iust, for grace and pittie both,
   no Realme hath had her like;
She pardons them full oft y would be loth
   to hold if they durst strike,—
   Elizabeth lord saue.
She is y Iuell makes vs glade,   18
a greater good cannot be had;
whilst we haue her, who can be sad?
   Elizabeth so braue.
Doth never tread from vertues trace,
her hart and mind are full of grace,
from pittie she tournes not her face.   24

Gods word with sword, & eke her crowne,[2]
   from foes she doth defend;
yet pagon pope, y filthy sort of Rome,
   y devill doth legat send
   To spoile o Juell braue.
But god will haue nosing[3] ill don;   30
he teacheth england how to shonne,
and traitors to y gallows runne—
   Elizabeth lord saue,
and still defend her with thy hand,
her happie daies to passe y sand,
so shall this be a blessed land.   36

The spanish spite,[4] which made y papiste boast,
   hath done them little good;
god dealt with them as w king Pharoes host,
   who were drowned in y flood,
   Elizabeth to saue.

---

[1] Besmear.

[2] Two wordes are added here, but worn away so as to be illegible; it seems to be "wt frowne," but query.   [3] *sic.*

[4] This seems to fix the date of the poem, as having been written after the episode of the Spanish Armada, 1588.

The lord him selfe wth streached arme   42
did quell ther rage y^t sought o^r harme;
ther threatning brathes ye lord did charme—
     Elizabeth so braue.
The lord did quite from tirant swaye,
and traitors lost ther hopèd daye:
grant all her foes, lord, like decaye!   48

The subtill engines y^t her foes prepared
   to worke o^r fatall fall,
are tourned to snares wherew^t them selues are snard,
   and brought to shame w^thall.
     Elizabeth so braue
Did not in strength of navie trust,   54
nor yet in steell y^t is but rust,
but in her lord, who is most Iust,
     wch lord and god doth saue
o^r land & vs from wo and teene
so wondrously as never was seene,
even for ye vertues of o^r Queene.   60

Thou England, thou maist say thou happie art,
   aboue a thousand soyles;
thou feelst no parte of other countrees smarte;
   god giues thy foes ye foyles,—
     Elizabeth most braue;
for how it is god doth vs spare,   66
one her he hath a fervent care,
to giue him thankes England prepare,
     o^r Juell he doth saue,
and all we haue els be it knowne,
his mercies great wch he hath showne,
all for her sake, not for o^r owne.   72

God for her cause doth cloath ye ground w^t store
   of plenty and encrease;
O^r barnes are full, o^r barkes can bere no more,[1]
   and blest we are w^t peace,—
     Elizabeth most brave;

---

[1] Shakspere, with courtly flattery, has also dwelt upon the prosperity of the reign of Elizabeth:

     "She shall be lov'd and fear'd: her own shall bless her;
     Her foes shake like a field of beaten corn,

for thee doth england feell all this, 78
we nothing want y^t needfull is,
this Iuell england cannot misse,—
    Elizabeth lord save,
that england may be happie still;
confound all those y^t would her ill:
so lawd thy name ye faithfull will. 84

Though god do this, yet, london, learne to feare;
  all england do ye like;
away w^t prid, shun hores, and shame to swere,
  or els ye lord will strike,—
    then no good can we haue;
but all o^r good we shall forgoe, 90
and feele his plagues, both hye and lowe;
o^r vices vile doth greeve him so,—
    and still our queene to saue,
the lord his Iustice still forberes,
as he hath done these manie yeares;
then let vs morne o^r sines with teres. 96

Do this, and live in Ioye & happie case,
  In favour of ye lord;
from vices past ye lord will tourne his face:
  then let vs all accord
    to praie y^t england braue
may florish everie howre and day 102
fresh and greene, like greenest baye,
and y^t her foes come to decaye,—
    Elizabeth lord saue,
That england may, as it hath beene,
be fruitfull, and peace in it be seene;
loung live and Raigne o^r gratious Queene. 108

finis.

And hang their heads with sorrow: good grows with her:
In her days every man shall eat in safety,
Under his own vine, what he plants; and sing
The merry songs of peace to all his neighbours."
       —*Henry VIII.* act v. scene 5.

[Ash. MS. 36, fol. 149.]

A Poem in Praise of Queen Elizabeth.

THE first five pages are a translation of the famous satire against women attributed to Simonides, commencing—

Χωρὶς γυναικὸς θεὸς ἐποίησεν νόον.

The whole piece is dull, and possesses but little merit. The author is unknown.

Thus farre the foule-mouth'd Greeke Simonides;
I wonder not his Nation cross'd the Seas,
And in a Ten yeares warre themselves engag'd
With their Allyes like men more-then-enrag'd,
Onely back to their Contry to restore   5
One woman faire, althoughe She was a whore.
   Had they not wanted beautyes, or not thought
A stranger Soyle had on her manners wrought,
And made her chaster then their worser Clyme,
Troye might perhapps haue stood vntill this tyme;   10
And this Satirique Poet found a waye,
In steed of nettles, to be crownd with Baye.
   Had he been blest but once to looke vpon
The heavenly beautyes of our Albion,
What raptures had his Soule possest! how hye   15
Had his Muse flowne in praise of Brittany!
His flagging Verse, lowe groueling on the Earth,
As those from whome he form'd his woemens birth,
Had danc'd on topps of Trees, and on the flowres,
Sweet as the Graces, nimble as the howres.   20
His fancy then had ledd him to the woods,
Or pritty Shrubbs, or to the silver floods,
Where he had mett the Snow-beclowded Swan,
The loving Turtle and the Pellican,
The harmlesse Robin, charming some sweet vale   25
With the sweet accent of a Nightingale,
The Ladye-decking Silkeworme, or vpon
The Phœnix in her bedd of Cynamon;

He woulde haue wrought on all the Spring discloses,
The   [1] children Lillyes, Roses :   .   30
To his imagination Earth had all
Discover'd, in her choice of minerall,
Azure, vermilion ; and the Ocean girle
Had shewd to him her Corrall & her Pearle,
And from the virtues to them all assign'd   35
He had describd a woman and her minde,
Not from a Catt or Ape, as he[2] Muse ran,
Nor from himselfe, althoughe he was a Man.
But had he seen the quintessence of all,
(To whose sweet Maiesty my numbers fall),   40
The Queen of Hearts, and masterer of Death,
Honor'd, admir'd, belov'd *Elizabeth :*
Had he been made of marble and noe more,
Like to that famous Statue heertofore,
W^{ch} yeelded forth a harmony each daye   45
When yt was shone on by the Sun's bright raye :
By the more powerfull beames of her faire Eyes,
What Musick had we heard ! what rapsodyes
Had he been lost in ! and at last all fir'd,
Like Phaeton, in suche a heate expir'd,   50
And never wrought his Muse so farre to tell
Where we might finde for Her a paralell.
    The taske had been too hye for him, for we,
That in divine things more inlightned be,
Stand all astonish'd at soe bright a raye,   55
And (having nothing else) can only saye,
From all that was in Eden good & faire
She had her birth ; of yt She hath the ayre,
The flowres' sweets, colours, breath of every spice ;
And if she be noe second Paradise,   60
Tis for the want of this one thing alone,
That Eden had a Serpent, *She hath none.*

---

[1] Blank in MS.   [2] *sic.* Query, as the muse can.

[Ash. MS. 36, 37, fol. 296r.]

Vpon the Death of Queen Elizabeth.

THIS ballad is not without a certain amount of vigour, which is
gratifying after the learned platitudes we have for some time
been perusing.   Its author I have not been able to trace.

I tell ye all, both great and small,
  & I tell yee all truly,
That we haue now a very good cause
  for to lament and cry.   4
O fye, O fye, O fye, O fye,
  O fy thou cruell death !
For thou hast taken away from us
  Our good Queen Elizabeth.   8

He might haue taken other folkes,
  That better might haue been mist,
And let us alone with our good Queene,
  That lov'd not a Popish Priest.   12
She ruld this Nation by her selfe,
  & was beholden to no man ;
O shee bore the Sway, & of all affaires,
  & yet shee was but a woman.   16

A woman (quoth I), and that is more
  Then anie man can tell :
How faire shee was, & how chast shee was,
  There's no man knew it well.   20
The Mounsieur[1] came himselfe from France,
  On purpose for to wooe her ;
And·yet she liv'd and dyed a maid,
  Doe what he could do to her.   24

She never did anie wicked act,
  To make her Conscience pricke her ;
Nor ever would submitt to him
  That calld himselfe Christs Vicar ;   28

---

[1] "The Mounsieur," the Duke of Anjou, see *antè* pp. 67, 68. This senti-
mental episode in the reign of Elizabeth is well known to all readers of history.

But rather chose couragiously
  To fight vnder his Banner,
'Gainst Turke and Pope & King of Spaine,
  And all that durst withstan her.   32

In Eighty Eight how shee did fight
  Is knowne to all and some,
When the Spaniard came, her courage to tame,
  But had better haue stayd at home: 36
They came with Ships, filld full of Whipps,
  To haue lasht her Princely Hide;
But she had a Drake made them all cry Quake,[1]
  & bang'd them back and side.   40

A wiser Queene never was to be seen
  For a woman, or yet a stouter;[2]
For if anie thing vext her, With that wch came next her,
  O How shee would lay about her!   44
And her Scholarship[3] I may not let slip,
  Forthere she did so excell,
That amongst the Rout, without all doubt,
  Queen Besse shee bore the bell.   48

And now, if I had Argus eyes,
  They were all too few to weep
For our good Queene Elizabeth,
  That here lies fast asleep;   52
A sleep shee lyes, & so shee must lye
  Untill-a the day of Doome;
But then shee'l arise, & p—e out the Eyes
  Of the proud Pope of Rome.   56

---

[1] Here we have the beginning of the pleasantries on the name of Sir Francis, which have been so frequently varied in modern songs. No little honour was done the English hero when he was made the subject of an epic by one of Spain's most celebrated poets, in which every abuse that national hatred could suggest was freely lavished.

[2] Bolder, the original meaning of the word, still preserved in Dutch.

[3] Respecting her scholarship, *vide antè* pp. 66, 67.

[Ash. MS. 36, 37, fol. 296v.]

Vpon Sir Francis Drakes returne from his Voyage about ye world & the Queenes meeting him.

THIS is a somewhat spirited ballad. The events which it commemorates are well known. Sir Francis Drake sailed from Plymouth, on his voyage round the world, Dec. 13, 1577, and returned in 1580, was visited on board his ship by the Queen, and knighted. Out of the fragments of this celebrated vessel a chair was made, which is still preserved in the Bodleian Library at Oxford, and has formed the subject of a very pleasing poem by Cowley. The career of Drake has been so often described, that, instead of recapitulating its leading incidents, it would be better perhaps to refer the reader to the two following curious tracts in the British Museum, where he may find some of the original authorities of the modern biographies.

"Newes ovt of the Coast of Spaine. The true Report of the honourable seruice for England perfourmed by Sir Frauncis Drake in the moneths of Aprill and May last past, 1587, vpon Cales. etc. Imprinted at London by W. How for Henry Haslop . . 1587. 4to."

"A Summarie and Trve Discovrse of Sir Francis Drakes west Indian Voyage, etc. London, 1589. 4to. Dedicated by T(homas) C(ates) to Robert d'Evreux, Earle of Essex."

Sr Francis, Sr Francis, Sr Francis is come;
Sr Robert, & eke Sr William his Sonne,
And eke the good Earle of Huntington [1]
March'd gallantly on the Road.   4

Then came the Ld Chamberlain wth his white staffe,
And all the people began to laugh;
And then the Queen began to speake,
"Yo^r wellcome home, Sr Francis Drake."   8

---

[1] Henry Hastings, the twentieth earl of the line. He succeeded to the dignity in 1560; summoned to Parliament in the lifetime of his father as Lord Hastings; Knight of the Garter. Died in 1595, leaving no issue.

You Gallants all o' th Brittish blood,
Why don't you sayle o' th Ocean floud?
I protest you're not all worth a Philbert,
If once compared to Sr Humphry Gilbert.[1]   12

For he went out on a Rainy day,
And to the new found land found out his way,
With many a Gallant both fresh & green,
And he n'er came home agen. God blesse the Queene! 16

[Ash. MS. 38, fol. 167*r*.]

On Queene Elizabeth Queene of England.

THESE lines furnish another proof of the popularity of the
Queen, with whom the greatness of the nation was identified.
The author is unknown.

Kings, Queens, mens, Iudgments eyes,
See whear your Mirrore lies:
In whome hur frinds hath seen
A kings state In a Queene;
In whome hur foes suruayde   5
A mans hart In A Mayde:
whome, least men, for her pietye
should Iudge to haue bine a dietye,[2]
Heauen since by death did summon,
To shew she was a woman.   10

T. (?) B.

---

[1] Born in 1539, and lost at sea in 1584. His tragical fate has formed the
subject of a poem by Longfellow:
" Southward, with fleet of ice,
Sailed the corsair death."
—Gilbert had accomplished two voyages to North America, and in 1583 had taken
possession of Newfoundland in the name of the Queen. On his return from the
latter, his ships were caught in a violent storm: the Admiral, one of those fine
austere spirits so peculiarly abundant in that age of vigorous manhood, was last
seen sitting in the stern of the ship, and was heard by the crew of one of the
vessels, ere the tempest separated them for ever, to cry out with a calm voice
that heaven was as near by sea as by land.
[2] Probably means a person who should live for ever, to guess from the etymology.

[Ash. MS. 38, fol. 172.]

On Queen Elizabeth.

Eliza, that great Maiden Queen, lies here,
Who gouernd England fower an forty yeare;
Our Coynes Refined,[1] Ireland Tamde,[2] Belgia protected,[3]
Frinded Fraunce,[4] foyld Spaign, and Pope reiected:　　4
Princes found her powerfull, the world vertuous,
Hir subiects wise and fast, and God religious.
God hath hur soule, the world hir Admiration,
Subiects hur good deeds, Princes hur Imitation.　　8

finis Char: Best.[5]

---

[1] In 1560, the base money which had been in circulation during the reign of Edward VI. was called in, and proper money issued in its place.

[2] Shane O'Neil rebelled against the English in the year 1565, but was murdered by his own countrymen at a banquet in 1567. Sir Walter Devereux, Earl of Essex, in vain attempted to plant colonies in Ulster. This was followed by the rebellion of the Earl of Desmond, who was assisted by the Spaniards, and for some time resisted the English, but was ultimately driven out as a fugitive, and killed while hiding in a miserable hut (see Lingard). His head was struck off, and Elizabeth caused it to be placed on London Bridge. Thereupon followed the vigorous rule of Sir John Perrot, who was recalled, however, owing to Court intrigues, and died in the Tower (Dec. 1591). The last great rebellion was that of Hugh O'Neil, who completely defeated the English at the Battle of the Blackwater (1598). His subsequent interview with Essex and fate will be spoken of afterwards in the notes to the ballads on that unfortunate favourite. To understand the Ireland of Elizabeth's time the tract written by Spenser is invaluable: there is a very curious description also in Borde's "Introduction of Knowledge" (edited by Furnivall, 1870, p. 131). The account is additionally important from being one of the earliest.

[3] Elizabeth's assistance of the Dutch in their revolt against Philip the Second is well known, and has been told by Motley.. The Netherlanders may be pardoned for not feeling any great gratitude on this score: they were compelled to endure the insolence of Leicester, and had to make a very solid return for the favours which they received.

[4] In 1562 Elizabeth sent forces, under the Earl of Warwick, to assist the Huguenots; they took Havre, but were ultimately compelled to capitulate. See also afterwards the notes on the career of Essex.

[5] Of this person I am unable to furnish any information.

NONCONFORMITY IN THE TIME OF ELIZABETH.

THE development of Nonconformity—a very natural sequence of the principle of private judgment so loudly proclaimed by the Reformation, and the new subjective authority upon which all religion was to be based—is a very interesting feature in the reign of Elizabeth. The exiles, who had fled the Marian persecution, brought back the more advanced opinions which they had cherished and openly exhibited among their Calvinist brothers on the Continent. Great irregularity began to be exhibited in the celebration of the Service, especially with reference to the administration of the Sacrament and the Sign of the Cross. But it was from one point of view especially that Elizabeth was but little likely to tolerate these irregularities. She was extremely tenacious of her ecclesiastical supremacy, and the great principle upon which it is based, viz. that the Church is dependent upon the political constitution of the country. "The Queen," says Neal,[1] "inherited the spirit of her father, and affected a great deal of magnificence in her devotions, as well as in her Court. She was fond of many of the old rites and ceremonies in which she had been educated. She thought her brother had stripped religion too much of its ornaments; and made the doctrines of the Church too narrow in some points." About 1563 the era of Protestant Nonconformity in England may be said to begin, and two years later Humphreys, Regius Professor of Divinity at Oxford and Principal of Magdalen, and Sampson, Dean of Christ Church, were deprived of their emoluments. Humphreys, however, ultimately conformed, and was made Dean of Winchester.

Those of the Puritans who remained in the Church became itinerant preachers or chaplains: many, however, openly deserted it, and began to form conventicles. The Queen caused information to be conveyed to them, that if they persisted in deserting their parish churches, they must look to a speedy and severe punishment. Matters had now come to a crisis, and the Nonconformists were resolved to try the legality of these proceedings by holding a meeting in London. They had hired a room at Plumber's-Hall, under pretence of celebrating a wedding, on the 19th of June, 1567, intending to have a sermon and a communion.[2] The London authorities, however, interfered; the recalcitrant religionists were handed over to the law, and some of

---

[1] "History of the Puritans." London, 1837. Vol. i. p. 86.
[2] Neal, i. 161.

them on the following day brought before the Bishop of London and other ecclesiastical and civil dignities. On this occasion, as on many subsequent, they presented a bold front, and freely discussed religious controversies with their aristocratic persecutors.

In the Eastern Counties, however, Puritanism found especially its stronghold, where it continued to flourish long after the Elizabethan period. It was from this part of England, as is well known, that the Roundheads drew their most valuable supporters, soldiers and statesmen of the type of John Winthrop, the founder of Boston, a man of whom Quincey Adams says, that if America had been a Roman Catholic country, he could not have failed to have attained canonization. Neal tells us that about 1574 Norwich had become a very celebrated centre of Nonconformity, and the Archbishop of Canterbury (Parker) was ordered to send a peremptory message to the Bishop of Norwich (Parkhurst), insisting that the conventicles and meetings of persons for "prophesying and expounding Scripture" should be put an end to. The Bishop was reluctantly compelled to assent, although he was notorious for very strong leanings in that direction.

In spite, however, of the regal thunders, the Puritans were no whit abashed, but openly set at defiance the ecclesiastical commissions. At a meeting held at Mr. Knewstub's, at Cockfield, in Suffolk, they framed a body of rules for their governance, with especial reference to the use of the Common Prayer Book, apparel, holidays, fastings, and other grievances.

It was in the diocese of Norwich, also, that the notorious Robert Browne, founder of the sect of the Brownists, first acquired his celebrity. Two of his disciples, Mr. Elias Thacker and Mr. John Copping, had the misfortune to be hanged in 1583, at Bury St. Edmund's, for disseminating his opinions. Their indictments were "for spreading certain books seditiously penned by Robert Brown against the Book of Common Prayer, established by the laws of this realm. The sedition charged upon Brown's book was, that it subverted the constitution of the Church, and acknowledged Her Majesty's supremacy civilly, but not otherwise." It was in 1583 that the Puritans of Suffolk sent the following petition.

The introduction of the piece may perhaps be allowed, as it gives a good idea of the state of religious feeling in the Eastern Counties in the reign of Elizabeth.

[Douce MS. 363, fol. 129*r*.]

The copie of the petition, by the gentlemen of Suffolk, to the Lords of the Counsaile. An° Doɱ. 1583, July.[1]

Wee see, by the longe & lamentable experienꝫ that the state of the Churche, especially in oure partes, growethe eueri daie more syckꝫ then outher, and they whome it moste consernethe have beene so carelesse provideng the meanes, as the hope of reamedy wexith almoste desperat w*hi*ch inforceth us, as in all former tymes, so now especially, to resorte unto youre good Lordes, whose harttes god hath seasoned with a tender care of his glorie in the bweaty of his Sion, the painefull pastures & ministers of the worde, by what meanes wee know not, are now of laate at every assyze browghte to the barr marshalled with the worst malefactors, presentid, indited, arrained, & condemned for matters as wee perceive of very smalle moment, some for leaving owte holly-daies unbydden, some for syngeng the salme nunc dimittis in the mornenge, some turning the question in Baptisme conserneng faithe, from the infantes to the godfathers, w*hi*ch is but you for them, some for leaving oute the crosse in baptisme, sumꝫ for leaving oute the ringe in marriage, wheretoo neither the Lawe, nor the lawe maker, had ever in oure judgmentes regarde, but ment indeede to bridle the enemy. Yet now a moste petifull thynge to see, the backe of the lawe is turned to the adversarie, and the eadge withe all the sharpnesse is layde uppon the firme and true hartted subiect. We grante order to bee the rule of the spirite of God, we desire one uniformity in all dewties of the churche, the same being agreable to their proportion of the faithe. But theise weak Seremonies, & there lyke, be so indifferent as there use or not use maye bee lefte to the discretion of the minister.

---

[1] This Petition is given by Strype in his Annals, vol. iii. pp. 183, 184. Strype has modernized it throughout, and made other alterations, e.g. the original copy has "*parting* of the Church & commonwelthe, or bothe," etc., clearly prophetic of the great divisions in religion and politics, then in their dawn. Strype takes all the force out of the argument by the substitution of *perilling* for *parting*. Neal, Hist. Puritans, vol. i. p. 254, gives a mutilated copy of this supplication, with every strong and intolerant expression carefully expunged.

We thinke it with oute duetye, and under the favorable
condition wee speak it, very harde to goe under so harde
handelynge to the uttar discredit of the whole ministery &
profession of truthe, and that which is moare, we that bee
maiestrates understande hir maiestie, are as wee think)
equivalent of voyce, and know that lawe & iustice is one,
& maye not bee devided, doo forebeare to speak what wee
knowe, lest by *our* severance in opinion, Lawe shulde bee
rent, & justice cut in twayne, and so the middest of the
people *which* are so easely distracted bee caried hither &
thythar to the moveng of further inconveniances. And so
by our lycence, ministerie & maiestracie, is browght into open
contempte, yf therfore it maye bee lawfull for us to speake
but truth for oure selves. This is oure course, we serve her
maiestie in the countery, not according unto oure fanticis
as the wordle (*sic*) falsely beares us in hande, but accordeng
to the lawes & statutes of the Realme of England. We doo
reverence both the lawe & the lawe makers, lawe speeketh
& wee kepe sylence, Lawe cõmandeth & wee obaye, with out
lawe no man can possess his owne in peace, by lawe we
procede against all offendors, wee touch) none that lawe
spareth, we spare none that lawe toucheth. Hinc illa
lachrima, we alowe not the papists their trecheris subtill
practizes & herizis. We alowe not the family of love an
egg of the same neste, we alowe not Anabaptistes nor there
comunite. We alowe not of Browne the overthrower both
of the churche & of the cõmon wealthe. We allowe (not)
all those, but we humbely uppon oure knees, we praie your
good lordshippes to geve us leave to advertise you, how the
adversarie very cunningly hathe new christenid us with an
odyous name of puritanisme; we defie & detest bothe the
name & the herezy, it is composed of all her herezis afore-
saide. The papistes bee pure & imaculate, he hath stoare
of goodnesse for him self) & plenty for outhers. The
family of love cannot sinne, they bee so pure that God is
homified in them, & they deified in God: but wee, thanckes
bee to God, doo crye out in the bytternesse of *our* soules,
peccavimus cum patribus nostris, and groane under the burden
of *our* sinnes, wee confesse that there is none worse before
God. And yet before the wordle wee laboure [to] keepe oure
selves and oure profession unblameable; this is oure puritanisme, it pleaseth them to use ministars, magestrates, &

outhar, especially suche as have eye to jūgelynges,[1] & the name being odyous, oftentymes with the ignorant it makes the person odious. A shrewde devise, & herewith seemith daingerous, for wee know that every simple man in these partes, thanckes bee to God and hir Maiestie, by hering the worde of God redd & preached, doo condemne & contemne the grosse erroures & trumpery of Roome, but the subtiltes of rome are not soone aspied. *Jesuites & Seminaries* are not odious names with the papistes, & yf in tyme suche meght be lykened & lodged by the popes harbengars, & good subiectes cunnengly wounded with lcwde titles & names falsely applied, God save the churche, the Queene, & the Realme. God send us peace in Christ. Amen. Wee very humbly desire, right honorable, not to become offensive unto you, eyther in the length or plaine delivery of this matter, for weare the cause but oures only, we coulde beare and forbeare, but when it retcheth even unto the parting of the Churche & comon wealthe or bothe; for they cannot but as twynnes lyve & dye together. Then unlesse wee wolde forget all dutye unto God & man, we cannot but unfolde before your honors judgments the particulars of theise so great discomfortes: if your good lord shippes shuld call us to triall & proofe of these matters, yt is the thinge wee moste desire; yf outherwise you shall thinck) to dispose any outher course as wee are moste bounde, so are wee moste readye to submitt all unto your greater wisdome. Oure lord, for his Christes saak, blesse all your studies & laboures imployed for the preservation of hir maiestie. The godly & peacable gover[n]ment of this lande, & the free passaige of the gospell, the roote of all the rest, that not we aloane, but the ages to come) may speak of your praises in all the streates & cornars of oure Cyties. And so comending oureselves & our beste services to youre continuall comandmentes, we doo tak oure leave.

Robart Germin,	Robart Ashefilde,
Robart Wingfield,	Robart fforth,
Nicholas Bakon,	William Thomson,
Phillip Barker,	Thomas Jeoley,
John Heigham,	Richard Wingfelde.

---

[1] Jugglings; the sentence is thus given by Neal: "This is our Puritanism; a name given to such magistrates and ministers and others that have a strict eye upon their juggling."

It was in 1589 that the celebrated Martin Mar-prelate tracts began to make their appearance, in which the opinions prevalent against the Church of England found a very violent and somewhat humorous expression. All attempts to discover the authors of these pamphlets—and there were probably several—failed, even though Burghley himself issued a proclamation. Whitgift and Bancroft were very active in the same direction, but with no better result. Here and there an unfortunate Puritan brought himself within the arm of the law, but the spirit of Nonconformity for all that was hearty and flourishing.

The close of the reign of Elizabeth saw the Puritans slowly increasing : the questions which divided the English Church were to be again debated with fresh violence in the reigns of her successors. The subjoined poem is probably the work of some Nonconformist sympathizer—certainly of one who rejoices in the changes brought about by the Reformation—

> "In each towne and cittie, her grace doth delight it,
>   To have gods word preached at large."

So also

> "What Realme on earth
>   May be compared to this,
>   That hath ye gospell plainly taught ?
>   It is a heavenly blisse!"

[   ]¹

A hartie thankes giuinge to god for our queenes most excellent maiestie, and is to be sounge to pe tune of pe medley.

I² prepare with speed,
crist commyng is at hand;
as by straing signes and tokens both
the learned sort haue stand.   4
gods workes plainly declares
each day vnto us all,
yᵗ soddenly an end shalbe
of things on earth mortall.   8
fyre fearce abroad shall flye,
from east vnto yᵉ west,
consumyng things yᵗ be earthly,
the greatest wᵗh yᵉ least.   12
no succor shalbe found
for favour, gould, nor fee;
but even as all yᵉ world was drownd,
so bournt shall all things bee.   16
Wherfore I say, make no delay,
vnfolde and hould
on Christ oʳ only stay,
for it is hee yᵗ remedie   20
must be we see;
or els with open crye
we shall to hell fire, oʳ deeds deserue no les,
meet meed for oʳ hire, oʳ liues do so expresse. 24

---

¹ The transcriber of this poem somewhat carelessly neglected to indicate the source from which it was taken, and subsequent search has not tracked it, but it is hoped that it may be added in the errata.

² Ay, so frequently written formerly. This has given rise to frequent puns. Cf. Shakspere's "Two Gentlemen of Verona," act i. scene 1.

Proteus: But what said she? [*Speed* nods.] Did she nod?

Speed: I.

Pro.: Nod, I; why that's noddy.

So also in the Sonnets we have the following curious quibble (Sonnet cxlviii.). "Love's eye is not so true as all men's 'No'"—where see Mr. Staunton's note.

then vnto o[r] Christ inclyne quickly,
and fly from follies desire,
and aske of him mercie for remedie,
he will not be any denier :   28
while life doth last, linger not if you may haue it,
he askes but a penitent harte ;
to late will it be when tyme is gon to craue it:
make speed therfor, ere you departe.   32
    Imbrace gods holy worde
    for fear of watchfull sword ;
    loue well y[e] pouertie,
    and then god will blesse thee.   36
What Realme on earth
may be compared to this,
that hath y[e] gospell plainly taught ?
it is a heauenly blisse !   40
allso a maiden meeke
amongst vs hee hath sent,
to shew his glorious wonderous workes
and power omnypotent.   44
she sitts in princly throwne,
and rules y[e] Relme in quiet;
she hath allso y[e] trew touchstone,
gods word her only dyet.   48
though foes do frett & fume,
yet god will blesse her still
with maiestie and eke with crowne,
as is his blessed will.   .   52
wherfore to pray let vs not stay,
but be redie
to aske of Christ alwaye,
that she from strife may lead her life   56
among vs longe.
let these prayers be reefe[1]
amonge all good christians, both day, night & howre,
y[t] god will indue her with his mightie powre ;   60
then neede we not feare any forren foes,
Christ wilbe her only defence.
o[r] queene she hath plentie to plucke down all thoes
that setteth by subtill pretence.   64

---

[1] Rife.

In each towne and cittie her grace doth delight it,
to haue gods word preached at large;
all thinges done amisse to haue them saue righted:
the maiestrats all she doth charge,   68
let each poore haue his wright,
oppresse no man with might;
then god y^t sits aboue
will knitt vs all in loue.   72

God grant to us
y^t we may haue ye grace
to loue o^r queene with faithfull harte,
and his word to imbrace,   76
y^t at ye latter day,
with him we may assend
to heavenly ioyes for vs prepard
by him world w^thout end.   80
god saue England so smale,[1]
and nobles of ye same;
god grant eachon y^t liue in thrale
may assend wth christs name;   84
o^r commons so direct,
o lord, we thee desire,
that none of them may be infect
to taste thy wrathfull ire;   88
and then I know, both hye and lowe
will iudg smale grudg
in england for to growe,
y^t vnitie mongst men may be: 92
god graunt it haunt,
and vsen in each degree.
then shall we be glasst [2] to each towne & cittie;
wher loue doth last loung tyme spight hath but smale pittie,
as tyme is ye tryall for truth to be tride,   97
so all things ther beinge shall haue,
till death doth come that will haue no denial;
bring kinde out of mind vnto graue.   100

---

[1] Here we see how different was the position of the England of those days from that which she occupies at the present time: our forefathers were proportionably meek. Waller, at a subsequent period, could only utter the mild boast—
  "Beneath the tropics is our language spoke,
   And part of Flanders hath received our yoke."
[2] *i.e.* mirrored.

then riches nor beauty nor nothing will saue vs,
if we do not help o^r pore brother;
and if we live well ye lord god will haue vs:
we are his owne and for none other;   104
he bought vs wth his bloud
to taste ye heauenly foode;
god grant vs ther for aye
both rich and pore to staye.   108

finis.

<hr>

Queen Elizabeth's Rejoycing.

CONCERNING the authorship of this poem, which resembles a
style of writing earlier than the Elizabethan period, I am not
able to furnish any accurate information.[1]

[Rawl. MS. C. 86, f. 155b.]

Myne hert is set vppon*e* a lusty pynne;[2]
I praye to venus of good continuaunce,
For I reioyse þ^e case þat I am in:
Delyu*er*d from sorow annexed to plesaunce,
Of all*e* comfort havynge habundaunce;
This ioy and I, I trust shal neu*er* twynne,
Myne hert is set vppon*e* a lusty pynne.   7

I pray to venus of good continuaunce,
Sith*e* she hath*e* set me in þ^e wey of ease,
Myne hertly *ser*uyse wit*h* myne attendaunce,
So to contynue, þat eu*er* I may please;
Thus voydyng from all*e* pensful disease;
Now stand I hole fer from all grevaunce,
I praye to venus of good continuaunce.   14

<hr>

[1] For the prolonged use of the thorn (þ) in MSS., see some good remarks by
Earle ("Philology of the English Tongue," 1st edition, 1871). This is a very
suggestive book, and the production of a scholar, who has thoroughly appreciated
the genius of the English language.
[2] In a merry humour.—*Halliwell.*

For I reioyse þᵉ case þ*at* I am in,
My gladnesse is such*e* þ*er* greuyth*e* me no payne,
And so to s*er*ue neuyr shal I blyⁿne,[1]
And thogh*e* I wolde, I may not me refrayne,
Myne herte & I so set is c*er*tayn*e* ;
We shal neu*er* slake, but eu*er* new begyn*e*,
For I reioyse þᵉ case þ*at* I am in.   21

[f. 150.]

Delyu*er*d from sorow annexed to plesaunce,
That all*e* my ioy I set as aught*e* of ryghte,
To please as after my symple suffisaunce,
To me þᵉ goodlyest most beauteous insight*e*,
A verry lanterne to þe al oþ*er* lyght*e* ;
Most to my comfort onⁿ her remembraunce,
Delyu*er*d from sorow annexed to plesaunce.   28

Of all*e* comfort havyng*e* habundaunce,
As whan*e* þ*at* I thynke þᵉ goodlyhed,
Of þᵉ most femyne and meke in countena*u*nce,
Verray myrrour and ster of womanhed,
Whos ryght*e* good fame so large a brod doth*e* spred :
Ful glad to me to haue congnossaunce,
Of all*e* comfort havyng habundaunce.   35

This ioy and I, I trust shall*e* neu*er* twyne,[2]
So þ*at* I am so fer furth*e* in þᵉ trace ;
My ioyes bene dovbil wher oþ*er* be but thyne,
For I am stabely set in suche a place,
Wher beaute cresith*e*, & eu*er* wellyth*e* grace,
Whiche is ful famous, & borne of nobil kyn*e* ;
This ioy and I, I trust shal neu*er* twyn*e*.   42

Finis quod Quene Elyzabeth.

---

[1] Cease. "Til he had torned him, could he not blin."—*Chaucer*, "The Chanones Yemannes Talc" (Tyrwhitt's ed.).
[2] Separate.

Latin verses on Elizabeth's proposed Marriage with Anjou.

For the circumstances under which these verses were written, see page 68 : we here get a contemporary pasquin, the form of expression which public opinion takes, where free discussion is denied.

[Douce MS. 363, fol. 144*r*.]

Vera Copia.

This copie was from a libell that some had set on a post in London.

Sola precor vel iuncta uiro sit Virgo Britannio [1]
Et ferat ex proprio pignora grata solo :
Viue domi, ne non viuas Francisse, recusat
Nostra peregrinum regio ferre Iugum.
Virgo valet, spirat, Regnat quo longior absis
Tutior enge redde (*sic*) Gallia, larga satis.[2]
Pectora fide (*sic*) Deo, bona corpora, corda, corone [3]
Dantur, nil restat ni velis arma tibi.
      Principes (*sic*) consilio viuat ut
        opto anima suo, Octr A° 1579.

A Method, not sharply Englished.

The kinge of ffrance shall not advañce his shippes in English
    sande,
Ne shall his brother ffrancis haue the Ruleng of the lande:
Wee subiects trwe untill oure queene, the forraine yoke defie,
Where too we plight oure faithefull hartts, our lyñies, our
    lyves & all,
thereby to have our honor rize, or tak our fatall fall.
Therefore, good ffrancis, Rule at home, resist not our desire ;
for here is notheng else for thee, but onely sworde & fyer.

---

[1] *sic.* ? Britanna.
[2] This line seems hopelessly corrupt. Perhaps
          Tutior: en regi Gallia larga satis
might be suggested.
[3] For "fide" and "corone" read fida and coronæ. By these alterations some
sense may be extracted from the original.

Teshe's Verses on the Order of the Garter.

THIS poem has already been printed by Sir Harris Nicolas in his "Orders of Knighthood," vol. ii., 1842. The MS. is on vellum. In the British Museum there is "A boke containing divers sortes of Hands, as well the English, as French Secretarie, with the Italian, Roman, Chancery and Court Hands. Also the true and just proportion of the capital Romans. Set forthe by William Teshe, of the Citye of Yorke, gentleman. 1580." It is dedicated to the Queen, and he begs that she will deign to accept it "among the noble presents of more higher estate." Teshe was probably the son of a certain Tristram Teshe of Yorke who lies buried in the Cathedral with the following inscription on his tomb: "Of your charity pray for the soul of Margaret Tesh, wife unto Mr. Tristram Tesh, of the cittye of Yorke, Notarie and principal Register of the Archbishopricke of Yorke, which Margarett departed unto the mercy of Allmighty God the viiij day of December, An. Dom. 1537." Teshe's verses are inscribed to the Earl of Bedford.

[Harl. MS. 3437.]

[lf. 1.]

Within a Place, or Pallace, richlye dight,
did sitt a Prince, and Princely Peer's attend,
Braue Lord's, faire Dames, and many a courtly wight:
the Knight*es* of th'order—eachone wore a Bend
aboute the Arme—all wayting, as it weare,
some heeauenly sighte, or happy tale to heare.   6

And in each Bend, enbrodred Bracelett wise,
weare certayne wordes, ymporting seuerall sence,
as best did pleas*e* their Honors to devise,
the more to shewe theire loyall harts pretence;
ffor as the Garter shew's what th'order sayth,
So by the Bend was knowne ye wearers fayth.   12

Myselfe, (alas!) the meanest of the Sorte
that stoode in place to see this princely sight,
and harde the wordes which here I shall reporte,
God know's howe muche vnto my hart*es* delight,
Behelde the Queene stande vp emoungst them all,
Herault's cryde scylence, husht was all the Hall.   18

[lf. 2.]   [drawing.*]

"Shame to the mynde that meanes" (quod shee) "amisse,"
whereby was seene her mynde did meane no ill:
"Lo! thus, my Lordes, our verdict geuen vp is,
lett them do well that looke for our goodwill,
A quj mal pense a luy tout honj Soit:
and for myselfe, Mon Dieu *et* seul mon droit.   24

"Highe God" (quod shee) "be alwayes our right hand,
and thinck on me, semper eadem, still.
He is the staye on which our harte shall stand,
our stronge defence from those that thinck vs ill;
where wronge makes warre, we must with patience arme;
Tyme trieth truthe, good myndes can meane no harme."   30

And so, me thought, shee satt her downe againe,
with Princely grace attending for the rest.
Then euery one, from hartes which coulde not fayne,
shewed forth th' aboundance of ech faithfull brest.
The Earle of Lincolne there did foremost stand,
and gaue his bend thus to her highnes hand.   36

[lf. 3.]   [drawing.]

"Renowned Queene, cheif Souereigne of our weale,
whose happie raigne hath made vs fortunate,
Trewe were the wordes which late you did reveale,
highe God is hee that hath vpheld your state;
What elce was said, wee all agree in this,
Shame be to hym that thincks or meanes amiss.   42

"A faithfull mynde doth sildome merritt blame,
which makes me saye, that Loialte n'ha hont:
Fidelitie can neuer purchase shame;
yt springes from faith and farre doth Fame surmount:
for what maintaynes your Princely roialtye
But love of God and Subiects Loialtye?   48

---

* The drawings are the Coats of Arms of each Noble as he is described, with
the bends containing their mottoes.

"Longe maye you lyve, in peace and happie dayes,
to double twice the tracte of Nestors date,
that after worldes maye singe vnto your praise,
in golden verse, the Tryumphes of your fate!
Thus doo I ende, and wishe, as is my wont,
rather death then shame, Loialte n'ha hont."   54

[EDWARD FYNES-CLINTON, 13TH LORD CLINTON and (in 1572
    created) EARL OF LINCOLN, who had been elected a Knight
    by Edward VI.   His motto was "*Loyaulté n'a Honte.*"   He
    was Lord High Admiral, and died 1584, being ancestor of
    the present Dukes of Newcastle, Earls of Lincoln.]

[lf. 4.] [drawing.]

"It is a prouerbe vsed everie-where,
a perfect frend is good in tyme of need;
But well is them, that either farre or nere,
in all assayes can stande themselves in steed.
But who be they?   Then Deus propter me,
for none I fynde but Virtus propter se.   60

"Virtue alone sittes euer by herselfe,
full poore yclad, and all to totters torne;[1]
shee' stemeth skyll, shee forceth not of pelfe,
shee laughes the worlde and worldlings all to scorne:
Fortune and shee are allwayes at a Jarre,
and vice gainst virtue maketh open warre.   66

"Thus, sacred Prince, vouchsafe here to receaue
my little Poesie, Virtus propter se,
which, as you maie, with wisdome well conceaue,
So thinck I wishe, but Deum propter me,
Et sicut Virtus viuit sola spe,
Sic viuit Spes, et Virtus propter se."   72

[THOMAS RATCLIFFE, 3RD EARL OF SUSSEX, LORD FITZWALTER,
    etc.; also elected a Knight by Edward VI.   The motto of
    this family, "*Virtus propter se.*"   He died 1583 sans issue,
    but the title did not become extinct till 1641.]

---

[1] To tatters.

[lf. 5.] [drawing.]

" Sith Virtue is with Reason well sett owte,
Souereigne," q*uod* hee, " Ie ne pense rien que bon',
in euerie cause of certaintie or doubte
auoir respect tousiours que veut Raison,
Car la Raison en chascun chose est bon' ;
Garde vous donc que vous suiuies Raison.　　　　78

" Over each member Reason is the Kinge,
who in the Head doth keepe his highest Courte,
and by the eyes surueyeth euerye thinge,
and throughe the eares doth harcken each reporte ;
But forth the mowth, as throughe a gate, he sendeth
suche rules of Reason as each faulte amendeth.　　　　84

" For Reason shewes the secrett of effecte,
and what th'effects of each thinge will insue.
to Reason, then, lett all men haue respect,
least wante of care doe lack of Reason rewe :
The sage affirme, and you shall finde it bon'
that I haue saide, tousiours Suiuez Raison."　　　　90

[ANTHONY BROWNE, VISCOUNT MONTAGU (so created in 1554);
 elected a Knight by Queen Mary.　His motto, " *Suivez
 raison.*"　He died 1592.　The title is supposed to have become extinct in 1797, though there are many claimants to it.]

[lf. 6.] [drawing.]

Then stepped forth an other Princely Peere,
and from his Arme he plucked of his Bende,
with stately looke, and with a plesaunt cheere—
" I not compare " (quoth hee) " nor yett contende,
But in fewe wordes my Poesie is, and shall,
whilst lyfe of myne doth last, *Droict et loiall.*　　　　96

" Right is the course which Reason doth direct,
firme is the faith that stedfast doth abide,
Iust is the mynde which vice cannot detect,
True is the knott that Truthe herself hath tide :
Right, firme, Iust, true, what euer shall befall,
my worde importes my will, *Droict et loiall.*　　　　102

" And so vouchsafe, sweet Souereigne, to thinck
what's saide is right, and what is right is true,
what's true is firme, whats firme can neu*er* shrinck,
the staff nott fall's that is vpheld by youe :
Wherfore in fine, I saye, and euer shall,
durant ma vie, *Droict et Loiall*." 108

    [ROBERT DUDLEY, EARL OF LEICESTER (so created 1563), who
        had been elected a Knight by Queen Elizabeth in 1559.
        The motto of this celebrated favourite of the Queen was
        " Droit et loyal." He died without legitimate issue 1588,
        when his honours became extinct.]

[lf. 7.] [drawing.]

" The redie mynde respecteth neuer toyle,
But still is prest t' accomplish hartes intent :
A broad, at home, in euerie Coste or soyle,
the deed performes what inwardly is ment ;
which makes me saye, in euerie virtuous deed,
I still am prest t'accomplish what's decreed. 114

" But byd to goe, I redie am to ronne ;
But byd me ronne, I redie am to ryde :
To goe, ronne, ryde, or what elce to be done,
speek but the worde, and soone it shalbe tryde :
tout prest Je suis po*ur* accomplier La chose
per tout Labeur que vous peut faire repose. 120

" Prest to accomplish, what you will commaunde ;
Prest to accomplish, what you shall desire ;
Prest to accomplish, your desir's demaunde ;
Prest to accomplish, Heaven for happie hire :
Thus doe I ende, and at your will I rest,
as you shall please in euerie Action prest." 126

    [GEORGE TALBOT, 6TH EARL OF SHREWSBURY, EARL MARSHAL
        OF ENGLAND ; elected a Knight 1561. The motto of this
        family, which is still in existence, is *" Prest ·d'accomplir."*
        He died 1590.]

[lf. 8.] [drawing.]

The Earle of Warwick next approched there,
whose Sentence shew'd the Imprese of his harte—
"God sees our harts" (q*u*od he) "and secret*tes* here,
and he rewards the Righteous by desarte:
To hym, and you, I doe protest that Foy,
that sayes, Vng Dieu, vng Roy, seruir Je doy.　　　　132

"By Kinge I meane my service to the Crowne,
and so to you, whome God hath crowned so;
Which God I praie to plucke those traitors downe
that hate your state or seeke your overthrowe.
In God and you doth rest my onlye Ioy
that vowes vng Dieu, vng Roy, seruir Je doy.　　　　138

"One God I haue by grace to searue and love;
One Queene by his commaund to loue and serve;
the one doth rest, to see in Heauen above
what wee on Earth of this one will deserue;
Whome who meanes yll God lend hym little Joy
and lett me still, Seruir vng Dieu vng Roy."　　　　144

> [AMBROSE DUDLEY, EARL OF WARWICK (so created 1567),
> eldest son of John, the celebrated Duke of Northumberland
> and brother to the Earl of Leicester above named; elected
> a Knight 1563. His motto, "*Ung Dieu, ung Roy, servir Je
> doy.*" He died sans issue 1589, when his honours became
> extinct.]

[lf. 9.] [drawing.]

"Many reporte as they of others here;
But, as for me, Je di cõe Je trouue;
even as I fynde, my meaning shall appeare,
en toutes choses cõe Je proue;
Even as I proue, and as by proofe I fynde,
So shall by proofe apparaunt be my mynde.　　　　152

"In trust sometyme is secret falshoode founde;
but yett by triall is each treason spide:
Since triall, then, of truth descries the grounde,
tyme must bring Truth, that triall maie be tride
ere trust be geuen. Wherefore, quand Ie proue,
I then will saye but, Come Ie trouue.　　　　158

" Where Truth I finde, there will I builde my truste;
Where trust I finde, I will not be vntrue:
Whence fauore com's due faithfull seruice must
approue true Mynde, that only honors you,
for virtues rare, Que veritè proue
and I, by proofe, saye, Cõme Je trouue."   164

> [HENRY CAREY, LORD HUNSDON, so created 1559 by the Queen,
> to whom he was first cousin; elected a Knight 1561.   His
> motto was, *" Comme je trouve."*   He died 1596, but the title
> continued in his descendants till the death of the 8th Lord
> in 1765, when it became extinct.   In 1832 Lucius Bentinck
> Cary, Viscount Falkland in Scotland, who descended from
> a common ancestor, was created Baron Hunsdon in the
> United Kingdom.]

[lf. 10.]   [drawing.]

" Some sorte of men contynually forecast,
and doe dyvine of thinges which maye insue,
neuer respecting what is gone and past,
but what's to come, that deeme they wilbe true,
Though falce in fine; for why? by proofe we see,
che sara, sara, What shalbe, shalbe.   170

" No fatall feare, or dread of destenye,
can daunte a mynd which euer is resolv'd.
Mans thought is fraile, his forecast vanitye,
which when I ofte within my mynde revolu'd,
I tooke my pen and writt this worde for me,
Che sara, sara, what shalbe, shalbe.   176

" Per quant' a me non stimo dj Fortuna
ch'ognj cose è al voler d' Iddio,
non credo che Fortun' ha forz'alcuna:
mà che sara sara, ben dico Io,
proui che vuol *et* egl'in fin dira
fa tutto Iddio, che sara sara."   182

> [FRANCIS RUSSELL, 2ND EARL OF BEDFORD; elected a Knight
> 1564.   His fatalistic motto of *" Che sara sara "* was adopted
> by his father, who, having, by his knowledge of Italian and
> Spanish, been able to be of the greatest use to the Archduke
> Philip, when shipwrecked off Weymouth, owed his favour-
> able introduction to the English Court and his subsequent
> advancement to that piece of fortune.   He died 1585, being
> ancestor of the present Dukes of Bedford.]

[lf. 11.]   [drawing.]

"Strange be th'events, Most Sacred Maiestye,
which hap to man whilst hee doth breathe on earthe.
Somemen are borne to care and miserye,
and othersome to lyue in Ioye and Merthe;
Somemen by trauaile passe both Land and Seas,
Whilst some at home doe lyue in rest and ease.   188

"Which when I thinck and meditate vpon,
I smile at some, and pittie others hap:
But lett that pass:—why shoulde I muse theron?
All men cannott haue place in Fortunes lap.
As for myselfe, I doe not meane to trie,
But Quo me fata vocant, there will I.   194

"You Fatall Sisters, websters[1] of my lyfe,
Spin slowe, wynde softe, and cutt not yet my twyne.
Sweet Atropos, vnsheathe not yet thy knyfe;
But lett mee lyue, to searue this Prince of myne,
Abroade, at home, or where your Highnes please,
Or, Quo me Fata Vocant, Land or Seas."   200

[SIR HENRY SYDNEY; elected a Knight in 1564, being then
    Lord President of Wales.   He was subsequently three times
    Lord Deputy of Ireland, and was brother-in-law to the
    Queen's favourite—the Earl of Leicester, whose sister he
    had married.   By her he was father of the celebrated Sir
    Philip Sydney and of Sir Robert Sydney, created in 1618
    Earl of Leicester, a title which became extinct in 1743.
    His motto of *"Quo Fata vocant"* is used by his present
    representative, the Lord De Lisle and Dudley.   He died in
    1586.]

[lf. 12.]   [drawing.]

"To chaunge, or feare, proceed's of Dastard mynde:
to doe the one or other I despise.
Fonde be those men that tourne with euerie wynde,
and feares ech blast or storme that doth arise.
As for myself, I trust in God, and you,
neuer to chaunge, or feare what shall insue.   206

---

[1] Weavers.   The feminine of weaver.

" Chaunge will I not the constant loue I beare,
Feare will I not the force of Fortun's spighte:
Thus doe I meane to neither chaunge or feare,
But in a staye to settle my delighte.
Lett fleeting mynd's of Fortune be afraide;
Where firmnes rest's, the harte is well apaide. 212

" In choise of Chaunge, Feare doth affirme the worss;
In Feare, the Harte can lye at little rest;
and restles Hart's can haue no greater curss;
and curssed Hart's are seeld [1] or neuer blest:
Itane? sic. cum hoc tam certum cerno
dicam, Mutare vel timere sperno." 218

> [WILLIAM SOMERSET, 3RD EARL OF WORCESTER; elected a
> Knight 1570. His motto, " *Mutare vel timere sperno.*" He
> died 1589, being grandfather of Henry, the loyal Marquess
> of Worcester (so created 1642), and ancestor of the present
> Dukes of Beaufort, Marquesses and Earls of Worcester.]

[lf. 13.] [drawing.]

" Of God and Man, what more esteemd then Truth?
Of Prince and Peere, what more then truth in price?
Not glozing [2] Iests that euerie gallante doth.
The Truth is that is honored of the wise;
And though that Truth vnwares maie purchase blame,
Truth wilbe Truth, in spite of all defame. 224

" The purest golde lyes hidd in dross and mire,
And precious stones mongst ragged Rocks do growe;
But as the one is purified by fire,
So are the other pullished also.
And as they both by Art are made most bright,
So Tyme bringes Truth by triall vnto light. 230

" Thoughe burnisht Brass maie shyne as bright as golde,
Yet Truth the Touchstone fyndeth it but brass;
Thoughe foyled glass seeme precious to beholde,
yett truth will knowe it for a peece of glass:
So Truth in all thinges doth the virtue trie:—
In veritate victoria, therfore, saye I." 236

---

[1] Seldom.　　　　　　　　　　[2] Deceitful, flattering.

[HENRY HASTINGS, 3RD EARL OF HUNTINGDON; elected a
Knight 1570. Died sans issue 1595. The motto, "*In veritate
victoria*," was doubtless used by him, but that on his Garter
plate is "*La Victoire vient de Dieu.*" The title is still
enjoyed by the descendants of his younger brother.]

[lf. 14.]　[drawing.]

With that stept forth a graue sage Lorde indeed,
with countenaunce milde, and with as comely grace.
"Madame," quod hee, "not many wordes shall need
to shewe in summe where virtue keeps her place;
per quanto a me, questa è sententia mia,
proua che vuol.　Cor vnum vna via.　　　　　242

"One Harte to Prince, state, selfe, and Cuntries heale,
one Loue, one losse, one Joy, one greife, one gall,
one mynde, one meane, one will, one wishe, one weale,
one good, one god, one but one all in all,
one happ, one Heauen, which vna sola via,
Cor vnum querit, quel mio, quella mia."　　　248

And therwithall, hee gaue her from his Arme
a brave riche Bende, wheron was rarely writ,
aboute a Harte, that neuer meaneth harme,
and but one waye seekes happie Heauen to hitt.
"Nel Cuore mio, questa è sententia mia,
Proua Troua, Cor vnum vna via."　　　　　254

[WILLIAM CECIL, LORD BURLEIGH (so created 1571), the
celebrated Lord High Treasurer; elected a Knight 1572.
The motto, "*Cor unum, via una*," although doubtless used by
him (as it is by his descendants), is not the one given in his
Garter plate, which is "*Honneur loyer et loyaulte.*" He died
1598, and was succeeded by his son, created 1605 Earl of
Exeter, and was the ancestor of the present Marquesses of
Exeter, and of the Marquesses of Salisbury.]

[lf. 15.]　[drawing.]

By order next a Baron then came forth,
and humbly there—"Renowned Queene," quod he,
"by due desarte esteeme eche vertues worth,
I saye no more, but fort' en loyalte:
my greatest force, I thinck, I best bestowe
in service suche as maye my duety showe.　　　260

"If Fortune frowne, why then in her despight;
and yf shee smyle, I trust her nere ye more:
doe what shee can, I feare not of her might:
lett fortune goe, sett only God before
in all affaires, ho detto et diro,
che dio volendo, Io lo faro."   264

And therwithall he plucked from his Arme
theis wordes in golde enbrodred faire to see,
"Dogge be his death that meanes *Diana* harme,
Dominus videt, Fort' en loyalte."
Then stood he by, when as, with reuerence lowe,
an other Peere his seemely selfe did showe.   270

> [ARTHUR GREY, 15TH LORD GREY DE WILTON; elected a
> Knight   . The motto here assigned to him, *"Forte en
> loyalte,"* is not the motto on his Garter plate, which is "*At
> Vincit pauperiem Virtus,*" and which was also used at his
> funeral. He died 1593. By the attainder of his son in
> 1604, this title became forfeited. But in 1784 Sir Thomas
> Egerton, who descended from a sister of the attainted Lord,
> was .created Baron Grey de Wilton (which became extinct
> on his death in 1814). In 1801, however, he had been
> created Viscount Grey de Wilton and Earl of Wilton, with
> a special remainder to the Grosvenor family, by whom those
> titles are still enjoyed.]

[lf. 16.] [drawing.]

"Weake is the faith that fleet's with everie wynde;
True is the harte that neuer meanes to starte;
A stedfast course maie shewe a stayed mynde,
and carefull zeale express a constant harte,
that in despight of Tout mortal daunger,
shall searue but you, et tousiours sans chaunger.   276

"Lyke to the Moone, that Moonthly chaungeth newe,
I maie compare a fleeting fickle mynde;
For when her full shee geues the worlde to vewe,
her wayne is nearest then by course of kynde:
So wavering witt's the farder that they raunge,
theire suddeyn wane presadgeth speedy chaunge.   282

III.   L

"But constant Myndes are lyke vnto the Sonne,
whose certayne course doth neuer runne astraye;
For thoughe with Clowdes it ofte be overdonne,
yett shyneth it in darcknes wismen saye:
So thoughe with cares sweet virtue clowded be
yet Sans chaunger virtue will virtue be."   288

 [HENRY STANLEY, 4TH EARL OF DERBY, whose wife was first
  cousin (once removed) to the Queen, being grand-daughter
  of Mary Tudor; elected a Knight 1574.   His motto, "*Sans
  changer*," is the same now used by the present Earl of
  Derby, his heir male.   He died 1592.]

[lf. 17.]   [drawing.]

A worthy Earle in place there did appeare,
who thus began, "Bien, vng Je seruiray.
One I will searue, which one in presence here;
and one aboue, whome no one maie saye naye,
which one on high is but that only one,
that makes my harte to serue this one alone.   294

"To serue and love, to love and eke to serue;
to serue with loue, and loue by service showe;
to shewe the due that fauore maye deserue;
to merritt well, and wish ech one do so:
to wish, and will, to serue, and still to loue,
one Queene on Earth, one God in heauen above.   300

"A Phenix hath no fellowe to be founde;
Blest be the Birde, and she that is as rare:
Excellence shewes where virtue is the grounde,
suche fruicts doe growe as only Heauenly are,
and ending thus, Je di e*l* bien diray,
Vng Je ayne, et vng Je seruiray."   306

 [HENRY HERBERT, 2ND EARL OF PEMBROKE; elected a Knight
  1574.   His motto "*Ung je serviray*."   He was the husband
  of the lady immortalized by Ben Jonson as "Sydney's
  sister, Pembroke's mother," who died 1621.   The Earl died
  1601, being ancestor of the present Earls of Pembroke and
  Montgomery.]

[lf. 18.] [drawing.]

Then did approche A Baron standing by,
"Souereigne," quod hee, "Je vous diray vne chose;
You maie Conceaue, and he that list to trye
shall finde by proofe, que Desir n'ha repose;
Myselfe haue tride, and harde it ofte confest,
that iu respect Desire doth neuer rest.   312

" Desire doth sett both witt and will to worke,
Desire doth worke in secrett of devise,
Desire doth seeke where secrett's closlye lurke,
Desire discryes the dutye of the wise,
Desire is suche as worlde cannot inclose,
which makes me saye, Desir n'ha repose.   318

"Desire sometyme doth sore aboue the skyes,
Desire agayne doth penetrate the Earth,
ore Sea and Lande Desire fleeting flyes,
· one while in care, an other while in Myrth :
So that Desire, amid'st Ten thowsand wose,
both lyves and dyes, Et iamais n'ha repose."   324

[CHARLES HOWARD, 2ND LORD HOWARD OF EFFINGHAM;
    elected a Knight in 1575; created Earl of Nottingham 1597;
    Lord High Admiral, etc. His motto, " *Desir na repos.*" He
    died 1624, and was succeeded by his two sons in succession,
    on the death of the last of whom, in 1681, the Earldom of
    Nottingham became extinct, but the Barony descended to the
    descendants of a younger son of the first Lord, and is still
    enjoyed by the present Earl of Effingham.]

[lf. 19.] [drawing.]

Then last of all came forth, with comlye grace,
a grave good Sir, who saide, " Iudicio meo ;
Fortune dothe beare a duble dealing face;
I seeke for noughte but Auspicante Deo,
And helpe me, God, my harte hath his desire,
no hap to heauen, once there I wish no higher.   330

"If God before I followe with goodwill ;
If god geue helpe, I wishe no better hap ;
If God geue hap, it cannot fall owte yll :
well springes the tree where god doth geue ye sap :
wherfore saye I, that in Iudicio meo,
nothing thryues well but Auspicante Deo.   336

" And God at hand nothing can thrive amiss,
for God doth helpe the hoping harte at need :
Both highe and lowe will all agree in this,
God guyde the hand, the worke will better speed ;
Then take of me this worde, Judicio meo,
I worke and wishe but Auspicante Deo."   342

> [Sir Francis Walsingham, Principal Secretary of State,
> appointed Chancellor of the Order 22 April, 1578, which
> he resigned ten years afterwards. His motto, *"Auspicante
> Deo."* This office has since 1671 been held by the Bishop
> in whose diocese Windsor is situated.]

[lf. 20.]

Thus when eche one had geuen vp his Bende,-
her Highnes rose from forth her cheare of state—
" I thancke you all," quod shee, " and for an ende,
Longe maie your dayes with myne rest fortunate !"
Wherwith they all made humble reverence then,
and all th'assembly saide thereto, " Amen !"   348

The Trumpett*es* blewe, and Heralds lowd did call,
" Sortez, Seigneurs, chascun a son Logis."
The Nobl's rose, and thence departed all,
them to disrobe, as vse and custome is ;
And as the Earle of Bedforde past by,
" nowe, good my Lorde, remember me," qu*o*d I.   354

Wm. Teshe.

Guilielmus Tesheus .·. composuit, scripsit, *et* pinxit :
An° Doɱ 1582.

In an old MS. in the Herald's College, marked "2ᵈ E. 8,"
part 2, page 2, occurs : " The proper words of the Lords of the
Order of the Garter.

The Quenes,	*Semper eadem.*
The Empror,	*Plus ultra.*
The Kinge of Spayne,	*Nec spe nec metu.*

The Duke of Sayvoye,	*Fert, Fert.*
The Duke of Memorancy,	$A\pi\lambda\alpha\nu\circ\varsigma.$
The Duke of Holst,[1]	
Erle of Arundell,	*Virtutis laus actio.*
Erle of Darby,	*Sans changier.*
The Marques of Wynchester,	*Aymes loyalté.*
Erle of Penbrok,	*Une je serviray.*
The Duke of Norfolke,	*Sola virtus invicta.*
The Lord Clynton,	*Loyalte na honte.*
The L. Pagett,	*Per il suo contrario.*
The Mquis Northamp,	*Amour avecque loyalte.*
Erle of Westmoreland,	*Esperance me comforte.*
Erle of Rutland,	*Pour y parvenier.*
The L. W. Haward,	*Desire na repos.*
Erle of Sussex,	*Virtus propter se.*
Erle of Shrewsbery,	*Prest accomplir.*
L. of Loughborough,[2]	*La victoire vient de Dieu.*
Viscount Montague,	*Suyves raison.*
Erle of Lesteter,	*Droict et loyal.*
L. Grey Wylton,	[illegible.]
L. of Hunsden,	*Come je treuve.*
Erle of Bedford,	*Che sara sara."*

In 1582 three stalls were vacant, and of the foreign knights— viz. The Emperor Rudolph (of Germany), The King of Spain, The King of France, The King of Denmark, Duke of Holstein, Casimir Count Palatine—our author takes no notice, giving the mottoes only of the sixteen English Knights and of the Chancellor, which (with the above nine) makes up the complete number of twenty-five. It is somewhat curious that the Chancellor of the Order is treated by Teshe in the same way as an actual Knight.

---

[1] "Jealousy of the power of Eric (King of Sweden) had induced the King of Denmark to set up a rival suitor in the person of Adolphus, Duke of Holstein. The prince was young, handsome, and (which exalted him more in the eyes of Elizabeth) a soldier and a conqueror. On his arrival, he was received with honour, and treated with peculiar kindness. He loved and was beloved. The Queen made him Knight of the Garter; she granted him a pension for life; still, she could not be induced to take him for her husband."—Lingard, vol. vi. p. 32.

[2] Henry Hastings, who succeeded his father in 1560 as Earl of Huntingdon, had been previously summoned (viz. in 1558) as Lord Hastings, and from his connexion with Loughborough was doubtless often called Lord of Loughborough.

[Ash. MS. 36, 37, fol. 303.]

To the blessed Sainct of famose memory Elizabeth The humble petition of her now wretched and contemptible ye Commons of Englande.

THIS lamentation is, on the whole, not a dull production. The writer, whoever he was, must have been an enthusiastic admirer of the "Maiden Queen." Perhaps the lines—

> "No snuffling raskall, with his horne pipe nose,
> Shall tell thy story in his ill-tun'd prose—

show him to have had a certain hostility to the Puritans. We seem to have a foretaste in them of some of the happiest passages of Hudibras.

> If Sa^{cts} in heauen can either see or heare,
> Or helpe poore mortalls, O then lende thine eare ;
> Looke doune, blest S^{ct}, and heare, o heare vs now,
> Whose humble heartes low as o^r knees do bow.　　　　4
> Looke on our sufferings, thinke but on o^r wrongs,
> That hardly can bee spoke wth mortall toungs.
> O bee not now lesse gratiouse then of olde,
> When each distressed vassall might bee bolde[1]　　　8
> In to thy open handes to put his greife,
> And thence receaue timely and faire releife ;
> Bee not lesse good, lesse gratiouse then before.
> In Heauen, ye supplications of ye poore　　　　12
> Are hearde as soone as suites of greatest kings.
> If o^r petitions, then (Blest Sct), want wings
> To mounte them to the Iudge of Iudges throne,
> O helpe then (mighty Soueraine !) wth thine owne ;　16
> Carry o^r iust complaintes, since Iust they ar,
> And make a tendar of them at y^t Barr

---

[1] The same method of hearing petitions is alluded to hy Puttenham in the poem previously given (*antè* page 90, lines 507-9) :

> "And take the hills with thine owne hande
> Of clowne and carle, of knight and swayne,
> Who list to thee for right complayne."

It is the well-known and favourite trick of personal goverument. Miss Strickland ("Lives of the Queens of England," vol. vii. p. 127) has told us :

"In her progresses she was always most easy of approach; private persons, and magistrates, men, women, and children, came joyfully, and without any fear, to wait upon her and to see her. . . . . She took with her own hand, and read with the greatest goodness, the petitions of the meanest rustics, and disdained not to speak kindly to them, and to assure them that she would take a particular care of their affairs."—That Elizabeth knew how to make herself a popular sovereign in this respect and all others is palpable to any one who studies her character fairly.

Where no corruption, nor no Freinde, nor Bribe,
Nor griping Lawier, auaritiouse Scribe,   20
No Fauorite, no Parasite, nor Minion,
Can either leade, or alter y° opinion
Of y^t greate Chancellor;—theire lay them doune,
And meritt praise on earth, in heauen renowne.   24

Where to begin (deseruar of all glory),
Or how to tell our vnexampled story,
Heauen knows wee do not know; nay, wch is worst,
Thy once blest subiects haue so oft been curst   28
For offering vp petitions in this kinde,
As still wee tremble, till wee call to miude
Thy woonted goodnesse: that, ôh y^t doth cheare vs,—
That only giues vs hope y^t thou wilt heare vs.   32
When Heauen was pleasd (Blest S^{ct}) to call thee hence,
And so make wretched (for some great offence)
This littell Ile, Oh then began our feares;
Oh had wee then y° kingdome drown'd in teares,   36
And in y° floods conuaied our soules to Heauen,
To waite on thine, we had not now beene driuen
To cry, and call thee from thy fellow Saincts
To heare, and pitty these our iust complaintes.   40
O pardon these our grosse omissions,
And deigne to furthar these our poor petitions,
And wee will make the name of great Eliza
Equall y° honors of y^t great Maria.   44
No snuffling raskall, wth his horne pipe nose,
Shall tell thy story in his ill-tun'd prose;
Nor show thy statue to each petty groome:
Thy monument wee'le builde shall make proude Roome 48
On Pilgremage to come, ãd at thy Shrine
Offer theire giftes, as to a thing diuine.
And on thy altar, fram'd of richest stones,
We'le daily tendar teares, and sighs, and grones.   52
Eternity shall sleepe, and long-tounged fame
Forget to speake e're wee forgett thy name.
Reade (blessed Soule), o reade it, and beleeue vs;
Then giue it to his handes y^t can releeue vs.   56

Thy perpetuall and faithfull Beadesmen
the distressed cõmons of Englande.

[Harl. MS. 367, leaf 151.]

𝕿𝖍𝖊 𝕬𝖓𝖘𝖜𝖊𝖗𝖊 𝖙𝖔 𝖙𝖍𝖊 𝕷𝖎𝖇𝖊𝖑𝖑 𝖈𝖆𝖑𝖑𝖊𝖉
𝕿𝖍𝖊 𝕮𝖔𝖒𝖒𝖔𝖓𝖘 𝖙𝖊𝖆𝖗𝖊𝖘 :
𝕿𝖍𝖊 𝖜𝖎𝖕𝖊𝖗 𝖔𝖋 𝖙𝖍𝖊 𝖕𝖊𝖔𝖕𝖑𝖊𝖘 𝖙𝖊𝖆𝖗𝖊𝖘,
𝕿𝖍𝖊 𝖉𝖗𝖞𝖊𝖗 𝖚𝖕 𝖔𝖋 𝖉𝖔𝖚𝖇𝖙𝖘 𝖆𝖓𝖉 𝖋𝖊𝖆𝖗𝖊𝖘.

OF this poem, which breathes the very spirit of the servile reign of the First James, I cannot discover the author. Whoever he was, he was well penetrated with the doctrine of the divine right of kings, one of the favourite points advocated by the British Solomon. His adulation reaches its height in such lines as—

"God and kings doe pace together."

O stay your teares, you who complaine,
  and saye as babes doe all in vaine.
Purblind people, why doe you prate?
  too shallowe for the depth of state,   4
You cannot iudge whats truely myne,
  who see noe farther than the rine.[1]
Kings walke the milkye heavenly way;
  but you by bye pathes gad astray.   8
God and Kings doe pace together;
  but vulgars wander light as feather.
I should be sorry you should see
  my actions before they be   12
brought to the full of my desires:
  god aboue men Kings inspires.
Hold you the publique beaten way;
  wonder at Kings, and them obey;   16
For vnder God they are to chuse
  what rights to take, what to refuse.
Whereto, if you will not consent,
  yet hold your peace, least you repent,   20
And be corrected for your pride,
  that Kings designes dare thus deride,
by raylinge rymes and vauntinge verse,
  which your Kings breast should neuer peirce.   24

---

[1] Rind. "d has a great affinity for n, and often is brought into a word by the n as a sort of shadow. In the words *impound, expound,* from the Latin *impono, expono,* the d is a pure English addition; so likewise in *sound* from French *son,* Latin *sonus.* Provincial phonetics go still further, and call a gown *gownd.*"—Earle, Philology of the English Tongue, 1st edition, 1871.

Religion is the right of Kings,
  and they knowe best what good it brings;
Whereto you must submitt *you*r deeds,
  or be puld vp like stinkinge weeds.   28
Kings euer vse there instruments,
  of whome they iudge by the events;
The good they cherish and advance,
  and many things may come by chance.   32
Content *you*r selues with such as I
  shall take neare me & place high.
The men·you mou'd seru'd in there tyme,
  and soe may myne, as cleare of cryme.   36
All seasons haue there prop*er* vents,
  and bringe forth seuerall events;
Whereof the choice doth rest in Kings,
  who punish and reward them brings.   40
O, what a callinge were a Kinge
  if he might giue or take nothinge
  but such as you shall to him bringe!
Such were a Kinge but in a playe,   ,   44
  if he might beare noe greater swaye;
leaf 151 b. And then were you in worser case,
  if soe to keep *you*r ancient face;
Y*ou*r face would soone outface his might,   48
  if soe you would abridge his right.
Alas! fond men, play not w*i*th Kings,
  w*i*th Lyons clawes, or serpents stings;
They kill euen by there sharpe aspect;   52
  the proudest mynde they can deiect;
Make wretched the most mighty man,
  though he doe mutinye what he can.
yo*u*r censures are a hurryinge round,   56
  that rise as vapours from the ground.
I knowe when it shalbe most fitt,
  w*i*th whome to fill and empty it.
The Parliam*en*t I will appoint   60
  when I see things more out of ioynt.
Then will I sett all wrye things straight,
  and not vpon yo*u*r pleasure waite;
where if you speake as wise men should;   64
  if not, by me you shalbe schoold.
was euer Kinge calld to account,
  or euer mynde soe high did mount

as for to knowe the cause and reason, 68
 and to appoint the meanes and season,
when Kings should aske there subiects ayde?
 Kings cannott soe be made afrayde;
Kings will command, and find the way 72
 how all of you may easiest paye,
which they'le lay out as they thinke best,
 in ernest, and sometymes in iest.
what counsells should be ouerthrowne 76
 if all were to the people knowne!
And to noe vse were Counsell Tables,
 if State affaires were publique bables.
I make noe doubt all wise men knowe 80
 this were the way to all our woe;
For ignorance of causes makes
 soe many grosse and foule mistakes.
The modell of our Princely match 84
 you cannot make, but marre or patch.
Alas! how weake would proue your care!
 wish onely you his best welfare.
your patience cannot waite our ends, 88
 soe mixt they are twixt foes & frends;
whereof againe, ne're seeinge people,
 straine not to see soe high a steeple:
Looke on the ground whereon you goe, 92
 higher aspects will bringe your woe.
Take heed your places all be true;
 doe not discontents renue;
Meddle not with your Princes cares: 96
 for who soe doth, too much he dares.
I doe desire noe more of you,
 but to knowe me as I knowe you;
Soe shall I loue, & you obey, 100
 & you loue me in a right way.
O make me not vnwillinge still,
 whome I would saue, vnwillinge kill:
Examples in extremity 104
 are neuer the best remedy:
Thus haue I pleasd my selfe, not you,
 and what I say you shall find true.
Keepe euery man his ranke and place, 108
 and feare to fall in my disgrace.

You call our children chidds[1] of state,
    you claime a right vnto their fate;
But knowe you must be pleasd with what   112
    shall please vs best in spite of that.
Kings doe make lawes to bridle you,
    which they may pardon, or imbrue
there hands in the best blood you haue,   116
    and send the greatest to his graue.
The Charter, which you great doe call,
    came first from Kings, to stay your fall:
From an vniust rebellion, moued   120
    by such as Kingdomes little loued.
Imbrace noe more you well may hold,
    as often doth the ouerbold.
As they did who your Charter sought   . 124
    For there owne greatnesse, who soe wrought
    with Kings and you, that all prou'd nought.
The loue that Kings haue to you borne
    moud them thereto for to be sworne;   128
For where smale goods are to be gott
    were knowne to them that knowes vs not.
yet you, that knowe me all soe well,
    why doe you push me downe to hell   132
    by makeinge me an Infidell?
Tis true I am a cradle Kinge,[2]
    yet doe remember euery thinge
That I have heretofore put out,   136
    and yet begin not for to doubt.
Oh how grosse is your device,
    change to impute to Kings as vice!
The wise may chaunge, yet free from fault;   140
    though change to worse is euer nought.
Kings euer overreach you all,
    and must stay you, though that ther all fall.
Kings cannot comprehended be   144
    in Commons mouths, coniure ye
all what you can, by teares or termes,
    deny not what the Kinge affirmes.

---

[1] Probably the same as the word "chits" still found in provincial dialects. Cf. Halliwell, Chit, a forward child.

[2] Probably referring to the circumstance that James was proclaimed king while an infant of little more than a twelvemonth old, owing to the deposition of his mother (July 24, 1567).

He doth disdaine to cast an eye 148
  of anger on you, least you dye,
euen at the shadowe of his face ;
  yet giues to all *that* sue for grace.
I knowe my freinds, I need noe teachinge ; 152
  prowd is the foolish ouerreachinge.
^{leaf 152 b.} Come counsell me when I shall call ;
  wherefore beware of what may fall.
Kings will hardly take advice 156
  of Counsells ; they are wondrous nice ;
Loue and wisedome lead them still
  there Counsell tables vp to fill :
They need not helpes in there choice ; 160
  the best advice is there owne voice,
And be assured *that* such be Kings
  as they vnto there Counsell brings,
w*h*ich alwayes soe commended are 164
  as some would make, & some would marre.
If I once bend my angry browe,
  yo*ur* ruine comes, though not as now ;
For slowe I am reuenge to take, 168
  and yo*ur* amendm*en*ts wrath will slake.
Then hold yo*ur* pratlinge, spare yo*ur* penne,
  be honest and obedient men ;
vrge not my Iustice, I am slowe 172
  to giue you yo*ur* deserued woe :
If p*r*oclamac*i*ons [1] will not serue,
  I must doe more peace to p*r*eserue,
To keep all in obedience, 176
  to driue such busie bodies hence.

---

[1] By statute 31 Henry VIII. the proclamations of the sovereign were declared as valid as acts of parliament, although, it is true, certain restrictions were imposed. Many of these *rescripts*, as they might justly be called, were very whimsical. Thus in 1580 the erection of houses within three miles of London was forbidden, on account of the too great increase of the city.

[Ash. MS. 36, 37, f. 303.]

To the most high and mighty, the most piouse and mercifull, ye cheife Chancellor of Heauen and Judge of Earth;
The most humble Petitions of ye poore distressed Commons of long afflicted Englande.

THE production of some poetaster who, at the beginning of the reign of James I., bewails the lost glories of the Elizabethan epoch. The lamentation upon the death of Prince Henry, James's eldest son, which occurred Nov. 6th, 1612, probably shows the author to have been a Puritan, and will assist in fixing the date of the poem.

If bleeding soules, deiected heartes, find grace,
  Then, all disposer, turne not back thy face
From vs thy supplicants. Thrice Heauens Suns have worne
  Their Summer sutes, since wee began to mourne;   4
Egipts ten plagues wee haue indur'd twise tolde,
  Since blest Eliza was with Saincts inrol'de.
Thy messengers of wrath theire violls power
  Each day vpon our heads; nay, euery hower   8
Plagues begett plagues, and fruitefull vengeance growes,
  As if there were no ende sett to our woes.
Haue our black sinnes (O God) raised such a cloude
  Twixt Heauen and vs, as cryes, though ne're so loude, 12
Can get no passage to thy mercy seate?
  Are our iniquities (good God) so greate,
So infinite, as neither grones nor teares
  Can entertainement gett? Remember but ye yeares 16
Of oʳ affliction; then forgett, we craue,
  Our sins; bury them in ye deepest graue
Of darke obliuion; hide them in ye side
  Of our Redeemer: o let them bee tide 20
In chaines, yᵗ they may neuar rise again.
  Lett vs no longer sue, or cry in vaine;
Lett this our supplication, this complainte,
  Tendered by our late Souereigne thy Sainct, 24

At last finde grace.   Wast not, wee humbly pray,
　　Enough y^t first thou tookest y^t Queene away ?
Was not y^t Doue, y^t Lambe of innocence,
　　Sufficient sacrifise for our offence ?　　　　　　　28
Ah, no ! our sins oute liu'd her, and our crimes
　　Did threaten to outeliue ye last of times.
Thou didst remoue her y^t shee might not see
　　The sad beginnings of our misery.　　　　　　　32
Had Egipt thicker darkenesse then had wee,
　　When clearest eyes at mid day coulde not see ?
Vnholsom mistes, strange foggs, rumors of warrs,
　　Euill portending Commetts, blasing starrs,　　　　36
Prodigiouse births, and most vnnaturall seasons,
　　Putting Philosophers quite besides theire reasons,
Frightning ye poore, and ye ritch exhorting
　　To leaue theire downy beds, wheare they ly snorting.　40
Heauen in combustion seemes, ye sky in armes,
　　The starrs beate drums, ye Spheares do sounde alarums,
The aire did often bloody cullers spredd,
　　And all to rouse vs from ye lazy bedd　　　　　　44
Of base Security : yet nought woulde fright vs,
　　Till wee weere rob'd of what did most delite vs,
Henry our ioy.[1]　Henry, whose euery limme
　　Threatned to conquer death, and not death him :　　48
Henry ye pride, eauen Hen^e2ry ye blest,
　　On whome great Britaine sett vp her greate rest :
Who had not in y^t one an ample share ?
　　What Subiect had not rather lost his Heyre ?　　　52

---

[1] Prince Henry, eldest son of James, to whom Queen Elizabeth was god-mother, born Feb. 19, 1593, died Nov. 6, 1612. The young prince was very popular, especially among the Puritan party, who were in the habit of saying—

"Henry the Eighth pulled down the abbeys and cells,
　　But Henry the Ninth shall pull down bishops and bells."

Very extravagant hopes were formed of this youth, which perhaps had in reality but little foundation. He died suddenly of a fever, and suspicion was even cast upon his father, so extravagant was the national sorrow. This may perhaps have been augmented, if not originated, by the well-known fact that the King and his son had not been always on the best of terms. Lingard says : "There existed but little affection between him and his father. James looked on him with feelings of jealousy, and even of awe ; and the young prince, faithful to the lessons which he had formerly received from his mother, openly ridiculed the foibles of his father, and boasted of the conduct which he would pursue when he should succeed to the throne."—Lingard, ed. 1854, vol. vi. p. 64.

[2] This letter was added above by the copyist, who observed that the line wanted another syllable.

What tendar Mother did not wish y^t darte
  Had glanced from him, and strooke her Darlings harte?
All y^t weere vertuose, all y^t weere good,
  Turned theire weepings (sic) eyes to streames of blood. 56
But thine anoyted (sic) needes must leaue ye Citty
  Before it bee distroyed, such is thy pitty,
And such thy pitty. Are theire yet full ten?
  Is theire (greate God) a number les of men   60
Whose innocence may slack thy kindled ire,
  And keepe this Sodom Britaine from ye fire
Of thy just anger? Is there yet a soule
  Whose vertue power hath but to controle   64
Thine heau'd vp handc of iustice? If there bee,
  For his or her sake rouse thy clemency,
Awake thy mercy, let thy iustice slumberr,
  And saue ye greater for ye lesser numberr.   68
For his or her sake, we do humbly pray
  Respitt of time: giue vs a longer day;
And then, inabled by thy grace and Fauor,
  Wee'le purchesse Pardon by our good behauior.   72
Plague,[1] famine, darkenesse, Inundations,
  We haue indured; feare of innouations,
Wth expectation of ye worst can follow,
  Daily torments vs: and wee howerly swallow   76
Our very spittell eauen wth feare and horror;
  We nightly sleepe wth care, awake wth terror.
Nor are wee all this time from vermine free—
  The Catterpiller hanges on euery tree: 80
Lousy Promoters,[2] Monopoly-Mungers [3]
  A crew of vpstarte rascalls, whose firse hungers

---

[1] In 1604 the plague raged in England: in that same year (the first Parliament of James) an Act was passed that no one should leave his house, while suffering from the plague, under the penalty of death; provision was also made for a rate for the support of the infected.

[2] Informers. Cf. an epigram by Sir John Harrington against "Promoters," beginning—

    "Base spyes, disturbers of the publique rest,
      With forged wrongs the trew mans ryght that wrest."

(From a MS. copy of the epigrams in my possession in the handwriting of Sir John.)

[3] The question of monopolies, which had become a standing abuse in the reign of Elizabeth, was very keenly debated in the reign of James I., who had freely betaken himself to this method of recompensing his needy courtiers. In 1621 Sir Giles Mompesson and Sir Francis Mitchell,—the former of whom sat for the portrait of Massinger's *Sir Giles Overreach,*—having been detected in very gross

Can ne're bee satisfied : a sorte of slaues,
 Far more insatiate then are whores, or graues :   84
A sorte of vpstarte Parasites yᵗ rise,
 And do more mischeif then Egiptian flyes.
Haue wee no froggs? o yes, in euery ditch,
 Deuouring yᵉ poore, impouerishing yᵉ ritch,   88
Busy Intelligencers, base Informers,
 Like Toades and froggs, by croking in all corners,
Promoting rascalls, whose inuenom'd toungs
 Have donne thy suppliants infinite of wronges. 92
Where they desire to enter, there's no defence,[1]
 No ancient title, no Inheritance,
Can keepe them oute : they search and strech yᵉ Law,
 Keepe Magistrates and officers in awe :   96
They pluck yᵉ Ballance from faire Iustice fist,
 And make her Ministers do what they list.
There is no equity, no Law, nor Right ;
 All causes go by fauor or by might.   100
O God of Mercy, what more can bee saide ?
 Iustice is-bought and solde, becom a Trade :
Honor's confer'd on base vnworthy groomes,
 And Clownes, for gaine, may perch in highest Roomes. 104
Jobb had full many scabbs, yet none so bad
 As wee these one and twenty yeares haue had.
Egipte had botches, many soares yᵗ smarted,
 But yet they lasted not, they soone departed. 108
Halfe fowerty yeares in this sad wildernesse
 Wee now have trauael'd ; is there no redresse ?
Bowman, and Iolex, Ringwood and his Mate,[2]
 Compar'd wᵗʰ vs, are in a better state :   112

---

abuses of this privilege, were degraded from knighthood and fined. The matter
was temporarily set at rest by 21 Jac. I., which declared all monopolies to be
contrary to law, and all such grants to be void. Charles I., however, in his
straits, produced by the constant antagonism of the Parliament, attempted to
renew them, and, as Clarendon says : " Obsolete laws were revived and vigorously
executed, wherein the subjects might be taught how unthrifty a thing it was, by
too strict detaining of what was his, to put the King as strictly to inquire what
was his own." An ingenious but unsatisfactory defence.

[1] The great height to which this scandalous custom of granting patents had
reached is well shown in the third volume of Lodge's " Illustrations of English
History."

[2] Who these individuals were I am unable to ascertain after a careful search
in the Calendar of State Papers for the reign of James I., including other
probable sources of information.

They can be hearde, they can bee rewarded,
  When wee are curst, sleighted, and vnregarded.
Is there a People (o Heauen) fallen a degree
  Below ye Condition of a dogg but wee? 116
Was there a nation in the Vniuerse
  More daring once, more bold, more stoute, more feirce?
And is there now vpon ye worldes broad face
  Any y^t can be reconed halfe so base? 120
Is there a people so much scornd, despis'd,
  So laught at, baffled, and so vassaliz'd?
Where's auncient nobility becomme?
  Alas! they are suppress'd, and in theire roome, 124
Like proud insulting Luciferrs, there sitts
  A sorte of vpstarte fawning Parasitts.
        Where's ye Gentry?[1]

---

[1] The piece terminates thus somewhat abruptly. On the next page of the MS. is an amatory poem, beginning—"Diana cecill, that rare beauty thou doest shew."

THE CANDLEWICK LETTERS.

Letter from John Downynge to his friend Bland.[1]

THIS is an epistle from a certain John Downynge, of Rye, in Sussex, to his friend, who has left the neighbourhood suddenly: it begins in verse, but ends in prose. Candlewick Street, A.S. *wic;* cf. Alnwick, Smethwick, Norwich, etc.: so called from the Candlemakers, who originally inhabited it; it was in the ward of Thomas de Basinge. See Memorials of London, by Riley, p. 3. To them succeeded woollen-cloth weavers from Flanders, who were settled in this street by Edward III. "There were then," says Stow, "in this city weavers of divers sorts, to wit, of Drapery, Tapery, and Napery." Cf. also Lydgate, in the Ballad of "The London Lyckpenny"—

> Then went I forth by London Stone,
> Throughout all Canwick Street:
> Drapers much cloth me offered anon;
> Then comes me one cried 'hot sheep's feet;'
> One cried mackerel, rushes green, another gan greet,
> One bad me buy a hood to cover my head;
> But, for want of money, I might not be sped.

John Bland was an old name in the City; a John Bland was Mayor in 1303 (Stow's Survey, ed. Strype, book i. p. 60), but perhaps the name is more correctly given as John Blount, or John le Blund.

[Tanner MS. 306, fol. 181.]

To wryte you comendations, : or send you salutations,
seyng your yll fashyons, : yt were but in vayne.
I leave yt therefore, : & kepe yt in store,
where maners are more, : I tell ye in playne;
for what maye I Iudge : of suche a suvege[2]
awaye so to truege : with out takyng his leave?
I tooke ye, my frend, : as ye do pretende;
but nowe, in the ende, : ye do me dysceave.
ye cam) in the evenyng, : & found me a wryting,
about letters sendyng : consernyng my charge.
in goynge your waye, : then dyd ye not saye
that the next daye : we shulld taulke at large?
in the mornyng I went : for the same intent,

---

[1] On the back of the letter is the following superscription: "To his frend Mr. Bland, drape*r*, in Candlewicke Strete, be this *delivered*. London, to his owne hands." The handwriting and orthography of these four pieces present great difficulties, which are increased by the torn and soiled condition of the paper. In many instances conjecture has been of necessity employed.

[2] *sic*. ? savage.

with hart well bent, : to the place where ye laye;
but you were gon), : & I ther vpon)
to formans[1] anon) ; : but you hastyd[2] awaye
with out all honestye, : or part of humanyte,
as voyde of Scyvyllytye, : Lyke one out of kynde.
in *which* you*r* sayde part : there wantyd good hart,
as sayde my consart, : who ys of my mynde;
for she thought verylye : we shulld have lawghfft merylye
at dynner, I assure ye, : & so had preparyd ;
but nothyng mystrustyng : you*r* suddyng dep*a*rtyng
with out further metynge, : she was cleane desevyd.

forcyd for want of tyme to a brevyate my meter, I conclude the rest in prowes: surelye & off my faythe I & my wyfe bothe were offendyd at you*r* sudden) dep*a*rture; patyens[3] [and] I ment to have taulkyd w*i*th you conse*r*nyng thyngs for your comodyte: & a part towchyng my frend m) carmarden) : to home ommytt not my hartye comendations, w*i*th thaynks *for* my great chere; when oportunytye shall se*r*ve, I shalbe redye to requytt parrt. to m) p*a*rker my frend; to m) greve̦s, your frend and my adoptyde Sonn, & heyre off the halff aker beyonde S. georgs,[4] Do my comendat*ions* : the Lyke omytt not to good m) champyon: & leave not out the rest of the Crewe: god blesse you all, & send my sonn̦e greves quyetnes w*i*th an vnytye & p*er*fitt amyttye bytwen) hym) & m) edward p*a*rker !

& thus restyng yowrs: requyrynge you myne the lyke vnfaynyd as p*er*fitt frends, & lovyng bretherin of one howsse & consanguynytye: leave not in oblyvyon my hartye salutations to m) Io[n] smythe.

& yff ye wyll, saye the lyke to mystrys coldwell. fare ye well & god send vs peace. Amen.

f*rom* Rye, the 18 of everell, 1561, you*r*s In° downўnge, in hast, I assure you, as aperythe.

---

[1] Perhaps related to Sir Wm. Forman who was Lord Mayor in 1538 (Gough MS. List of Lord Mayors and Sheriffs).

[2] So corrected by the writer from *were ryd*.

[3] Patience; no doubt the name of his wife.

[4] Perhaps St. George's, Southwark. Cf. Stow, book iv. p. 27 (ed. 1720). "In this Lane (Paris Garden) is Groves Court, consisting of small houses." It will be observed that the names of most of these citizens recur in the letters: they were, no doubt, good, substantial, and "proper" men of their time, but it would be idle, in the majority of instances, to disturb their ashes.

Letters from the Deventer Crew[1] to the Candlewick Crew.

Two letters in verse from Paul Peresonne and Arthur Mawd, Wardens of the Deventer Crew, to the Crew in Candlewick Street, and the answer. The history of these singular compositions appears to be, that in April, 1561, some wild young English merchants settled at Antwerp played a practical joke on some grave London citizens by addressing them in a set of rhymes, as if they were roystering free-livers like themselves. The first letter remained unanswered, and then probably, determined to elicit a reply of some kind, the writers despatched a second letter, merely an altered version of the other, with the addition of a prose preamble, which produced a strong poetical remonstrance from the worthy seniors, who are greatly scandalized at the imputations cast upon them. These pieces, and the answer of the Candlewick Crew, are undoubtedly original. The paper is worn and soiled, and so damaged at the edges that the words bracketed had to be supplied. The hand is a coarse secretary one, with numerous flourishes and contractions. The two letters from the "Deventer Crewe" were written by different persons. The handwriting and orthography are those of the London citizen of the time, precisely as we find in the Diary of Henry Machyn.

These pieces of quaint doggerel have no value except as giving us an insight into the manners of the time, and showing us the hearty geniality and too-often coarse horse-play of our ancestors. The City guilds were in a very flourishing condition in the time of Elizabeth : we were fast making our country the great shop of Europe : the nickname of "la nation boutiquière," which the baffled rivalry of a neighbouring nation has fixed upon us, was becoming more than ever appropriate. This is not the place, however, to attempt anything like a sketch of the history of the Great English Companies.

---

[1] Deventer on the Yssel, formerly the capital of Overyssel: a strong place, with extensive trade. Thomas à Kempis died there. It was besieged and taken by Maurice of Nassau, 1691.

[Tanner MS. 306, fol. 178.]

Lawes Deo Semp*er*! Le .3. iour De Aprell, 1561.   Stillo
[Romano].[1]

Hauynge opportunytye of tyme to cawłłe to memorye your
Jentełł Commendacyons Lattelye by vs Receyvyd, for the
w*hic*h as yett we Reste your Dettares, ettc.   The Cawes
where off was onłłye for Lacke of A trustye frynde for
Dellyuerye ther-off: w*hic*h Resonnable Exskewess we Dowte
not Butt you wiłł Exsepte, and o*ur* Loue, ettc.

So Lycke as your Commendacyons, by vs in ałł poynts hathe
    byn vzid,
So hoppe we in Lycke Case of your ples*ure*, owres shałł not
    be Refusyd,
whiche thynge nowe beynge Donne, att ower Reqwestess,
yow bynd vs at ałł tymes, here-aftar, to ffullfyłł yower be
    hestes.   4

And fyrste we wyll Be gyn, with owr moste welbe Lovyd,
and frend Redye at ałł Dayes, as we haue wełł provyd;
his name for to Re herse, as yow shałł vnder stand,
A propper man of parson, whoos name ys John Bland.   8

A man for his Acktes moste prompte, and ałł wayes Redye
To breeke his faste at the Snylle, where he hawthe byn full
    merrye,
of ałł men to A begger, I dowe Compare hym Beste,
for when his skryppe ys full, he will laye his townge to
    Reste.   12

And thus owr menynge is, to tacke ałł owr frendes in order,
for w*it*h yow nychollas Spencer, we wiłł p*ro*sede further.
Vnto yow nowe owr hartye Comendacyons we will Dereckte,
Trustynge you will them of yowr ples*ure* wełł Exsepte.   16

---

[1] Thus addressed on the back of the letter: "To ower Lovynge frendes the
Crewe of Candellwicke Strette, this our Lettar be *delivered.* London. To Eyther
of·ther handes."

And further owr Comendacyons we mowste in no wyse for gett,
of yow to be Donne, to mysteres wełł mett,[1]
Dwellynge at the hande in hande with in Saynte Clements
   Lanne,[2]
ałł Evenyngs of yow to be Done, or ells yow are mowche to
   blame.   20

We Reqwyer you Dowe owr Commendacyons, to Robarte in
   the hand in hand,[3]
A man of marvellus oneste quałłyttes, By Re porte off Iobn
   Bland.
yf thes owr Commendacyons showld you in anye poynte
   offennd,
At yower Awnswer here off, we will them amend.   24

And thus myndynge to haue ałł owr frendes in Remembrances,
with yow Rychard Champyon [4] we procede owr Enterances,
who is on of the Crewe that oftentymes Dowthe macke merrye,
with fygges, Reysons and allmondes, Bowghte in Buclares
   Berrye.[5]   28

---

[1] Query, "masters, well met."

[2] "On the north side of this ward, at the west end of Eastcheap, have ye St. Clements Lane, a part whereof, on both sides, is of Candlewick Street Ward."—Stow, book ii. p. 183.

[3] Probably the name of a drawer, with whom the young idlers of the day affected familiarity. "Sirrah," says Shakespere's Prince Henry, "I am sworn brother to a leash of drawers, and can call them all by their Christian names."
"Your first compliment shall be to grow most inwardly acquainted with the drawers, to learn their names, as Jack, and Will, and Tom."—Decker's Gull's Horn-Book, 1610.

[4] "Master Champion, draper," who, in August, 1558, "was chosen Shreyff of London by the comens of the cete" (H. Machyn's Diary, p. 170). The Sheriff was son of Richard Champion, of Godalming, Surrey. He was afterwards knighted. Lord Mayor of London 1566, died 1568. His epitaph is in Stow, beginning—

   "The Corps of Richard Champion, Knight,
    Maior and Draper, here doth rest."

Sir R. Champion died without issue. His wife was Barbara, widow of Alderman Heardson. In Machyn's account of the christening of Thomas White (Feb. 3rd, 1560-1) she figures as "Masteres Champyon, (the) altherman(s) wyff, godmother." She erected a monument in St. Dunstau's-in-the-East, with kneeling effigies of herself and her two husbands.

The name was a good one in the city, and well reputed, if we judge by its civic honours: the following occur among the number:

  1529, 21 Hen. 8. Wm. Champion, Sheriff.
  1530, 22 Hen. 8. Richard Champion, Draper, Sheriff.
  1558, 6 Mary. Richard Champion, Draper, Sheriff.
  1566, 7 Elizabeth. Sir Richard Champion, Draper, Lord Mayor.

[5] "Bucklersbury falls into Walbrook, almost against St. Stephen's Walbrook

Wythe plentye of wyne, ffyttyd at the Bores hedd,[1]
with whiche yow macke the goodman often tymes to go
    druncke to Bedd;
and then, I dowte nott, But with the wyffe you maye Dowe
    your plesure,—
Everye man in his course, at his owne Laysare.   32

Church. After that (in the reign of Henry VI.), the pepperers or grocers had seated themselves in a more open street, to wit, in Bucklesbury, where they yet remain" (Stow). Bucklersbury took its name from the owner of "one antient strong Tower of stone," given by Edward III. to St. Stephen's, Westminster. In course of time it became the property of one Buckle, who set about taking it down, to build into a house. But the said Buckle, greedily labouring to pull down the old Tower, a piece thereof fell upon him, which so bruised him that his life was thereby shortened. "This whole street called Buckleshury, on both the sides throughout, is possessed by Grocers and Apothecaries toward the west end thereof."—Stow, ed. 1720, book iii. p. 27. See also Memorials of London, p. 25.

The apothecaries of those days were herbalists. Shakespere has alluded to this, when he makes Falstaff speak of the young gallants "as a many of these lisping hawthorn buds, that come like women in men's apparel, and smell like Bucklersbury in simple time." There must also have been a celebrated tobacconist's shop there in the time of Ben Jonson, for he seems to allude to the sign: "I thought he would have run mad o' the black boy in Bucklersbury, that takes the scurvy roguy tobacco there" (Bart. Fair, act i. scene 1).

[1] The first mention of this celebrated tavern occurs in the testament of William Warden, temp. Richard II., who gave "all that tenement called the Boar's Head in Eastcheap" to a college of priests, or chaplains, founded by Sir W. Walworth, the Lord Mayor, in the adjoining church of St. Michael, Crooked Lane. The presence of "Prince Hal" in this house was no invention of Shakespere: history records his pranks, how one night, with his two brothers John and Thomas, he made such a riot that they had to be taken before the magistrate. No wonder then at the proud inscription on the sign, which still existed in Maitland's time: "This is the chief tavern in London." At one time the portal was decorated with carved oak figures of Falstaff and Prince Henry; and in 1834 the former was in the possession of a brazier of Eastcheap, whose ancestors had lived in the shop he then occupied since the Great Fire. On the removal of a mound of rubbish at Whitechapel, brought there after the Great Fire, a carved boxwood bas-relief boar's head was found, set in a circular frame formed by two boar's tusks, mounted and united with silver. An inscription to the following effect was pricked at the back: "Wm. Brooke, Landlord of the Bore's Hedde, Estchepe, 1566."

"The original inn having been destroyed by the Fire, was rebuilt, and continued in existence until 1831, when it was finally demolished, to make way for the streets leading to new London Bridge. Its site was between Small Alley and St. Michael's Lane. The ancient sign, carved in stone, with the initials J. T. and the date 1668, is now preserved in the City of London Library, Guildhall."—Hotten's History of Signboards, p. 379. See also a notice in Catalogue of Works of Art exhibited at Ironmongers' Hall, vol. ii. pp. 465-66. The site is now occupied by the monument to William IV.

Hotten mentions two other Boar's Head inns—one in Southwark, another without Aldgate. Of the Snylle (snail) mentioned in the first letter, and the Snype in the second, no mention can be found. They were perhaps both the invention of the writers.

Ower welbe Lovyd hamares[1] Clyffe in no wise mowste Be for
    gotten ;
yf his parson were absente, the Crewe wold Downne the
    Brocken,[2]
who with his Lewte Dowthe make the hotte Crewe merry,
with (   ) Small yes,[3] Syngynge, mrs wett mett, shatt
    I Rowe in your wherrye ?   36

And then Lowcke you cawtt Robarte to fyll a pott off alle,
whitte yow, hamers Clyffe, are skowrynge off her Taylle ;
and then, Robarts Braynes Beyng troubled in that same Tyme,
Dowthe brynge you for atte a pott of Frenche wynne.   40

And thus, hamers Clyffe, with you we witt macke an Ende,
prayenge god off his grace unto vs a merye metynge to send.
yff tyme wold par-mytt, we wold wrytte you more at Large,
and thus we praye god, Kepe yow owt off wellses Barge.[4]   44

John Graves, we here Saye, ys on off your Crewe,
which newes vnto vs Dyd Seme verrye newe ;
And knowynge that he the good fettowe Can playe,
owr mynde ys to haue hym in for on by the waye.   48

In playenge on the Vergenatts he ys wett skyttyd,
And on his fyddett manye tymes wett wittid,
attso on the gyttarne he playes verye well ;
yett hammers Cliffe on the Lewte Dowthe him far Exsett.[5]   52

When att thes Instruments are Com to gether,
no mar-vett thoughe yow haue there-in grette plesure ;
the mettodye there-of By Reson showld be so whette,[6]
That John blandes howes should be in Dawnger to be
    Dawnsid Down with yowr ffette.   56

---

[1] *sic* in this and the following verses. ? Thomas. See Letter immediately
succeeding.

[2] Perhaps this phrase may have arisen from Broken Wharf, "a water gate or
key, so called, of being broken and fallen down into the Thames."

[3] There is a gap here in the original, and it is very difficult to make any sense.

[4] A cant name for the Fleet Prison. The Fleet was anciently the River of
the Wells, or such a term might well date from the time of King John, who
"by his patent, dated the third of his reign, gave to the Archdeacon of Wells
the custody of the said King's House at Westminster, and his Gaol of the Fleet."
Stow, book iii. p. 256.

[5] These stanzas fill the leaf, the date is again superscribed on the v° side as
follows : Laude A Dio .3. Aprell, 1561. Stillo Romano.

[6] O.E. wethe, sweet. A.S. wette.

Yett on ther ys of yore Crewe w*hich* to vs ys vn-knowne,
The fame off his Dawnsynge to andwarpe is blowne ;
Syde ys hiss name, as we wiь yow teь,
a-mownge aь the Crewe for Dawnsynge he beres the beь. 60

To aь the Reste of the Crewe w*hich* we haue not namyd,
we aske p*ar*don of yow, and not to be Blamyd;
for this owr worcke to yow aь we haue Deryctid,
prayenge yow aь at *yo*ur ferste metynge yt maye be En-
 actyd. 64

And forther that when So Ever this owr worcke shalbe Redd,
That on off *yo*ur Crewe for ower Suckses maye go droncke
  to bedd ;
whiche Requeste off you fuьfyьid, we Reste yowr Dettar,
hoppynge owr nexte Comendacyons shaь plese yow bettar. 68

And now thes owr Comendacyons for this tyme beynge Donne,
from vs yowr owld frendes, arthur maude and pawьe peresonn,
and aьso not for-gotten, off an other frend as yett vn-knowne,
Rycharde Carmarden,[1] who hathe hym comendid to yow
 Everye on. 72

The Tyme passythe A-waye, we moste nedes macke an Ende,
prayenge to the Lyvynge god yow aь to Amend],
And aьso To Send vs aь-wayes off his grace,
And in the hevens Terestyaь A Dweьynge place. 76

yower Lovynge frendes,
pauьe peresonne,
arthur mawd.

The Second Letter of the Deventer Crew.

THIS letter is bound up so as to precede No. 1, of which it is
in the main a repetition, with occasional variations. It is written
by Arthur Mawd in a much coarser hand than the first, which is
in Pereson's handwriting. Each of the young men affixed his
own signature, both to the letter of April 3rd and that of the 25th.

---

[1] Probably the son of "my frend Mr. Carmarden," in John Downynge's letter.

[Tanner MS. 306, fol. 177.]

Jhesus.[1]   At Barrowe[2] the 25 of Aprell.

Moste Trustye and welbe Louyd Frendes, with [Loue]
Vnfaynnyd we Commend vss vnto you, wyshynge [all]

---

[1] A very common way of commencing a letter at the time. Thus the celebrated letter of Mrs. Alleyn to her husband, preserved in Dulwich College, in which Mr. Collier so strangely found the allusion to Shakespere. "Jhesus. My intyre and welbeloved sweet harte, still it joyes me," etc.

[2] Most probably Bergen-op-Zoom. Compare Eng. Barrow, A.S. beorh, same as the German *berg*. Or perhaps, according to an ingenious suggestion, it may be Berchem, a small place formerly at a short distance from Antwerp, but now forming a suburb of the city. Barrow is mentioned by Boorde (See Mr. Furnivall's edition, p. 150), where the Brabander says:

> "I was borne in Braban, that is both gentil and free;
> All nacyons at all tymes be well-come to mee.
> I do vse martes, dyuers tymes in the yere;
> And of all thynges, I do loue good Englysh bere.
> In Anwarpe and in Barow I do make my martes;
> There doth Englysh marchauntes cut out theyr partes."

Mr. Furnivall suggests Breda: with which opinion I am unable to agree, as I cannot see how that name can have been corrupted into Barrow. He quotes Hall's Chronicle: "In this yere (A.D. 1531) was an olde Tolle demaunded in Flaunders of Englyshmen, called the Tolle of the Hounde, wbich is a Ryuer and a passage: The Tolle is .xii. pence of a Fardell. This Tolle had been often tymes demaunded, but neuer payed; insomuche that Kyng Henry the seuenth, for the demaunde of that Tolle, prohibited all his subiectes to kepe any Marte at Antwerpe or Barow, but caused the Martes to be kepte at Calyes." —p. 786, ed. 1809. "If this warre [with the Emperor in 1527] was displeasaunt to many in Englande (as you have hard), surely it was as much or more displeasant to the tounes and people of Flaunders, Brabant, Hollande, and Zelande, and in especiall to the tounes Andwarpe and Barrow, where the Martes wer kept, and where the resorte by Englishmen was."—*Ib.* p. 746. Perhaps these young men were factors in the Low-Countries for some great London house or houses. Their mode of living and boldness of speech have a parallel in Master Hobson's story of his factor in France, "A merry conceited youth," "Pleasant Conceits of Old Hobson," p. 14 (Halliwell). Their morals were probably not improved by their sojourn among the Flemings, who were noted for their deep potations. Thus Sir Thomas Gresham complains in the Privy Council that his health is suffering from the heavy carousals he is obliged to partake of with the Flemish merchants, "for all their cheer is in drink." Compare also Nash's "Pierce Penniless's Supplication to the Devil" (ed. by Payne Collier for the (Old) Shakspere Society, 1842, p. 52): "From gluttonie in meates, let me discend to superfluitie in drink, a sinne that, euer since we have mixt our selues with the Low Countries, is counted honourable, but before we knew their lingring warres, was held in the highest degree of hatred that might be. Then, if wee had scene a man goe wallowing in the streetes, or line sleeping vnder the boord, wee would have spet at him as a toade, and cald him foule, drunken swine, and warned all our friends out of his company: now, he is no body that cannot drinke super uagulum,[1] carouse the hunter's hoope, quaffe vpseg freze crosse,

[1] "Drinking super nagulum, a devise of drinking new come out of Fraunce; which is, after a man hath turnde up the bottom of the cup, to drop it on hys nayle, and make a pearl with that is left; which, if it slide, and he cannot mak stand on, by reason thers too much, he must drinke againe for his penance."

heꝛthes, wythe good Sowckeces in aꝛꝛ yower Dowengs. By
this ower frennd and Ghyllde brewer hawnsyd[2] a[nd]
Sworen in to ower Compane and preve Leged. not Long
Synes we thoughte good to Caweꝛꝛ to memorye the owllde
and Accustoomabeꝛꝛ frenshippe vzid and frequentid Amonge
vs towerdes you, not Longe Synes sent By hym to Adrese
the Same, who ys on of the Ryghte Stampe, and vallewyd
of vss. Conveniute in aꝛꝛ places for the Lycke valleue whoes
*pr*esenes vnto you hath Longe Synes from you byn absente,
yett I truste his *per*con in no poynto for gotton, and hauynge
*per*vzid ower owlld and ansyente Regester we fiynd that of
Longe Synes we haue vnto *your* Crewe Adressyd A Lettar,
w*hic*h as yett we never haue R*eceive*d awnsuer; wherrefore
at this present hauynge not moche ·to trobell you with at
this tyme we Dowe menne to pute you in memorye ther of,
as tyme and place shall Sarve, ettc.

And fyrste we wilbe gyn w*it*h ower moste welbe Louyd,
ower frend at aꝛꝛe Dayes, as we haue well [prouyd];
his name to Reherse, as you shall vnders[tand],
A proper manne of *per*con, whoes name ys Jhone [Bland].   4

A man for his Acktes moste prompte and Re[dy]
to brecke his faste at the Snype, where he hathe byn f[ull
      merrye] ;
of aꝛꝛ men to a Beger he ys comparid Be[st],
for when his Skryppe ys fule, he Layes hym Downe [to rest].   8

---

with leapes, glones, mumpes, frolickes, and a thousand such dominering inuentions.
He is reputed a pesaunt and a boore that will not take his licour profoundly;
and you shall heare a caualier of the first feather, a princockes that was but
a page the other day in the court, and now is all to be frenchified in his souldiours
sute, stand vpon termes with. ' God's wounds! You dishonour me, sir, you doo
me the disgrace if you do not pledge me as much as I drunke to you;' and,
in the midst of his cups, stand vaunting his manhood, beginning euerie sentence
with ' When I first bore armes,' when he neuer bare anie thing but his lord's
rapier after him in his life. If he haue been ouer and visited a towne of
garrison, as a trauailer or passenger, he hath as great experience as the greatest
commander and chiefe leader in England. A mightie deformer of men's manners
and features is this vnnecessarie vice of all other. Let him bee indued with
neuer so manie vertues, and haue as much goodly proportion and fauour as
Nature can bestow vpon a man, yet if hee be thirstie after his owne destruction,
and hath no ioy nor comfort but when he is drowning his soule in a gallon pot,
that one beastly imperfection wil vtterly obscure all that is commendable in him,
and all his goode qualities sinke like lead downe to the bottome of his carowsing
cups, where they will lye, like lees and dregges. dead and vnregarded of any
man."   [2] hanselled.

and thus to tacke att ower frendes in order,
with you Rychard Champyon we witt prosede further
as on of the Crewe that oftentymes makes merre
with mane Dyllycatts Boughte in Bouclares Berre.   12

wythe plentye of wynne fyllid at the Bores hedd,
where with yow macke the good man go droncke to Bedd,
and we feare nott But with the wyfe yow can Dowe *your*
        plesure;
Evere man in his Corse, at his owen Layser.   16

and thus with yow, Ryc*hard* champyon, we witt macke an end,
prayenge god of his grace a mere metynge to vs Sende.
ower welbe Louyd thomas Clyfe in nowyse moste be for gotten,
yf that his *per*con were absent, the Crewe wolld Su[re be
        brocken].   20

who wythe his Lewte Dowthe macke the Crewe [merry],
with [   ] Small yes, Syngynge, heye Derrye D[errye];
and then Lowcke you Cawtt Robarte to fytt [a pot of ale],
whylle yow, thomas Clyfe, arre skowrynge his m$^{rs.}$ taytt.   24

and then, thomas Braynes Beynge trobled in that tyme,
Dowthe Brynge you in Stedde off atte A potte of wynne:
yf tyme wolld *per* myt we wolld wrytte you more at Large,
and thus we *pra*ye god keepe you ought of wellses Barge.   28

Jno. Graves, we herre Saye, ys on of yower Crewe,
w*hi*ch newes vnto vs Dyd Seme verre newe,
and knowynge that he the good fellowe can [playe],
ower mynd hys to haue hym in for on by the [waye].   32

In playenge on the Vergenalles he ys well skyllid,
and on his ffyddell mane tymes well willid,
allso on [the] gyttarne he playes verre well;
yett thomas Clyfe on the Leute dothe him [far exsell].   36

When att thes Instrumentes are Com to gether,
no marvett though you haue therre in grette plesure;
the mellodye there of By Rezon sholld be So Swette,
that Jn° Blandes hows shall be in danger of dawnsynge down
        with your fette.   40

Yett on therre ys of yower Crewe w*h*ich to vs ys unknowen,
the fame of his Dawnsynge to andwarp ys Blownne;
Syde ys his name as we wiłł you tełł,
amonge you ałł for dawnsynge he berres the Bełł. 44

To ałł the Reste whiche we haue nott namyd,
we aske p*ar*don of you, and not to be blamid;
for this ower workes to you ałł we haue dedycatid,
p*r*ayenge you at yower metynge yt maye be enactid. 48

and when So Ever yt shałł chanes this owr worke be redd,
that on of yo*u*r Crewe maye go droncke to bedd;
w*h*ich Requeste of you fullfyllid, we Reste yower Dettar,
hopynge ower nexte Comendacyones shałł plese you better. 52

The tyme pasythe Awaye: we moste macke an end,
prayenge to the Lyvynge god you ałłe to amend;
and allwayes to Sennd vs of his grace,
and in the hevenes terestyall A dwellynge place. 56

yours, The m*aster* wardens
of The Deventer Crew,
arthur mawd,
pawłłe peresoñn.

Answer of the Candlewick Crew.

W*E* now give the answer of the worthy members of the Candlewick Crew, who are greatly indignant with the liberty which
has been taken with them, and rebuke their juvenile assailants
accordingly. There is something very quaint in these laboured
efforts of the Aldermanic muse: apparently they considered it
a matter of honour to retaliate in rhyme: poetical "flytings"
of this description ornament the literature of both the fifteenth
and sixteenth centuries. Cf. Dunbar with Kennedy, and Skelton
with Garnesche. The antiquary finds no little amusement in
these highly-spiced fragments of ancient virulence.

[Tanner MS. 306, fol. 179.]

your letter large of lewde effecte we longe synns have re-
    ceyvyd,
wherin your myschevous meanyng mynde in wryting is
    perceyvyd ;
your proper preface pend in prowesse, by way of commen-
    dations,
shewyth a smorye[1] symple style, in ower ymagynations.   4
an] introduction] to a trade, off rvde & Rechelesse rymyng,
a craftye cloke to culler crymes, which after coms in wrytyng.
your fantzye forgeth fyrst to name, as orderlye we stand,
owr fayth full, freke,[2] & frendlye mate, and lovyng brother
    bland,   8
whome we both love, & lyke also, and think hym moche
    more better,
then dothe your rvde and rompcnte style: compares him to
    a begger.
a shamelesse sort, a synfull syghte : emonge ye trulye be,
that so wyll wryte to his dyspigt : & he no wursse then] we.
A modest mate & merye man] : a fythfull ffrende at nede,   13
a hatelesse hart, a wyttye wyght : & trew in word & dede.
from bland, our best belovyd frend, to champyon], then] ye
    com :
althoughe good choyce of chere we vse, yet ye myght leave
    owte som].   16
but bucklers berye ye bryng in, & other suche lyke places,
& thervnto ye Joyne such gere, that I perceyve ye grasles.
I shame to shewe, & wyll not wryte, the rvdenes of your style,
but ye remayne suche as ye were, and have byn] of longe
    whyle.   20
we would ye wete, & well dyd knowe, & kepe yt in your
    mynde,
that champyon cheyfe emong vs ys, and one both trewe &
    kynde :
an] honest hartye man] he ys, of lyffe most pure vnspottyd,
whose fame & bruyte[3] & doynges [y]ett were never staynd ne
    blottyd ;   24

---

[1] ? Sorry.   [2] Brave, firm. See instances quoted by Halliwell.
[3] Rumour or report, a word of Keltic origin.

but as in name he Champyon ys, the lyke, be sure, at nede,
ye shall hym͒ fynde in force & myght : & fyrme in word &
    dede.
with Curtyous clyffe ye followe next, lest he shulld be for-
    gotton͒,
and yf he were not well in lyfe, ye saye owr crew were
    broken,   28
as thoughe the fredom͒ of owr faythe dependyd but one clyfe.
no, wytles wryter, know thou well, our state ys not so breyfe :
thoughe one or twooe or thre dep*ar*te, the crewe ys not
    dyssolvyd ;   31
therefore be sure, ye sawcye syr, your dowbt therein resolvyd.
hys life doth lyke, & eke delyght, & please owr fantzyes well ;
but to recite the Rest ye wryte, my eares doth glo to tell.
ohe, shamelesse secte of sathans sewte ! how dare ye so to
    wryte ?   35
what cawsse doth clyffe compelle ye thus of hym so to indyte ?
alas ! good clyffe, o curtious mate ! ohe gentle harte &
    mynde !
was never none that yet colld saye, o clyff, thou art vnkynde !
our brother braynes ye also blame, who ys of good reporte.
now welses barge, I swere, ys mete to furnyshe suche a sorte.
procedyng forth, ye bryng in graves : m*ar*veyll moche we do
that he, in lyke as others are, ye do not slawnder so.   42
ye Saye ye mynde to make hym one emong vs to be placyd ;
naye, make som͒ meanes to place your selves : for whye ? ye
    ar dysgracyd.   44
owr orders onlye dothe p*er*mytt, no brother in our crewe
By havyng made vs sore offense, shall lenger then ensewe
emonge vs to be fre thenceforth, wyth out owr whole consent,
and that Som͒ prowff ther maye be had that he doth sore
    repent.   48
nowe whether that ye have all lost the fredom of owr crewe,
your letter late ye sent vs both doth large ynowff condempn
    you.
Lesyd[1] the sort of other sins whereof ye be suspectyd,
as powll at barrowe by two wentches hath byn late infectyd,
and mawd at andw*ar*p hath the lyk : small ioye we have to
    wryt yt,   53

---

[1] *i.e.* setting aside. (Cf. out-taken, except.) The word is not common in this
sense.

& Randle eke ys not to seke :[1] & hawes at brussells[2] hath yt;
this trulye we do touche apart : in brefe you*r* great abvse,
thoughe you at large in lyeng sort, w*i*th slawnders vs accvse.
wherefore yt is awardyd here, w*i*thout ye do submyt ye, 57
ye lese the tayle of that ye had, whereof we do dyscharg ye ;
yet at the great request of *some*, of you*r* part vndeservyd,
ye maye w*i*th hvmblyng of you*r* selves by gratis now receyvyd. 60
vpon som hope of happyer lyfe then hereto-fore was uzyd,
or ells be sure yt ys decreede ye shalbe cleane Refusyd.
ohe bayres bolld, howe dare ye wryte so lewdlye vs vnto,
and theñ at ende to wry_te so rvde, vnmete for you to do ? 64
as thoughe we culld not Rede you*r* byll wyth-out we went
  to drynke;
and thoughe we had, yt yll becomes you so of vs to thynke,
that we, as wyse & Sober wyghtes, Owre selves shulld so
  abvse
to drynke so muche tyll we be dr*u*ncke, as ye emonge ye vse !
also we cannot merye be when we be so dysposyd, 69
but th*a*t our brother blande ys lyke to have hys howsse downe
  dancyd.
no, no, ye selye sorye shaddes[3] : we ar not of those sort,
a medyo-cryte we vse in all owr acte & sport. 72
well were yt wyth ye all, I saye, yf ye culld do the lyke ;
but youth herto cannot attayne : theyre wytts be far to syeke.
wherfore we wyll beseche the lorde to sende ye of hys grase,
that ye maye sett you*r* wytts & mynde a whyle to Run]
  owr Pace ; 76
That you by vs in Tyme be brought t*o* so*me* confyrmytye,
& by beholdynge of our steppes may lerne hvmanytye.
And thus we ende, & here conclude : we send ye comendations,
And hope to here that by thys byll ye wyll amend your
  fashyons ; 80
so shall we all ryght Joyfull be : & ye receyve to grase,
& yeld agayne the thyng ye lost, omytting you*r* trespace.
  By yours somtymes, when ye were cowntyd mete,
   the Crewe & brotherhede of candellwycke strete. 84

---

[1] Perhaps a relation of Thomas Randall, merchant, to whom, on October 9th, 1559, " was master Row Alderman(s) dowthur mared " (Machyn's Diary, p. 215).
[2] Perhaps son to Master Hawes, clothworker, who was made sheriff on August 1st, 1558, with Richard Champion (Machyn, p. 170). [3] Mean fellows.

POEMS RELATING TO CAMPION,

OF the following poems the earliest (I. pp. 164, 165) is that entitled "A libel touching Campion," in three parts, of four, three, and two verses respectively, in different measures. This, of course, was not so called by the author, but by the transcriber who sent a copy of it for the information of the Council, and thereby caused its preservation among the State Papers. It refers to Campion's disputations and rackings in the Tower, but not to his death; its date is therefore in September or October, 1581. I cannot hazard a guess as to the author.

The next batch (II. pp. 166-179) is the collection of "certayne verses made by sundrie persons," annexed to an 8vo. book, the title of which will be found prefixed to the poems. They are four in number; two on Campion's death; one, a dialogue between a Catholic and Consolation, and the fourth, the complaint of a Catholic. They are all, especially the two first, very good and smooth for their day, and were well received. They were the productions of persons of some mark—"haud ignobilium poetarum acute commenta," says Bombinus, in his life of Campion. In stanza sixteen of the first poem we read:

> "You bloody jury, Lea and the eleven,
> Take heed your verdict, which was given in haste,
> Do not exclude you from the joys of heaven."

Among the Puckering papers in the British Museum is a letter from this Lee to the Lord Keeper, dated in 1595. He was then for the second time "a prisoner restrained from bodily travel," and complained of the conduct of the Catholics to him. "I have been persecuted by them for my verdict, given in haste, as Vallenger rhymed, against Campion and his traiterous companions." This seems to ascertain the authorship of the first poem; and it is confirmed by the notice in Bridgewater's *Concertatio* (fol. 225 and 408), which informs us how Vallenger had his ears nailed to the pillory and cut off, for verses he wrote on Campion's death.[1] Vallenger was a known ballad-writer of the

---

[1] The records of Vallenger's trial in the Star Chamber are lost (the sentences in criminal cases were all burnt at Clerkenwell in the Gordon riots in the last century), otherwise we should find there one of the poems attributed to Walpole, if More (*Hist. Prov. Ang.* lib. v. No. 33) is correct in saying that the law was first put in action against him, before he was known to be a Catholic, for a poem he had written on Campion's happy death.

day, and the smoothness of these verses is surprising, after Gabriel Harvey's information that Spenser ironically called him Noble Master Vallenger, on account of his supreme carelessness of English quantity and accent.   (Three proper and familiar letters between Harvey and Spenser, 1581.)

With regard to the authorship of the other three poems, one was written by Henry Walpole, the young heir of the great family in Norfolk, who was converted to Catholicism on the occasion of Campion's execution, became a Jesuit, and returned to England to be captured and hanged in 1595.[1] Thomas Pounde is, I think, the author of the short sketch of Munday, which will be quoted below, and as he also was a versifier, may have written one of the poems to boot.[2] Possible writers of the others are Francis Tregean, Robert Parsons, and even Philip Earl of Arundel; but this is a mere guess, founded on the fact that they did all write religious verses. These poems were published in 1581—that is some time between Dec. 1, 1581, and March 25, 1582.

The next batch of poems (III. pp. 180–190) consists of four paraphrases or glosses upon the four previous ones; these are by Anthony Munday. This kind of serious travestie was common in Queen Elizabeth's age; Father Southwell's *Sinners Complaint*, founded on Dyer's *Fancy*, is well known, as is also Fulke Greville's version of the same poem. Munday had cause for being angry with the publication which he glozed upon. Apart from his having been the chief witness against Campion and his companions, and a spectator of their execution, he had published an account of the matter, the substance of which may be found in Holinshed's Chronicles. It is in Hallam's judgment characterized by "a savageness and bigotry which I am sure no scribe of the Inquisition could have surpassed." He had also been attacked by Pounde in a short

---

[1] John Gerard, in his autobiography (Morris's Translation, p. xci), says of Walpole, "He used to be at Court before the death of Father Campion, in whose honour he also wrote some beautiful verses in the English tongue, declaring that he and many others had received the warmth of life from that blessed martyr's blood, and had been animated by it to follow the more perfect counsels of Christ." This description does not apply to any of the following poems with any accuracy. Possibly the first may be his, and only attributed to Vallenger by Lee in ignorance.

[2] Pounde was probably the author of a long poem, in two parts, in the Record Office, Dom. Eliz. 1582, No. 58. The first part is a criticism on Fox's Martyrology; the second, a very carefully-executed summary of the troubles of Catholics under the penal laws. A long extract was printed in the *Rambler* for Sept. 1859, p. 373. The whole poem deserves printing.

biographical sketch prefixed to the four poems. "Kogging Munday," he says, "first was a stage player (no doubt a calling of some credit), after an aprentise, which tyme he wel serued with deçeauing of his master; then wandring towardes Italy, by his owne report became a coosener in his iourney. Comming to Rome, in his short abode there, was charitably relieued, but neuer admitted in the seminary, as he pleseth to lye in the title of his booke; and being wery of well-doing, returned home to his first vomite againe. I omite to declare howe this scholler now come out of Italy did play extempore; those gentlemen and others whiche were present can best giue witnes of his dexterity, who being wery of his folly, hissed him from his stage. Then, being therby discouraged, he set forth a balet against playes; but yet (O constant youth) he now beginnes againe to ruffle vpon the stage. I omit among other places his behauiour in Barbican, with his good mistres and mother, from whence our superintendent[1] might fetch him to his court, were it not for loue (I woulde save slaunder) to their gospel."

The steps which Munday took to refute some of these imputations may be seen in the biographical sketch prefixed to his *John a' Kent and John a' Cumber,* published by the (old) Shakespeare Society. To the notices of him there, I may add, that he continued for some years in the profitable calling of informing against Catholics; he attached himself to Topcliffe, the priest-catcher, by whom he was employed to guard and to take bonds of recusants, and who wrote about him to Puckering (Sept. 20, 1592, Harleian MS. 6998, p. 31) as "a man that wants no wytt." How he used his wit in his vocation is told us by PHS (Phellippes?), one of Walsingham's agents, in a letter to the Secretary of State (Record Office, Domestic Papers, 1590, No. 138 A). "He hath been in divers places where I have passed; whose dealing hath been very rigorous, and yet done very small good, but rather much hurt; for in one place, under pretence to seek for Agnus Deis and hallowed grains, he carried from a widow £40, the which he took out of a chest. A few of these matches will either raise a rebellion or cause your officers to be murdered." He lived to a great age, was pageant poet to the City, and appears also to have had some office in the law courts. I find Anthony Munday, gent., employed in the transmission of the documents relating to the foundation of Falmouth to the Corporation of Penrhyn in the reign of James I. (Gilbert, Historical Survey of Cornwall, 4to., 1820, vol. ii. p. 793.) Munday's paraphrases are dated 1581.

---

[1] *i.e.* the Bishop of London.

Vallenger's poem, "Why do I use my paper, ink, and pen?" (p. 166) and the next, "What iron heart that would not melt in grief?" (p. 173) are found in MS. with variations, the chief of which are given in the notes, at the end of a copy of the 1581 edition of Watson's ʽΕκατομπαθια, which was formerly in the possession of Hearne the Antiquary, and came into the Bodleian with the Rawlinson MSS. The transcriber has headed the former poem 𝔄 𝔤𝔬𝔬𝔡 𝔳𝔢𝔯𝔰𝔢, 𝔲𝔭𝔬𝔫 𝔞 𝔟𝔞𝔡𝔡 𝔪𝔞𝔱𝔱𝔢𝔯, and after the 180th line, and the word "finis," has added the following gloss:

☞ What is it yᵗ those flattered of the Popes will shame to speake, to winne and continue their favour?

To the latter poem he has prefixed the title 𝔄𝔫 𝔬𝔱𝔥𝔢𝔯, 𝔬𝔣 𝔱𝔥𝔢 𝔰𝔞𝔪𝔢 𝔢𝔯𝔯𝔬𝔲𝔯, and after the 54th line, and word *Finis*, has added the gloss:

Is he you thus commend cald Campion?
Is this your Sainct, whose prayers you so singe?
Then Campion, the Popes thiefe Champion,
At Tiburne trust[1]: To heauven sent in a stringe.
   For whose sweet soule I ringe this lowde alarum:
   His mendacia sunt opes et aurum.   qᵈ *Iω:λ.*   60

The signs at the end, qᵈ *Iω:λ*, mean "quoth John Lilliat." John Lily, the author of Euphues, has a commendatory piece prefixed to Watson's book, "John Lily to the Author his friend," which is signed "Farewell, John Lilliat." The poems and songs of this MS. may appear in a future publication, but the copy we have of them shows that John Lilliat cannot have been the same man as the famous author of Euphues.

The fourth specimen of these Campion ballads (IV. page 191) consists of an original stanza, followed by a few stanzas inaccurately quoted from Vallenger's poem. They seem to have been put together by a person who signs himself in cypher or anagram, as a ballad hortatory to persuade some one to suffer death for his religion, after the example of Campion. The indorsement seems to show that the person addressed was George Jarves, Priest, hanged at London, April 11, 1608.

Among the many publications respecting Campion, either extant or noticed in the Stationers' Registers (see *Collier's Extracts,*

---

[1] trust = trussed.

pp. 136, 149, 162, 176), the following is the only title which seems to refer to a ballad:

"Mr. Campion, the seditious Jesuit, is welcome to London." Licensed to Richard Jones, July 24, 1581.

Other ballads against the Pope were licensed July 19 and 20, but no mention of Campion is made in their titles.

EDMUND CAMPION, son of a citizen and bookseller of London, was born there Jan. 25, 1540, educated at Christ's Hospital in Newgate Street, selected to recite a congratulatory harangue to Queen Mary when she passed St. Paul's on her solemn entry into London Aug. 3, 1553, sent to Oxford by the Grocers' Company, selected by Sir Thomas White in 1557 to be Fellow of his new foundation of St. John's College. He made the English oration at the funeral of Amy Robsart in 1560; in Feb. 1564, was Orator in the schools, and in the same year preached the funeral sermon for Sir Thomas White, and took his M.A. degree. Displayed his eloquence before Queen Elizabeth and Lord Robert Dudley on their visit to Oxford 1566, after which Dudley, then created Earl of Leicester, sent for him, and became his good patron, giving him a private opportunity of exhibiting his talents before the Queen at Woodstock. Campion at this time was the most hopeful scholar at Oxford. In 1568 he was Proctor. He had been for some little time reading divinity, which led him to doubt about the Anglican Church; but he fell into the hands of Cheney, the anti-Calvinistic Bishop of Gloucester, who calmed his scruples, and ordained him deacon. But his scruples revived, and he left Oxford in August, 1570. He went to Ireland, where he became an adviser of Sir Henry Sidney for his scheme of a Dublin University, a friend of Sir James Stanihurst, Speaker of the Irish House of Commons, whose son Richard had been his pupil at Oxford; and of Sir Christopher and Lady Barnwell, of Turvey. Here he definitively left the Protestant communion, and wrote his "History of Ireland," which Richard Stanihurst afterwards made into the groundwork of the Irish part of Holinshed's Chronicles. His nonconformity was observed in Ireland, pursuivants were sent after him, and he had to escape to England. Returning to London, he was present at the tragedy of Dr. Storey in June, 1571, and then fled across the Channel to Douai, where, in the English College, he received minor orders. After spending a year there, he went to Rome, and for some time was dependent on Cardinal Gesualdi; but in June, 1573, he joined

the Society of Jesus, and was sent to undergo his noviciate first
in Prague, then at Brünn, in Moravia. Then he returned as
a professor to the College at Prague, and became famous, not
only for his orations, but for his Latin tragedies, which were
played with the highest applause before the Emperor Maximilian
and other distinguished spectators. Here also he renewed an
old acquaintance with Sir Philip Sidney, who visited Prague in
1576. In 1579, at the urgent request of Dr. Allen, the founder
of the English College at Douai, the Jesuits determined to send
some of their number to England, and fixed upon Parsons and
Campion as the pioneers of the mission. Campion first returned
to Rome, and an account is extant of his journey homewards,
and of a controversy he had with Beza in his passage through
Geneva. Campion landed at Dover June 24, 1580. He pro-
ceeded to London, and immediately began to preach. The
enthusiasm of the young converts was excited, and the Council
soon found that something more than ordinary was occurring.
The young Catholic gentlemen were swept up and confined in
sundry prisons, or committed for safe custody to different clergymen, aldermen, or other responsible persons. Campion, seeing
that he might any day be shut up in forced silence in prison,
had written a declaration of his motives and objects in coming
to London. This he committed to the custody of Thomas
Pounde, an enthusiastic young Catholic of Hampshire, and a
relation of the Earl of Southampton, who had played the part
of Mercury in a masque at Kenilworth, during the famous
revels there in 1575, and who still dabbled in poetry and other
literature. Pounde was so excited by this able document, that,
in spite of his pledges, he distributed copies in MSS. from his
prison. Some of the first of these were sent to his own neighbourhood, and the earliest copies which reached the Council were
captured in Hampshire. The document had however become too
public to be suppressed, and the press teemed with replies to
Campion's "great brag and challenge"—for in the paper he had
challenged to single combat all the divines of England on public
controversial hustings. The effect was only a redoubled vigilance
on the part of those who had to stop all controversy on the
Catholic side, and Campion had to transfer his presence from
London to the Provinces. In Yorkshire and Lancashire he spent
his time in preaching, and in composing a little book, his "Decem
Rationes," ten reasons which seemed to him so incontrovertible,
that on the strength of them he had dared with confidence to
make the challenge. The little book was secretly printed at a
flying press set up for the occasion in Stonor Park, near Henley,
and distributed by hundreds at the commencement in Oxford,

June 27, 1581. Among the refined critics of the day this book made a great sensation. It was cried up as the quintessence of Latin scholarship; and the divines of Oxford and Cambridge had to rebuke solemnly the frivolity of the young men who were ready to sacrifice their religion to beauty of phrase; just as in 1589 they had to lament over their enjoyment of the libellous jokes of Martin Marprelate.

A fortnight after this triumph, Campion was taken at the house of Mr. Yate, of Lydford, Berks, by means of one. George Eliot, who had lived as a Catholic in the service of Sir William Petre, and who for his exploit was rewarded by the Catholics with the name of Judas Eliot, and by the Queen with the red coat of a yeoman of the guard. Campion, with two other priests found with him, was taken to London, and made to ride through the City to the Tower, his elbows tied behind him, his hands in front, and his heels under his horse's belly, with a paper in his hand, like a perjurer, inscribed CAMPION THE SEDITIOUS JESUIT. This was on Saturday, July 22, 1581. A week after, the Council ordered Norton and others to examine him, and if necessary to deal with him by the rack. The chief point to be discovered was the names of the gentlemen at whose houses he had been entertained. By the beginning of August information had been obtained, the Council said from him, but more probably from some of the others captured with him, of a great many of the houses where he had stayed. The proprietors of all were imprisoned, and many of them subsequently very heavily fined by the Star Chamber. After he had been twice racked, he was allowed to have some discussion in the Tower—not in public, but before a select audience. Of course each side claimed the victory for its own champion; and the printed account of the controversy issued by Deans Nowel and Day differs very much from the MS. accounts circulated by Campion's friends. Campion, however, made one illustrious convert, Philip Earl of Arundel. After three of these conferences, the Council determined to treat the matter in another way, and to make an example of the priests in prison.

At this time the Duke of Anjou was in England as Elizabeth's accepted suitor. The prospect of her marriage to a Catholic husband filled half England with dismay. The politicians thought it would be a good stroke to hang a batch of priests upon the occasion, for this would prove that the marriage, if it was to come off, would make no difference in the religious policy, or possibly, if Anjou was a man of spirit, might drive him off in disgust. Hence, after several futile attempts to get up a case, it was determined to arraign eleven priests and two laymen for a con-

spiracy against the Queen's life, entered into at Rome and Rheims.
The proof of the plot depended on the testimony of Sled, Munday,
and Caddy, three young men who had pretended to be Catholics,
or perhaps were so, and had thus gained admission to the foreign
Colleges. But their testimony amounted to very little. "The
prosecution," says Hallam, "was as unfairly conducted, and
supported by as slender evidence, as any, perhaps, that can be
found in our books." The trial took place on the 20th of
November, 1581. Chief Justice Wray presided. One Lee was
foreman of the jury. The prisoners were all found guilty. On
the 1st of December Campion, Sherwin, and Briant were dragged
on hurdles from the Tower to Tyburn, and there hanged, drawn,
and quartered. In the following poems reference will be found
to the circumstances of the day—how it began in clouds and
rain, and cleared up just as Campion was hanged; and how there
was a most remarkable flood tide on the Thames.

For the life and times of Campion, see *Edmund Campion, a Biography, by
Richard Simpson.* Williams and Norgate, 1867. The above particulars are
extracted from this book.

I.

[From *Domestic State Papers, Elizabeth*, Vol. 150, No. 72 (Public Record Office).]

A Libell touching Campion.

Campian is a Champion,
him once to ouercumme,
The rest be well drest,
the sooner to mumme.   4

he lokes for his liffe,
they saye to dispute;
and doubtes not our doctrine,
he bragges to confute.   8

yf in steede of good argument
we deale by yᵉ racke;
the papistes maye thinke
that learninge we lacke.   12

come forthe, my fine darling*es*,
and make him a dolt;
you haue him full fast,
& y^t in stronge holte.   16

A Jesuite, a Jebusite, wherefore I you praye,
because he dothe teache you ye onely right waye;
he proferethe ye same by lear*n*inge to proue,
and shall we from lear*n*inge to racke him remoue.   20

his reasones were redie, his growndes were most sure,
the enemye cannot his force longe endure:
Campyon in campinge in spyrituall feild;
in godes cause his liffe is reddy to yeld.   24

Our preacher*es* haue preached in pastime & pleasure,
and nowe they be hated farre passi*n*ge all measure;
There wiues and there wealthe haue made them so mute,
They can not nor dare not *with* Campyan dispute.   28

let reason rule & racki*n*ge sease,
or els for eaer hold *your* peace;
you can not *with*stand god*es* powre & his grace,
no, not *with* ye tower nor ye rackinge place.   32

A golden verse, w*hi*ch truly saithe,
let reson goe, hold fast thy faithe:
A mayde to be a mother & god a man,
let reason go, man, and beleue thowe ye mother,
set faithe aboue & lett reason goe vnder.   37

II.

[From "A true reporte of the death and martyrdome of M. Campion, Jesuite and preiste, and M. Sherwin and M. Bryan, preistes, at Tiborne the first of December 1581. Observid and written by a Catholike preist, which was present therat. Wherunto is annexid certayne verses made by sundric persons." (British Museum.) In the black letter original, the proper names in the poems are printed in Roman type: this has not been made italic here.]

𝔙pon the Death of 𝔐. Edmund Campion, one of the Societie of the holy name of Jesus.

1.

Why do I vse my paper, inke, and penne ?
and call my wits to counsel what to say ?
such memories were made for mortall men,.
I speak of Saints whose names can not decay :
an Angels trumpe were fitter for to sound
their glorious death, if such in earth wer found.   6

2.

Pardon my want, I offer nought but will ;
their register remaineth safe aboue.
Campion exceedes the compasse of my skill,
yet let me vse the measure of my loue,
and giue me leaue, in lowe and homeli verse,
his hye attempts in England to rehearse.   12

3.

He came by vow : the cause to conquer sinne ;
his armour prayer, the word his targe & shield ;
. his comfort heauen, his spoyle our soules to win,
the diuel his foe, the wicked world the field :
his triumph ioy, his wage eternall blis,
his Captaine Christ, which euer blessed is.   18

Variations in the Oxford MS.: Line 3. earthly *for* mortall.   11. humble *for* homeli.   16. His badge the Crosse *for* the diuel his foe.   17. The Diuell his foe *for* his triumph ioy.

4.

From ease to paine, from honour to disgrace,
from loue to hate, to daunger being wel;
from safe abode, to feares in euery place,
contemning death, to saue our soules from hel:
our new Apostle, comming to restore
the faith which Austine planted here before.   24

5.

His natures flowres were mixt with herbes of grace;
his mild behauiour tempered wel with skil;
a lowly minde possest a learned place;
a sugred speach, a rare and vertuous wil;
a saintlike man was set on earth below,
the seede of truth in erring hartes to sow.   30

6.

With tung & pen the truth he taught & wrote,
by force wherof they came to Christ apace;
but when it pleased God, it was his lote
he should be thrald, he lent him so much grace,
his patience then did worke as much or more,
as had his heauenly speeches done before.   36

7.

His fare was hard, yet mild & sweet his cheere;
his prison close, yet free and lose his minde;
his torture great, yet smal or none his feare;
his offers large, but nothing could him blinde.
O constant man, O mind, O vertue strange,
whom want, nor wo, nor feare, nor hope coulde change!   42

8.

From rack in Tower they broght him to dispute,
bookeles,* alone, to answere al that came:
yet Christ gaue grace, he did them all confute
so sweetly there, in glory of his name,
that euen the aduers part are forst to say,
that Campions cause did beare the bell away.   48

Variations in the Oxford MS.: Line 26. by *for* with.   30. lowe *for* sow.
42. When *for* whom.

* In his disputations in the Tower, Campion was allowed only to have his Bible; not even a copy of his *Decem Rationes.*

9.

This foyle enragde the minds of some so farre,
they thought it best to take his life away,
because they saw he would their matter marre,
and leaue them shortly nought at al to say :
traytor he was, with many a seely slight,
yet pact a Jury that cried guylti straight.   54

10.

Religion, there was treason to the queene ;
preaching of penance, warre against the lande ;
prests were such dangerous men as haue not bin ;
prayers & beads were fight and force of hande ;
cases of conscience, bane vnto the state ;
so blind is error, so false a witnes hate !   60

11.

And yet behold, these lambes be drawen to dye ;
treason proclaymed, the queene is put in feare ;
out vpon satan ! fye ! malice, fye !
speakst thou to them that did the guildles heare ?
can humble soules, departing now to Christ,
protest vntrue ? Avaunt, foule fend, thou lyst !   66

12.

My soueraigne Liege, behold your subiects end—
your secret foes do misenforme your grace :—
who in your cause their holy liues would spend
as traytors dye, a rare and monstrous case !
the bloudy wolfe condemnes the harmeles shepe
before the dog, ye whiles the shepherds* slepe.   72

13.

England, looke vp, thy soyle is staind with blood,
thow hast made martirs many of thine owne ;
if thou hast grace, their deaths will do thee good,
the seede wil take, which in such blood is sowne ;
and Campions lerning, fertile so before,
thus watered too, must nedes of force be more.   78

Variations in the Oxford MS.: Line 49. but this *for* This foyle.   54. They
part *for* yet pact.   57. byn scene *for* bin.   59. were bane *for* bane.   61.
are *for* be.   65. vnto *for* now to.   70. straunge *for* rare.

  * *Orig.* sherherds.

14.

Repent thee, *Eliot*,* of thy Judas kisse,
I wish thy penance, not thy desperate ende;
let *Norton* † thinke, which now in prison is,
to whom was said, he was not Cæsars friend;
and let the Judge consider well in feare,
that Pilate washt his hands, and was not cleare.   84

15.

The witnesse false, *Sledd*,‡ *Munday*, and the rest,
which had your slanders noted in your booke,
confesse your fault beforehand; it were best,
lest God do find it written when he doth looke
in dreadfull doome vpon the soules of men:
it wil be late (alas!) to mend it then.   90

16.

You bloody iury *Lea*,‖ and all the leauen,
take heede your verdit, which was giuen in hast,
do not exclude you from the ioyes of heauen,
and cause you rue it when the time is past:
and euery one whose malice causd him say
Crucifige, let him dread the terror of that day!   96

Variations in the Oxford MS.: Line 86. with all *for* which had. **88.** *omit* doth. **91.** rest *for* leauen. **92.** *omit* which was. **93.** place of blest *for* ioyes of heauen.

* George Eliot, the man who found and betrayed Campion by pretending to be a good Catholic.

† Norton, a commissioner for putting Campion to the torture. For an account of him see Wood, *Athenæ Oxonienses;* also some notices in Collier's *Dodsley's Old Plays*, i. p. 110. There is much about him in Bridgewater's *Concertatio*, fol. 64, 73, 77, 127-129, 223, 229. His imprisonment here referred to was not for treason, as Allen suggests (*Concertatio*, fol. 221 *verso*), but for taking part in the contraband printing of a Puritan book.

‡ Sledd had entered the Roman Seminary as a Catholic, but, as he professed, with the intention of betraying his associates there. *Concertatio*, fol. 62, 95, 121. (For Munday, see the Introduction, pp. 158, 159.)

‖ Lee was the foreman of the jury.

17.

Fonde *Elderton*,* call in thy foolish rime,
thy scurile balates are to bad to sell ;
let good men rest, and mende thy self in time,
confesse in prose thou hast not meetred well ;
or, if thy folly can not choose but fayne,
write alehouse toys, blaspheme not in thy vain.　　102

18.

Remember, you that would oppresse the cause,
the Church is Christes, his honor can not dye,
though hel her selfe reuest † her gresly iawes,
and ioyne in league with schisme and heresie ;
though craft deuise, and cruell rage oppresse,
yet skil wil write, and martirdome confesse.　　108

19.

You thought perhaps, when lerned Ca*m*pion dyes,
his pen must cease, his sugred tongue be still ;
but you forgot how lowde his death it cryes,
how farre beyond the sound of tongue and quil ;
you did not know how rare and great a good
it was to write his precious giftes in blood.　　114

20.

Liuing, he spake to them that present were,
his writings tooke their censure of the viewe ;
now fame reports his lerning farre and nere,
and now his death confirmes his doctrine true.
his vertues now are written in the skyes,
and often read with holy inward eyes.　　120

Variations in the Oxford MS.. Line 105, revert her greedie *for* revest her
gresly.　　114. death *for* giftes.　　115. lightninge *for* liuing.

* Elderton, one of the most industrious of the ballad-writers of the day. He
is often referred to by Nash, Deloney, and others. Many of his productions have
survived, and some have been reprinted by Mr. Collier.

† "reuest" should probably be revert.

21.

All Europe wonders at so rare a man ;
England is fild with rumor of his ende ;
London must needs, for it was present than,
when constantly three saints their liues did spend,
the streets, the stones, the steps you hald them by,
proclaime the cause for which these martirs dy.   126

22.

The Tower saith, the truth he did defend ;
the barre beares witnes of his guiltles minde ;
Tiborne doth tell he made a pacient ende ;
on euery gate* his martirdome we finde.
in vaine you wroght y^t would obscure his name,
for heauen and earth will still record the same.   132

23.

Your sentence wrong pronounced of him here,
exemptes him from the iudgments for to come ;
O happy he that is not iudged there !
God graunt me too to haue an earthly dome !
your witnes false, and lewdly taken in,
doth cause he is not now accusd of sin.   138

24.

His prison now the citie of the king ;
his racke and torture, ioyes and heuenly blisse ;
for mens reproch, with angels he doth sing
a sacred song, which euerlasting is :
for shame but short, and losse of small renowne,
he purchast hath an euer during crowne.   144

25.

His quarterd lims shall ioyne with ioy agayne,
and rise a body brighter then the sunne :
your blinded malice torturde him in vayne,
For euery wrinch some glory hath him wonne,
and euery drop of blood which he did spend,
hath reapt a ioy which neuer shal haue end.   150

Variations in the Oxford MS.: Line 129. godly *for* pacient.   141. reports *for* reproch.   144. sempiternall *for* euer during.   148. wring *for* wrinch.

* The quarters of persons executed for treason were usually nailed up on the town gates, where their heads were also placed.

26.

Can dreary death the*n* daunt our faith or paine ?
ist' lingring life we feare to loose, or ease ?
no, no, such death procureth life againe,
'tis only God we tremble to displease,
who kils but once, and euer stil we dye,
whose hote reuenge tormentes eternallye.   156

27.

We can not feare a mortal torment, wee ;
this Martirs blood hath moystned all our harts,
whose partid quartirs when we chaunce to see,
we lerne to play the constant christians parts ;
his head doth speake, & heauenly precepts giue,
how we y^t looke, should frame ourselues to liue.   162

28.

His youth enstructs vs how to spend our daies ;
his flying bids vs how to banish sinne ;
his straight profession shews the narrow waies
which they must walk that looke to enter in ;
his home returne by danger and distresse,
emboldens vs our conscience to professe.   168

29.

His hardle drawes vs with him to the crosse ;
his speeches there prouoke vs for to dye ;
his death doth say this life is but a losse ;
his martird blood from heauen to vs doth crye ;
his first and last and all conspire in this,
to shew the way that leadeth vnto blisse.   174

30.

Blessed be God, which lent him so much grace,
thanked be Christ, which blest his martir so ;
happy is he which sees his masters face,
Cursed are they that thought to worke him wo ;
bounden be we to geue eternall prayse
to Jesus name which such a man did rayse.   180

Amen.

Variations in the Oxford MS.. Line 164. so *for* how.   166. to *for* that.
178. which *for* that.

𝔄n otḥer, upon tḥe same.

1.

What yron hart that wold not melt in greefe?
what steele or stone could kepe him dry from teares?
to see a Campion haled like a theefe,
to end his life, with both his glorious feares,*
in whose three deathes vnto the standers by,
euen al the world almost might seeme to dye.　　6

2.

England must lose a soueraigne salue for sinne,
a sweet receit for suttle heresie:
India a saint her seely soules to winne,
Turky a bane for her idolatrie;
the Church a souldier against Babylon,
to batter hell and her confusion.　　12

3.

The skowling skies did storme & puff apace,
they could not bear ye wrongs y^t malice wroght;
the sunne drew in his shining purple face,
the moistned clouds shed brinish tears for thoght;
the riuer Thames awhile astonied stoode
To count the drops of Campions sacred blood.　　18

4.

Nature with tears bewaild her heauy losse;
honesty feard her selfe should shortly dye;
religion saw her Champion on the crosse;
Angels and saints desired leaue to cry;
euen herisie, the eldest child of hell,
began to blush, and thought she did not well.　　24

5.

And yet, behold! when Campion made his end,
his humble hart was so bedewde with grace,
that no reproch could once his mind offend;
mildnes possest his sweet and cherefull face;
a pacient spectacle was presented then,
in sight of God, of angels, saints, and men.　　30

Variations in the Oxford MS.: Line 4. peers *for* feares.　　6. did *for* might.
11. Champion *for* souldier.

* "feares" = feres, or comrades, viz. Sherwin and Bryaut.

III.　　　　　　　　　　　　　　　　　　　　　　O

6.

The heuens did cleare, y^e sun like gold did shine,
the cloudes were dry, the fearful riuer ranne :
nature and vertue wypt their watred eyen,
religion ioyed to see so mild a man ;
men, angels, saints, and al that saw him dye,
forgot their grief, his ioyes appeard so nye.   36

7.

They saw his pacience did expect a crowne ;
his scornful cart, a glorious heauenly place ;
his lowly mind, a happy high renowne ;
his humble cheare, a shining angels face ;
his feare, his griefe, his death, & agonie,
a ioy, a peace, a life in maiestie.   42

8.

From thence he prayes and sings in melodie
for our recure, and calleth vs to him ;
he stands before the throne with harmonie,
and is a glorious suter for our sinne :
with wings of loue he jumped vp so hye,
to helpe the cause for which he sought to dye.   48

9.

Reioyce, be glad, triumph, sing himmes of ioye,
Campion, Sherwine, Brian live in blis :
they sue, they seeke the ease of our annoy ;
they pray, they speake, and al effectuall is ;
not like to men on earth as heretofore,
But like to saints in heauen, and that is more.   54

Finis.

A Dialogue betwene a Catholike and Consolation.

CATHOLIKE FIRST SPEAKETH.

Is righteous Lot from sinful Sodome gone ?
is olde Elias left alone agayne ?
and hath the earth no iust man, no not one,
the cause of Christ and Christians to sustaine ?
if holy life with true religion fayle,
then farewell faith, for falsehood will preuayle.   6

CONSOLATION.

No, Lot, thou hast some felowes in this land,
Elias, there are left seuen thousand yet ;
reioyce, thou earth, thou hast a warlike bande
for our good Lord in martial order set,
by life and death this quarel to beginne,
to vanquish falsehood, satan, hell, and sinne.   12

Although a worthy Champion of your trayne
were slayne of late, and yet not vanquished,
into his place another stept againe ;
whom Christs spouse our common nurse hath bred ;
lament not then, for there are in his rome
as good as he, expecting martirdome.   18

CATHOLIKE.

Such men, no doubt, are very hard to finde,
for dainty things are seldome sifted out ;
the Phenix hath no partner of her kinde ;
a man perhaps may seeke the world about,
ere he may find one Campion agayne ;
wherfore his losse makes me the more complaine.   24

Where shal you find so many giftes in one,
a wit so sharpe, ioynd with such memory,
a great diuine, hating promotion,
a lusty man professing chastitie,
a worthy roope* spronge vp of basest kinde,
a lerned man to beare a lowly minde.   30

---

* "roope," probably root.

Solon for pith, for wisedome Salomon,
Peter for style, and Paule for eloquence,
Dauid for trueth, for beautie Absolon,
for personage Saule, a Jobe for patience :
all that for which the fame of these began,
(a thing most strange) were ioynde in this one man.   36

Not rack nor rope cold daunt his dredles mind,
no hope nor hap could moue him where he stood,
he wrote the truth as in his bookes we finde,
which to confirme he sealed with his blood,
which makes me dout there are no mo such men,
send workmen, Lord, into thy vineyarde then !   42

CONSOLATION.

Dispaire thou not, thou seely mournful wight,
for there are mo haue tooke this match in hand ;
we needs must win, our lord himself doth fight,
the Cananites shal be expulsd the land,
for Edmund liues and helpeth godly men
by prayers, more then erst with tongue or pen.   48

His quarters hong on euery gate do showe,
his doctrine sound throgh countries far and neare,
his head set vp so high doth call for moe
to fight the fight which he endured here,
the faith thus planted thus restored must be,
take vp thy crosse, saith Christ, and folow me.   54

As well as preists the lay men too shall frame
their skillesse heads to take so good a vowe,
God can of stones rayse seede to Abraham ;
doubt not, therfore, for there will be enowe.

CATHOLIKE.

Fiat voluntas Dei, then say I,
we owe a death, and once we needes must dye.   60

Finis.

The complaynt of a Catholike for the Death of M. Edmund Campion.

O God, from sacred throne beholde
    our secret sorrowes here,
Regard with grace our helplesse griefe,
    amend our mournfull cheere.   4
The bodies of thy Saintes abrode
    are set for foules to feede,
And brutishe birds deuour the flesh
    of faithfull folke in deede.   8
Alas ! I rue to thinke vpon
    the sentence truely scande,
No prophet any honor hath
    within his natiue lande.   12
Thy dolefull death, O Campion, is
    bewayld in euery coste,
But we liue here & litle knowe
    what creatures we haue loste.   16
Bohemia land laments the same,
    Rodulphus court is sad,
With deepe regarde they now recorde
    what vertues Campion had.   20
Germania mourns, al Spayne doth muse,
    and so doth Italy,
And Fraunce our friend hath put in print
    his passing tragedie.   24
They that wuld make these men to seeme
    to be hir highnes foes,
O Lorde, it is a worlde to see
    the fayned fraude of those,   28
For when they had in dastard wise
    deuised to dispute,
And could not finde in al their craft
    the cause for to confute,   32
And that their winnings was so well*
    they needed not to boste,
And that in consciens they did know
    new found is lightly loste,   36

---

* *Query* small.

They suttly seeke a further fetche
  contrary to all reason,
To say he is not Cæsars frende,
  accusing him of treasone.   40
But shal we mutche lament the same,
  or shall we more reioyce,
Such was the case with Christ our lord,
  sutche was the Jewish voyce.   44
So wer their wrathful words pronounst,
  so was their sentence wrong,
For Christ did giue to Cæsar that
  which did to him belong;   48
So Christ his true disciples here
  no treason do pretend,
But they by Christ and Christ his lore
  their fayth till death defende.   52
Though error haue deuised now
  a visard so vnfit
To cloke her craft to change the case,
  to blear ech simple wit,   56
Because she taught vs long before
  that none for poynts of fayth,
According vnto Christes lore
  ought to be done to death.   60
Her wilines wer soone bewrayed,
  had they but once recanted,
No doubt therof they had not then
  not life nor liuing wanted.   64
Thus who so ways her works & words,
  with fraude shal find them fraught,
And how they now performe the same
  that heretofore they taught.   68
God knowes it is not force nor might,
  not warre nor warlike band,
Not shield & spear, not dint of sword,
  that must conuert the land: 72
It is the blood by martirs shed,
  it is that noble traine,
That fight with word & not with sword,
  and Christ their capitaine.   76
For sooner shall you want the handes
  to shed sutch guiltles blood,

Then wise and vertuous still to come
   to do theyr country good.   80
God saue Elizabeth our queene,
   God send her happie raigne,
And after earthly honors here,
   the heauenly ioyes to gayne.   84
And all sutch men as heretofore
   haue misinformd her Grace,
God graunt they may amend the same
   while here they haue the space.   88

Finis.

III.

[From "A breefe Aunswer made vnto two seditious Pamphlets, the one printed in French and the other in English, contayning a defence of Edmund Campion and his complices, their moste horrible and vnnaturall Treasons against her Maiestie and the Realme. By A. M." London, 1582. (Lambeth Library).]

Verses in the Libell, made in prayse of the Death of Maister Campion, one of the societie of the holie name of Jesus; heere chaunged to the reproofe of him and the other Traitours.

WHY doo I vse my paper, inke, and pen,
   and call my wits in councell what to say?
Such memories were made for woorthy men,
   And not for such as seeke their Realms decay.
     An Angels trumpe exalts ye Subiects trueth,
     When shame rings foorth ye Traitors fearful rueth.   6

Pardon my want, I offer naught but will,
   To note downe those, at whome the Skies do skowle:
Campion his treasons do exceed my skil,
   The cause, his comming, & the deede too fowle.
     Yet giue me leaue in base and homely verse,
     His lewd attempts in England to rehearse.   12

He came by vowe, the cause, his Princesse foyle,
   His armour, Treason, to his Countryes woe:
His comfort, blood, slaughter & greeuous spoyle,
   The Deuill his Author had incenst him so.
     His triumphe, Englands ruine and decay:
     The Pope his Captaine, thirsting for it aye.   18

From ease to paine, from honour to disgrace,
   From looue to hate, to daunger beeing well:
Thus dyd he fall, flying his natiue place,
   and Countrey, where by duty he should dwell.
     Our no Apostle comming to restore,
     The bloody sway was sometime heere before.   24

His natures flowers were mixt with hunny gall,
  His lewd behauiour, enimie to skill ;
A climing minde, reiecting wisedomes call,
  A sugred tongue, to shrowde a vicious will ;
    A Saintlyke face, yet such a deuillish hart
    As sparde no trauaile for his countries smart.   · 30

With tongue and pen, the trueth he did suppres,
  Stopping the way that Christians did desire,   ·
Which pleased God for his great wickednes,
  To stay his race, wherein he dyd aspire.
    Then his behauiour witnessed the more
    What he was then, as also long before.   36

His fare was good, yet he a scornefull cheare,
  His prison fayre, yet he a froward minde ;
His councell good, yet deafned was his eare,
  Perswasions large, he obstinate and blinde.
    Oh stubborne man, oh minde & nature straunge !
    Whome wisdom, pittie, grace, nor looue could chaunge.   42

After great pause, they brought him to dispute,
  With Bookes as many as he could demaund ;
His cheefest cause, they quickly did confute,
  His proofe layd downe, reprooued out of hand.
    So that the simplest present there could say,
    That Campions cause did beare the shame away.   48

After his foyles so often to his face,
  It was thought good, Justice his deedes should trie ;
Upon appearaunce of so fowle a case,
  Nature her selfe, wild doome deseruedlie.
    Traitour he was, by prooues sufficient found ;
    The Jewrie sawe his Treasons so abound.   54

Her Maiestie to be depriu'd of lyfe,
  A forraine power to enter in our Land ;
Secrete rebellion must at home be rife,
  Seducing Preests receiu'd that charge in hand ;
    All this was cloaked with Religious showe,
    But Justice tried, and found it was not so.   60

Then rightfull doome bequeathed them to dye,
  Whose treasons put her Maiestie in feare;
Out on the fiend, whose mallice wrought so slie
   Hath wun a number, part with him to beare.
    But thinketh he, his enuie can preuaile?
    No, little Dauid did the Giaunt quaile.   66

My gratious Princesse, see your Subiects mone,
  Such secret foes among them should be found,
Who serue your Grace in duety euery one,
   though treason seek to make their harts vnsound.
    The bloody woolf prayes on yᵉ harmles sheepe,
    So treason seekes in loyall harts to creepe.   72

England, looke vp, thy Children doo rebell;
  Unreuerent actes haue entred in their minde;
The subiect seekes his rightfull Prince to quell,
   Yea, his natiue Countrey prooues vnkinde.
    Campion, who sometime yᵘ didst sweetly sourse,
    Prepares his venome to destroy his Nourse.   78

Eliot reioyce, that God prolonged thee
  To take the man, who meant vs all such yll:
As for thy slaunders, take them patiently,
   Enuie drawes blood, and yet hee can not kyll.
    Those who by words he seemde to put in feare:
    Haue washt their hands in iudgement sound and cleare.   84

Myselfe a witnesse, Sled and all the rest
  who had their treasons noted in our Booke,
Account our selues of God most highly blest,
   who gaue vs grace to such attempts to looke;
    And hauing giuen our witnes sound & plaine,
    We feare not mallice, nor his spightful train.   90

The well aduised Jewrie on this cause,
  Who with discretion pondred euerie thing,
Beholde their treasons with such heedfull pause,
   That they found out the depth of Enuies sting.
    Whereby they saw the stirrers of this strife
    Were farre vnwoorthy any longer life.   96

Yea, Elderton dooth deskant in his rime,
  The high offences of such gracelesse men,
Which causeth him to yrke at euerie crime,
  And gainst their treasons to prouide his pen ;
    Yet not without wisedome and modestie,
    To warne all other that liue wickedlie.   102

Remember you that would oppresse the cause,
  Our Church is Christes, his honour cannot die,
Though hell him selfe reuest his griesly iawes,
  And ioyne in league with treason & poperie.
    Though craft deuise, and cruel rage oppresse,
    Christe will his chosen styll in safetie blesse.   108

You thought, perhaps, presumptious Campion could
  disseuer those, whom Christ hath ioynd in one,
And that our gratious louing sheepheard would,
  Before the woolfe, forsake his flock alone.
    No, he preserues his Sheepe for greater good,
    And drownes ye rauener in his enuious blood.   114

We knowe that Campion liuing did intreate
  The Snbiect from his vowde humilitie ;
Nowe therefore shame his dealings dooth repeate
  Throughout the world to his great infamie.
    The skies themselues, with lowring angry face,
    Adiudge his deedes, woorthy of all disgrace.   120

All Europe woonders at this shamelesse man,
  England is fild with rumor of his race ;
London must needes, for it was present than,
  when Justice did three Traiterous minds deface.
    The streets, ye stones, ye steps they halde them by,
    Pronounst these Traitours woorthy for to die.   126

The Tower sayeth he Treason did defend;
  The Barre beares witnesse of his guilty minde ;
Tiborne dooth tell he made a Traitours ende ;
  On euery gate example we may finde.
    In vaine they work to laude him with such fame,
    For heauen & earth beares witnes of his shame.   132

The rightful sentence giuen of him heere,
  Will charge his conscience in the time to come ;
Although they say he is excused there,
  And shall not taste Gods iudgment & his doome.
    Saint Paul dooth say, in reuerence of yᵉ highest,
    We all shall come before the seate of Christ,   138

There to make aunswer vnto euerie thing,
  And to receyue reward accordinglie ;
If well, the Cittie of our heauenlie king
  Shall recompence our former miserie,
    Where we with Angels voice continuallie,
    Shall laude the gaine we haue so happilie.   144

Then blinded mallice shall perceyue and see
  His owne deuises, Author of his rueth ;
And how true Subiects haue felicitie,
  In recompence of their assured trueth.
    The one condemnd for his disloyaltie,
    The other crownd for his fidelitie.   150

Can Treason then preuent our happy peace ?
  Or blustring winds assayle our Sprouting Tree ?
No, soueraine Faith sends down her due encrease,
  And shroudes her Plant in sweete tranquilitie ;
    So that the foe, presuming on his might,
    Is forste to know : Faith can preuent him quite.   156

Let vs not feare a mortall Tirant then,
  Seeing Faith and Trueth dooth eleuate our harts,
God hath reserued one to conquer ten,
  Let vs then learne to play true Christians parts.
    The head of him that sought our Countries wo
    Dooth witnesse shame to all that seeke it so.   162

His youth dooth byd vs bannish filthy pride,
  his fleeting hence, to serue our Prince in trueth ;
His lewd profession dooth lay open wide,
  To fall from God, how greeuous is the rueth.
    His home returne, his Challenge, & deface,
    Saith : Subiects, keep true harts in euery place.   168

His Hardle drawes his sect vnto like ende,
  His speeches there, vnfolde their tretcherie;
His death dooth say : Who so his life dooth spend
  In faith and trueth, reapes ioy eternallie.
    His first and last, and all agree in one :
    Ther's none to helpe vs, but our God aloue.   174

Blessed be God, who cut him off so soone,
  Thanked be Christ, which blest his seruants so ;
Happy are we, that haue such comfort woon,
  curssed are they that thought to work vs woe !
    Bounden we be to giue eternall prayse
    To Jesus name, who did such refuge rayse.   180

Finis.

¶ Another vpon the same.

What iron hart, that would not melt in woe,
  what steele or stoone could keepe him drie from teares ?
To see a Subiect fall from duetie so,
  And arme him selfe vnto his Countries feares?
    In their three deaths, ye standers by might see
    The ende of hatred and disloyaltie.   6

England may mone a Subiect erred so,
  Without respect of God and Natures lawe ;
And we our selues may show some signe of woe,
  That treason should our brother from vs draw ;
    That Antichrist should gain our Campions hart,
    And make him Soldier to his countries smart.   12

The skowling skies did storme and puffe apace,
  they could not beare ye wrong y^t malice wrought;
The Sun drew in his golden shining face,
  ye moistned clowds shed brinish teares with thought ;
    The Riuer Thames against his course would run,
    To count the treasons Campion would haue doon.   18

Nature her selfe, with teares bedewd her face,
  Duetie in countenaunce looked pale and wan ;
Shee, for to think her worke should her disgrace ;
  He, to be wanting in an *English man.*
    Euen Antichriste, the eldest childe of hell,
    Began to blush, and thought he did not well.   24

For loe, beholde, when Campion made his end,
  His hardned hart refused soueraigne grace ;
His owne reproche did so his minde offend,
  That treason did appeare vpon his face :
    An yrksome spectacle was presented then,
    In sight of God, of Angels, Saints, and men.   30

The heauens did cleere, y Sun like gold did shine,
  The Clowdes were drie, the fearfull Riuer ran,
Nature and Vertue wipte their watred eyne,
  To see that Iustice cut off such a man.
    Men, Angels, Saints, and all that saw him die,
    Gaue thankes to God in heauenly melodie.   36

They saw Peruersenes had withdrawn his minde,
  And Treason quite supplanted Dueties awe,
Presumptuous thoughts did humble Patience blind ;
  There was no place for Graces, well they sawe.
    His falsehood, treasons and impietie,
    With blame and shame, did ende in infamie.   42

By whose example, euerie Subiect maye
  Be warned howe they fall in such abuse ;
And all their thoughts on loyaltie to staye,
  Least they likewise doo taste like sharpe refuse ;
    For Honour dooth exalt the Subiect iust,
    When Horrour throwes y Traitour in y dust.   48

Reioyce, be glad, triumph, sing Himnes of ioy !
  Campion, Sherwin, Brian, haue their due !
They are supprest, that sought our great annoy ;
  I hope their fellowes shortly shall ensue !
    For faithfull minds doo lothe y they should liue,
    Who to their Countrey doo dishonour giue.   54

Finis.

A Dialogue betweene a Christian and Consolation.

Christian speaketh first.

Is chaste Susanna in the Iudges handes?
  Is Daniell left vnto the Lions iawes?
Doo Subiects breake bothe God & Natures bandes?
  And Enuie seeke to put downe Peace her lawes?
    Dooth perfect awe and true Religion fayle?
    Then may I feare that falsehood will preuayle.   6

Consolation.

No, Susans foes the Lord will cut in twaine,
  and stop the mouthes of Danielles enimies:
Reioyce therfore, thou hast a noble trayne,
  Armde by the Lord in most triumphant wise;
    Whose life and death, thy quarrell will begin,
    To vanquish falsehood, Sathan, hell and sinne.   12

Beholde of late, a Champion of their traine,
  Confuted, foyled, yea, and vanquished,
With those who did like tretcheries maintaine,
  In their deuises, they soone perished:
    Lament not then, for Justice holds yᵉ swoord,
    Who to them all, will like desert affoord.   18

Christian.

Alas! I mourne, and sit with sighing minde,
  To see my natiue Countrey-men rebell
Against the onely Phœnix of her kinde,
  Who dooth in grace and goodnesse all excell.
    And could proud Campion thinke to worke her woe?
    O Lord, confound them all yᵗ seeke it so!   24

What were his giftes, if we recount ech one?
  A pregnant wit, I graunt to tretcherie;
A bad Diuine, seeking promotion;
  A lustie man, detesting chastitie;
    A gracelesse impe, sprung vp of basest kinde;
    A simple man, to beare a loftie minde.   30

His pithie wisedome, style and eloquence,
  Comparde with those of fame and dignitie,
Dooth open plaine his freends insipience ;
  His confutation prooues it worthilie.
    All the reportes whereby his fame began,
    Were neuer found to harbour in the man.   36

Then boast no farder of his dreadlesse minde,
  Which rack nor roape could alter, as you say ;
Recount his treasons, cruell and vnkinde,
  And then his prayse will soone be layd away.
    Your prayse, his pompe, nor al you haue in store,
    Can make the man the woorthier ere ye more.   42

CONSOLATION.

Tis true in deede, their follie is in sight,
  vnto their shame that take like thing in hand ;
We needs must win, our Lord himself doth fight,
  The Cananites shalbe expulst the Land ;
    Yea, all the deedes of such vngodly men
    Shalbe confounded, nere to rise agen.   48

Campion, his* quarters on the gates doo showe
  His treason, doctrine, and his lyfe too yll ;
His head set vp, dooth daylie call for moe
  Of those that leane vnto like wicked wyll :
    Well may they flaunt & florish for a space,
    But trueth in ende their dealinges will disgrace.   54

Not hell it selfe our iniurie can frame,
  But we shall prosper as the sprouting Baye ;
God can of stones rayse seede to Abraham ;
  He is our hope, and he wyll helpe vs aye.

CHRISTIAN.

Fiat voluntas Dei, then saye I,
I trust in God, whether I liue or die.   60

Finis.

---

* Campion his = Campion's

The Complaint of a Christian, remembring the vnnaturall treasons of Edmund Campion and his Confederates.

O God, from sacred throne beholde
    our secret sorrowes here;
Regard with grace our helpless case,[1]
    amend our mournfull cheere.   4
The creatures whome thou hast appoint
    to liue in Princesse awe,
Forsake their duetie, looue, and feare,
    and spurne at dueties lawe.   8
Alas! I rue to thinke vppon
    their factes so lately scand;
Howe they did seeke their Princesse death,
    and spoyle of natiue land.   12
Thy Treasons, Campion, is bewaylde
    of many farre and neere,
To thinke what vnkinde actions, thou
    wouldest haue perfourmed heere.   16
Bohemia Land may well reioyce,
    Rodulphus Court be glad:
That thou to recompence thy paine,
    such due desart hast had.   20
Germania maye leaue off to mourne,
    yea, Spayne to muse, and Italie,
And Fraunce may rent that false report
    of thy surmised Tragedie.   24
They that would make these men to seeme
    as not her Highnesse foes;
O Lorde, it is a world to see
    the fayned fraude of those!   28
For when as Campion had presumde
    to challenge a dispute,
His craftie cloake was soone pulde off;
    Learning did him confute.   32
Albeit his cauilles, skornes, and coyle,
    he bare with shamelesse face,
Yet trueth pulde off his craftie vayle,
    and shewed his wretched case;   36

---

[1] *Orig.* grace.

So that although they did withstand
  eche cause of right and reason,
Yet Justice soone found out the depth
  of their most wicked treason.   40
Justice perceiu'd how, vnder cloake
  of their Religion,
They comprehended trayterous guile
  and false sedition.   44
Justice perceyued howe they sought,
  within their natiue Soyle,
To mooue rebellion and debate
  to worke our secrete spoyle.   48
Justice perceyued howe the Pope,
  with forraine Princes might,
Would vse our England as him pleasde,
  and put our Queene from right.   52
How that these men were sent before,
  by his perswasion,
To make all ready gainst the tyme
  of his inuasion ;   56
So that destruction suddenlie
  should come vpon vs all;
Those onely sau'd, had holie Graynes,
  or could the watch-woord call.   60
All this did Justice playne discerne,
  with many matters more,
Where-through they had the iust desart
  that they deseru'd therefore.   64
God saue Elizabeth our Queene !
  God sende her happie raigne !
And after earthlie Honours heere,
  the heauenlie ioyes to gaine !   68
And all that secke her secrete harme,
  or to annoy her Grace,
God turne their hearts, or that they may
  enioy but lyttle space.   72

Finis.   *Anthony Munday.*

IV.

[From *Domestic State Papers, James I.,* Vol. 32, No. 32, 11 April, 1608 (Public Record Office).]

Remember Campione, how he died, that worthy wight,
Ralph Sherwine, and the rest besied, for Jesus right ;
thow canst not allwaies liue & lest stand stiff Dear frend,
this breckish Liff is but a breth onct suer to end.   4

This Campione was for wisdom Salamone ;
peter for stiell & Paull for eloquence ;
Dauid for truth, for beuty absolone,
for personadg saull ; a Job for paciens,   8
all thing*es* of w*hi*ch in thes the sam begon,
two thing*es* most strang was Joind in this on man.

No rack nor roap could daunt his [d]redles mynd,
noe hop nor hap could moue hym wher he stood ;   12
he wrot the truth w*i*thin our bock*es* wee find,
w*hi*ch to confirm he sealed w*i*th his blood :
I am in Doubt ther ar noe moor such men ;
send workmen, Lord, into thi vinyard then.   16

Dispair thow not, thow sealy mornfull wight,
for ther are moor hath taken this match in hand,
and Edmund liues & help*es* the godly mene
by prayers moor then herst by tong or pen :   20
God cane of ston*es* rayse sied to Abraham,
therfor Doubt not ther wilbe Inne.
Fiat voluntas Dey, then say wee,
wee ove a death & onct must Die.   24

Fynis p*er* me Kebche in Sasene na exe.

_{Indorsed.} Georg Jarves Prist, suffred for god and his truth at
London the xith of Aprijll, 1608.

TWO POEMS BY JOHN LILLIAT.

As a specimen of the poems of John Lilliat, mentioned above, p. 160, we give the following two, of which the latter utters the writer's grievances. No information about the author seems attainable. There is no mention of him in Wood's *Athenæ Oxonienses*, nor are any productions by a person of such a name in Carew Hazlitt's Handbook. The edition of Watson's poems, previously alluded to, contains many other MS. poems at the end, besides those cited here, and at the conclusion are the following lines :—

> "Quisquis in hunc librum sua lumina verterit unquam
> Nomen subscriptum perlegat ille meum."

Many of these pieces, however, cannot possibly be the production of John Lilliat; for instance, we find copied out the delicious old bucolic, so world-renowned, beginning,

> "Come live with me, and be my love."

Some of the songs in the MS. are accompanied by the music to which they were sung; among them is "A dittie vpon the death of Dulcebell Porter, my scholler: whose Mother died the 20 of Nouember, beinge Munday, 1598, and this her daughter, Januarii 20, 1598."

> "Thy like not left for Musiek's skill
> Waighinge thy age and arte togither."

It would seem probable that Lilliat was a teacher of music.

[Rawl. MS. 148, fol. 43.]

The Spider's Web
(or Anacharsis sayinge of Solons written Lawes).

1.

I meruayle much at spitefull spiders giues,
In such slight sort, that weaue their web so thin :
Sith none. but Bees, or silly harmeless flies,
Intangled are, and fetterd fast therin.
Their wile approues them parciall as I win.
    For if ye Drone should once anoy their Net,
    She rendes ye web, and soone therout doth get.

7

2.

The drowsie drone thus easly scapes we see,
which only lives vpon poore others toyle;
when little flie, and paynefull busie Bee,
Is left behinde, alone to beare the broyle,
whose fault but small, & yet to take the foyle:
   The Spider rather should the Drone enthrall;
   Not Bees nor flies, wch doe no harme at all.   14

3.

Herin contayned ys a Misterie,
wch I refrayne in termes to vtter flat:
Perhapps our Lawes this web may signifie,
But mum, be mute; no more I say of that,
Let cease y^ie tongue, & learne to charme y^ie chat.
   If I offend, in Spider, or in Bee,
   Blame *Anacharsis*[1] then, and blame not me.   21

Ιωλ.
John Lilliat.
Lex exlex.

[Rawl. MSS. Poet 148, fol. 37.]

Lilliat, his Malecontent.

1.   Attend awhile,
      The ragged stile,
  That from my Muse doth flo:
      Whose lowd lament,
      Of discontent,
  Copartner of my woe.   6

2.   As men are friended,
      So Lawe ys ended,
  The adage olde doth say;
      And with the moste,
      In evry Coast
  Affection bears the sway.   12

---

[1] Who was a noble philosopher borne in Scythia, and formed the first Potters wheele.

3.   Lewd Barabbas
        acquitted was
  And sett at libertie :
        when *Jesus Christ*,
        sonne of the hig'hst,
  Condempned for to die.   18

4.   The innocent,
        in discontent,
  finds fewest friends, God knowes :
        when greater sway,
        bears all away,
  with bigg bravado showes.   24

5.   Let little flie,
        but looke awry,
  Rewarded with a rapp :
        When bigger bug
        doth striue & strug,
  And feareth not the slapp.   30

6.   True iustice flead,
        Playne dealing dead,
  The weakest to the wall :
        Wronge sets a face
        Right to disgrace,
  The Judge pleads parciall.   36

7.   Yet in all this,
        Not one ther is,
  My wronge will seeme to right ;
        But for myne ease,
        am glad to please,
  And say the Crowne is white.   q^d *Iω λ.* 42

Lucæ. 21, 19.

Per patientiam vestram,
possidete animas vestras.
St. Barnard.
Deiectum, non eiectum.

POEMS REFERRING TO THE EARL OF ESSEX.

THE career of the unfortunate Essex, one of the most brilliant favourites of Elizabeth, must always form an astonishing episode in her reign. While, however, we lament the caprice of the Queen, we see in this, as in corresponding reigns, that when a female sovereign holds sway, the Court must necessarily become a mere exercising ground for the most unscrupulous and indefatigable adventurers. Of course this remark only holds good in the case of a semi-civilized country. As the rights of the citizen are more and more respected, the outrageous development of personalism—to coin a word—becomes in proportion impossible. The history of the Russian Court during the whole of the last century furnishes a very striking parallel—a peculiar grossness, however, being added by the remoteness of the scene of action from the more polished centres of the west. In Essex's short life of thirty-four years many events of surpassing interest were crowded. In early youth—and we must remember that his life was destined at best to be little more than youth—he served in the Netherlands with the Earl of Leicester, where he held the commission of a captain-general of the cavalry. On the approach of the Spanish Armada, he was appointed to the like command, although at the time only twenty-one years of age. But a vigorous mind and a striking person had already marked him out as one of Fortune's favourites. On the death of Leicester, he succeeded him as the most prominent courtier; but his active temperament, rendering him disinclined to sink into the mere drawing-room honours of a carpet knight, urged him to join expeditions to France, where he was sent to assist Henry IV., and to Portugal, in an attempt to place Don Antonio on the throne, and thereby weaken the power of Philip of Spain, the uncompromising enemy of England. The ballad-writers have not failed to speak of this exploit, and we are told how he challenged the proudest in Lisbon to combat; and when they dreaded the English champion, he stuck his dagger in the gate in scorn of them, like the legendary Oleg of Russian history hanging his shield derisively on the walls of trembling Constantinople. But his grandest achievement was the capture of Cadiz in the year 1596, when a combined fleet of English and Dutch, numbering 150 sail, and carrying 14,000 men, sailed under the command of Essex in conjunction with Lord Howard. This is the celebrated exploit which is entitled in the Percy Collection the "Winning of Cales." When they arrived at Cadiz, they attacked the shipping in the harbour, and the Spanish commander was obliged to order the vessels to be burnt, to prevent them from falling into the hands of the English. Essex landed and captured the town, which he gave up to plunder. He wished to hold Cadiz; but a council of war would not support him. The fleet therefore returned to England, laden with booty, and having inflicted on the Spaniards a loss of four millions sterling. Two ships of the enemy were also brought back—the St. Matthew and St. Andrew. Macaulay speaks of this expedition as "the most brilliant military exploit that was achieved on the Continent by English arms during the long interval which elapsed between the battle of Agincourt and that of Blenheim."[1]

Essex displayed great ability in the affair. He set at liberty some Moorish galley-slaves, and through them entered into communication with the revolted Moors of the south of Spain, who had been shamefully oppressed by Philip.

In 1597 a fleet sailed under the Earl of Essex and Sir Walter Raleigh against the Azores. This is the celebrated "island voyage," and the following prayer is attributed to the Queen on the setting out of the expedition.

---

[1] The readers of Percy's Reliques—and who has not at some time or other familiarized himself with that epoch-making book? (an edition of the Percy Folio has fortunately been lately published by Messrs. Hales and Furnivall more suited to the critical wants of the age)—will not have forgotten the ballad of the Winning of Cales (or Cadiz). The verses are rather doggrel, but are fresh and accurate: the story of carrying off the two prize vessels is very circumstantially detailed—

> "The great St. Phillip, the pryde of the Spaniards,
> Was burnt to the bottom, and sunk in the sea;
> But the St. Andrew, and eke the St. Matthew,
> Wee took in fight manfullye and brought away."

The story of the number of gentlemen whom Essex knighted, and the rhyme in consequence, is too hackneyed to need repetition. The spoil of "Cales" formed a pleasant theme for song and jest for many a year. Thus we find in Hall's Satire (Singer's ed., 1824, p. 65), when he is describing the gallant:

> "Yet for all that, how stiffly struts he by,
> All trapped in the new-found bravery;
> The nuns of new-won Cales his bonnet lent,
> In lieu of their so kind a conquerment.
> What needed he fetch that from farthest Spain
> His grandam could have lent with lesser pain."

The plunder from this expedition seems to have been most ample, but many of the adventurers who joined in it were discontented. From a recently-published Calendar of State Papers we get some curious details. All who shared in the voyage and contributed to the outlay seem to have looked upon it as a good investment. Thirty chests of armour were taken, of which twenty-three were delivered at Plymouth to Sir Gilly Merrick.

[Harl. MS. 6986, leaf 58.[1]]

THE QUENES MA. PRAYER AT THE GOINGE OWT OF THE NAVYE. 1597.

O god, all-maker, keeper, and guider, Jnurement[2] of thy rare-senc, vnused and seeld-heard-of goodues, powred in so pleutifull sort vpon us full oft; breeds now this boldnes, to craue with bowed knees, and heartes of humilitye, thy large hande of helping power, to assist with wonder oure iust cause, not founded on Prides-motion nor begun on Malice-stock; But, as thou best knowest, to whome nought is hid, grounded on iust defence from wrongcs, hate, and bloody desire of conquest. For scince, meanes thou hast imparted to saue that thou hast giuen, by enioying such a people, as scornes their bloodshed, where surelie ours is one: Fortifie (deare God) such heartes in such sort, as their best part may be worst, that to the truest part meant worst with least losse to such a Nation, as despise their lines for their Cuntryes good. That all Forreine Landes may laud and admire the Omnipotency of thy worke: a fact alone for thee only to performe. So shall thy name be spread for wonders wrought, and the faithfull encouraged, to repose in thy vnfellowed grace: And wee that mynded nought but right, inchained in thy bondes for perpetuall slauery, and liue and dye the sacrificers of oure soules for such obtayned fauoure. Warrant, Deare Lorde, all this with thy command.

Amen.

The two commanders however quarrelled. They ravaged the island, but did not succeed in capturing the Spanish Plate Fleet: two or three galleons, however, returning from the Havannah, worth £100,000, were taken.

From this period is said to date the bitter animosity which raged between Essex and Raleigh during the few years of life which remained to the former. It is sad to find the unfortunate Earl's enemy gloating over his end by watching his execution from an upper window in the Tower. There is an undoubted allusion to Raleigh in lines 189, 190, on p. 30 of this volume:

> " But Rawe-bones layde on lies at large,
> And howrelic sought to see his fall."

For two years the Earl seems to have remained inactive,

---

struggling, no doubt, between the various factions, which at this period harassed the Court. In 1599, however, he was, at his own request, sent against the redoubted O'Neil, who had during the previous year totally defeated Sir Henry Bagnal at the battle of Blackwater (August 14th, 1598).[1] He landed at Dublin April 15th, 1599. The army placed under his command consisted of 18,000 men, the best levies in the counties, and many veterans from the Netherlands.

His commission gave him unprecedented authority: he had the power of pardoning all crimes and treasons without exception; and he might continue the war or bring it to an end at his discretion. He was to direct his whole force as much as possible against Ulster, as this was the great centre of the rebellion. His first act, however, on arriving in Ireland, was to disobey the commands of the Queen. He appointed the Earl of Southampton commander of the cavalry, in direct opposition to Elizabeth's express order, to whom Southampton had given offence by a forbidden marriage. Nor did he remove him till a peremptory mandate from the Queen convinced him that she was no longer to be trifled with.

Essex did not proceed to Ulster. On the contrary, he marched into Munster, reaching Limerick, and taking Cork and Waterford on his way, returned to Dublin. He had only to boast of having made himself master of two castles, and received the submission of three native chieftains.

Three months had already been consumed, and his army was greatly diminished by desertion, disease, and other casualties. About the end of August, with only 3000 men out of the 18,000, he met O'Neil on the banks of the Brenny; but instead of fighting, concluded an armistice with him, to be renewed every six weeks during the winter, on condition that Essex should transmit to the Queen O'Neil's demands, which were not likely to be very acceptable to her.

In an interesting paper communicated by Mr. E. Shirley, of Eatington, to Notes and Queries (4th S. viii. p. 34), the true site of the celebrated interview between Essex and O'Neil on Sept. 7th, 1599, is said to have been "at a ford (since bridged over), called Anagh Clint, on the river Lagon, where at present passes the road between Carrick Macross and Ardee, on the borders of the counties of Monoghan and Louth, and the provinces of Ulster and Leinster."

---

[1] The letter of Essex announcing his appointment will be found in the *Nugæ Antiquæ*, vol. i. p. 245. He adds (with a "good mouth-filling oath"): "I will beat Tyr-owen in the feilde; for nothynge worthy hir majesties honor hathe yet beene atchievede."

[Harleian MS. 1291, leaf 40 back.]

A BRIEF RELATION OF W*hi*CH HAPPENED IN THE EXPEDITION OF THE LO*rd* LIEUT*enant* GENERALL OF IRELAND TO-WARDS Y^{e} NORTH PARTE OF THAT KINGDOM FROM THE 28 OF AUGUST VNTILL THE IX. OF SEPTEMBER, 1599.

No rebell in Ireland being able to contynew long w*ith*out holdinge correspondency w*ith* Tyrone,[1] and receyuing of ayde from him; I can not thynke they erre, who are of opinion that he (before any other rebell) were by her ma*ie*stis forces first to be taught his obedience, w*hich*, no doubt, hath beene, and is, the iudgme*n*t of the lo*rd* leiute*nant* generall of Irelande. But that kingdome, being at his lo*rdship*s first landinge, either wholly entred into rebellion, or enclyninge to favor them w*hich* were allready in action, the northeren frontiers being (besides their naturall sterillyty) soe wasted by Tyrone, that they denyed meanes not to susteine me*n* but catle : and w*hich* is of as great consequence as any other consideration, his lo*rdship*s army being then raw and vnex-perienced : yt seemeth to my weake sence to haue beene agreable to all pollicy, both of state *and* warr, to haue first visited ye weaker rebells. Against whome his lo*rdship* having performed so much as hath beene declared in my former relations; and assured the south *and* west frontiers of ye english pale, [leaf 41.] by sufficient garrisons : he de-parted from Dublin towards castle Kerran, a village not farr from Kelles in East meath, where he mustred 2700 foote and 300 horse, conducting them by the shortest way towards Donnemaine in ferny, purposing to plant there a garrison*ne*, for that from that place might be offended co*m*-modiously, all the rebells bordering vpon Blackwater. In his iorney his lo*rdship* visited Louth, w*hich* towne, althoughe yt stande conveniently to receiue a garrison*ne*, yet bycause yt could not be fortefied w*ith*out much chardge, tyme and travell; his lo*rdship* repayred [to] Ishleragh, a village neare Louth, placing in the same, two dayes after, seaven companyes of foote and a troope of horse. Whilst this worke was in

---

[1] The struggle of Hugh O'Neil, surnamed Ruadh or the Red, forms the subject of a curious poem in Hardiman's Irish Minstrelsy. The author supposes himself at Rome, where he has a vision over the graves of the Celtic chieftain and his brother.

hand, S*i*r Willim Warren obteyned leaue of his *lordshi*p
that he might treat w*i*th Tyrone (who laye then encamped
not aboue thre myles from vs w*i*th ten thowsand foote and
a thowsand horse) for the deliuerye of capt*ain* John more,
taken prisoner not many daies before in ophaly.[1] Tyrone,
profess*in*ge to S*i*r willim warren to haue had a longe tyme
a great desyre to make his submission, And entreated the
lo*rd* lieuet*enant* by him that he would be pleased to receiue
a message from him by Henry Agen, his constable, who,
being p*er*mitted to haue accesse vnto his *lordshi*p that night,
entreated that his lordship would vouchsafe to parly w*i*th
his master the next daye.   To w*hi*ch the lo*rd* lieut*en*an*t*
[   ][2] [leaf 41 bk.] and saide that he would in the morning draw
forth into the field and be readdy by ten a clocke to p*ar*ly
w*i*th him, w*i*th his sword in hand.   And that Tyrone might
know him, he comaunded to be shewed to Agen his horse
and armes, sayinge that he would send to Tyrone to know
the markes lykewise of his, to the end they should not
mistake one the other in the field, where sayd he to Agen,
"yf thy master haue any confidence, either in the iustnes of
his cause, or in the goodnes *and* nu*m*ber of his me*n*, or in
his owne vertu, of all w*hi*ch he vaynelye glorieth; he will
meet me in the field so farr advanced before the head of his
kerne[3] as my selfe shalbe separated from the front of my
troopes, where we will pa*r*lie in that fashion w*hi*ch best
beco*m*meth soldiors," w*hi*ch sayd, he licensed him to departe.

Early in the mornin*g*e the lo*rd* lieutenant havinge appointed a sufficient nu*m*ber both of foote and horse, w*hi*ch
he ordered in forme of a saltier or sanct Andrews cross,
placing vpon eche flancque (w*hi*ch served for winges) 100
hors, appoyntinge lykewise to follow the army not much
behynde the Rearewarde an entier grosse of 100 horse, that
out of the same might both be sent out seconds to any
distressed parte, and also that in a generall adversytye yt
might stand to make the retreat of the whole army: In
this order his *lordshi*p marched through an open champion,

---

[1] "The lord deputy, the Earl of Sussex, distinguished himself by the vigour
of his government.   He recovered from the native Irish the two districts of
Ofally and Leix, which he moulded into counties, and named King's County and
Queen's County, in honour of Philip and Mary."—Lingard, v, 236, ed. 1854.

[2] There is a gap in the manuscript here.

[3] An Irish foot soldier.   The word occurs in Shakspere.

vntill he came within a myle or thereaboutes of Tyrone's camp, which (besydes the naturall strength thereof) was so strongly fortefyed by arte *and* industrye as yt appeared to them who had seene the woorkes, impossible to be [leaf 42.] forced by twenty tymes our number.

When the lo*rd* lieut*e*nant expected in this place some howres in battell, a small nu*m*ber of Tyrones horsmen shewed themselues a farr of from *our* troopes, one of w*h*ich callinge to ours, tould them that Tyrone desyred much to speake with his lo*rdshi*p: And hvmbly entreated the same. But that tyme and place he thought not fitt, for that their p*a*rlye might be a cause to bringe the troopes to blowes, which he studying by all meanes to prevent, had purposely conteined himselfe, with his whole forces, w*i*thin the lystes of his campe, w*h*iche so soone as the lo*rd* lieut*e*n*ant* vnderstoode (makinge his Reare the vantguard), he returned to his campe in his first order. Tyrone beinge resolued not to fight vpon equall grownde, And the lo*rd* lieut*e*n*ant* not having sufficient forces to attempt his campe, he resolued, by the advice of his counsell, to returne backe into meath. And directing his march accordingly, the next mornynge, towards Nabber, where his lo*rdshi*p had porposed to fortefye and to plant a garrison*ne*, he was overtaken by Hen: Agen, who, having don*e* his dutye to his lo*rdshi*p, he lett him vnderstand (speaking so lowd as all might heare that were present) That Tyrone desyred the queenes mercy, and intreated to speake with his lo*rdshi*p concerninge the manner of making his submission: addinge, further, that Tyrone attended his lo*rdshi*ps at a forde called Bellaclyne, not halfe a myle out of the waye of the army vpon the right hand of the march, w*h*ich being instantly viewed, by such as his lo*rdshi*p sent thither, they fownde the place convenient, and Tyrone attendinge there vnaccompanied; to whome his lo*rdshi*p hasted, but not before he had sett a guard vpon the Baggage, and put both foote and horse in p*er*fect order to fight. Bycause that tymes of treaties and p*a*rlies haue ever beene held for moste suspected.

[leaf 42 bk.] Before the lo*rd* lieutenant was fully aryved at the foarde, Tyrone tooke of his hatt, and enclyninge his body, did his duty vnto his lo*rdshi*p: with very hvmble ceremony, contynewynge the same observancy the whole tyme of the parlye. It was first emparled betweene themselues in pryvate, and then before six on either partye. With the lord lieutenant were the earle of Southampton, Sir Georg Bourchier, Sir warham St. leger, Sir Henry Danuers, Sir willim Constable, Sir willim warren. On Tyrones parte were Cormoc mac Baron, mac Guinies, Evard mac Cowleye; mac Guyre, Henry ovengton, *and* Richard owen; where yt was concluded that there should be a cessation from armes for six weekes, And the warr to be renewed at the lord lieutenant pleasure, gevinge 14 dayes warninge. It was further agreed, That yt should be lawfull for all them that were now in action, to participate of the benefyte of this cessation, which if any refused or neclected, they should be lefte by Tyrone and all his adhearents, to be prosecuted by her maiesties army, for performance of which agreement the lord lieutenant bownd him selfe in the honor of his woorde, And Tyrone tyed him selfe by oath taken the next daye followinge by 4 comyssioners, Sir warham sen leger, Sir willim Constable, Sir willim warren, *and* Henry wootton,[1] secretary to the lord lieutenant, of whome he is as worthely esteemed for his rare quallities as he is deservedly loved of all others for his vertues, And therefore thought the onely man in the armye fittest among the rest of the comissioners, that by the weight of his iudgment might be couunterpoyzed the sharpnes of Hen: ovengtons witt, Tyrones cheefest counsellor. There were sent with the commissioners [leaf 43.] for their guarde certeine troopes of horse, with whome remayned as pledge vntill the returne of the commissioners Evard mac Cowlye, Hen: Agen, and Shane mac Donnell. Henry ovengton (without whome Tyrone deliberateth of no matter of moment) was nomynated for the fowreth pledge; but Tyrone intreated the commissioners *that* they would rest satisfied with the others, and that ovengton myght remayne with him selfe.

If there be either fayth in Tyrone, or truth in them that are moste of his counsell, he desyreth nothing more then peace, which at this tyme had beene concluded; but that he resteth bownde to the Spaniarde by oathe, to contynew in armes, yf the spaniard shall lande such forces[2] in England

---

[1] The celebrated Provost of Eton. See subsequent remarks upon him and his connexion with Henry Cuffe, the Earl's Secretary.

[2] Throughout the struggles of O'Neil considerable countenance had been lent him by Spain. It is to the assistance of this country, together with that of France, that the old Irish national songs, in the native language, always point.

as might possesse and holde any place in that kingdome, w*h*ich not succeedinge by the end of this moneth he hath faythfully promysed to the lo*rd* lieut*enant* to submitt himselfe to the queenes mercy. Of the p*er*formance of w*h*ich promisse there is more hope for some important reasons, then for any truth w*h*ich hath beene fownd in him selfe. ffor first his yeares (w*h*ich are drawinge to threescore) may moove him to desyre quiet. next, the establishment of his greatnes in his posterytye, w*h*ich he can not doe by the custome of Tamistrye[1] if he should dye and leaue his children yonge. Thirdly, the feare w*h*ich he may conceiue of her ma*i*esties power, if she shall once resolue to presse him in dyvers partes at the same instant. And, lastly, a desyre w*h*ich he may haue to preserue that infinite masse of wealthe w*h*ich he hath by iniustice and rapine heaped togeather, w*h*ich els wilbe in shorte tyme exhausted, by the maynteyninge of his Bonaghs[2] [leaf 43 bk.] and susteyninge them whom he hath robbed.

So soone as this conclusion was made w*i*th Tyrone, the lo*rd* lieuetenant dissolued his army, and havinge lodged in such garrisons as served beste to preserue the subiect, he retyred himselfe to Droghedagh, from whence, after some few dayes, he returned to Dublin.

---

[1] Or Tanistry. Spenser shall explain this word for us:

"*Eudon.* What is this which you call Tanist and Tanistry? They be names and termes never heard of nor knowne to us.

Nen. It is a custome amongst all the Irish that presently after the death of any of their chiefe Lords or Captaines, they doe presently assemble themselves to a place generally appointed and knowne unto them to choose another in his steed, where they doe nominate and elect for the most part, not the eldest sonne, nor any of the children of the Lord deceased, but the next to him of blood, that is the eldest and worthiest, as commonly the next brother unto him, if he have any, or the next cousin, or so forth, as any is elder in that kinred or sept, and then next to him doe they choose the next of the blood to be Tanist, who shall next succeed him in the said Captaincy, if he live thereunto."—View of the State of Ireland, Spenser's Works, Todd's edition, p. 505.

[2] Cavalry soldiers. There was also a bonaughty, which was a tax levied on the people to support the bonaughts.

[Ashmole MS. 219, fol. 133.][1]

KNIGHTES MADE IN ERLAND 1599 BY THE E. ESSEX.

The Erel of rutland, mentioned in Ash. MS. 862, art. 44.
The Erell of Kildare.
The Lord Cromwell, Ash. MS. 862, art. 44.
The Lord Gray.
The Lord Mountigell, see Ash. MS. 862, art. 44.
Sr Robart Vernome, *do.*
Sr Georg Manners.
Sr Thomas Weste, *do.*
Sr Henry Carey.
Sr Jaslen percey.[2]
Sr Carewe Lennalls.
Sr william godolphin.
Sr william Constable, *do.*
Sr william Courtney.
Sr Arter Champnon.
Sr Jhon Davyes, *do.*
Sr Jhon polley.
Sr fraunces Lacon.
Sr huet osborne.
Sr Thomas Moston.
Sr Thomas Tosborowe.
Sr Fraunces Knight.
Sr Fraunces hartley.
Sr Georg thornton.
Sr Terence odersey.
Sr fraunces deverox.
Sr Richard Masterson.
Sr Robart Lasket.

Sr Robart Coñstabell.
Sr Edward Warren.
Sr Cuthberte halsey, 31. (After this name the knights are numbered.)
Sr heugh oconardou, 32.
Sr Jhon Maholand, 33.
Sr Make Swindon, 34.
Sr Thomas baldillon, 35.
Sr Thomas burke, 36.
Sr William warren, 37.
Sr henry lindley, 38.
Sr william gaskon, 39.
Sr thomas oflos, 40.
Sr Jhon Wagon, 41.
Sr William Louelesse, 42.
Sr Jhon harington, 43.
Sr Edward blunt, 44.
Sr Robarte Digbey, 45.
Sr Henry goddard, 46.
Sr Edward Essex, 47.
Sr william Cornwallis, 48.
Sr william Reed, 49.
Sr Edward morgan, 50.
Sr Henry Carewe, 51.
Sr Richard worsand, 52.
Sr Edward Michelborn, 53. Ash. 862.
Sr Jhon haidon, 54.
Sr fraunces micrek, 55.
Sr Jhon Thrastes, 56.
Sr georg lester, 57.
Sr Charells willmote, 58.

What could have been the motives of Essex for this extraordinary conduct, it is not easy to discover. By his many gallant actions we can easily see that he was no coward. The ballad-writer speaks (p. 29, line 167) of a plot, and it is generally believed that the unfortunate Earl hurried back, divining but too surely that his enemies were busy against him during

---

[1] The MS. throughout is in Forman's handwriting.
[2] Is this name the same as Jozaphell Pearsey in Ash. MS. 862?

his absence. Great expectations had been formed of this campaign, but they were to be rudely dashed to the ground. Shakespere only uttered the common opinion when he spoke of (Henry V. act v. Prologue, Chorus)—

> "——— the general of our gracious empress,
> (As in good time he may), from Ireland coming,
> Bringing rebellion broached on his sword."

The "Synon" who "subtellie did charme" was, no doubt, Cecil, whom Essex repeatedly mentioned as one of his bitterest enemies.[1]

He now conceived the desperate design of suddenly appearing before the Queen, and effecting a reconciliation in person. He abruptly presented himself at Nonsuch on the 28th of September, soon after she had risen, and was at first favourably received, and also at an audience accorded to him subsequently on the same day; but he was shortly after delivered over to the Lord Keeper to be in his custody. Meanwhile the public voice asserted itself loudly in favour of Essex. With the people he was

---

[1] The allusion is of course to Virgil, Æneid II. At some particular period of his disfavour, Essex had broken out into the following lines, which are preserved in the Ashmolean MS. 781. They have been already printed in Knight's London, vol. ii. p. 159.

> "Happy were he could [he] finish forth his fate
> In some unhaunted desert, moste obscure
> From all societies, from love and hate
> Of wordly folkes: then might he sleepe secure:
> Then wake againe, and give God praise.
> Content with hippes and hawes and bramble berrie,
> In contemplation spending all his dayes;
> And change of holy thoughts to make him merrie.
> Where when he dyes his tombe may be a bush,
> Where harmeless Robin dwells with gentle Thrush."

From the same MS. I also extract the following, "Annother of his to her Matie upon his commaund to goe for Ireland:"

"From a minde delightinge in sorrowe, from spirits wasted with passion, from a harte torne in peeces with care and greefe and travell; from a man that hateth himself and all thinges that keepe him aliue, what seruice can yor ma^tie expect since my service paste deserves noe more then banishment and proscription into the cursedest of all countreyes; nay, nay, it is your Rebells pride and success that must give me leave to Ransome my life out of that hatefull prison of my loathed bodie, which if it happen soe yor ma^tie shall have not cause to mislike the fashion of my death, since the course of my life would never please you.

> "Yo^r maties exiled servant,
>
> "Ro. Essex."

Just at the period, when he might have commenced a new lease of favour with offended majesty, appeared the book of Dr. Hayward—"The first part of the Life and Raigne of King Henric the IIII., extending to the first yeare of his raigne." Here the Queen, from some cause or other, imagined that she traced allusions to herself in the discussions upon the misgovernment of Richard II.; and in the usurpation of Henry she saw a representation of the aspirations of Essex. The unfortunate author, on these frivolous grounds, was committed to prison.

III.   Q

a great favourite, as many lines in the accompanying ballads will amply testify. He had always opposed religious persecutions, and thus had gained friends both among Puritans and Roman Catholics: he had also many staunch adherents among the military. On the 5th of June, 1600, Essex was examined before the Council, and ordered to keep himself to his own house. He had been in the custody of Lord Keeper Egerton since the preceding October. Upon the conclusion of this commission, Elizabeth deprived him of every office which he held by patent, and ordered him to remain a prisoner in his own house during her pleasure. He was however, at the end of three months, released from custody, but forbidden to present himself at Court without leave. Soon after, a valuable patent which he held expired; but Elizabeth refused to renew it, saying, "that in order to manage an ungovernable beast, he must be stinted in his provender."

The repeated efforts of Essex to gain the Queen's favour having been as repeatedly repulsed, made him more desperate. He entered into negociations with James of Scotland, representing that Cecil and his partisans were aiming at excluding that prince from the succession, and meditated bestowing the crown on the Infanta. These eccentric proceedings gradually oozed out: accordingly Sir Thomas Egerton, Henry Somerset, Earl of Worcester, Sir William Knollys, and Sir John Popham were sent by the Queen to see what he was doing, and to summon him to appear before the Council. The scene of their arrival at the house of Essex presented all the characteristics of a riot. A large mob had collected. When Egerton desired Essex to privately explain his grievances, several voices exclaimed: "They abuse you, my Lord. They are undoing you. You lose your time." It was in vain that Elizabeth's emissary ordered every man to lay aside his arms in the Queen's name. The angry crowd, of whom Essex had long been the darling, shouted, "Kill them, keep them for pledges, throw the Great Seal out of the window." Finally they were locked up in a room, and detained as prisoners.

On Sunday, February 8th, 1601, Essex, pretending that his life was in danger, marched into the City, leaving the lords in the care of Sir John Davyes, Francis Tresham—of whom we shall find mention in the Gunpowder Plot conspiracy—and Owen Salisbury; but they were released in a few hours, and before Essex could return.

The infatuated favourite rushed forward, exclaiming, "For the Queen! for the Queen! a plot is laid against my life." Not a citizen, however, joined him: the astonished crowd simply

looked on in amazement, exclaiming, " God bless your honour ! "
After passing through Ludgate and Cheapside, Essex, at a loss
what step to take, entered the house of a supposed friend, then
one of the sheriffs, who, " seeing the multitude, avoided himself
out at a back door, when presently, in divers parts of the city,
Essex was proclaimed a traitor, to the no less grief of the citizens
than fear of his followers."

Many of his friends now forsook him, and about two o'clock
in the afternoon he came to Gracechurch Street, and attempted
to make a stand there ; but although the Mayor and others were
at the end of the street, no one arrested him.   He retired again
to St. Paul's, intending to pass by Ludgate the same way that
he came ; but his progress was impeded by a barricade of empty
carts, and some companies of troops hastily got together by the
Bishop of London.   The Earl was forced back, having been twice
shot through the hat.   Sir Christoper Blount was taken prisoner,
and another associate named Tracy slain.   Essex then continued
his retreat, and in an agony of thirst desired drink of some of
the citizens, which was given him.   At Queenhithe he took boat,
and succeeded in reaching his house in the Strand, which he
fortified, intending to die in its defence.   The place was, however, soon stormed, and its inmates compelled to surrender.   One
of his companions, Captain Owen Salisbury, stood bareheaded
at an open window, eager to rush upon his fate.   A bullet from
some one in the street struck him in the side of the head.   " Oh !
that thou hadst been so much my friend as to have shot a little
lower ! " he exclaimed.   The wound, however, proved fatal, for
he died on the following morning.   By ten o'clock that evening
Essex had surrendered, and was first conveyed to Lambeth,
and subsequently to the Tower.   On the 19th of February he
and Southampton were arraigned before Lord Buckhurst, as Lord
Steward, and twenty-five other peers.   The indictment charged
him, among a variety of treasonable acts, with having en-
deavoured to raise himself to the royal dignity.   The crown
lawyers were Yelverton, Coke, and Bacon.   We cannot here
enter into the question how far the latter can be justly charged
with having betrayed his friend.   The matter has certainly assumed a new phase since the publication of Mr. Hepworth
Dixon's book ; and Mr. Spedding also considers that Bacon was
not guilty of treachery towards Essex (Spedding's Bacon, vol. iii.
pp. 136–138).

The Earl could only stoutly deny that he had nourished any
idea of injuring the Queen, although his step-father, Sir Christopher Blount, confessed at his execution, a few days later, that
the conspirators, rather than fail in their ends, were prepared to

have "drawn blood even from herself." He affirmed that he had taken up arms solely in defence of his own life, which was threatened by Lord Cobham and Sir W. Raleigh. The peers declared Essex and his companion Southampton to be guilty of high treason. The latter earl—who has earned the gratitude of posterity by his patronage of Shakspere—remained in the Tower till the next reign, when he was released and restored to his title and estates.[1] Essex was privately executed in an inner court of the Tower. The circumstances of his death, and the threefold stroke of the headsman, as recorded in Williams's ballad, are circumstantially correct (p. 33, line 274); but the reader who cares to have a more minute account of the event will find it amply described in the two following narrations, now first published.

The first, a touching "ACCOUNT OF THE DEATH OF ESSEX," from the Memories of Mr. Thomas Cook and Mr. Kidman, is taken from the Cambridge University MS. Kk, 1, 3 :—

Execucion [of] Erle [E]ssex: 25° [F]ebr; 1600 [in] the tower. The 25th of februarie 1600;[2] beinge Ash Wedensdaie, aboute 8fo of the clocke in the morninge, was the sentence of death executed against the Erle of Essex within the Tower of London; where a scaffolde beinge set vp in the middest of the courte, & neare vnto it a fourme placed, where-onne satte the Earls of Cumberland & Hartford; the Lod Viscounte Byndon; Lod Thomas Haward then Lord Constable of the tower; Lod Darcey; & Lod Compton; Sir Jhon Peyton Lieutennant of the towne; with about 16tn partizens of the guarde, was sent to bring the earle prisoner; whoe camme in a gowne of wrought veluet, a satten suite, & felte hatte all blacke; and a litell ruffe band about his falling band; and aryvinge onne the scaffold with 3ree chapleines Dr Mountford, Dr Barlowe, and Mr Asheton, Hee vailed his hatte, and makeinge reverence to the Lordes, laied it awaie, and spoake to this effecte; "My Lordes, and yee my christian bretheren, whoe are to bee witnesses of this my iuste punnishment, (at theis wordes and all the while after liftinge vp his eyes moste intentiuelie to heauen), I confesse to the glorie of god, that I am a moste wretched sinner, and that my sinnes are moe in number, then the haires of my heade; that I haue bestowed my youth in wantonnes, luste, and vncleannes; and that I haue beene puffed vp with pride, vanitie and loue of this worlds pleasure;

---

[1] See the fine lines addressed by Samuel Daniel to Southampton.
[2] Old style: 1601 new.

and that notwithstanding diuers good motons inspired into mee from the spirit of god; The good w*hi*ch I would I haue not donne; and the evill w*hi*ch I woulde not, that haue I donne; for all w*hi*ch I humblie beseeche my saviour Christe to bee mediator to the eternall ma*j*estie for my pardon; especiallie for this my laste sinne, this greate, this bloudie, this cryinge, this infectous sinne, whereby so manie for loue to mee, haue bene drawne to offend god, to offend their sovereigne, and to offende the worlde; I beseech god to forgiue it vs, and to forgeue it mee the moste wretched of all; I beseeche her ma*j*estie & the state, and Ministers thereof; to forgeue it vs; and I beseache god to send her ma*j*estie a prosperous reigne, & a longe, if it bee his will; O Lord graunte her a wise & an vnderstanding hearte; O Lord blesse her & the Nobles, and Mynisters of the church & of the state; And I beseeche youe and the world, to houlde a charitable opinion of mee, for my inten*t*ion to her-wards, whose death I protest I never meante, nor violence to her p*er*son; Allso I desire all the world to forgiue mee, even as I doe freelie and from my harte forgeue all the world: I was never I thanke god Atheiste to denie the power & omnipotencie of god; never Papiste trusting in my owne meritts, but hope for my salua*t*ion, from god onelie, by the mercie & meritts of my saviour Jesus: This faith was I brought vp in, and herein am nowe readie to die; beseech-inge yee all to ioyne your soules w*i*th mee in praier, that my soule maie bee lifted vp by faith aboue all earthlie things in my praier, for nowe I will giue my selfe to my private praier; yet for that I beseeche youe to ioyne w*i*th mee; I will speake that youe maie heare;" Then putting of his gowne & ruffe, and presenting himselfe before the blocke, hee was, as it seemed, by one of the chapleines incouraged against feare or death; to whome hee aunsweared, that "haveing byne diuers times in places of daunger, yet where death was neither so present nor certeyne, hee had fealte the weakenes of flesh, and therfore desired god nowe, in this greate conflicte, to strengthen him;" and so preparing him-selfe to kneele downe, asked for the execu*t*ioner, whoe onne his knees all-so asked him pardon, to whome hee said, "thou art welcome to mee, I forgeue thee; thoue art a minister of Justice:" and soe w*i*th like fixed eyes on heaven and w*i*th long & pass*i*onate pawses in his speache; beganne his praier;

"Oh God creator of all things, and Judge of all men, thoue haste let mee knowe by warrante out of thie word, that Satan is then moste buisie, when our ende is neareste; and that sathan beinge resisted will flie; I humblie beseech thee to assiste mee, in this my laste combate, and sithence thou accepteste even of all our desires, as of actes, accepte of my desire to resiste him even as of true resistaunce and perfecte by thie grace, what thou seeste in my flesh to bee fraile & weake; giue mee patience to beare, as becommethe mee, this iuste punnishment inflicted onne mee, by so honorable a tryall: graunte mee the inward comforte of thie spirit; let thie spirit seale vnto my soule an assurance of thie mercies: lifte my soule aboue all earthlie cogitatons, and when my life & bodie shall parte, sende thie blessed Angells, which maie receave my soule, & convey it to thie ioyes in heaven." Then sayinge the Lords praier, (hee iterated this petition, 'Lord Jesus forgeue vs our trespasses,') and the creede; hee added, "Lord Jesu receaue my soule, into thie hands O Lord I commend my spirit;" And so desiringe to bee infourmed of what was fitte for him to doe, for desposinge him selfe fittlie to the blocke, (sayinge 'hee would onelie stretch out his armes thus,' spreading them wide out,) his doublet taken of, in a scarlet wascoate, hee was willed by one of the doctors, to saie the beginninge of the 51st psalme; whereof when hee had said 2 verses, the executioner beinge then readie, hee bowed towards the blocke, and saide: "In humilitie and obedience to thie commaundment, in obedience to thine ordinaunce, to thie good pleasure O God, I prostrate my selfe to my deserued punishment;" so lyinge flatte a-longe onne the bordes, his armes streached out, hee saide, "Lord haue mercie vpon mee thie prostrate servaunt:" and then layinge downe his heade and fittinge it on the blocke, with theis laste wordes in his mouth, "Lord Jesu receaue my soule;" in the middeste of that sentence, yt was severed by the axe from his corps, at 3xle blowes, but the 1rste deadlie and absolutelie depriveinge sense and motion. All this was M. Thomas Cooks memorie; a few other wordes uttered by the said Erle, Mr Kidman remembered; & Mr Cooke to when hee heard them; viz. "I am by nature fearefull of death as other men, and therfore if I beare it pacientlie and constantlie as a christian oughte to doe, I beseeche youe ascribe the glorie to god *that* dooth strengthen me by his spirit, and not to mee."

The following is another MS. account of the death of the Earl of Essex :—

[MS. R. 5. 12, Trin. Coll. Camb. Baker's copy, MS. : Mm. i. 44, fol. 81, Cambridge Univ. Library.]

The Earle of Essex suffred one Ashwednesday, the 25th of Februarie 1600 within the tower of London, betweene 7: & 8: of the clocke in the morninge. The man*er* of his death, & the whole sume of such woords, as hee did speek to the guard ou*er* night before he died, & such woords as he did deliver from his Chamber to the scaffold & also uppon the scaffold, to the hower of his death.

One tuesdaie at night about eleven of the clocke he opened the casm*ent* of his windowe, & spake to the guard; "My good Frends praie for me & to-morrowe I shall leave an example behind. mee, that you shall remember, & you shall see a stronge god & a weak man. I haue not anie thinge to give you, if I had, I would give it to you, but I haue nothing left, but that I must paie unto the Queen to-morrowe." In the morninge he was brought out by the liftenant w*hi*ch attended one him, w*i*th 3: Divines exhortinge him, & at his cominge foorth of his chamber, he called verie hartelie to god, that he would give him strength & patience to the end, & all the waie as he came from the chamber to the scaffold he praied, sainge, "O lord, give me true Repentance & true patience, & true humilitie." Hee entreated those that went w*i*th him to praie for him, sainge, "O god be mercifull to mee the most wretched sin*n*er one the earth." Then he turned him to the nobellmen, that satt one the scaffold, & put of his Hatt, and said, " R^t: Honble Lo*rds* & right wor^p: & *Christ*ian Bretheren, that come hither to bee a witness of my death, I doe confesse before god & you all, that I have been a most miserabell & wretched sinner, & a notorious wretch, & that the sines of my youth have beene more then the haires of my head, for I have beene given to pride & to lust, vaine glory, & divers other greivous sines, accordinge to the fashion of this world, wherein I have most greiuously offended my God, & therefore o Lord my God forgive mee my sines & especiallie this last & bloudie fact this deadlie sine w*hi*ch I have comitted & was ledd into, & also manie men have ventured for the love of mee both their lives, goodes & soules, w*hi*ch

is as great to mee as maie bee. Lo: Jesue forgive mee &
them, and for this bloudie fact. I have received an Honble:
triall and am iustlie condemned, p*r*otestinge on my salvacou⁹
before God, that I never intended to hurt the p*er*son of her
Matie: my Soveraigne, & wheras I was condemned for my
Religion, I p*r*otest before God and you all as I hope to [be]
saved, I neu*er* was Atheist nor Papist, for I doe defie them
both with all my hart, nor was I eu*er* anie other, then a
true *Christ*ian by profession, for I never denied the power
of my God, nor I neu*er* beleived to be iustified bye workes:
but the Religion w*h*ich I p*r*ofesse is, that I shall be re-
deemed by the death & passion of Jesus Christ crucifyed
for mie sines, in w*h*ich profession I have all waies beene
brought upp from my youth hitherto, & nowe bye Gods
grace will die in the same, desireinge the God of Heauen, for
Christs sake, not to suffer the flesh to have anie power ou*er*
mee, but send thy holie Angell to bee neere mee." Then
liftinge upp his hands & eies to Heaven, he entreated the Lds:
& his *Christ*ian Bretheren to assist him in praier, as Christ
himselfe taught us, entretinge them not w*i*th eies & lipps
onlie, but to lifte upp y^r harts & mindes also w*i*th him to
the Lord alsoe for him. Then he invocated one God zealous-
lye, & praied for the good estate of her ma^{ties}: most Royall
person ferventlie, for the longe continuance of her life &
Raigne amongst us. He praied also for the whole estate
of the nobillitie, & alsoe for the comonaltie. Then he
said, "Right Honble: Right wo^p: and *Christ*ian Brethren, I
will kneele down to praier & will praie aloud, because you
shall hear mee what I saie, intreatinge you to praie w*i*th
mee & for mee." Then he kneeled downe before the Blocke,
& entreated God to forgive him all his sins, & especiallie
this last sin, this crynge sin, & most greivos sin, most
humblie beseechinge her Matie: to forgive & pardon him.
Alsoe the like he desired of all Estates whatsoever. Then
hee repeated the Lords Praier, & when he came to, "As we
forgive them y^r trespasses against us," he first reapeted it
as it was written, & then againe ov*er* thus, "as we forgive
them all y^r trespasses against us," & so to the ende of the
Lords Praier. Then one of the Divines putt him in minde
to saie the Beleife, w*h*ich he did, the Doctor sainge it softlie
before him. Then hee beinge remembred by the Divines to
forgive and praie for his enemies; he praied for them all

& desired God to forgive them freelie, as hee did, sainge, "for that they beare the Image of God, as well as my selfe." Then he called for the Excecutioner, who came one the Scaffold to him, & there besought him to forgive him, and hee looked upon him & said, "god forgive thee, for I doe, thou art the minister of true iustice. O God thou knowest, I have been in danger of deathe manie times in beinge fitinge against mie enemies, and I never was afraide of death, wherefore I praie thee O God, give mee true patience, & trulie to be humbled to the end."

Then he asked the Executioner, what he must doe and howe hee must lie, the w*hi*ch he did as he was told. Then hee said, "I praie you praie for mee, & when you shall see mee strech foorth my Arms, & that mie necke bee laide on the blocke, & the stroake redie to be given, that it would please God to send his holie Angell to carrie my Soule upp p*r*esentlie before the mercie seate of the Everlastinge god." Then he kneleed downe & liftinge upp his Eies devoutly to Heauen, he thus said, "Lo: God, as one unto thine Altar doe I come, offeringe my bodie & bloud as a sacrifice." Then he laide his necke one the Blocke, & the coller of his Doublet did hinder the Execution, because it did cover his necke. Then himselfe did saie, "my Doublet dothe hinder thee, dothe it not," & w*i*th that he rose upp again & pulled it of, sainge, "what I must doe, I will doe," & then givinge his Bodie to thee Blocke againe & spreadinge his Armes abroad, & streatchinge his bodie at large, he repeated these his last woords, his necke beinge upon the Blocke, & bid the Executione*r* strike home, & said, "Lo: Jesu come Lo: Jesu, receive my soule," and soe at three strokes hee stroke of his Head, & when his head was off & in the Executione*r*s hand, his Eyes did open & shut, as in the time of his praier; his bodie, feete, Armes, Leggs, Armes, nor fingers never stirred, neither anie p*ar*t of him noe more then a Stone, neither at tho first nor at the thirde stroke.

Finis.

The Excecucon[s] of the somtime good Earle of Essex (MS. Coll. Trin. Cant. 2, 5, 12).

Williams, in his ballad, is evidently so great an admirer of Essex that he is unwilling to make mention of his delinquencies in Ireland, or of his subsequent rash enterprise against the Queen. It is quite possible that he may have been an old soldier who served under Essex : there are many minute points of detail in the poem which seem to show a personal experience of the campaigns of the ill-fated general. Thus he praises him for his anxiety in securing the soldiers' pay.

Most of the ballads here printed will probably be censured by the reader as dull and tedious : he will however find ample proof of the great popularity which Essex enjoyed among all classes, owing to his real or affected sympathy with the doctrines of universal toleration.

Like all fashionable favourites, he was destined to have his epoch, "borne like bubbles onward," and among other proofs we find the following dance named from him (Harleian MS. 367, leaf 178) :

"The Earle of Essex.

"A double forward, and a single backe, 4 times ; then to singles, sides, with a double forward and a double backe ; all over againe, and so end."

Let it remind the reader of the bright time of the Earl, his joyous days, his gallant show at Court, before the poems speak of his 'hard waie' to the grave and death. That there must have been something more in the man than mere vapouring bravado and the insane flourishes of a swash-buckler, we may conclude from his expedition to Cadiz, even if we do not go quite so far as the words of Hallam, who speaks of that "too noble and high-minded spirit, so ill-fitted for a servile and dissembling Court; . . . . . . the consistent friend of religious liberty, whether the Catholic or the Puritan were to enjoy it" (Hallam's *Constitutional History*, i. p. 167). Sir Henry Wotton, who had been "taken into a serviceable friendship with the Earl of Essex, did personally attend his Concels and Imploy-ments in Two Voyages at Sea against the Spaniard, and also in that (which was the Earl's last into Ireland)," and had been obliged also to leave the kingdom at the time of the disgrace and execution of his patron, has ·left us a curious parallel be-tween Essex and George Villiers, Duke of Buckingham, in which he speaks thus of the former : "In the Earl we have two examples of his severity, the one in the Island Voyage, where he threw a Souldier with his own hands out of a ship ; the other in Ireland, where he decimated certain troops that ran away, renewing a peece of the Roman Discipline."

This last act of severity corroborates the account of the strict régime which he exercised over his soldiers, as mentioned in the ballad composed by Richard Williams.

The body of Essex was buried in St. Peter's Chapel in the Tower. He left three legitimate children—1st, the great Parliamentary general, Robert Devereux, the third Earl of Essex, born in 1592, restored in blood and honours in 1603, who died in 1646 without issue, when the earldom became extinct; 2nd, Frances, who married first the Earl of Hertford, and afterwards the Duke of Somerset; 3rd, Dorothy, who married Sir Henry Shirley, and then William Stafford, of Blatherwyck, in Northamptonshire.[1]

Lowndes gives the following list of books, etc., on and by Essex :—

A Declaration of the Practises and Treasons attempted and committed by Robert late Earle of Essex, and his Complices. Lond. 1601. Supposed to have been drawn up by Sir Francis Bacon.

An Apologie of the Earle of Essex; against those which jealously and maliciously tax him to be the Hinderer of the Peace and Quiet of his Country. Penned by himself in Anno 1598. Lond. 1603. 4to. Published by Lord Bacon. Reprinted under the title of the Earl of Essex's Vindication of the War with Spain in an Apology to Mr. Anthony Bacon, penn'd Anno 1598. London, 1729. 8vo.

Honors Fame, or the Life and Death of the Earle of Essex. 1604. 4to.

Histoire de la Vie et Mort du Comte d'Essex, avec vn Discours grave et eloquent de la Royne d'Angleterre au Duc de Biron sur ce Subject. 1607. 12mo.

The Earl of Essex his Letter to the Earle of Southampton in the Time of his Troubles. Lond. (1642). 4to.

A Letter from the Earl of Essex to the Earl of Southampton in the latter Times of Q. Elizabeth's Reigne. Lond. 1643. 4to.

Memoirs of the Life of Robert Devereux, Earl of Essex. Lond. 1573. 8vo.

To these may be added—

The Arraignment, Tryal, and Condemnation of Robert Earl of Essex, and Henry Earl of Southampton, at Westminster the 19th of February, 1600, and in the 43 year of reign of Queen Elizabeth, for Rebelliously conspiring and endeavouring the Subversion of the Government, by Confederacy with Tyr-Owen, that Popish Traytor, and his Complices; of whom these following, viz.: Sir Christopher Blunt, Sir Charles Danvers, Sir Gillie Merrick, Henry Cuffe.[2] Counsel for the Queen, Sir Henry Yelverton, the Queen's Serjeant, Sir Edward Coke, the Queen's Attorney-General, afterwards Lord Chief-Justice of England, Mr. Bacon, afterwards Lord Chancellor. London, Printed for Tho. Basset, at the George in Fleet Street, Sam. Heyrick, at Grayes-Inn Gate in Holborn, and Math. Gillyflower, in Westminster Hall, 1679.

---

[1] Williams speaks of two "gallante Impes," and the second must be an illegitimate son named Walter, see *Biographia Britannica*, 1793, vol. v. p. 155; also for a complete pedigree of the family *Baronagium Genealogicum*, vol. iii. 1784.

[2] See the poems written by this man, who is said to have been one of the worst advisers of Essex.

"The ballad of 'Essex's last good night' is," says Mr. Chappell (Popular Music, vol. i. p. 175), "on the death of Walter Devereux, Earl of Essex (father of Queen Elizabeth's favourite), who died in Dublin in 1576 (Sep. 22)." "The Paradise of Dainty Devises" (1580) has a poem called "The Complaint of a Sinner, and sung by the Earle of Essex upon his death-bed in Ireland." The poem begins,

"Oh! heavenly God, O Father deere, cast down thy tender eye."

This production alludes to the death of Walter, Earl of Essex, which occurred under somewhat suspicious circumstances, his own wife not escaping from the loud echoes of a common censure, which her subsequent hasty marriage did nothing to allay.

Upon Essex himself, besides the poems here printed, we have "A lamentable dittie composed upon the death of Robert Lord Devereux, late Earle of Essex, who was beheaded in the Tower of London, upon Ash Wednesday, in the morning, 1601. To the tune of *Well-a-day*. Imprinted at London for Margaret Allde, etc., 1603." Reprinted in Collier's Old Ballads, p. 124, 8vo. 1840; and in Evans, vol. iii. p. 158. Copies are also in the Bagford and Roxburghe Collections.

[Harl. MS. 6910, leaf 177.]

Verses vpon the report of the Death of the right Honorable the Lord of ESSEX.

THIS is a somewhat tedious poem, of unknown authorship.   The
verses, however, show the great popularity which Essex enjoyed.
At the conclusion we have one of the pastoral dialogues so much
in vogue at the period.

GOOD GOD ! what will at lenght become of vs ?
What hope haue wee, when all our hope is gone ?
Wee hope in vaine, if thou wilt plague vs thus,
To take the good, and let the badd alone.
Send him agayne, Great Joue, let him returne,
Whose losse wee greeue, whose death wee nought but
  mourne.   6

Send him againe to vs, that now at last
Our sommer season may returne agayne;
That those cold nights *which* wee in teares haue past
May prooue effectuatt, ne be spent in vayne.
O let him come, that now my teares may end :
Els send me, Ioue, more store of teares to spend. 12

Not longe it is since that wee had him heere :
And yet tis long since I his death gan mourne :
Each minute seemes an howre, each howre a yeare,
Each yeare an adge to them *that* liue forlorne.
An adge in pleasure seemes but an howre or twayne ;
An howre witt seeme an adge, if spent in payne. 18

Could I but soare with Eagle winges on hye,
And flye to Heauen as Orpheus went to hett,
So thou mightest liue, I would not care to dye,
Let Ioue but suffer mee my Tale to tett :
If Orpheus mou'd th' infernatt Gods to pittye,
Ioue coulde not chuse but heere my wofull dittye. 24

Orpheus did trauaill with his well tun'd Lute,
And gott his wife by his alluring stroake;
But my sadd tale should first begin my sute, [lf. 177 bk.]
Hoping to mooue a hart as harde as oke,
If teares and prayers might preuayle as well,
As Hermes pipe, or Orpheus Lute in Hell. 30

The many ey'd Argus was induc'd to sleepe,
Whilst Hermes played vpon his slender reed,
And lull'de therwith forgat his charge to keepe.
Twas Hermes pipe, Twas it *that* did the deed.
O happie Lute, o happye pipe of thyne,
His Lute, thy pipe prevaild, and so may myne. 36

I haue a pipe which shall I hope preuaile,
The selfe same pipe that Hermes vsde of late.
My Pype ile vse if all meanes els do fayle.
With it Ile sweetly singe at heauen gate.
Joue must be Lull'd a sleepe, *and* ere it be day,
With mee my harts delight shall wend away. 42

But how to find the way is all my care;
The way to Heauen is straight *and* perillous;
There stand*es* the Lyon, Bull, the Ramme, the Beare,
A Hundreth beasts besyd*es* as daungerous.
Therfore I will with teares intreate once more
That Joue will heare mee, *and* my deare restore. 48

Oh how mee thinkes I feele my slubbred cheekes
From foorth myne eyes greife-easing-teares to call:
A burning feauer still for moisture seekes:
That place must wither, wher no rayne doth fall:
No meruaile then if *that* my face doth wither;
For why, my teares are gon I know not whither. 54

Yet were my cheekes so throughly wett of late
With flood*es* of teares in such aboundance falling:
That litle streames did flow wheras I sate:
That now, alas! my teares are past recalling: [lf. 178.]
So long I spared not for teares that now
To weepe on more, Alas! I know not how. 60

Yet though mine eyes are drie, my hart is wett,
From whence full streames of luke warme blood do fall.
And if my teares cannot this fauour get,
My blood is thyne, my hart, my life and all:
Because my teares are dry, my hart shall mourne,
Crying (deare ESSEX) for thy quicke returne.   66

Oh let my teares yet mooue thee (gentle JOVE),
Behould my greife, respect the paynes I suffer:
Thou that behouldst each creature from aboue,
Accept this last oblation that I offer.
My teares are dryed, my blood still wastes away,
How long (sweet ESSEX), how long wilt thou stay?   72

Come quickly, ESSEX, els thou stayest to longe;
Thou stayest to long, although thou com'st to-day;
Although thou com'st to-day, thou dost vs wrong;
Thou doest vs wrong, come therefore, come away:
Come, come, each groue doth nought but ESSEX cry;
Each shore cries ESSEX, ESSEX; so will I.   78

Looke how each tree begins to hang his head,
And letts his fadeing leaues with sorrow fall.
See euery plant and euery hearb lookes dead;
The greenest grasse for sorrow waxeth pale;
Each litle streame aboue his bankes doth swell;
Greiuing for him whome all things lou'd so well.   84

For greife the fountaines inly troubled are;
ffor greife eche tree hath chaungd his sommer coate;
ffor greife away the swallow flyeth farre;
ffor greife each pretty bird hath chaungd his noate;
ffor greife each beast and bird is prest to dye;
ffor greife my ESSEX dyed, and so will I.   [lf. 178 bk.] 90

Then let me liue no longer, let me dye;
Let Sunne no longer see my weary boanes;
But let my spirit to his sweet soule vp flye,
That lives among the saintes and holy ones.
Come, death, I praye thee, fye! how long thou art!
Why bend thy bow, let fly, heere, heeres my hart.   96

The Heauens I thinke sufficiently haue wept,
That both the earth below, *and* seas cries "hoe!" [1]
The Heauens knew well for whome those teares they kept,
They knew on whome they might them best bestow.
And now I thinke they haue not spared the same:
The earth shall Judge for whome, and whence they came. 102

They came for Essex, but they came from heauen;
They came for him whome wee would haue agayne;
They came from heauen to make all recknings euen,
To cleare the counts that were betweene them twaine.
Now all accompts are clear'd, why dost thou stay?
Now all is euen, why comst thou not away?   108

Then let him come, sweete Joue, and send him downe.
I know he's happie, make vs happie to.
Come quickly, Essex, and receiue thy crowne,
Which wee haue made for thee with muche adoe;
This *Laurell Crowne*, which never yet was worne,
But kept for thee against thou didst returne.   114

I know thou hearst, thou canst not chuse but heare;
And hearing, wilt thou not do thus much for me?
Come downe a while, thou shalt not stay, my deare.
Why comst thou not? alas! doest thou abhorre me?
After a while with leaue thou shalt returne,
And then shall I haue leaue *and* tyme to mourne.   120

Then shall I to the woods with Philomell,   [lf. 179.]
And there consume my wreatched dayes with mourning;
The prickly Briers shall be my Centinell,
And keepe myne eyes awake against the morning,
That then the woodes maye heare the plaintes I make,
For thy sweet soule (sweet Essex), for thy sake.   126

---

[1] " And at a stert he was betwix hem two,
 And pulled out a swerd, and cryed, Hoo."
     —Chaucer, *Knight's Tale.*

Some darkesome denne, and ouergrowne with mosse,
I shaɫɫ fynd out, where I may rest my boanes.
And there Ile sitt, and there bewayle my losse,
There wiɫɫ I rest, my pillowe made of stones,
The earth my bed; *and* this is all for thee,
ffor thee (deare ESSEX) whome I long to see.   132

A Hermits life shall best become my state,
A Hermits weede shaɫɫ best become my backe,
A Hermits dish instead of siluer plate,
Nought shall I haue, yet nothing shall I lacke.
Ile walke and weepe, Ile nought but sight all day,
And all night longe Ile sitt me downe *and* pray.   138

Ile praye, Ile weepe; Ile pray for thy retourne,
Ile weepe because thou art so long away.
Ne cease to pray, tiɫɫ fyre shall cease to bourne:
Nor cease to weepe, till sunne shall cease by day
To shew his glorious face.   Ile pray, Ile weep—
I made a vow to thee; my vowe Ile keepe.   144

Thus like a Hermite will I walke alonge,
And muse on nought but of thy glorious acts:
Thy speare, thy *Launce*, thy *Sheilde*, shall be my songe;
Ile singe of nought but of thy Noble facts.
Are *Pompeys* warrs, or *Ceasars* conquests knowne,
And shaɫɫ not thyne all-passing-acts be shewne?   150

Their deeds were graced by the singers songe,
That could at large discribe what they had done.
Direct my pen, Great IOVE, I may not wronge   [lf. 179 bk.]
Nor clipse his fame, that hath more honoure woone;
Ceasar nor *Pompey* may compare with thee,
Thrice happye DEVORAX, if thrice may bee.   156

What shall hearafter after adges say,
If all thy conquests wonne be straight forgotten?
The body dyes, thy name shaɫɫ ne're decay;
Thy fame shall liue, thy body dead and rotten.
And thou shouldst liue, if I might haue my wiɫɫ,
But sith thou canst not liue, thy name liue stiɫɫ.   162

III.   R

And art thou dead, my deare, and couldst thou dye?
And leaue vs thus in this tempestious tyme?
Thy soule, to good for earth, to heauen doth flye,
More fitt, indeed, for that celestiall Clyme.
There shalt thou haue the meede of all thy labour,
Though heere on earth thou hast had litle fauour. 168

This is the fauour that thou hast receiued,
Thou art with *Scipio* into exile sent;
At least, thou art of common Ayre bereaued;
At least, thou art (Alas!) in prison pent.
After such conquests wonne, so *Scipio* far'de:
Thou hast with *Scipio* this for thy rewarde. 174

Thou, that hast grac'st so much this litle laud,
And with the victores garland crown'd her head,
Whome *Spaniards* dread for thy victorious hand,
And *Irish* rebells feare, What! art thou dead?
Once more I pray thee, Ioue, let him returne,
That wee *that* lou'd him so may cease to mourne. 180

And yet it may bee that hee will not deigne
That this ingratefull Land agayne should haue him;
But tell him, Ioue, how hee is wisht agayne,
How much wee want him, and how much wee craue him.
Giue him these lynes, for these I hope shall mooue him,[lf. 186.]
These shew our harts *and* mynds, and how wee loue him. 186

Wee loue him still, and still wee wish him heare,
Wee loue *and* wish for him, that want him most;
Should wee not wish him, whome wee held so deare
Before the parting of his blessed ghost?
Aliue wee lou'd him; dead, we loue him more:—
They loue him dead, that lou'd him not before. 192

But had wee lou'd him as our duty was,
Our dutie was t' haue crown'd his head with bay,
And not t' haue caus'd him, as wee haue, alas!
Ingratefull wee to make such hast away,
Ingratefull wee that were the cause of this,
Wee onely loosers are, yett hee a winner is. 198

Though hee hath lost his life, yet hath he wonne
A Crowne of Glorie in the highest spheare,
A Crowne that farre excells the midday Sunne,
The midday Sunne when as it shynes most cleare :
His Crowne excells an earthly Crowne as farre
As doth the Sunne excell a lesser starre. 204

Whom could it then haue greiu'd, if hee had seene
his manly face a Laurell garland weare ?
This honoure was his due, if it had bin
Ten tymes—nay, if a Thousand tymes—more deare ;
But some haue Crown'd his head, in stead of bay,
With foule reproach, as much as in them laye. 210

That head that was more fitt a crowne to weare,
Nor must, nor dare, I say, a crowne of Gold :
A Crowne of Gould, alas ! it were to deare ;
'Twere deare to gett, but dearer farre to hould.
Nor do I wish to see more Crownes than one,
And none to raigne but faire ELIS' alone. [lf. 180 bk.] 216

And let her raigne, Good God, as long as I
Or any other drawes his vitall breath ;
And let her liue, *and* let her neuer dye,
But rule till Christ shall come *and* conquer death.
Weare thou thy Crowne, ELISA ! 'tis thyne owne,
And keepe it still in despite of thy foen. 222

Weare thou thy Crowne, ELISA ! weare it still,
And prosper still, God graunt, vntill the end !
This haue I pray'd for thee.   Now, be it thy will,
That I may pray this one thing for a freend.
I can but wish It him, I can but craue it ;
If I could giue it him, he should surely haue it. 228

I wish him, then, a Crowne,—a Crowne of Bayes,
That he might triumph in his victors weed ;
Me thinks this might, Great QUEENE, prolonge thy dayes,
To see that Crownes should be thy subiects meede
Is't not an honoure, is't not a grace to thee,
To gouerne those that like Kings Crowned be ? 234

Although there bee I knowe, although not many,
Yet too, too many, if there be but two,[1]
That frett and grind there teeth, if there be any,
To whome we bend *and* more obeisaunce doe,
Some envie thee, wee envie stiłł *our* better :
Their better then thou art, but must remaine their debter. 240

Thou must remaine their debter for a tyme ;
And if thou neuer shalt discharg thy detts,
Yet know they liue that liuing still are thyne ;
Thy Sonnes wiłł truly tread their father's stepps,
Nor cease vntiłł they haue appeasde thy ghost,
With offering vp their blood to him they hated most. [If. 181.] 246

I cannot sleepe one winke, thy troubled spirit
Doth still pursue me wheresoere I goe.
I cannot rest by day, nor sleepe by night,
Thy Ghost still askes me what I meane to doe.
Reuenge ! Reuenge ! nought but revenge I heare ;
Revenge ! thy Ghost still soundeth in myne eare. 252

Me thought I saw Alecto stand amaz'de ;
Tisiphone did shake her ougly head,
And in my face the fell Mega'ra gaz'de,
And weeping sayd, looke, looke, here lyes hee dead.
The furies wept, the furies wept amayne :
What hart so hard that could from teares refraine ? 258

The furies wept to see earth's wonder lye,
And neuer stirre, nor mooue, nor draw his breath ;
They stood amaz'de to thinke that he could dye,
That foyled Mars in feild, and fear'd not death ;
They went to see him in his winding sheete,
And with there watery teares they washt his feete. 264

Three tymes they lifted vp his heade from grounde,
Three tymes I saw them kisse his paler browe,
Three tymes they daunc'de his sencelesse corps arounde,
Three tymes they stand stone stiłł, Three tymes they bowe
Them selues a-crosse, Three tymes I heard them sing
Haile, ESSEX ! hayle to thee ! all haile, our King ! 270

---

[1] Raleigh and Cecil are probably here alluded to.

With that mee thought I sawe them post away,
And carye him betweene them in the ayer,
And in a stately tombe his corps to laye,
Whither they may at their due tymes repayre,
And there solemnize with continuatt cries
His death, whose body there intombed lyes.   276

Mee thought againe I sawe when as my deare   [lf. 181 bk.]
Went to the Elisian plaines to take his place;
Mee thought I sawe when he aproched neare,
Thousandes of Soules stand stareing in his face :
They wondred much to see earths wonder there;
They wondred most of all that knew him heere.   282

I sawe how euerie Ghost did bend full lowe,
And crouche to him as soone as hee came nye :
Greene herbes, and Roses sweete, I saw them strowe,
As if some bridgrome were to passe therby.
Some looking stood, some gaz'd, mo prest to see;
But most did wonder who the same might bee.   288

As if some Commet, or some blasing starre,
Or strangest Meteor in the ayre had been,
Or els as if a flaming fyre from farre
In sylent night were on a suddaine seene ;
So stood each Ghost amazde, *and* could not tett
What they might thinke to see such ghosts in hett.   294

Or as a wearie trauailer should tread
His foote by chaunce vpon a deadly snake,[1]
Starts backe agayne, *and with* pale feare lookes dead :
Feare of the danger past doth make him quake.
Each ghost did quake and tremble for to see
Such Ghosts to passe the river Styx as hee.   300

Mee thought I sawe how Pluto was agast,
When sudayne newes was brought into his courte,
How DEVORAX the Stygian lake had past,
And thousandes dayly did to him resort :
Pluto for anger looked pale and wanne,
Till on a suddaine thus a Ghost began.   306

---

[1] See Virgil, ii. 379 :   "Improvisum aspris veluti qui sentibus anguem
Pressit humi nitens."

Most Soueraigne Lord, kinge of th' infernall deepe,
Prince of Auernus *and* of Acheron,
Lord of those plaines where blessed soules do sleepe,
Ruler of Lethe and obliuion ;
Great Pluto, whome th' infernatt Ghosts do feare,
Marke well my word*es, and* to my talle giue eare.　　312

There hath of late arriued at *our* Coast,
And hath already past the Stigian lake,
Some Princes spirit, some mightie monarchs ghost,
At sight of whome ech ghost in hell doth quake ;
Such glory shinneth in his manly face,
That Phoebus rides not w*ith* so great a grace.　　318

My self did see him, soone as ere he came ;
Come step by step, w*ith* such a maiestie,
That sure he was a man of muckle fame,
Of great renowme, *and* greater dignitye :
His gesture, gate, and cariage doth declare
He was not as the basser co*m*mons are.　　324

I surely thinke he was some goddese child,
For sure he cannot be of mortall blood ;
Or els some Nimph hath bin by chaunce beguil'd,
As shee was sporting in some pleasant wood :
Ioue surely spied some Nimph whereas she lay,
Shrouding hir self from heat of so*m*mers day.　　330

No mortall wight, no man, had euer power,
That such a mirhour from his loynes should springe ;
'Twas Ioue him-selfe that through the tiles did shower,
'Twas Ioue that mounted w*ith* the Egles winge,
'Twas Ioue that for Europa crossed the seas,
'Twas Ioue that like a Swanne did Leda please.　　336

Then lett me speake what I in hart conceaue,
That Ioue his father was, not any other ;
Why might not JOVE, that did so ofte deceiue
So many Queenes, also deceaue his mother ?
Nor is it any shame at all, but rather
A grace to one haue a God ones father.　　342

And if the ofspringe of the Gods may die,
And that their threed is by the sisters spunne,
Then sure I thinke (if none thinke so but I)
Some God his father is, he some Gods sonne.
No sparke of earthly mould in him is seene,
And such a Ghost as hee heere hath not bin.   348

But Looke you yonder, I need say no more,
See yonder where he comes, with what a grace !
Pluto, I thinke, ne're saw such Ghosts before,
Or seldome saw his like wit*h*in this place,
But marke his stature well, he is so tall,[1]
That by the head in height he exceeds them all.   354

Behould his foote, his legge, his comely knee,
Behould the round proportion of his thighe ;
Behould his wast, vouchsafe his breast to see ;
Behould his necke, his cheeke, his burning eye ;
Behould his mouth, his head, *and* all the rest :
Each member striues which shall become him best.   360

Men speake of Hector, of Achilles stoute ;
Oft haue I heard of Alexanders name ;
Of Ajax, Pyrrhus, all the Gretian route ;
Of Scipio, Pompey, and of Ceasars fame :
Yet that this one is dead, it greeues me more,
Then all the rest, whome I haue nam'd before.   366

It greiues my hart to see him in this place,
Because by right he should haue never dyed ;
And yet it Joyes me more to see his face
Then 't doth the Bridgrome to behould his Bride :   [lf. 183.]
One while it grieves me, then it maks me glad ;
One while I ioyfull am, one while more sadd.   372

My Soule is sad euen for their sakes aboue,
For them that haue so great a cause to playne,
For them *that* liue, and him so dearely loue,
For them *that* do so great a losse sustayne :
Iudge thou if they haue cause to mourne or noe ;
Iudge thou, great Pluto, if it be not so.   378

---

[1] MS. *tale.*

So spake the Ghost, when Pluto thus began,
I know right well, *and* marke what thou hast spoke ;
Nor hast thou lyed, for why, I know the man
Whose death so many doth to teares provoke ;
And, by my Crowne, my selfe can hardly keepe
Myne eyes from teares, but *that* they nedes witt weepe.   384

And I could weepe, if teares did not beseeme
A womans face, *and* not a manly spright ;
A womans teares men comonly esteeme
As *ignis fatuus* in a darkesome night :
Therfore, because myne eyes are teares forbidden,
My hart shatt shead his teares that there lye hidden.   390

My hart foregaue me soone as ere I heard,
Thy tongue but ginne so hard a tale to tell ;
And, by my scepter, How I was affraid,
Least some vnhappie chaunce there had befell.
Yet could I not suppose the end of it,
That hee was dead, that should not haue dyed yet.   396

Well, then, dispatch, make hast, and quickly runne,
You know the place wheras the sisters keepe,
Tett them from me *that* I witt haue them come,
They *that* haue caus'd so many eyes to weepe :
Goe fetch those haggs : why flyest thou not ? be breife. [lf. 183 bk.]
Although their sight witt nought decrease my greife.   402

They that haue made so manie weeping eyes,
Such heauie harts for his vntimely death,
For him whose corps on earth intombed lyes,
Whose soule with vs remaineth here beneath,
For him whose soule *and* body death could seuer,
For him whose body dyed, whose soule liues euer.   408

And shall they laughe when others nought but weepe ?
And shall they sing when others nought but crye ?
When others wake, shall they securely sleepe ?
And shall they lyue when as their betters dye ?
As I am Pluto, I witt make them know,
What 'tis for them to make their freind their foe.   414

As I am Pluto, and as Pluto liues,
As Pluto liues, *and* hath power to command,
As he hath power to punish him *that* striues,
Against his sacrede witt it to withstand,
So shall the fates soone see what Pluto can,
What Pluto witt do for so worthy a man.   420

Come, cursed Haggs.   Clotho, hould vp thy head;
Looke not a-squint, it will not serue thy turne:
Thou doest not heare the prayers for the dead,
Thou doest not see the teares of them *that* mourne,
Thou doest not heare the sighes of them *that* plaine,
For him whom thou, vile Hagg, of late hast slayne.   426

Is this the threed thou spunst, that should haue bin
A threed that should from East to West haue runne—
A threed the like wherof was neuer seene—
A threed the like wherof was neuer spunne?
Did I not charge thee that this threed should bee
No common one, but one as muche as three?   [lf. 184.] 432

And Lachesis striue not to hide thie head;
Thou hidest thie head, but canst not hide thie shame.
Thy sister   ¹ *and* thou drewst out the thred,
Which of you two deserves the greater blame?
Come, cursed hag, thie face thie fact bewrayes,
And thou that guilty art, thie guilty conscience sayes.   438

Is this that threed I charg'd thee draw in lenght,
That Nestors threed should not be halfe so longe?
Is this that threed I said should haue the strenght,
That Hector's threed should not be halfe so stronge?²
And is this thread, this stronge threed, drawen so weake,
That one poore little pull could make it breake?   441

Didst thou but heare the bitter plaints menn make
For losse of him whos threed to weake was spunne,
The heavy grones *and* outcries for his sake,
That should haue had a longer course to runne.
No, no, thou doest not heare the sighes they breath
ffor him whom thou, vile hag, hast done to death.   450

---

¹ Blank in MS.   ² MS. *longe*.

My eyes are wearied with continuall cries,
And often prayers which they daylie make.
One sayes he will a fat lame sacrifice,
One sayes he'le give a yong kid for his sake :
Thus euery one doth promise lesse or more,
If I would heare them, and their deere restore.　　　456

O that I could ! but now it is to late :
This threed is cutt that should haue lasted longe,
This threed is cutt by thee, thou cursed fate ;
Thou didst mistake the threed, thou didst him wronge.
See, Atropos, see how thou didst mistake ;
Thou didst him wrong, amendes thou canst not make.　　462

I knowe not if thou didst mistake or not ;　　　[lf. 184 bk.]
This threed, thou seest, hath not the lenght I bad :
Or yf thou didst of purpose Crosse me soe,
This threed hath not the strenght *that* should haue had.
Hold vp thie head, thou witch ; speake, answere me,
Thie fault is ne're the lesse, how so ere it be.　　　468

And, by myne honour, were it not for shame,
And that I thinke the god*es* would be displeas'd,
Y*our* wheele, yo*ur* spindle, and yo*ur* cursed frame,
Soone should be burnt, *and* ye soone should be eas'd,
Nor should my court.　　But that Ile beare in minde,
Till, for revenge, a fitter place I finde.　　　474

So Pluto spake, mee thought,[1] and more then this,
Much more then I in minde could safely keepe,
Nor beare away.　　My head so troubled is,
That eu*er*y sence seemes, as it were, a-sleepe :
My head so troubled is with greefe and care,
That all my sences, as no sences are.　　　480

My weeping eyes cannot discerne aright,
Dim'd with those teares that fell as fast as raine ;
Excesse of teares hath cleane obscured their light,
That blacke seemes white, *and* white seemes blacke againe.
Blacke seemes the swanne, white seemes the blacker crowe ;
Thus blacke frome white, my poore eyes scarcelie knowe.　486

And when I heare poore Philomela's songe,
Her mornfull songe, when she bewayles her fate,
Her wofull tunes in token of the wrong
W*h*ich wicked Tereus offred hir of late,
Her sweetest songe seemes but the screeching Cries
Of some vnlucky Owle by night that flies. 492

And when I smell the sweetest Gilliflower,
The faire Carnacian, and the lovely rose,
The sweetest odour seemes to me most sowre, [lf. 185.]
The sweetest smell doth make me stop my nose;
The stinckinge Carrion seemes to me to *smell*
More sweet then doth the sweetest daffadill. 498

And when I tast, my tast so altred is,
That gall seemes hony, hony gall anone;
And yf by Chaunce, my ladies lippes I kisse
Their tast to me seemes as I kiss'd a stone;
Yea Mopsaes lipps seeme to my tast as sweet,
As yf Pamelas lipps *and* myne should meet. 504

And when I feele, my feeling quite is gone,
That soft seemes hard, and heavy streight seemes light;
Soft, hard, light, heavy, is to me all one :
No sence I haue that can discerné aright.
I see, I heare, I tast, I feele, I smell,
And yett no sence I haue that Iudgeth well. 510

Alas! what shall I say? or who is neare
To whome I may my wofull case complaine?
Lives any one *tha*t will with equall care
Behold my greef *and* pittie me my payne?
O no, ther's none, ther's none *tha*t lives, I knowe,
That once will pitty me, sith I am so lowe. 516

But though that mortall men will neuer deeme
To see my teares, *and* heare the plaint*es* I make,
Yett will the god*es*, I hope, my teares esteeme,
Esteeme my teares *and* deepe sighs for his sake,
For his sweet sake, whose death so deere we see
That thousand*es* rather might haue dyed then he. 522

But if there bee one rose amonge the rest,[1]
That shewes aboue the rest his ruby head,
One tree that shewes aloft his lofty crest,
Soone are they blasted, soonest are they dead.
The fairest flower, the rose, is pluckt anone,   [lf. 185 bk.]
Whereas the stinckinge weed is lett alone.   528

MY ROSE is pluckt, my CEDAR hanges his head,
    Of my sweete flowre nought but the stalke remaynes,
My Ioy is quickly gon, my deare is dead.
Oh! how I heare how all the earth complaynes!
Oh! that my death might haue suffis'd for thyne!
Thy life was life to me, thy death is myne!   534

If euery member of my body were
A Body by it selfe substantiall:
Had I ten liues I should not count them deare,
So they from death to life my deare might call.
Could my life saue but one haire of thy head,
Thou doest not know how soone I could be dead.   540

And should I not vouchsafe to dye for thee,
Who whilst thou liued'st didst suffer so much wronge?
The wronge thou hadst it did pertayne to mee.
The bodyes payne runnes all the part*es* among;
Each member greeues when as the whole is troubled:
Though what one feeles is in the whole twise doubled.   546

What wronge thou hadst the earth may Iudge full well;
Though what thou didst deserue each man may gesse:
Great is the wrongs, the w*hi*ch no tongue can tell;
Great is the wronges, which no pen can expresse.
Ingratefull soyle! for what shall vertue serue,
If this be their reward that best deserue?   552

What was the cause why worthy Scipio did
Forbid vngratefull Rome his boanes should haue?
The same that might haue caus'd the to forbid

---

[1] In tho MS. this line was re-written at the end of the stanza by mistake in beginning a new one.

That this ingratefull land should be thy graue. [lf. 186.]
Thy bones, with Scipioes, might haue found a place,
A place more thankfull then *our* Ingland was. 558

But thou art dead, and thou hast left us thus :
I would thou wert not dead, or that I could
Steale fyre from heauen with Prometheus,
And make one like to thee of earthly mould.
Thy like?   That cannot be of earthly creatures,
Are faynt, effæminate, and tender natures. 564

Or that I knew where good Sybilla keepes,
She should conducte me to the golden bowe ; [1]
With her I would into th' infernall deepes,
And passing Styx, vnto the ghosts belowe.
There in ELISIUM would I spend the night,
In happy talking with my hart*es* delight. 570

But let me see the cause wherfore my deare
Was thus exiled from his soueraignes gate. ˄
We haue a Lawe cal'd Ostrocismus here,
A certayne Lawe the Athenians vs'd of late.
My Lord was by this lawe exiled I fynd :
The good must packe, the bad must stay behynd. 576

For this was Aristides forc'd to leaue
His natiue soyle, the place where he was borne ;
This Lawe of Ostrocisme did him deceaue ;
It makes some laugh, but many moe to mourne :
This Law of Ostrocisme by force doth make
My Lord this Land, and all his freend*es* forsake. 582

Well, then, sith Ceasar doth example giue,
Syth he 's fled from vs, from our selues wee'l fly ;
Then let vs dye, *and* not desyre to liue,
And let vs liue, *and* yet desyre to dye.
Lett's dye, lett's liue ; to dye or liue be loth : [lf. 186 bk.]
Let neither please vs, yet desyre them both. 588

---

[1] bough.   See Virgil, vi. 204 :
    " Discolor unde auri per ramos aura refulsit."

Now hee is gon, why should I stay behynd?
Why should I wander on this earth alone?
Nothing but shaddowes heare beneath I fynd:
I often talke, yet talke but to a stone;
And when I seeme far off a man to see,
Alas! alas! it is a silly tree.   594

And as I walkt alonge, my selfe and I
I spyed a man farr of vpon a playne;
He stoode stone still, till I had passed by.
I spoke to him; hee answered not agayne,
Yet bowed his head: alas! the wind did blow,
And made him stoope, and bend his head full lowe.   600

Why do I stay, sith that my deare is gone?
Hee rests aboue; why do I stay belowe?
Why should I wander on this earth alone?
ffayne would I dye, and yet I know not how.
Earth, swallow me, or ells permitt some tree
May fall vpon my head and murther mee!   606

I dye, yet liue, I dye a lingring life,
I liue, yet dye, I liue a lingring death;
Bothe life and death are with themselues at strife;
My sence is gone, and yet I draw my breath.
Fye, death! fye, fye, how long shall life withstand?
How long shall feeble life resist thy mightie hand?   612

O fatall howre when first I was begott,
yet farr more fatall was myne howre of birth,
Most fatall howre when as it was my lott
To see earths hope so soone departe the earth,
My life forespent, a life I cannot call;
Come quickly, death, and make amends for all.   [lf. 187.]   618

Heere will I sitt, and neuer hence depart,
This broad leau'd beech shall bee my canapie.
I will not hence till death hath throwne his darte,
Then shall I Tryumph in my victorie.
Heere sitt I downe, let me not rise agayne,
Then heare me, death, and ease me of my payne.   624

Viator.—God speede, my freend, why sittst thou heere so
    sadd ?
Thy lookes bewraye a discontented mynd.
Menalcas.—Indeed, my freend, more cause I neuer had,
    I seeke for that which in no place I fynd.
Viat.—Why, what ? if I so much may freely crauo.
Mena.—Nay, nought but that which I alreadie haue.   630

Viat.—Why seekest thou that of which thou art possest,
    And yet to fynd thou makest so much adoe ?
Mena.—I seeke it farre, though heere I sitt and rest,
    I haue it not, and yet I haue it to.
Viat.—And hauinge it, why doest thou seeke it more ?
Mena.—For more I want it then I did before.   636

Viat.—How canst thou want the thing that now thou hast ?
    Thou hast it not, *and* yet thou hast it to.
Mena.—I haue it now, but cannot hould it fast,
    I hauing, haue it not, *and* want it so.
Viat.—Thou hast, hast not. I pray thee tell mee plaine.
Mena.—I haue not now, and now I haue againe.   642

Viat.—I pray thee, man, deale plainly with thy freend.
    Why sitst thou heere ? why doest thou weepe so sore ?
Mena.—Still must I weepe, my teares must have no end ;
    Here must I sitt, and I must rise no more.
Viat.—No more ? Alas ! what art thou ? let mee know.
Mena.—Attend a while ; that I shall quickly shew.   648

Whilome I was, till fortune cross'd my fate,   [lf. 187 bk.]
A shepheard happye for my fruitfull flocke ;
And on those playnes pipinge I dayly sate ;
I fed my sheepe, and they increas'd my stocke ;
Heere had I tyme to tune my oaten reede,
Whilst my poore flocke did round about me feede.   654

I knowe there dwells no shephard on this coast,
Whose flocke did yeeld him more encrease then myne ;
There was no one that had more cause to boast,
Till fortune turnde her wheele, and ganne declyne :   ,
My Ewes came euery day twise to the payle,
But now scarce once, I know not what they ayle.   660

Vnless they sight, because I nought but weepe,
And will not feede, because I cannot eate.
Alas! poore soules! alas! poore sillye sheepe!
Why do you for my sake forsake your meate?
Feede on, my lambes; feede on, my tender kidds;
Spare not to eate; spare not, your master bidds.　　666

Let not the cause that keepes myne eyes from sleepe
Cause you refraine your foode thus euery day,
Let not the cause that makes my hart to weepe
Cause you, alas! thus causles pyne away,
Then cease to sight, poore sheepe! ye do me wrong;
Myne onely is the greife, to me it doth belong.　　672

Oh, how I lou'd my flocke! what care I tooke!
I loue it still, yet once I lou'd it more.
Both loue and hope made mee more nearely looke;
I loue it still, though not as earst before.
I lou'd my flock, although it was but smale,
Yet one poore one I loued best of all.　　678

The leader of my heard, for him I weepe;
My selfe haue lost my hope, my flocke their guide:　　[lf. 193.]
My hope is gone, the stay of all my sheepe;
So hee had liued, would all the rest had dyed!
Hee kept the rauenous wolfe *and* fox away;
And whilst he liued, my flock did ne're decay.　　684

Now hee is gon, the wolfe is waxen bould,
The Fox doth dare molest my tender lambes,
And fetch my kiddes out of the very fould,
And steale my simple sheepe out of my hands,
The wolfe *and* fox (thee dead) now dare do more,
They dare doe that they durst not doe before.　　690

Poore shepheard I, how my poore sheepe do stray!
And wander vp and downe they know not whither.
Alas! they know not in what place to stay,
Nor where to shrowd themselues from winters weather.
The wind, the rayne, snow, hayle, *and* every showre,
To kill my Kidds, and tender Lambes haue powre.　　696

Alas! my hope, my deare, my onely ioye!
O, ESSEX! ESSEX! whither art thou gon?
And what about shall I my witts employe,
To wayle thy death, thy absence to bemone?
Heare must I sitt *and* still bewayle thy death,
Whilst poore Menalcas liues *and* drawes his breath. 702

Viat.—What doest thou mumble thus? speake, speake it
      plaine,
Reueale thy greife, *and* so thou mayst fynd ease:
To keepe it in doth more augment thy payne;
To make it knowne doth it in p*ar*t apease.
Reueale thy greife, impart me halfe thy care,
Bee rul'd by me, *and* let me beare my share. 708.

To men may with more ease a burthen beare,
Two riuers do receue more store of rayne,
Two oxen w*i*th more ease the ground do reare,
Two Barnes do receiue more store of graine: [If. 188 bk.]
Then let two beare which is to much for one,
And let vs greeue alike, or both, or none. 714

Mena.—Why should I doubt my seacrets to reveale?
Why should I hyd them from so true a freend?
Why should I to my selfe my greifes conceale?
Why should I not bewray what I intend?
My paynes are ripe, my teares not farre behynde,
Yet still more cause of greife and teares I fynde. 720

Longe haue I wept, longe haue my watry eyes
Stream'd forth there sea-salt teares adowne my face.
Long haue I mourn'd, the wood*es* haue heard my cryes.
The trees haue seen my teares that flow'd apace,
The wood*es and* trees shall with me wittnes beare,
They heard mee weepe when all refused to heare. 726

They sawe me weepe, they saw me bownde to dye;
See in there barkes, see where my plaints are carued;
They heard mee nought but ESSEX! ESSEX! crye,
And weepe for him that best my teares deserued:
I wept for him, for him my teares I spend,
ffor him still must I weepe, my teares must haue no end. 732

III. 8

Viat.—What meanst thou, man? why doest thou ESSEX
    name?
  Or why is ESSEX wholly in thy mouth?
Mena.—Because hee was a man of mickle fame,
  Whose like hath neuer liued in all the south.
Viat.—Because hee was: why doest thou say because?
  As though he is not now, as ere before he was.   738

What though hee liues a prisoner for a tyme!
What though his body they in prison pen'd!
The name of prisoner nought augment*es* his cryme:
The bones obey, the mynd wiłł neuer bend;
Nor doth this dimme at ałł, or clipse his fame,
But soone shall adde more honoure to his name.   [If. 189.] 744

Looke how the sonne, when first he shewes his face
Out of a Misty Cloude, doth shine most cleare:
So likewise, after this supposd disgrace,
The name of ESSEX greater shall apeare.
A flaming fyre is farthest seene by night,
In clowdy tymes shałł vertue sbine most bright.   750

Because hee was? thou doest him double wronge,
As though his worthy fame were ought decayd,
He yet surviues, *and* shall, I hope, liue Longe
To helpe his freend*es*, and make his foes afraid.
He yet suruiues, he liues, his name doth liue,
Whose life doth life to many thousand*es* giue.   756

Mena.—What doth Menalcas heare? Alas! hee dreames!
His eares but flatter him, hee is deceaued;
His eyes are dimmed, gazeing on Titan's beames;
Each obiect hath eche sence of sence bereaued.
And can he liue? Oh, no! it cannot bee!
And could hee dye? Dead, dead, alas! is hee.   762

Viat.—What sayest thou, man? whome doest thou meane is
    dead?
Knowe this, that ESSEX liues; how could hee dye?
Each member dyes when they haue lost their head.
Had hee bin dead, I should not now bin I.
He liues, I liue, his life is life to mee,
Had hee bin dead, dead should I also bee.   768

Mena.—Alas! let not vaine hope my hart beguile,
Thou flatterest mee; how shall I trust myne eyes?
Let not vayne hope reuiue me for a while,
But let me end my wreatched dayes with teares.
If ESSEX liue, tell true, Oh! then, liue I!
If he be dead, Oh, then, alas! I dye!   774

[lf. 189 bk.]
Viat.—Why should I iest?   Hee liues, by heauen I sweare,
Nor do I flatter thee, but tell thee troth;
Then blest art thou, thou needst no longer feare,
And blest am I, so are wee happy boath:
Then sith suche happie newes Menalcas heares,
Cease now to weepe, at lenght abstayne from teares.   780

Mena.—O Heauens! O Earth! O all ye powers diuine!
Great JOVE! what sacrifice shall please thy mynde?
What shatt I offer at thy Holy shryne?
A Kydd? A Lambe? or ells a tender Hinde?
Great JOVE! and hast thou heard my wofutt prayer?
And doth my deare enioy the common Ayer?   786

Now is the tyme that I could wish to dye,
Sith that my deare doth yet aliue remayne.
I neede not weepe, I need no longer crye,
Why haue I wepte? giue me my teares agayne.
Could teares doe this, I haue moe teares in store,
Then keepe them still, I will not haue them more.   792

Finis.

A Poem made on the Earle of Essex (being in Disgrace with Queene Eliz): by mr henry Cuffe his Secretary.[1]

CONCERNING Henry Cuffe, who was executed[2] with Sir Gilly Merrick on March 13, 1601, less than a month after Essex himself, we have the following curious details from Wotton's Life, which I quote from the *Reliquiæ Wottonianæ* (London, 1651): "And whereas he (Wotton) was noted in his youth to have a sharp wit, and apt to jest; that, by time, travell, and conversation, was so polish'd and made usefull, that his company seem'd to be one of the delights of mankind. In so much, as Robert Earl of Essex (then one of the darlings of fortune and in greatest favour with Queen Elizabeth) invited him first into a friendship, and after a knowledg of his great abilities to be one of his Secretaries; the other being Master Henry Cuffe, sometimes of Merton Colledg in Oxford, and there the acquaintance of Sir Henry Wotton in his youth; Master Cuffe being then a man of no common note in the University for his learning, nor after his removall from thence for the great abilities of his mind, nor, indeed, for the fatalness of his end." We have also the following further

---

[1] Another copy of this poem, in Add. MS. 5495, fol. 28 bk., has this title: "These verses were pend by Robert late Earle of Essex in his first discontentment in þe moneths of July and August." Variations in this copy given in the footnotes are referred to as B. Another copy is in Douce MS. 280, fol. 123, but the variations are in most instances confined to ridiculous blunders. There are two other copies, one in Sloane MS. 1303, fol. 71, the other in Add. MS. 15,891, fol. 244 bk., the chief variations of which are given in the footnotes. See also Harl. MS. 4910, fol. 167.

[2] In the Tanner MS. 76, fol. 98, we have a copy of Henry Cuffe's speech at his execution at Tyburn, March 13th, 160$\frac{0}{1}$. It consists of a series of curious quibbles in the antithetical style of the period.

"MR. CUFF'S SPEECH AT HIS EXECUTION AT TIBURN.

"I am adjudged to Death for plotting a plott never acted; and for acting an Act, never by me plotted. The Law will have its course. Accusers shall be heard; Greatness must have the victory; Scholar & Martialist (whose Valor & Learning in Engld shd have priviledged, yet) in Engld must die like Dogs & be hanged. To dislike this is but Folly; to gainsay it is but Time lost; to avoid it impossible: But to endure it manly: & to scorn it magnanimity. The Prince is displeased; ye Law injurious; ye Lawyers uncharitable; & Death terrible. But I ask pardon of ye prince, forgive ye Lawyer; beseech ye world to pardon me; & welcome Death."

To this is appended the following allusion: "A strange prediction of his unfortunate end made by a Wizzard whom he consulted, 20 years before it happened."

account of this unhappy man, about whom, whether he was instigator or dupe of the plot of Essex, there does not seem to be any trustworthy account. "There was among his nearest attendauts one Henry Cuffe, a man of secret ambitious ends of his own, and of proportionate counsells smothered under the habit of a Scholler, and slubbered over with a certain rude and clownish fashion, that had the semblance of integrity. This Person,[1] not above five or six weeks before my Lords fatall irruption into the City, was by the Earl's special command suddainly discharged from all further attendance, or accesse unto him, out of an inward displeasure then taken against his sharp and importune infusions, and out of a glimmering oversight, that he would prove the very instrument of his Ruine.

"I must add hereunto, that about the same time my Lord had received from the Countesse of Warwick (a Lady powerfull in the Court), and indeed a vertuous user of her power, the best advice that I think was ever given from either sex; That when he was free from restraint, he should closely take any out-lodging at Greenwich, and sometimes when the Queen went abroad in a good humour (wherof she would give him notice), he should come forth, and humble himselfe before Her in the field. The Counsell sunk much into him, and for some days hee resolved it: but in the mean time, through the intercession of the Earl of Southampton, whom Cuffe had gained, he was restored to my Lord's ear, and so working advantage upon his disgraces, and upon the vain foundation of vulgar breath, which hurts many good men, spun out the finall destruction of his Master and himselfe, and almost of his restorer, if his pardon had not been won by inches."—The Parallel, p. 31.

[Harl. MS. 6947 (art. 32), lf. 230.]

1. It was a time when sillie Bees could speake,
    and in that tyme I was a sillie Bee,
  who suckt on tyme, vntill my heart gan[2] breake,
    yet neuer found that tyme would favour me.
      Of all the swarme, I onlie could not thrive,
      yet brought I wax, and hony to the hive.

---

[1] It is curious to note how Wotton, with the characteristic prudence which had apparently served him well in many important passages of his life, speaks in an off-hand and depreciatory way of a man who had at one time been his college friend, and seems at a later period (while both were in the service of Essex) to have been in very close relation with him.

[2] Sloane and Add. MSS. *did.*

2. Then thus I bussed when tyme no sap would give,
  why is this blessed tyme to me soe dere ?[1]
sith in this tyme, the lazie drone[2] doth live,
  the waspe, the worme, the gnat, the Butterfly.
   mated[3] with greefe, I kneeled on my knees,
   and thus complained, vnto the kinge of Bees.

3. " My leige, god graunte thy tyme may haue no[4] end,
  and yet voutsafe to heare my plainte of tyme,
which euery fruitles[5] fly hath found a freind,
  and I cast downe, while Attomyes doe Clime."[6]
   The kinge replies but thus, " peace, peevish[7] Bee,
   Th' art borne to serue the tyme, the tyme not thee."

4. " The tyme not thee,"—this word clipt[8] short my winges,
  and made me, wormelike, creepe[9] that once did flie.
Awefull regard, disputeth not with kinges, [lf. 230 bk.]
  receaveth a repulse, not askinge whie :[10]
   Then from that tyme, I for a tyme[11] withdrew,
   To feede[12] on Henbaine, Hemlock, Nettls, Rue.

5. But from those leaves noe dram of sweet I draine,
  theire[13] headstrong fury[14] did my wittes bewitch,
The iuce disperste blacke bloud in euery vaine,
  for hony gall, for wax I gathered Pitch :
   my Combe a Rift, My Hive a leafe must be,
   Soe Changd that Bees scarce tooke me for a Bee.[15]

6. I worke on weedes, when moone is in the waine,
  whilst all the swarme, in suneshine tast the Rose ;
On blacke roote[16] fearne, I sitt[17] and sucke my baine,
  whilst on the Eglentine, the rest repose :
   Hauinge too much, they still repine for more,
   And cloide with fulnes,[18] surfit on the store.

---

[1] Sl. and Add. *drye.* [2] B. *ones doe* for " drone doth." [3] Sl. *In a tyme.*
[4] Add. *never* for " haue no."
[5] Sl. *whom euery fearelesse* for " which euery fruitles."
[6] The reader will be reminded of Shakespere's line, " Drawn with a team of little atomies."—*Romeo and Juliet,* act i. scene iv.
[7] Sl. *foolishe.* [8] Sl. *cutt.* [9] B. *stoope* for " creepe."
[10] Add. *Receives Repulse, dares aske no Reason why.*
[11] Add. *a time I me* for " I for a tyme." [12] B. *suck* for " feede." [13] Sl. *my.*
[14] Sl. *fortune.* [15] Add. and Harl. 6910 *omit* this verse.
[16] Douce MS. *wort-fearne.* [17] Sl. *ferne loe I seeke* for " root fearne I sitt."
[18] Sl. *sweetenesse.*

7. Swolne fatt with feastes, full merelie they passe,
 in sweetned[1] Clustres they[2] fallinge from the Tree,
Where findinge me to nibble on the grasse,
 some scorne, some muse, and some doe pittie me :
 And some[3] envy and whisper to the kinge,
 Some must be still, and some must haue no sting.[4]

8. Are Bees waxt waspes or spiders to infecte ?[5]
 doe hony bowelles make the sperit galle ? [1f. 231.]
Is this the ioyce[6] of flowers to stirr[7] suspecte ?
 Ist not enough to treade on them that fall ?
 What stinge hath patience, but a sigheing greefe,
 That stinges naught but it-selfe without Releife ?

9. True patience the[8] provender of fooles,
 Sad patience that waiteth at[9] the dore,
Patience that learnes, thus to conclude in schooles,
 Patience[10] I am, therefore I must be poore :
 Greate kinge of Bees, that rightest euery wronge,
 Listen to Patience in her dyinge songe.

10. I Cannot feed on Fennell,[11] like some flies,
 nor fly to euery flower to gather gaine ;
myne appetite weites on my princes eies
 Contented with Contempte, and pleasd with Paine ;
 And yet[12] expectinge of[13] an happie hower,
 When he[14] shall saie, this Bee shall suck a flower.

11. Of all the greefes that moves my patience great,
 there is one that fretteth in the highest degree,
To see some Caterpillers bred vp[15] of late,[16]
 Croppinge the fruite[17] that should sustaine the Bee :
 yet smiled I, for that the wisest knowes,
 That mothes doe fret[18] the cloth, Cankers the Rose.

---

[1] B. *sweetest* for "sweetned."
[2] Sl. *swarmes and clusters* for "sweetned clustres they." Add. *sweltned clusters falling on a tree.*   [3] Sl. *some me* for "some."
[4] Douce MS. *nothinge.*   [5] Add. *afflict* for "infecte."   [6] Sl. *juice.*
[7] B. *staie* for "stirr."   [8] Sl. *is fitt* for "the."
[9] Sl. *watcheth still and keepes* for "that waiteth at."
[10] B. *Patient* for "Patience."   [11] Sl. *Hemlocke.*   [12] B. *tyme* for "yet."
[13] Sl. *I still expect* for "expectinge of." Add. *such* for "of."   [14] Sl. *shee.*
[15] Sl. *bird bredd* for "bred vp." Add. and Harl. 6910 *omit* "vp."
[16] Referring probably to Raleigh or Cecil.   [17] Sl. and Add. *flower.*
[18] Douce and Sl. *will eate.* Add. *the moath the Cloth, the canker eates the Rose.*

12. Once did I see by flyinge in the feeild   [lf. 231 bk.]
   Fowle beastes to browse vpon the Lylly faire;
 vertue and bewtie could no succour yeild,
    Als prouender for asses, but the aire :
      The partiall world of this takes litle heede,
      To give them flowers that should on Thistles feede.

13. Tis onlie I must draine Egiptian flowers,[1]
    Having noe savor, bitter sapp they haue,
 And seeke out[2] rotten tombes, and[3] dead men's bowers,
    And[4] bite on *Pathos*[5] growinge by the grave :
      yf this I cannot haue, as haples Bee,
      witching Tobacco, I will flie to thee !

14. What thoughe thou die mens longes[6] in deepest blacke,[7]
    A morninge habit suites a sable hart !
 What thoughe thy fumes[8] sound memorie doe Crack,[9]
    Forgetfulnes is fittest for my smarte !
      Ô vertuous fvme,[10] let it be carved in oke,
      That wordes, hopes, wittes, and all the world is smoke !

15. Five yeares[11] twise told, with promises perfumed,[12]
    my hope-stuft[13] head was Cast in to a slumber ;
 Sweete dreames of gold, on dreames I then presumd,
    And mongst the Bees thoughe[14] I were in the Nomber.
      wakinge I founde Hive,[15][16] hopes, had made me vaine,
      twas not Tobacco stupified the braine.[17]

Finis.

---

[1] The author was thinking of Pliny, whose "Natural History," is the great authority for many of the curious beliefs of our ancestors. See bk. xxi. chap. 40, "Nam et in Ægypto sine odore hæc omnia."

[2] Add. *the.*   [3] Add. *the.*

[4] Add. *to.*   " B. *Potthos.* Add. *wormewood.* Harl. 6910 *night-shade.*

[6] Sl. *my lunges* for "mens longes."   [7] Add. *omits* the two last stanzas.

[8] B. *frynds* for "fumes."   [9] B. *lack* for "crack."   [10] B. *fame* for "fume."

[11] Sl. *tymes.*   [12] Sl. *promise vnperformed.*

[13] Sl. *hopes iust* for "hope-stuft."   [14] B. *thought* for "thoughe."

[15] B. *how* for "hive."   [16] Sl. inserts *but.*

[17] Tobacco must have been a great novelty in England at this time. "Sir Walter Raleigh was the first that brought tobacco into England and into fashion. . . . They had first silver pipes. The ordinary sort made use of a walnut-shell and a straw. I have heard my grandfather Lyte say, that one pipe was handed from man to man round the table. Sir W. R. standing in a stand at Sir Ro. Poyntz's park, at Acton, took a pipe of tobacco, which made the ladies quit it till he had done."—Aubrey.

[Tanner MS. 306, fol. 192*r*.]

Elegy on the E[arl] of Essex.

CONCERNING the authorship of this poem I am unable to furnish
any information.

O England, now lament in teares ;
in teares lament the dismall fall
of an heroick english peere,
as eu*er* liu'd or eu*er* shall,
whose soule so sweet doth rest on high,
to liue w*i*th christ eternally.   6

His neu*er* dying fame remaines,
although his bodies clad in Clay ;
w*i*th angels blest his soule it raines
in Joyes that neu*er* shall decay :
his vertuous life deserues to be
carud out in oke for men to see.   12

ffor by his hand o*u*r clime got fame,
by Essex helpe much gould we gaind,[1]
and by his force our foes were tamd,
for in his hart trew valor raind :
his hand, helpe, force, and vertuous hart,
hath bred o*u*r weale, and causd o*u*r smart. 18

ffor whilst he liud o*u*r weale was bread,
so was his death o*u*r cause of mone.
by whom shall souldiers now be led,
syth th*a*t theer Captaynes dead and gone ?
w*i*th teares they do his dath deplore,
but teares cannot his life restore.   24

O Poetes all, leaue of to penne
ffond trillinge toyes of Loues delight,
And frame *your* wittes t' advaunce such men
as Devorax, th*a*t worthy wight !
In polisht poemes sounde his prayse,
To Crowne *your* heades w*i*th lawrell bayes. 30

---

[1] Alluding to the capture of the ships on the expedition to Cadiz and the
Island voyage. For the abundance of the plunder see Lingard, vi. 275.

Learninge he healde in great regarde,[1]
Because therin none coulde him reache,
And schollers paynes he would rewarde;
And such as did the gospell preache
He reverenste still; vnhappy we,
That lost soe soone his companye!   36

A second Marce he was of myghte,
Appolloes witt ador[n]ed his minde,
Noe pen was able to recite
The gistes[2] of god to him assynde;
But envye, that foule monstrous feynde,
Hath broughte to death true vertues frynde.   42

The Spaniarde prowde can well reporte
The deeds of armes that he hath done;
So witnesse canne theyr battered forte;
And stately Cales[3] he manly wone,
And in despight of Spanishe pride,
Eyght dayes he did therin abide.   48

To see of Philippe wo[uld] re[deeme]
His conquered towne [with gold] of [Spayne],
But when he saw his light esteeme,
The towne on fyre he settes amayne;
But to his men strayght Charge he gave,
That Mayds & Wiues noe hurte should have.[4]   54

Wherin his mercy macht his mighte,
true Vertues giuen him from aboue,
Rich natures giftes on him were dighte,
Whiche drawe from men both feare & loue.
A moses mild in towne was hee;
In feyld forre Samson deemed to be.   60

Two stately shippes[5] he lickwise wone,
And Englands armes on them advanced,

---

[1] With reference to his manner towards his dependeuts, Macaulay says that Essex "conducted himself with a delicacy such as has rarely been found in any other patron. Unlike the vulgar herd of benefactors, he desired to inspire, not gratitude, hut affection. He tried to make those whom he befriended feel towards him as towards an equal." The Queen appears to have been irritated hy the amount of sermonizing in favour of Essex, which was practised by zealous clergymen.   [2] =gestes.

[3] Cadiz, frequently so called iu old poetry. See the ballad in Percy's Reliques.

[4] I have already alluded to the strict discipline maintained by Essex in his army.

[5] Two of the largest, the St. Matthew and St. Andrew, with an argosy, were taken.—Lingard vi. 275.

Which Cesars actes, when he had done,
Into the deepe he forthwith lancste ;
Hoystinge vp sayles to Cutte the streames
That shine agaynst the sunne bright beames.　　66

The fishes plaid in signe of Joy,
and mermaids carrold songs of glee ;
with wind the silken fluds did toye ;
and neptune chargd his tritons three :
for his returne the trumps to sound,
with ekkoing noyse they did abound.　　72

His Cullers he hath spred in france,
in honor of our Royall queene ;
where death hath sat vpon his lance,
wher as in battaile he hath bin :
the papish posts he sent to hell
that did against their king rebell.　　78

Rebellious townes he taught to know
allegance due vnto their king,
as quene Rene,[1] and other more,
with to subiection he did bring :
all france admird this english gere
& king therof held him full dere.　　84

when Don Anthonio was displaced
by spaniards from his princly throne,
and being so by them disgracd,
to Englands queene, he made his mone.
ten thousand men she him sent,
among them, then, braue Essex went.　　90

when as at Lisborn he ariud,
such haughty prowess he did show,
when at their gate his feet he draue,
which strook amasment to his foe :

---

[1] Alluding to the assistance sent by Elizabeth to Henry IV. "Rene" is
probably Rouen, which was invested by the Earl of Essex, assisted by some French
troops, in 1591. Don Antonio was an illegitimate nephew of Henry, King of
Portugal, and a pretender to the throne. The expedition, commenced by Drake
and Sir John Norris, and afterwards joined by Essex, was a failure. Sickness
was very rife among the English : the Portuguese viewed the pretensions of Don
Antonio with contempt, and the expedition returned to England with less than
half of its original numbers.

During the*ir* prowess to proue in fight,
Anthonio was their king by right.   96

" [op]en y[our] gates, therefore," quoth he,
"and entertaine with Joy your king,
your fo[rm]er faults forgotten be ;
from him I do yo*ur* pardon bring.
o doe not then your King depose,
that holds you deare and hates your foes." 102

But at his words they sett but light,
discharging shot at him amaine ;
yet ner dismayed o*ur* english knight
but valiantly did still remaine :
drawing his poniard from his side,
wheron a silken scarfe he tide.   108

And on their gate he lefte the same,
returning to his Company :
w*hich* deeds be eternized by fame
for noble acts of Cheualry.
Spaine, france and portingall did feele
his fauchions force of tempred steele. 114

As Phoebus brightnesse far exceeds
ech twinkling star and Lunas light,
so much and more did Essex deeds,
beyond all other shine far bright ;
what should I saie, god to him gaue
all vertuous gifts that man might haue. 120

when tilt and barriers force were seene,
sweet Deuorax still great honor wonn ;
for Courtiers weale and Englands queene,
ther were no dangers he would shun :
but dead he is, why should we mone ?
O yes, bycause he died so soone !   126

Long since was Alexander kild,
and haniball did feele like paine,
Pompeus, penis,[1] both were spoyled,
& scipio, Cirus, Cesar slaine :
in vertu and valor thes had p*ar*t,
yet subiect vnto deaths black dart.   132

---

[1] ? Pyrrhus.

Wit*h*in the tower he lost his head,
in view of many noble peres :
whi*c*h on there harts great sorrow bread,
and from their eyes ran perles teares.
on skaffould then ariued he,
attird in black, w*i*th prelats three. 138

Vayling his hat,[1] the lords to greet,
his velvet gowne he then layd by,
and spake to [them] theise words so sweet :
" my frends th*a*t come to see me die,
to god his glory I confesse,
my sinnes, like sands, ar numberles. 144

" yet papist haue I neu*e*r bin,
and Athisme still I did disdaine ;
I neu*e*r wrongd my Royall queene,
but prayd to god for her long Rayne :
and god w*i*th shame confound them all,
that seche to worke he*r* graces fall ! " 150

Then for the Counsell prayed he,
and for the Clergy of the land,
and for the pore comunalty,
that long in peace their weale might stand ;
then privatly his prayers he sayd,
desiring god of heuenly ayd. 156

Then headsman humbly on his knee,
be[gged] for his death forgiuen to be ;
" w*i*th all my hart I pardon thee,
and welkome, frend, thin act to me ;
& when thou seest me spread my handes,
vnto the taske see that thou standst." 162

then w*i*th thes wordes his life had end,
after on block his head was layd :
" sweet Christ, from heuen thy angels send,
my soule by them to be conveyd
Vnto thy throune of maiesty,
to liue in blise eternally." 168

. finis.

---

[1] This description of the conduct of Essex at his execution exactly corresponds
with the account given in the narratives of eye-witnesses, now for the first time
published, *antè*, pp. 208–213.

[Harl. MS. 6910, lf. 151.]

[Robert Earle of Esser against Sir Walter Rawleigh.]

HERE we have another lamentation over the malice of the enemies
of Essex. The "Cuckoo" may be easily identified, and is surely
an allusion to Raleigh. Another copy of this poem is found in
Add. MS. 5495, fol. 28, from which the above title and some
variations are given.

MUSES no more, but Mazes[1] be *your* names,
Where Discord[2] sound shall marre *your* concorde sweete,
Vnkyndly now *your* carefull fancye frames,
When fortune treads *your* fauours vnder feete :
    But foule befalle that cursed *Cuckoes* throt,
    That soe hath crost sweet *Philomelaes* note !   6

And all vnhappie hatched was that bird,
That parret-like can never cease to prate ;
But most vntymely spoken was that word,
That brought the world in such a woefull state,
    That *Loue* and *Likeing* quite are ouerthrowne,
    And in their place are hate[3] and sorrowes growne.[4]   12

Is this the Honoure of a Haughtie thought,
For *Louers* hap to haue all spight a Loue ?
Hath wreached skill thus blinded reason taught,
In this conceipt such discontent to mooue ?
    That *Beautie* so is of her selfe berefte,
    That no good hope of ought good hap is lefte ?[5]   18

Oh let no *Phœnix* looke vpon a *Crowe*,
Nor daintye Hills bow downe to dirtye dales ;
Let neuer Heauen an Hellish Humour knowe,
Nor firme affect[6] give eare to foollish tales :
    For this in fyne will fall to be the troth,
    That pudle[7] watter makes vnholsome broth.   24

Woe to the worlde, the sonne is in a clowde,
And darksome mists[8] doth ouerrunne the day,
In Hope[9] conceipte is not content[10] allow'd,
Fauour must dye *and* fancye weare awaye :   [151 bk.]

---

[1] Add. *Marzes* for "Mazes."   [2] *whose discords* for "where discord."
[3] *is greife* for "are hate."   [4] *sowen* for "growne.   [5] Add. *omits this stanza.*
[6] *aspect* for "affect."   [7] *filthy* for "pudle."   [8] *mist* for "mists."
[9] *high* for "hope."   [10] *content is best* for "is not content."

Oh Heauens what[1] Hełł ! The bands of Loue are broken,
Nor must a thought[2] of such a thing[3] be spoken.　　30

Mars must become a Coward in his mynde,
Whiles Vulcan stands to prate of Venus toyes :　　.
Beautie must seeme to go against her kinde,
In crossing Nature in her sweetest ioyes :
　　But Oh ! no more, it is to much to thinke,
　　So pure a mouth should puddle watters drinke !　　36

But since the world is at this woefułł passe,
Let Loues submission Honours wrath apease ;
Let not an *Horse* be matched with an *Asse*,
Nor hatefułł tongue an happie hart disease :
　　So shałł the world commend a[4] sweet conceipt,
　　And Humble fayth on heauenly Honour waite.
　　　　　　finis.　　Comes Essex.　　42

[MS. Bibl. Reg. 17 B. ʟ. leaf 2.][5]

𝖁erses made by the Earle of Essex in his Trouble.

Essex here laments the unmanageable character of the Queen, or
is represented as so doing.

The waies on earth haue paths and turnings knowne,
The waies on Sea are gone by needles light,
The birds of th'aire the nearest way have flowne,
And vnder earth the moules do cast aright :　　4
A way more hard then these I needs must take,
where none can teach, nor noe man can direct,
where noe mans good for me example makes,
But al mens[6] faults doe teach her to suspect.　　8

Her thoughts and myne such disproportion haue ;
All strength of loue is infinite in mee ;
She vseth the aduantage tyme and fortune gaue
Of worth and power, to gett the libertie.
Earth, Sea, Heaven, Hell, are subiect vnto lawes ;
But I, poore I, must suffer, and knowe noe cause.　　14
　　　　　　R : E : E :

---

[1] Add. *oh* for "what."　　[2] *word* for "thought."
[3] *thought* for "thing."　　[4] *your* for "a."
[5] There is another copy of these verses, with little or no variation, in Sloane
MS. 4128, fol. 14*b*.　　[6] MS. nens.

[Add. MS. 15,226, lf. 6b.]

The disparinge complainte of wretched Rawleighe for his treacheries wrought ag*ainst* the worthie Esser.

FOR allusions to the hostilities prevailing between Raleigh and Essex, see pages 30 and 197. Cuffe is said to have urged Essex to remove Cecil, Cobham, and Raleigh from the Queen's Councils at whatever cost. This poem, which is anonymous, must have been written by a great admirer of the unfortunate Earl—and he had many.

To whome shall cursed I my case complaine,
to moue some pittye of my wretchles state?
for thoughe noe other comfort dothe remaine,
yet pittye would my greife extenuate.
but oh! I haue deserued nought but hate,
 For I towards God & man my-self abused,
 & therefore am of god & man refused.   7

To heauen I dare not lifte my wretched eies,
nor aske God p*ar*don for my wicked deeds;
for I his word & service did despise,
esteeminge them of noe more worthe then weeds;
from w*hi*ch most vile conceite theise woes p*ro*ceeds.
 For now I finde, & findinge, feare to rue,
 theire is a god w*hi*ch is both iust & true.   14

And vnto men I likewise am affraide
to make complaint, of this my gnaweinge greife,
Least they, as well they may, should mee vpbraide
w*i*th scorne & pride, w*hi*ch in mee were most rife;
& therefore man will yeild mee not Relefe.
 Thus wretched I, w*hi*ch euery man did scorne,
 am now my-self of eu*er*ie man forlorne.   21

What shall I doe in thys p*er*plexed plighte,
Fearinge to moue to god or man for grace?
shall I to heavenly Saints my wooes recite,
in hope that they will moue my wretched case?
O noe: It is theire office and theire place
 To iudge such guiltie sinfull soules as I,
 and therefor noe releif may come thereby.   28

Yet one there is of that Cælestiall sorte,   [lf. 7.]
whoe sure I thincke would pitty my distresse;
For when hee liued here, in earthly porte,
hee was the patterne of all gentlenes.
Ah! but gainst him I greatly did transgresse:
   Then, traitor vile, how canst thou hope for grace
   from him whome thou by treason didst displace?   35

O yes, I knowe his vertues here were such,
Hee did abhorre to beare revengeinge minde;
and beeinge there, they bettered are by much,
because he liues remote from fleshlie kinde,
in perfect ioye to blessed Saints assigned.
   A worthy Essex! but for feare and shame,
   I would invoke thy honorable name!   42

But 'ere I can exspect Comiseracion,
I must intreat forgiuenes hartilie;
and 'ere forgiuenes can haue Confirmacion,
I must confesse howe I haue iniured thee:
For it with reason rightlie doth agree,
   That such a wrongfull wicked wretch as I
   should first confesse, and then for pardon crye.   49

Wherefore I will my clogged conscience cleere,
by true confession of my treacherie,
That God & angells, Saints and men may heare,
howe I thy honor wrong'd most shamefully,
which on my-selfe is lighted suddainely:
   For this my due deserts, now falne on mee,
   plainely declares my treason wrought gainst thee.   56

For when thy soueraigne did thee well respect,   [lf. 7 bk.]
as well thou didst deserue to bee respected,
I then with falshood did thy truthe infect,
whereby her princely Iudgment was infected,
and thou by her most causelessly reiected;
   Then I, which on occasion did attend,
   omitted nought which might thee mee offend.   63

III.   T

For then with open throate I did not spare
to taxe thy vertues most reprochfullie;
Thy vallour was ambition, I would sweare;
thy curteous bounty, hope of soueraigntie;
thy Justice, mallice and extremitye;
    And thy religious vale I ofte would call
    dissimulacion to deceaue with-all.   70

Thus with detraccion I did first assaile thee,
whoe did effect what shee did vndertake;
Then envie wrought that nothinge might availe thee,
Though truthe thy iust Apologie did make;
Then framed treason brought thee to the stake;
    That to assaile thee with theese furies fell,
    I pawnd my soule to fetch them out of hell.   77

I allsoe hadd assistance in this worke,
whose helpinge hands were in as deepe as myne,
though some of them aloof now slily lurke,
as if theire consciences were sole devine;
yet in a league with mee they did combine
    Thee to destroye by treasons pollicie,
    which was effected to our Infamye.   84

But some of my Confederates in this act,   [lf. 8.]
whose dates of mischeif did with myne expire,
are fallne with mee in this pretended fact,
prepar'd to paie our due deserued hire,
nowe, if it were not sinne, I would desire
    That all which wrought with mee in this disgrace
    might stand with mee in this my wretched case.   91

But what should I need doubt or stand in stare,
that they shall scape revenge, more bare than I;
sure hee whoe hath intrapt mee in this snare
can traverse them in theire owne pollicie,
and will, noe doubt, when hee due tyme dothe see,
    For hee will punishe everie treacherous case,
    either in this or in a worser place.   98

And therefore, thoughe they florishe for a tyme
in Grace, authoritye, and honors great,
w*h*ich maie pe*r*swade them they may easily climbe
vpp to y⁰ highest stepp of Fortunes state,
yet is theire one whoe can theire hopes deseate,
   For when they thincke themselues in highest respect
   then suddainely hee can them soone deiect.   105

Witnes my self, whoe thought my self as sure
as anie one of my associates all;
but now I finde treason caunott indure,
insultinge pride will likewise haue a fall,
for such offences doe for vengeance call;
   And bee w*h*ich is the remedie of wronge
   hathe said his vengance shall not tarry longe.   112

W*h*ich by experience I haue found most true;   [lf. 8 bk
for in the self same kinde that I offended,
hee iustlie hath repaide to mee my due;
his iustice therefore needs must bee comended,
w*h*ich hath it-selfe soe equallie extended,
   vsinge the meanes of my owne foule offence
   to giue to mee a righteous recompence.   119

For as by letters I procur'd thy bane,
w*h*ich of a pe*r*iur'd villaine I d*i*d buye,
whoe for comoditie hadd stollne the same
from her to whome thou sent'st them faithfully,
containeinge nought but truthe & modestie,
   Yet I, w*h*ich knew they would thee much infest,
   did spare noe cost till I hadd them possesst: 126

Soe I throughe lett*e*rs, of contrarie kinde
to those of thine, am now adiudged my meed;
for when all other p*r*omises did fayle
mee to offend in this pretended deed,
my opposites more strictlie did p*r*oceed,
   And then a letter did gainst mee p*r*oduce,
   for w*h*ich my cuninge lacks a cleane excuse.   133

And thus, as I by le*tt*ers thee offended,
by le*tt*ers nowe my owne offence was provde;
vile Traito*u*r I, that ill gainst thee intended,
whoe for desert I rather should haue lovde;
pride, spite, & mischief thereunto me movde,
　　And now mee-thincks dispaire dothe mee surprize,
　　settinge thy wrongs before my wretched eyes.　　140

For when I heard my-selfe exclaim'd vppon　　[f. 9.]
by him whose mouthe, Mastivelike, revilde thee,
then thought I howe I laughinge stood by one
whose cankred hart broke out & much defild thee,
and still wee laught, to thinke howe wee beguild thee.
　　I then did praise the barker's mouthe for spendinge;
　　but now he hathe mee plaug'd for then offending.　147

And now I finde it dothe my conscience gall,
that wee suborn'd a *Judas* to betray thee;
whoe tould thee, when the Counsell did thee call,
that I & *Cobham* by the waye would slaie thee;[1]
advisinge thee therefore for to staie thee;
　　And thus by fraud wee forc'd thee to offend,
　　by disobayenge when the lords did send.　　154

It now likewise dothe greeve mee, though too late,
that wee procurd thy Prince thee to imploye,
whilest in thy absence wee might worke thy hate,
by vrginge thou didst purpose to annoye
thy loueinge Country, & thy Prince destroye;
　　And more, to stare her with that foule intent,
　　wee raised force thy comeinge to prevent.　　161

But well wee knewe thy meaneing was not such,
thoughe wee pretended soe thee to abuse,
hoping thereby wee might encrease soe much
thy soueraignes hate that shee would quite refuse
to heare thee speake with truthe this to excuse;
　　And sure wee were wee should our purpose gaine,
　　if from her presence shee would thee restraine.　168

---

[1] Lord Cobham, one of the most uncompromising enemies of Essex: he was implicated with Raleigh in the conspiracy to place Arabella Stuart on the throne at the beginning of the reign of James I., and sentenced to death, but afterwards reprieved on the scaffold.

When falselie thus wee hadd the queene possest   [lf. 9 bk.]
with this conceite, that thou hadst plotted treason,
wee likewise then our pollicies addrest
to trayne thee over by some subtill reason,
whereof our consultations were not geason;[1]
  For I have heard, thoughe here it may seeme grosse,
  holy's the churche where sathan beares the crosse. 175

Then wee did blowe abroade the Prince was dead,
thinckinge thereby to further our intent;
for then we hopt thou sure wouldst gather head,
and come with speed invasion to prevent;
for wee before of cuninge purpose sent
  That Spanish expedicion was in hand,[2]   181
  the which wee knewe thou stronglie woldst withstand.

But here our expectacion somewhat faded,
because thou didst not come when wee expected,
nor in that manner as wee hadd persvaded;
thou men'st to come when first thou was detected,
yet wee soe wrought that thou wast quite reiected,
  And eke restrained of thy libertie,
  the which wee labored most incessantlie.   189

Now when wee hadd *our* wishes thus obtained,
we lefte noe tyme *our* mischeifes to devise;
For then false Articles wee forged & fained,
wherewith wee dimm'd thy soueraignes princely eyes;
and then did every one against thee rise,
  like as a single hound by Currs ore matched,
  once beeinge downe, by every Curre is snatched.   196

Then for Starrchamber wee did worke a-pace,   [lf. 10.]
pretendinge thou shouldst presentlie appeare,
and there by order answer face to face
such articles as should concerne thee neare;
but this was neuer meant, the case is cleare,
  for well wee knewe, if thou shouldst there haue spoken,
  our knott of treacherie might haue beene broken. 203

---

[1] scarce.—Halliwell.

[2] In 1598 the English were again apprehensive of a Spanish invasion. Preparations were apparently made by the ministers of Philip III, the new king, but they ended in nothing. The kingdom was, however, put in a state of defence. Essex was forbidden by the Queen to leave his command in Ireland: his enemies were apprehensive that he might return to England to drive them from court, and therefore procured the order. See Lingard, vol. vi. p. 292.

But wee a farre more clearer shifte devised
then that thou shouldst haue answered *our* obiection,
for wee *p*rocur'd thy falle to bee surmised;
thou beeinge absent, oh vile lawes infection !
and censured as wee hadd giuen direction ;
    for wee soe wrought thy prince by subtill sawes
    y^t what wee willed was of more force then lawes.   210

The yce was broken, then wee grewe more bold,
in course of violence forward to *p*roceed ;
for then all offices w*hi*ch thou didst hould
wee purg'd thee of, as wee before decreed,
thereby more discontent in thee to breed :
    thus when wee hadd occasion stirdd to ire,
    wee gaue the scope y^t shee might kindle fire.   217

But when wee sawe occasion, nought *p*revailed
w*i*th furious blast the fier to inflame;
but as the more she wrought, the more she fayl'd,
because coole patience still the heat orecame ;
for iuce of her by grace was on the same :
    wee then another stratagem devised,
    by w*hi*ch thou was most cuningly surpriz'd.   224

And this was slye & subtile subornac*i*on,   [lf. 10 bk.]
with *p*romis*es* of very large extent,
w*hi*ch gain'd vs one w*i*th thee in estimac*i*on,
and in thy private favo*ur* resident :
of him wee made our workinge instrum*en*t,
    thee to *p*erswade, to gaine thy form*er* grace,
    by vsinge meanes thy hinderers to displace.   231

But when hee tould vs thou was well contented .
to liue a private life, remote from care,
the modell of a *p*roiect wee invented,
wherein hee might his loue to thee declare,
by giueinge helpe the state for to repaire;
    to w*hi*ch, when hee had gotten thy consent,
    wee hadd our purpose & our whole intent.   238

For then wee doubted not to pricke thee on,
by subtill force of forged instigac*i*on,
w*h*ich wee alreadie hadd resolued vppon,
to stirre thee vpp to secrett consultac*i*on,
for resoluc*i*on and determinac*i*on,
   of meanes and tymes, of present execution ;
    loe thus wee wrought thy vtter dissolution.   245

Yet this my true detestable Confession
is but the abstract of my villanye ;
for I haue wrought more treacherous transgressions
against thy hon*our*, truthe, & loyaltie,
then now I can recall to memorye ;
   For w*h*ich, w*i*th sighes, all desp*er*ate of releefe,
    I crauo for p*ar*don to aszwage my greefe.   252

And as for this offence wee nowe intended,   [f. 11.]
I doe not doubt but I shall favo*ur* finde ;
but what can my estate bee thereby mended ?
for still I shall retaine a guiltye minde,
for w*h*ich I can noe place of refuge finde ;
   for every man will kill mee w*i*th his eye,
    & therefore twere most ease for mee to dye.   259

For I such Terror in my Conscience feele,
by thought of my most execrable deeds,
that [though] my hart obdurate bee as steele,
yet when I thincke thereon, it quakes & bleeds,
such peircinge passions from them still p*r*oceeds :
   Oh since I haue confessed then the truthe,
    Forgiue mee, then, and pittye this my ruthe !   266

But if thou wilt not daigne to pittye mee,
then must I eu*er* pittiles remayne ;
for all that liues laughes at my miscrie,
except some fewe, and they I thincke doe faigne,
fearinge I should theire falshood vile explaine :
   Thus like a Cursed Catiffe did I liue,
    and now my cursed case dothe noe man greive.   273

Finis.

SIR WALTER RALEIGH.

THE following poem was probably composed by one of the admirers of Essex, who keenly anticipates the disgrace and punishment of the unfortunate Earl's rival. Raleigh is accused of avarice, pride, sensuality, and lying. The verses seem to belong to the beginning of the reign of James I., when Sir Walter was implicated in the plot for placing Arabella Stuart on the throne, tried at Winchester in 1603 and found guilty. Cecil had now completely shaken off Raleigh, and the two confederates in the ruin of Essex were endeavouring to supplant each other.

Many of the accusations brought against Raleigh by the anonymous versifier are fully substantiated. He was one of the most flagrant instances of the gross abuses of the system of monopolies, having enjoyed a very lucrative patent for licensing the sale of wine, which was subsequently augmented as a reward for his services at the time of the Armada. He seems to have been at all periods of his life amenable to bribes, and some of the offenders implicated in the Essex affair were glad to purchase his good offices by large sums of money. A Mr. Littleton is said to have paid him £10,000. That his private life was licentious is well known, and Aubrey quaintly assures us that he was "damnable proud;" but we may perhaps be pardoned for an inclination to forget these defects, when we consider the gallant general, the man of courtly and chivalrous action, the scholar and poet.

If his memory pales among us, he will not be forgotten by our transatlantic kinsmen. In the earlier half of the seventeenth century America was the exercising ground of all the most rarely attempered, the noblest and the most gallant spirits; and among them all no finer one could be found than Raleigh.

To recapitulate the events of his life would be but to make a dry catalogue of facts known to every reader. Thus much may suffice. He was born in 1552 in Devonshire—one of Devon's choicest worthies—and was for some time a student at Oriel College, where, as Wood says, "he was worthily esteemed a proficient in oratory and philosophy." He afterwards served as a volunteer in France and the Netherlands; but his most interesting undertaking was the attempt to found a colony in Virginia in 1584—memorable for ever as the first English settlement on that continent, although the plan was not at first successful. It is thus that the name of Raleigh must be for ever associated with the "Old Dominion."

His intrigues against Essex I have already spoken of. They form the most discreditable passages of his life, and one would willingly forget the scene of Sir Walter viewing the execution of his fallen rival. After a long imprisonment, during which he composed his "History of the World," he was allowed to equip thirteen vessels in 1617, with a view of opening a mine in Guiana; but the expedition resulted in a complete failure, and his eldest son was slain at St. Thomas. On his return,[1] the Spanish ambassador complained of the expedition to James as being piratical; and the English monarch, who at that time was anxious to bring about the marriage of his son with the Infanta, readily sacrificed a man for whom he had never had a great predilection. In a Spanish life of Diego Sarmiento de Acuña, Conde de Gondomar, the ambassador previously mentioned, published at Madrid in the year 1622, we find it recorded with a flourish of triumph that he caused the head of the English General, Walter Raleigh, to be cut off (hizo cortar la cabeça al General Ingles Whaltero Rale); and of the same important individual we are told that he chastized the insolence of the bold English pirate, Francisco Draques.[2] Whatever the causes may have been, Raleigh perished on the scaffold on the 29th of October, 1618. In his last moments he comported himself with much dignity.

Of his literary works his "History of the World" is now but little read. It is a heavy performance, but has some fine outbursts of eloquence. Some of the poetical pieces assigned to him are beautiful, and contain many of the exquisite touches peculiar to the authors of the Elizabethan period; they were, however, for the most part, published anonymously, and cannot in many

---

[1] See Howell's Epistolæ Ho-Elianæ, 1645, page 6: "Sir Walter landed at Plymouth, whence he thought to make an escape, and some say he hath tampered with his body by Phisick, to make him look sickly, that he may be the more pitied, and permitted to lie in his own house. Count Gondamar, the Spanish Ambassador, speaks high language, and sending lately to desire audience of his Majestie, he said he had but one word to tell him, his Majestie wondring what might be delivered in one word; when he came before him, he said onely, 'Pyrats! Pyrats! Pyrats!' and so departed. Tis true that he protested against this Voyage before, and that it could not be but for some praedatory designe: and if it be as I hear, I fear it will go very ill with Sir Walter, and that Gondamar will never give him over till he hath his head off his shoulders; which may quickly be done, without any new Arraignment, by vertue of the old Sentence that lies still dormant against him, which he could never get off by Pardon, notwithstanding that he mainly laboured in it before he went; but his Majestie could never be brought to it, for he said he would keep this as a Curb to hold him within the bounds of his Commission, and the good behaviour."

[2] See *Notes and Queries*, 1st series, March 26th, 1853.

instances be attributed to him on the safest evidence. It was the great age of miscellaneous collections, into which the rare spirits showered the cornucopiæ of their wits. He was probably the author of the answer to Christopher Marlowe's "Come live with me," and if so, deserves a niche, be it but a small one, among his great contemporaries. Moreover, he was the friend of Spenser, and prophesied the glories of the "Faerie Queene."

Rawleighs Caueat to Secure Courtiers.

[From Add. MS. 15,226, fol. 11 back.]

I speake to such, if anie such there bee,
   whoe are possessed, through theire princes grace,
with swellinge pride, scorneinge insolencie,
   haughtie, disdaineinge, & abuse of place:
     To such I saie, if anie such there bee,
     come see theire vices punished in mee.   6

For I that am nowe as ye see abiected,
   by iust desert of former life ill spent,
was sometymes of my prince as well respected
   as anie nowe in this new Gouerment;
     But for I then my fauour misimployed,
     I now with punishment am much annoyed.   12

Then did I hold *Religion* but a Jest;
   farr more esteeminge my owne pollicie,
whereby I framed my accions as a beast,
   moved by beastlike sensuallitie.
     For what my fleshly humours did delight,
     That held I lawfull, were it wrong or right.   18

My whole endeavour was to please my sence
   with greedie avarice & fowle oppression,
divelishe disdaine, filthie incontinence,
   & false invencions were my cheife profession;
     those vices were by mee still exercised,
     and these haue caused mee to bee dispised.   24

And well hee dothe deserue despised to bee,   [fol. 12.]
   whose minde with such corrupcion is infected;
wherefore 'twere good yow should theire natures see,
   that soe they maie the sooner bee reiected;
     ffor anie one of them sufficient is
     bothe soule & bodie to deprive of blisse.   30

First looke on *Auarice*, that senceless beast,
   and yow shall see noe end of greedie scrapinge;
for thoughe her paumch bee stopt at Middaies feast,
   her still devouringe mouthe contynewes gapinge:
     most wise was hee whoe did her nature fitt,
     comparinge her to the infernall pitt.   36

If yow her reason should desire to knowe,
   why beeyond reason shee dothe ritches loue;
suerlie noe other reason shee could showe,
   but Covetous desire w*hi*ch dothe her move.
     The w*hi*ch enforceth her soe lowd to Crye
     ffor *Riches, Riches,* most incessantlye.   42

Then *Riches* come, and w*it*h her shee dothe bringe
   her God, her daughters, and her servants three;
her Enimies doe alsoe after flinge
   whoe dothe her much molest & terrifie;
     For Riches never doe approache alone,
     but is by Furies fierce attended on.   48

Pluto her God dothe guide her by the hand,   [fol. 12 bk.]
   and dothe dispose her when hee best dothe please;
her daughter, Pride, dothe swellinge on her stand,
   whoe, w*it*h sharpe prickinge, doth her much disease:
     ffilthy excesse for more, more still cryes,
     and ignorance dothe blinde her moth*ers* eies.   54

Blinde *Chance* her serv*ant* sometime doth availe her,
   and some times hee by losse sore dothe wrong her;
but Fraud & Vsurye doe never faile her,
   but like good serv*ants* still doe *pro*fitt bring her:
     Suspit*i*on, feare & greife, her enimies,
     doe waite advantages, her to supprise.   60

Now when vile Auarice is full possest
  Of riches, and this traine w*hi*ch doth attend,
Shee dothe account herself not meanely blest,
    and then to gaine a heaven she will not spend;
      but still dothe seeke her to increase w*i*th gaine,
      by all meanes possible w*i*th busie paine.   66

For when opp*re*ssion must his cunninge vse,
  In *Monopolies* and in tr[a]nsportac*i*ons,
whereby hee manie thousands dothe abuse,
    by sendinge that awaie to many nations
      w*hi*ch should bee dealt for gods sake to y*e* poore,
      whoe, wantinge, aske the same from doore to doore. 72

But *Avarice* for riches still dothe crye   [fol. 13.]
  Soe stronglie that the poore cannot be hard,
for shee hadd rather they should starue & dye
    then shee from gettinge riches should be barred:
      such is the nature of y*t* damned Spright,
      that riches onely are her whole delighte.   78

To pleasure her opp*re*ssion w*i*th his power,
  Of all the meaner sorte dothe make his praye,
like to a wide mouthd pike, w*hi*ch dothe devoure
    the smaller Fishe, w*hi*ch cannott gett awaye:
      and when the Foxes skinne can take noe place,
      then dothe oppression use the lyons Case.   84

If hee by strength of place dothe rule y*e* lawe,
  and suites decrees uppon long pleaded cases,
then if a matter haue a cracke or fflawe,
    Argentum must annoynt those Crazie places,
      Whereby in tyme it growes sufficient stronge
      to passe for curre*n*t, bee it right or wrong.   90

And if shee bee in place of Goue*r*ment,
  haueinge of meaner places ouersight,
then such as doe not bribes to him present
    are either pentioned or discharged quite;
      For avarice doth still crie out for Gaine,
      and the opp*re*ssor dothe noe wronge refraine.   96

When theise vile vices hadd my coffers filld, [fol. 13 bk.]
  my minde likewise was then filld with disdaine;
by whose approche all vertues quite were spilld,
  which doe in mind of anie man remaine;
    Yet in my minde shee found but few to spill,
    for (since it was a minde) the same was ill.   102

This hell-bredd *Monster*, of fowle divelish kinde,
  was gotten by proud scorne of scornefull *Pride*;
Nurst upp by *Envie* in a Cankred minde,
  which could noe other but itselfe abide;
    Deformitie her nature dothe expresse
    her nature poisones where it doth possesse.   108

Of this her nature was my minde possest,
  and with her poison was I all infected,
the which by me in fury was exprest,
  When anie but my self I sawe respected;
    For were hee farr my better in degree,
    Yet I disdaind hee should my equall bee.   114

This hatefull vice made mee soe odious seeme
  that for the same I hated was of all;
For as none but myselfe I did esteeme,
  soe none there was which did not wish my fall:
    wherefore if this in anie of y^w bee,
    Come, see the same now punished in mee.   120

I likewise, like a beast, much tyme did spend [fol. 14.]
  in that most beastly sinne of fleshly pleasure,
to which with filthy minde I much did bend,
  makinge noe spare of bodie, soule, nor treasure;
    For as a beast is moued still by sence,
    soe was I moued by fowle incontinence.   126

And for I would bee exquisite herein
  I vsed supernaturall devises;
powders, perfumes, paintings for filthy skinnes,
  Extraccions, distillacions, spiritts of spices;
    with theise and such like tricks I still was able
    to trimme a hackney for the Divells stable.   132

And as younge Apes doe learne by imitac*i*on
  of elder Apes theire friskinge Apeishe toyes,
soe many Apes & Monkeyes vse my fashion,
  and in the same doe places their cheifest joyes :
    never was beast to nature so vniust,
    as man & woman giuen to beast-like lust.   138

This sinne was my familiar recreac*i*on,
  wherein I gloried much w*i*th shameles pride ;
boastinge my self of easie acceptacion,
  p*r*otestinge that I neu*er* was denyed :
    Ah but if this in anie of yow bee,
    come see the same now iustly plaug'd in mee.   144

In false Invenc*i*on likewise I excelled,   [fol. 14 bk.]
  w*i*th w*hi*ch my Prince's eares I much abused,
whereby plaine truthe was oftentymes repelled,
  and such as did prevent her were refused :
    This sinne is onely p*r*oper to the devill,
    then I w*hi*ch vsed the same must needs bee evill. 150

Noe toothe of beast or subtile serpente stinge
  is halfe soe hurtfull as a lyars tounge ;
for those but paine to outward p*ar*ts do bringe,
  w*hi*ch maie bee cured well w*i*th medicines stronge ;
    but if a lyars tonge doe make a wound,
    noe salue can heale the same or make it sound.   156

When smoothd toung*e*d flatterie w*i*th falsehood ioyne,
  as seldome yow shall see them goe ap*ar*te,
then what the one in her false harte dothe coyne,
  the other publisheth by subtill arte :
    And such a Tincture on the same shee setts,
    that of the greatest it acceptance getts.   162

Surelie if Princes rightlie wold conceiue
  what danger lyes in fawninge flaterie,
how of theire sences shee doth them bereaue,
  and how shee doth impaire royaltie,
    noe doubt they would then hold it for good reason,
    to punishe her as they would punishe treason.   168

For if it bee offence deservinge deathe, [fol. 15.]
   To sett the princes shadowe on base coyne,
sure hee much more offends wh*i*ch w*i*th base breathe
    vnto the princes substance vice dothe ioyne ;
      and this dothe hee whoe makes an occupac*i*on,
      his prince to humo*ur* with bas*e* adulac*i*on.   174

Theise twoe united sinnes did first aduance mee,
   and by theise twoe I still my state sustain'd,
and theise in sinne soe highlie did inhance mee,
    that for the same this mischeif I haue gain'd ;
      wherefore if theise in anie of yo^w bee,
      come see theise & the rest now plaug'd in mee.   180

But do not come as Idle Gazers vse,
   whoe make noe vse of what they doe behold ;
but come & see how God dothe mee refuse,
    because myself to vice I wholly sould :
      Soe come & see ; behould theise plauges in mee,
      & fly my sinnes least plaug*e*d soe yow bee.   186

And doe not thinke that earthlie princes Graces
   can giue p*r*otecc*i*on to a life ill-spent,
nor doe not thinke authoritie of places
    can for one hower reu*e*rse due punishment ;
      for neither favor nor authoritie
      can staie God's hand from iust severitye.   192

Wherefore all yo^w whoe knowe yo*ur* selues infected [fol. 15 bk.]
   w*i*th these fowle sinnes w*hi*ch I haue now confess*e*d,
see y^t in tyme yo*ur* prayers bee directed,
    & that yo*ur* wrongs comitt*e*d bee redress*e*d ;
      For if yo^w doe not speedily repent,
      bee sure yo^w shall receaue iust punishm*e*nt.   198

bee not deceiued by vaine imaginac*i*on
  'of Gods remisse, forgetfullnes of wronge,
for hee sometymes vse p*r*ocrastinac*i*on,
    Yet will hee not deferre his comm*e*inge longe ;
      For when mans sinfull measures overfrothe,   203
      then powers he forthe his measures fill*e*d w*i*th wrothe.

Soe measure iust for measure shall yo^w haue,
　　if still *with*out remorse y^w doe offend;
and therefore if yo^w hope yo*ur* selues to saue,
　　leaue of in time & seeke yo*ur* liues to mend :
　　　　but if yo^w still contynewe in your sinninge,　　209
　　　　then shall yo*ur* ende paie deare for yo*ur* beginninge.

And do not hould this my advice for vaine,
　　because yo^w knowe mee vaine w*h*ich doth advise yo^w;
but rather doe thereby yo*ur* vice refraine,
　　least for the same both God & man despise yo^w;
　　　　For thoughe my owne confession p*rou*e me evill,　215
　　　　Yet truth hath some time come even from the divell.

And therefore since w*i*th truthe yo^w nowe are warn'd,[fol. 16.]
　　thoughe from a mouthe that truthe hathe seldome vs*e*d,
Yet speakinge truthe let not the same be scorn'd,
　　but lett the cause thereof bee well *perused*;
　　　　And yo^w shall find that God dothe soe ordaine it
　　　　for yo*ur* behalf, if yo^w can entertaine it.　　228

But if yow willfully advice refuse,
　　and, like as I did, growe from ill to worse;
then looke what paym*en*t God to mee dothe vse,
　　such or the like hee will to yo^w disburse;
　　　　For if my warninge cannott now advise yo^w,
　　　　my punishm*en*t shall shortlie then surprize yo^w.　228

Finis.

[Lansdowne MS. 777, leaf 64.   Variations given from another copy in
Harl. MS. 791, leaf 49.]

On S[r] Wa. Raleigh's Death.[1]

Great heart, who taught thee so[2] to dye,
Death yeelding thee y[e] victory ?
where[3] took'st thou leaue of life ? if there,
How couldst thou be so free from feare ?   4
But sure thou didst,[4] & quitd'st y[e] state
Of Flesh & blood before y[t] Fate.
Else what a myracle is wrought
To tryumph both in[5] flesh & thought ?   8
I saw in euery[6] stander by
Pale Death ! life onelye in thine eye.
The Legacy thou gau'st vs y[n],
wee'll sue for when thou dyest agen,   12
Farwell ; y[r] glory truth shall saye[7]
wee dyde, thou onelye liu'dst y[t] daye.   14

---

[1] This piece has been already printed.   See Hannah's "Courtly Poets,"
1870.   A copy occurs among the Rawlinsonian MSS. 699, p. 35, and also among
the Hawthornden MSS., vol. viii.
[2] Harl. thus *for* so.   [3] when *for* where.   [4] died'st.
[5] over *for* both in.   [6] all the *for* euery.
[7] For truth shall to thy glory say, *for line* 13.

LORD BACON.

The following lines are said to have been written by Dr. Lewis,[1] one of Bacon's chaplains, whom he afterwards caused to be made head of Oriel College at Oxford when a very young man, "not caring," he said, "for minority of years where there was majority of parts." The appointment, however, does not appear to have been a fortunate one, for he got into some scandal, and had to give it up. The verses relate to the fall of the "wisest, meanest of mankind," as Pope has it, in 1621, when Bacon was prostrate in the dust. Of course every one who wishes to read the life of this intellectually great man must go to the exhaustive work of Mr. Spedding, which is a $\kappa\tau\hat{\eta}\mu a$ $\epsilon i\varsigma$ $\dot{a}\epsilon\iota$ for everything connected with him; nor will the glowing rhetoric of Macaulay ever want its readers, although the study may not be so profound a one. All encomium upon Bacon as philosopher, essayist, and historian is idle: the pathetic words of his will, when he bequeathed his memory to foreign nations, and to his own countrymen when some generations were passed, have been amply fulfilled: he now stands a statuesque and colossal figure for all time. Those who cannot bring wits enough to fathom the depths of the Novum Organum, may admire the close-wrought gold, the subtle analysis, the delicate antithesis of the essays, or pause with delight upon the quaint reflections teeming with worldly wisdom introduced so copiously among his historical works—more neglected, but most unjustly so.

Three other copies of this poem are found in the British Museum: Sloane MS. 1792, leaf 109; Add. MS. 29,303, leaf 3*b*.; and Add. MS. 25,303, leaf 83, referred to for the various readings as V. X. and Z. There is also another among the Jackson MSS.. presented to the University of Edinburgh by Mr. Halliwell (p. 82), thus headed: "In laudem Francisci Baconis olim totius Angliæ cancellar."

---

[1] Dr. William Lewis, Provost of Oriel College (1618–1621). He resigned, and died at an advanced age in 1667.—See Gutch, *History of Colleges and Halls of Oxford*, 1781.

Dor. Lewis, his foolish inuectiue against the Parlament for proceedinge to censure his Loᵈ Verulame.[1]

[Sloane MS. 826, leaves 4, 5, 8: title from Add. MS. 25,303.]

When you awake, dull Brittons, and behould
What treasure you haue throwne into your[2] mould;
Your ignorance in pruming[3] of a state
You shall confesse, and shall[4] your rashnes hate : 4
For in your[5] senceles furie you haue slaine
A man, as farre beyound your[6] spungie braine
Of common knowledge, as is[7] heaven from hell
And yet[8] you tryvmph, thinke you haue done well. 8
Oh, that the monster multitude should sit[9]
In place of iustice, reason, conscience, witte,
Nay in a[10] throne or[10] spheare above them all !
For tis a supreame power that can call 12
All these to barre :[11] and with a frowning brow,
Make Senatours, nay mightie Consults bow.
Bould Plebeans, the day will come I know
When such a[12] Cato, such a[12] Cicero, 16
Shalbe more worth[13] then the first borne[14] can be
Of all your auncestours, or posteritie.
But hees not dead you[15] say : oh, that[16] the soule
Once checkt, controwld, that once[17] vsed to controwle, 20

---

[1] X. has, instead of this title, the following : "Certen verses made in the behalfe of Sʳ Francis Bacon, whoe was Lorde Keeper of Englande Anno 1620 ; but then put off by the Parlement howese for some occations to me vnknowen." V. *has only* "On Sir Francis Bacon."

[2] V. this; X. and Z. the *for* your. [3] V. and X. praving; Z. pruning.
[4] X. and Z. that *for* shall. [5] V. X. and Z. a *for* your.
[6] V. X. and Z. the *for* your. [7] V. *omits* is.
[8] X. *omits* yet; Z. has tryumphinge *for* you tryvmph.
[9] A marginal note in Add. MS. 29,303 to lines 9-13 says, "The maker hereof was too bould in his censure, and partiall in his loue, as maye appeere by the sequell."
[10] Z. the, and, *for* a, or.
[11] V. There to the; X. Such to the *for* All . . . to ; Z. *has* the *after* to.
[12] V. X. and Z. as *for* a.
[13] X. and Z. worthy *for* worth. [14] X. *omits* borne.
[15] V. you'll *for* you. [16] V. X. and Z. but *for* that.
[17] V. X. and Z. *omit* once.

Cowcheth her downie wings, and scornes to flye
At any game but faire eternitie.
Each spirit is retired to a roome,
And makes[1] his living body but a toombe;　　　24
On which such[2] epitaphs may well be read
As would the gazer strike[3] with sorrow dead.
Oh that I could but give his worth a name　　　[fol. 4 bk.]
That if not you, your sonnes may[4] blush for shame!　　28
Who in arithmatick hath greatest[5] skill
His good partes cannot number, yet[6] his ill
Cannot be calld a number; since tis knowne
He had but few that could be calld his owne:　　　32
And those in other men (even in these times)
Are often praised, and[7] vertues calld, not crimes.
But as in purest[8] things the smalest[8] spott
Is sooner found, then either staine or blott　　　36
In baser stuff; even so his chance was such
To haue of faults to few, of worth to much.
So by the brightnes of his owne[9] cleare light
The moates he had lay open to each sight.　　　40
If yee would[10] haue a man in all points good
You must not haue him made of flesh and bloud:
An act of Parliament you first must settle
And force dame Nature worke[11] in[12] better mettle.　　44
Some faults he had, no more then serve[13] to proove
He drew his line from Adam, not from Jove.
And those small staines[14] nature for its[15] offence
Like moones in armorie[16] made a difference　　　48
Twixt him and angells; beeing sure[17] no other
Then markes[18] to know him for their[19] younger brother.
Such spotts remooved (not to[20] prophane) he then
Might well be call'd a demie God mongst men.　　　52

---

1 V. and X. made *for* makes.　　2 X. *omits* such.
3 X. and Z. prick *for* strike.　　4 X. and Z. might *for* may.
5 X. *omits* greatest.　　6 X. but *for* yet.
7 X. prayses *for* praised and.
8 Z. purer, peorest *for* purest, smalest; X. purest *for* smalest.
9 Z. noone *for* owne.　　10 X. will *for* would.
11 X. to *before* worke.　　12 V. on *for* in.
13 V. X. and Z. serued *for* serve.　　14 X. in *before* nature.
15 V. X. and Z. forced *for* for its.　　16 V. X. and Z. were *before* made.
17 X. since *for* sure.　　18 X. made *for* markes.
19 X. a *for* their.　　20 X. *omits* to.

A diamond flawed, saphyers and rubies stained
But vndervalewed are, not[1] quite disdained;
Which[2] by a file[3] recoverd they become
As worthie of esteeme, yeeld no lesse sum*m*e.   56
The gardner finding once a canker growne
Upon a tree, that he hath frutefull knowne,
Grubs it not vp; but w*i*th a carefull hand
Opens the roote, remooves the clay or sand   60
That cawsed the[4] cancar, or w*i*th cunning arte
Pares of some rynde, but comes not nere yᵉ harte.   [fol. 5]
Only such trees yᵉ axes adge endure
As nere bare fruite, or else are past all cure.[5]   64
The prudent husbandman thrusts not his sheare
Into his[6] corne because some[7] weeds are there,
But takes his hooke, and gently as he may
Walke thróugh the[8] field, and takes[9] them all away.   68
A house of many roomes one[10] may com*m*and,
But yet it shall require many a hand
To keepe it cleane: and if some filth be found
Crope[11] in by[12] negligence, is't cast to th' grownde?   72
Fie, no; but first yᵉ supreame owner comes,
Examines everie office, viewes the roomes,
Makes them be clensed, and on some certaine paine
Com*m*ands they never be found so againe.   76
The temple else should over-throwne haue bin,
Because some money-brokers[13] were therein.
The arke had sunke and perisht in the floud,
Because some beasts crope[14] in that were not good.   80
Adam had w*i*th a thunderbolt bin strooke,
When he from Eve the golden[15] apple tooke.
But should the maker of[16] mankinde doe soe,   83
Who should write Man? who should to mans state grow?
Shall he be then put to th' extreame of law,
Because his conscience had a little flaw?   86

---

[1] V. but *for* not.   [2] V. Yet *for* Which.
[3] X. and Z. foyle *for* file.   [4] V. this *for* the.
[5] Z. omits the next twelve lines.   [6] X. the *for* his.
[7] X. such *for* some.   [8] X. his *for* the.
[9] X. pluckes *for* takes; V. pulls *for* takes.   [10] V. man *after* one.
[11] Crept. An instance of a strong perfect, which has since been changed into a weak form.   [12] X. Crept in through *for* Crope in by.
[13] X. changers *for* brokers.   [14] X. and Z. crept *for* crope.
[15] Z. tempting *for* golden.   [16] V. all *after* of.

Will ye want conscience cleane, because y^t he
Stumbled or tript[1] but in a small degree ?   88
No ; first looke back to all your owne past[2] acts,
Then[3] passe your censure, punish all the facts
By him committed : Then Ile sweare he shall
Confesse that you are vpright Chancellours all :   92
And for the time to come with all his might
Strive to out doo you all in dooing right.[4]
Oh could his predicessours goost appeare,
And tell how foule his Master left the chaire ![5]   96
How every feather that he satt vpon   [fol. 5 bk.]
Infectious was, and that there was no stone
On which some contract was was[6] not made to fright
The fatherlesse and widdow from their right.   100
No[7] stoole, no[7] boord, no[7] rush, no[7] bench, on which
The poore man was not sould vnto the rich.
It[8] would have[9] longer time the roome to aire
And what yee now call foule yee would thinke fair.[10]   104
He tooke to keepe (tis knowne), this but to live ;
He robd to purchace land, and this to give.
And had this[11] beene so blest in his[12] owne[13] treasure,   107
He would have given much[14] more with much more pleasure.
The nights greate lampe from the rich sea will take,[15]
To lend the thirstie earth,[16] and from each lake
That hath an overplus borrow a share,
Not to its proper[17] vse, but to repaire   112
The rivers[18] of some parcht and vp-dried hill :
So this vnconstant planet (for more ill
Envie cannot speake of him) tooke from some floud,   . .
Not for 's owne[19] vse, but to doe[20] others good.   116

---

[1] X. and slipt *for* or tript; V. and Z. slipt.   [2] X. and Z. passed *for* owne past.
[3] X. and Z. And *for* Then.   [4] Z. *omits* the next ten lines.
[5] "Eggerton was before him Lord Keeper." Marginal note to lines 95–98, in Add. MS. 29,303. Ellesmere, Thomas Egerton, Bacon (1540–1617). To his custody Essex was committed, see p. 206.   [6] *Sic.*   [7] X. nor *for* no.
[8] V. and X. you *for* it.   [9] V. give *for* have.   [10] X. would then be *for* yee would thinke.   [11] V. hee *for* this.   [12] Z. in's *for* in his.
[13] V. X. and Z. borne *after* owne.   [14] X. and Z. *omit* much.
[16] Cf. Timon of Athens, act iv. scene 3 :
> "The sun's a thief, and with his great attractiou
> Robs the vast sea : the moon's an arrant thief,
> And her pale fire she snatches from the sun."
The idea, however, dilated upon in these five lines, is a very old one, and can he found in the pseudo-Anacreon. (See Bergk.)   [16] V. X. and Z. lande *for* earth.
[17] V. X. and Z. her owen *for* its proper.   [18] V. and Z. ruines *for* rivers; X. raynes.   [19] X. his owen *for* 's owne.   [20] V. and X. for *for* to doe.

But such[1] misfortune dogg'd his honest will,
That what he tooke by[2] wrong, he gave as ill.
For those his bountie nurst, as all suppose
(not those he iniured), proov'd his greatest foes.　　　120
So foolish mothers from their wiser mates
Oft filch and steale, weaken their owne estates,
To feede the humor of some wanton boy;
They sillie women hoping to haue ioy[3]　　　124
Of this ranke plant, when they are saplesse growne.
But seld or never hath it yet bin knowne
That pamperd youth gave parents more releefe
Then what increastd their age with care[4] and greefe.　128
These[5] oversights of Nature, former times　　　[fol. 8.]
Have rather pittied then condem'd as crimes.
Then wher is charitie become of late?
Is her place begg'd? her office given[6] Hate?　　　132
Is their a pattent got for her restrainte?
Or a[7] Monopoly gain'd by false complaint?
If so, pursue the patentees, for sure
False information did the writt procure:　　　136
The seale is counterfeict, the referrees
Have taken bribes: then first examine these,
Restore faire Charitie to her place againe,
And he that suffers now may then complaine:　　　140
Set her at Justice feete, then[8] let the poize
By them directed be, and not by noise.
Let them his merritts weigh[9] with his offence,
And you shall finde a mightie difference.　　　144
Rase not a goodly building for a toy:
Tis better to repaire then to destroy.
You will not force his ashes to y[e] vrne,
Tush, thats not[10] it; himselfe, himselfe will burne.　148
When he but findes his honour sound retreate
Like a cag'd foule, himselfe to death will beate:
And leave the world when thers no healpe at all
To sight and greeve for[11] his vntimely fall.　　　152

---

[1] X. since *for* such.　　　[2] X. and Z. with *for* by.
[3] X. inioye *for* haue ioy.　　　[4] V. and X. payne *for* care.
[5] X. This *for* These.
[6] X. turned to *for* given; V. and Z. to *after* given.
[7] V. X. and Z. *omit* a.　　　[8] V. X. and Z. and *for* then.
[9] X. wright *for* weigh.　　　[10] Z. *omits* not.　　　[11] Z. at *for* for.

The skilfull surgeon cutts not of a lim*m*e
Whilst there is hope : oh deale you[1] so w*i*th him !
He wants not fortitude, but can endure
Cutting, incision, so they *promise* cure ;   156
Nay more, shew him but[2] where the ey-sore stands,
And he will[3] search and drest w*i*th his owne hands.
Would yee anotomize ? would ye desect [leaf 8 bk.]
For your experiment ? oh, yee may elect 160
Out of that house where yee as Judges sit,[4]
Diverse for execution far more fitt ;[4]
And when ye finde a monster overgrowne[5]
With foule[6] corruption, let him be throwne 164
At Justice feete, let him be sacrifiz'd,
And let[7] new tortures, new plagues be devised :
Such as may fright the living from their[8] crimes
And be a president to[9] after times ; 168
Which long-lived records to enseuing daies
Shall still proclaime, to your[10] eternall praise.[11] 170

---

[1] X. not *for* you ; V. and Z so then *for* you so.
[2] X. *omits* but.   [3] V. X. and Z. shall *for* will.
[4] X. reverses these two lines.
[5] V. farr oregrowne *for* overgrowne.
[6] X. frayle *for* foule.
[7] V. and X. there be *after* let, *omit* be *before* devised ; Z. *the same, but omits* and.
[8] V. like *for* their ; X. and Z. such *for* their.
[9] V. X. and Z. for *for* to.   [10] Z. his *for* your.
[11] Add. MS. 25,303 has the following lines appended by way of comment on the poem (leaf 86) :

Blame not the Poet, though he make such moane
For's Lord, since in his case he pleads his owne ;
if y*t* his Lord must such sharpe censure haue,
what then must hee y*t* was soe very a knaue ? ·4·
yet as his faultes were more, so may we say
his witts weare, for he quickely ruu away.
Like to the mau that saw his Master kisse
y*e* Poopes foote, feard y*t* a worse place was his,— 8
may y*e* Lords cure succeede his punishment,
and iustice him oretake that it ore went ;
Though scapd his first, he stay till y*e* last doome,
and cry Let hir (*sic*) alone till y*t* day come. 12

The following Verses on Bacon are printed in vol. i. p. 469, of "Prince Charles
and the Spanish Marriage," by S. R. Gardiner. Mr. Gardiner says :—

"The following verses are valuable as giving an idea of the mode in which
Bacon's case was regarded by a not unfavourable looker on."

Vicecomes Sanctus Albanus Cancellarius Anglicauus
Miris dotibus imbutus, ingeniosus et acutus,
Linguâ nemini secundus (ah! si esset manu mundus)
Eloquens et literatus repetundarum accusatus   4
Accusatus haud convictus (utinam haud rithmus fictus)
Tanquam passer plumbo ictus est ægrotus, aut sic dictus,
Morte precor moriatur reus antequam damnatur,
Morte dico naturali; (munus, non est pœna tali),   8
Ab amico accusatus; miser tu, at es ingratus.
Actæon tu propriis manibus, præda facta tuis canibus
Pereant canes hi latrantes te famamque vulnerantes. ·
Tua sors est deploranda, quid si culpa perdonata,   12
Fama est per orbem flata quod sigilla sunt sublata.
Mali semel accusatus, et si pœnâ liberatus,
Manet malum et reatus, absit hic sit tuus status.   15
Vive tu, si vitam cupis, vita cara ursis, lupis,
Et si quid fecisti malè, redime et bene vale.   17
—*State Papers, Domestic,* vol. cxx. 39.

[Harl. MS. 6938, leaf 27.][1]

𝔙erses made by an unknowne Author upon the falle of S[t] ffrancys
Bacon Lord Verulam, viscounte S[t]. Albons & Late lord
Chauncelor of Englande.[2]

Great *Verulam* is very-lame, the gout of[3] go-out feeling,
he humbly begs y[e] Crutch of State, with falling sicknes reeling:
diseas'd, displeas'd, greiues sore to see[4] that State by fate should perish;
Unhappy, that no hap[5] can cure, nor high protection cherish :   4
Yet cannot I but marvaile much at this in Common reason,
y[t] *Bacon* should neglected be when it is most in season.
perhaps y[e] game[6] of *Buck* hath vilified[7] y[e] Boare;
or else his Crescents are in war[8] y[t] he can hunt[9] no more.   8
be it *what* it will, the Relatiue *your* Antecedent moving,
declines a Case Accusatiue, the Datiue too much loving.
Young, this griefe will make thee Old, for care with youth ill matches.
Sorrow makes *Mutas* muse; that Ratcheus[10] under hatches.   12
Bushell wants by halfe a pecke the measure of such teares,
because his Lords posteriors makes the[11] buttons y[t] he weares.
Though Edney be casheir'd, greife moues him to compassion,
to thinke how[12] suddenly is turn'd[12] the wheele of his ambition.   16

---

[1] Other copies of this poem are found in Harl. MS. 367, leaf 187, and Harl. MS. 1221,
leaf 80*b*. ; the variations in which are here given, and referred to as B., A. respectively.
[2] This heading is found in Harl. MS. 367 only.
[3] B. or *for* of.
[4] B. greeueth soare *for* greiues sore to see.
[5] B. hope *for* hap.
[6] B. grace *for* game.
[7] B. doth vilifi *for* hath vilified.
[8] B. vaine *for* war.   [9] B. hurte *for* hunt.
[10] A. Ratchers ; B. Hatchers.
[11] B. *omits* the.
[12] B. that fate should bringe so lowe *for* how . . . turn'd.

had Butler liu'd he-ad vext a [1] greiu'd this dismall day [2] to see
the hogshead y[t] so late was broach'd, to run so neere the [lee].
Fletcher may go feather bolts for such as quickly shoot them ;
Now Cockins Combe is newly cut, a man may soone confute him.　　　20
The red[3]-rose house lamenteth much y[t] this unhappy[4] day
Should bring this fall of[5] leafe in March before the spring in May.
Albones much[6] condoles the losse of this great viscounts Charter,
Who suffering for his conscience sake is turn'd Franciscan Martir.　　　24

[Royal MS. 17 B. L., leaf 2 back.]

Verses made by Mr. Fra. Bacon.[7]

The man of life vpright whose giltles heart is free
From all dishonest deeds and thoughts of Vanitie ;
The man whose silent daies in harmeles ioyes are spent,
Whome hopes cannot delude, nor fortune discontent :　　　4
That man needs neither Towers nor Armor for defence,
Nor secret vaults to flie from Thunders violence ;
Hee onelie can behold with vnaffrighted eyes
The horrors of the deepe and Terrours of the skies :　　　8
Thus scorning all the care that fate or fortune bring,[8]
Hee makes the heauen his booke, his wisdome heauenlie things,
Good thoughts his onelie freinds, his life a well spent age,
The Earth his sober Inne, a quiet Pilgramage.　　　12

---

[1] A. and *for* a ; B. heed next have *for* he-ad vext a.
[2] B. so sudden for *for* this dismall day.　　　[3] B. whit *for* red.
[4] B. so fatall *for* vnhappy.　　　[5] B. the fallinge leafe *for* this fall of.
[6] B. *omits* much.
[7] This is printed by Mr. Spedding in his edition of Bacon's Works, vol. vii. p. 269, from Royal MS. 17 B. L. He does not mention the copy in Add. MS. 4128, which also ascribes the verses to Bacon.
[8] Add. MS. 4128, leaf 14, has *brings* for *bring*.

POEMS ON WARWICK AND FROBISHER.

THESE verses are addressed to Ambrose Dudley, Earl of Warwick, for a brief account of whom see page 120. He had been sent to France by Elizabeth to support the Protestants. For some notice of Dr. Simon Forman and his MSS. see also p. 70. He seems to have enjoyed a very dubious reputation: here we have the "wizard" quitting his criminal and deleterious drugs, and betaking himself to the humbler offices of a flatterer and small-beer poet. It is to be regretted that his curious diary, preserved among the Ashmolean MSS., has not been entirely printed. As yet only a few extracts have appeared—as, notably, the interesting mention of the production of Macbeth.

[Ashmolean MS. 208, leaf 260 bk.]

lord of Warrick.

What doth more glad the harts of men
    Then springe tim when hit comes ?
Or what doth pinch men more *with* care
    Then hyemps *with* her Bloms ?   4

For when that Ladie Ver appears,
    for good relife men hope ;
But when Againe A waie hit fares,
    Then Hiemps cuts their crope.   8

So wase ther nothinge, noble Lord,
    That more did make men glad,
Then when the folke of *your* coming
    Abundaunt newes they haid.   12

Then did their harts in bodyes lepe,
    for ioye of *your* comminge ;
And to behould your Louely cher,
    full great wase their Runninge.   16

for whye, they knewe Asuredly
    that comfort *with* youe came
In depe distres their harts to ease ;
    Therfore thei praise your name.   20

Therfore they praye continually,
  That here stiłł might byd,
And never wold w*ith* willing hart
  That youe from them should ryd.   24

And I my-self, O noble Lord,
  Could wishe youe her to dwełł
Continuallie with willing hart;
  for suer hit[1] lykes me węłł.   28

Ase Euphrates of Paradice,
  That flod Abrood doth spred;
So doth yo*ur* name in Ałł our costes,
  wher so ever youe goe or ryde.   32

The wind, Also, which Bloweth stiłł,
  Youre name Abrood doth Bare;
for prudent Iustice in youe flowes,
  which rids men out of care.   36

And ase The Węłł of Helicon,
  That never dryeth vpe,
So is yo*ur* name in ałł this land,
  for whye? none can hit stope.   40

Even ase the Culter of the plowghe,
  which makes the land to Reue;[2]
Soe doth your na*me* the harts of men
  with good report them cleue.   44

The which Report god still encres,
  And graunt youe happie daies,
And nestors yeares that youe maye Liue,
  And stiłł Augment yo*ur* praise.   48

And thuse farwełł, moste noble Lord;   [lf. 261 bk.]
  my hart hear at is sade:
But yet we hope to se the daies
  when youe o*ur* harts shałł glad   52

---

[1] MS. hits.   [2] To tear or be torn.

Againe, I meane At your Returne
  Againe even to this place;
Again, I saie, god graunt hit be,
  And that with in short space.   56

Noe other gifte I haue wher with
  I might present your praise;
for, certes, I am A scollare poor,
  In learning spend my daies.   60

But thus doe youe in mind, I praie,
  Receiue nowe in good part,
And not except the thinge hit selfe
  Aboue my willinge hart.   64

Simon fforman.

1578, Januari the 10th.

To write a life of Martin Frobisher is only to go over very old ground. He was born at Doncaster, of parents in a humble position. Being provided with funds by Ambrose Dudley, Earl of Warwick, he fitted out three ships in 1576, with a view of discovering a North-west passage to China. In 1577 he sailed from Harwich on another expedition, and returned towards the close of the same year. In 1588 he commanded the *Triumph*, and exerted himself vigorously against the Spanish Armada, and finally was sent, in 1594, with four men-of-war, to the assistance of Henry IV. of France. Here, in an assault on the fort of Croyzon, he received a wound in the hip, of which he died soon after his return to Plymouth. His adventures have found a chronicler in the indefatigable Hakluyt.

Of such a stamp and mode of life was old Martin Frobisher, one of the sea-lions of the Elizabethan epoch—a "shepherd of the ocean," to quote the rather fantastic appellation which Spenser gave to his visitant on the banks of

"Mulla mine, whose waves I whilome taught to weep."

But for these sea-glories, of course, we must go to Mr. Kingsley's fresh, vigorous books, which seem to be redolent of the brine and the bold roystering deeds of our forefathers. Like the Homeric heroes, they did not blush to unite the duties of the sailor and the wild adventures of the buccaneer. They founded, however, the maritime glories of England, and the maiden Queen gladly accepted their services, and gave them her countenance and support. She could grace the "Golden Hind" with her presence at a dinner; and when Master Frobisher set out on his first voyage, a regal hand was seen waving him an adieu as his vessels passed the Palace at Greenwich.[1]

[Ashmolean MS. 208, leaf 262.]

Thomas ellis in praise of frobisher.[2]

Yf gretians stout did right extoll
    Their Worthye Weights of fame,
And gaue to them great honors highe,
    Which did deserue the same;—   4

Yf they had cause for to Advaunce
    Alcydes for his might,
Which did subdewe ech sturdie foe
    And monster fierce in fight;—   8

Which brought fro*m* hesperus ylle ye frut
    Which glitterud lyke to gould,
And did enriche his Countrye soill
    wit*h* heaps of goulden mould:—   12

---

[1] "The first voyage of M. Martine Frobisher to the Northwest, for the search of the straight or passage to China, written by Christopher Hall, Master in the Gabriel, and made in the yeere of our Lord 1576.

"The 7 of June being Thursday, the two barks, viz. The Gabriel and the Michael, and our pinnesse set saile at Ratcliffe, and bare down to Detford, and there we ancred: the cause was, that our pinnesse burst her boultsprit, and fore mast athwart of a ship that rode at Detford, else we meant to have past that day by the Court, then at Grenewich.

"The 8 day being Friday, about 12 of the clock we mayed at Detford, and set sail all three of us, and bare downe by the Court, where we shotte off our ordinance and made the best shew we could : Her Maiestie beholding the same, commended it, and bade us farewell, with shaking her hand at us out of the window. Afterward she sent a Gentleman aboord of us, who declared that her Maiestie had good liking of our doings, and thanked us for it, and also willed our Captaine to come the next day to the Court to take his leaue of her.

"The same day towards night M. Secretarie Woolly came aboorde of us, and declared to the company, that her Maiestie had appointed him to give them charge to be obedient, and diligent to their captaine, and governours in all things, and wished us happie successe."—*Hakluyt*, vol. iii. p. 29.

[2] Who Thomas Ellis was I cannot discover. Did Forman compose the verses in his name ?

Or yf that theie deservedlye
  enrold the valiaunt facts
of the Adventrose Jason braue
  with Aℓℓ his noble actes,   16

And aℓℓ his noble knitlye trope
  from Cholchis ylle, the which
Did bringe A waie the goulden fleece,
  his Countrie to enriche :—   20

Yf thes, I saye, w*ith* flickeringe fame,
  wear lyke to loftie[1] skye,
That even tyℓℓ nowe in thes *our* daies
  Their fame A freshe doth flye ;—   24

Whie should not then *our* frobisher,
  Whoe sure doth them surmo*u*nt,
With goulden Trumpe of Thundringe fame
  be glad-in lyke acompte ?   28

His harte ase valiaunt is Ase theirs,
  His hazards wear more hard,
His good succes doth theirs surpase,
  Yf they be weℓℓ compard.   32

The glittering flece that he doth bringe,[2]
  In value suer is more
Then Jasons was, or Alcyds frute,
  wher of was mad such store.   36

And crueℓℓ monsters he doth tamc,
  And men of sauage kind,
And searcheth out the swellinge seas,
  And Countrise straunge doth find.   40

And brings hom treasur to his land,
  And doth enrich the same,
And Corage giues to noble harts
  To seke for fleight of fame.   44

giue place, therfore, youe greatia*n*s nowe,
  And to me giue Assent:
This worthy weight excells youre imps,
  The which befor him vent.   48

       finis.   qd. S. fo.

---

[1] MS. loftie.

[2] The second expediton of Frobisher in 1577 was fitted out with a view to the discovery of gold.

[Ashmolean MS. 208, leaf 263.]

John kirkham of martin frobisher.

THIS poem seems to have been composed by Forman in the name
of Kirkham, a person of whom nothing is known.

Youe Muses, guid my quiuering quill;
    Caliope, drawe near;
Sicilian nimphes, attend my suet,
    And to my hestes giue ear.   4

Your sacred ayd A whyll I craue,
    my shiueringe sence to staye;
such hewt exploits I take in hand,
    That men to me maye saye: 8

Thy ragged rime and rurall verse
    cannot Ascend soe hye
To toutch the tope of martins prayes
    which fleth the hiest skie.   12

Wher whirlinge sphers doe hit resound
    And deweshe staress containe:
With Thundringe Trompe of goulden fame,
    in Azure ayer soe plaine.   16

Whose hewtie acts not heavens allone
    contented ar to haue;
but earth And skyes, the surging seas,
    And Silvans Eccoughes braue,   20

Do all resound with tuned stringe
    of siluer harmonye,
Howe frobisher in every coste
    with flickering fame dothe flye.   24

A mertiall knight adventuros,
    Whose valure great wase suche,
That hazard hard he light estemd,
    his countrie to enriche.   28

To climb The height And heutie[1] hills,   [lf. 264 bk.]
   where Poets preach for praise;
To Vewe Pernassus and etna,
   I liste not spend my daies.   32

Nor yet to seke the water nimphes,
   nor fataƚƚ sisters three,
Nor yeat to teƚƚ of Acteons death,
   what thaunche be chamced (*sic*) he.[2]   36

Nor yet to teƚƚ of Arthurs Knits,
   in force that did exceƚƚ;
for certainlye suche men ar dead
   of whom the Poets doe teƚƚ.   40

god graunt to thee old Tythons age,
   And Creasus happie wealth;
Policrats haps god send youe to,
   And Gallens perfect healthe.   44

but sith my wit for sakes my wiƚƚ,
   I maye not what I wold;
Then, pardon wit, accept good wiƚƚ,
   That wills yf soe it could.   48

Thus wiƚƚ I end, And not contend
   your noble fame to scrye,
Whose excellent grace doth far surpase
   The clear and christaƚƚ skye.   52

To Abrams seat thy sowƚƚ shall com
   in lastinge ioyes to rest;
When from this earth thy sowƚƚ shaƚƚ pase,
   The heavens it shaƚƚ possese.   56

finis.   qd.   Simon forman.

---

[1] ? haughty.   [2] what thence bechanced he.

POEMS FROM THE JACKSON MS.

The following pieces are taken from a MS. volume presented
to the University of Edinburgh by Mr. Halliwell.   The contents
appear to have been copied out by one Richard Jackson, who
began the book in 1623, as this date is found with his name on
one of the opening leaves (see *Notes and Queries*, 5th series,
vol. iii. p. 99).   This book was at one time in the possession of
Haslewood the antiquary, and is alluded to by Mr. Collier,
" History of English Dramatic Poetry," vol. iii. p. 275.

𝔙icars on 𝔔ueen 𝔈lizabeth.

This piece, of which a duplicate is to be found (Ash. MS. 38, fol.
24), is the composition of John Vicars, who in his day obtained
the reputation of perhaps the most conspicuously "bad poet."
In Hudibras we find him coupled with Prynne and Withers (with
the latter certainly most unjustly) as one of those who write
against nature and their stars;   nor has he escaped the caustic
severity of Oldham.

Vicars was born in 1582, and died in 1652.   The following
amusing account of him is given by Anthony à Wood:—

"John Vicars, a Londoner born, descended from those of his
name living in the county of Cumberland, educated from his
infancy or time of understanding in school learning in Christ
Church hospital in London, and in academical partly in Oxon,
particularly, as it seems, in Queen's Coll., but whether he took
a degree it appears not.   Afterwards he retired to his native place,
became usher of the same hospital (which he kept to, or near,
his dying day), and was esteemed among some, especially the
puritanical party (of which number he was a zealous brother),
a tolerable poet, but by the royalists not, because he was inspired
with ale or viler liquors.[1]   In the beginning of the civil wars he

---

[1] This shows that Wood had been reading Hudibras, and did not think as
meanly of it when it first appeared as Mr. Samuel Pepys.

" Thou that with ale, or viler liquors,
Didst inspire Withers, Prynne, and Vickars,
And force them, though it was in spite
Of Nature, and their stars, to write."

shewed himself a forward man for the presbyterian cause, hated all people that loved obedience, and did affright many of the weaker sort and others from having any agreement with the king's party, by continually inculcating into their heads strange stories of God's wrath against the Cavaliers. Afterwards, when the independents began to take place, he bore a great hatred towards them, especially after they had taken away the king's life."

A long list of his works is given in Carew Hazlitt's Handbook, but the recapitulation of them would be a trespass upon the reader's patience. They are well known, however, to the antiquarian, and some of them, especially the "Prodigies and Apparitions, or England's Waruing Pieces," 1643, valued on account of their curious plates.

Among the Ashmolean MSS. No. 38, 170, we find *Vindiciæ Virgilianæ*, "Why, how now Mævius, art thou dabling still. Wrighten against John Vicars, the Usher of the Schole at Christ Church Hospitall, by E. C." The piece subjoined has been printed before.

A SUCCINCT MEMORIALL OF THAT MATCHLES MIRROR OF PRINCELY ROYALTY, QUEENE OF VERTUE, PATRONESSE OF CHRISTIAN PIETY, AND PATTERNE OF MOST WORTHY INIMITABLE VERTUES AND ENDOWMENTS OF GRACE AND GODNES, ANGELICALL ELIZABETH.

<pre>
Behold the pourtract of faire vertues Queene,
Rare paragon of time, by fame still seene,
Sweet nurse of loue, graue wisdomes darling deere,
Religions fortresse, fortitudes chiefe peere,   4
Chastities lampe, faiths nourceling, charitye,
Constancies bullwarke, gēme of pietye,
Delights faire arbour, pleasures pallace rare,
Where subiects hearts were freed frō woe and care :   8
The flower whose top foule envye nere could crop,
The Tree whose boughes Traytors could neuer lop ;
A piouse Deborah to ouerthrowe
Proud Sisera of Rome—Christ's mitred foe ;   12
The vine whose iuyce their subiects comfort gaue,
The Rose of England florishing most braue,
To whom since Venus deigneth to giue place
As to the mirror of perfections grace,   16
Whose princly, noble and heroicke mind
Bids bold Semiramis come far behind.
</pre>

Not chast Diana, with her nimphes most faire,
With chast Eliza dare attempt compare.   20
Whose learning, witt, and knowledge most profound
Parnassus nimphs with great applause resound.
Whose amitye what king did not desire ?
What potent nation dreaded not her ire ?   24
What puissant Keisar could her corage quell ?
Who ere in ought Eliza could excell ?
On whom as handmaides Peace and Plenty tended,
Whose life in glory led, in glory ended.   28
And tho grim death hath rob'd vs of this treasure,
And she an angell in celestiall pleasure,
Yet still on earth her neuer-dying name
Shall propagated be by sounding fame.   32
She was, she is, what can there more be said ?
In earth the first, in Heaven the second maid.
Praise her who list, he still remaines her debter,
For Art nere faign'd, nor Nature fram'd a better.   36

James the First.

THE character of James the First as a king has been frequently drawn, and his manuers are familiar to the general
reader by the somewhat highly-coloured portrait of Scott in the
"Fortunes of Nigel." As an author he is less commonly known,
but the pupil of Buchanan, if a pedantic, was certainly a learned
writer. He had not been under the eye of one of the greatest
Humanists for nothing. His "Essayes of a Prentise in the
Divine Art of Poesie," together with the "Counterblaste to
Tobacco," were reprinted by Mr. Arber in 1869. They are
deliciously quaint, and well worth reading: his Demonology may
also be consulted with advantage in these days of "levitating
theories."[1] The King's works were by himself presented to the
Universities of Oxford and Cambridge.

---

[1] *Vide* the passsge about how witches travel.

VERSES VPŌ THE KINGS WORKES TO CĀBRIDGE DEDICATED.

Rex pater est patriae, mihi clara Academia mater.

Thus in the deare memoriall of my duety,
  Into the tender bosome of my mother,
I light my father vp : O let her beutye,
    Mixt with his strength, each day beare me a brother,   4
      And let the spring tides of their fresh delight
      Make euery minute as a marriage night.   6

Crownes haue their cowmpasse, length of dayes their date,
Tryumphes their tombes, felicity her fate,
Of more then earth can earth make none partaker,
But knowlege makes the king most like his maker.[1]   10

Among the common-places books of fugitive verses made in the first half of the seventeenth century, and preserved among the Ashmolean and other MSS., we find here and there a few pieces assigned to James I., but on no very certain authority. As the King however, like Queen Elizabeth, was well known to be a "makir" in the Scotch sense of the word, they may possibly be his. In the Jackson MS. we have the following curious story :

"Two yeares before the King died, a carbuncle being in his hat, and he by the fire sleeping, by chance it fell in the fire and was burnt. Immediately after the King called to mind two propheticall verses that his scoolemaster Buchanan the night before in his dreame appeared to him and repeated to him, the verses being these :

      Sexte, verere Deum, iam te tua properat aetas,
      Cum tuus ardenti carbunculus vritur igni.

Soe he died two yeares after."

For some pleasant papers on James as a writer, see Isaac Disraeli's "Inquiry into the Literary and Political Character of James the First."

Physically weak, and the child of an unfortunate marriage, James passed his youth among the broils of the turbulent and savage aristocracy of Scotland. His early days were further embittered by the acrid Calvinism of the Kirk-squabbles of the

---

[1] The last four verses have been already printed, and contain some noble truths pungently expressed.

country.   All these experiences left a deep impression upon him:
he became a supporter of the divine theory of kingcraft in its
most exaggerated type, and an Episcopalian of the most approved
constitutional pattern.   In the intervals of his buffoonish sallies,
he uttered many wise things, and showed considerable political
sagacity.   Thus he foresaw the great constitutional struggle which
was approaching, and prophesied the mischief which Laud would
work in the kingdom.   The pageant of royalty—the very first
principles of which were shortly to be debated—was however to
be made ridiculous by a king whose personal cowardice, whose
uncouth and waddling gait, whose tedious and pedantic platitudes,
made him an object of contempt to his Court, and were such that
his very wife and children blushed for him.

Vpō the death of Queene Anne—the verses of King James.

(Anne, wife of James I. and daughter of Frederick II. of Denmark, died in 1619.)

> Cara Deo, taedis clarissima, prole beata,
> Anna soror regum, filia, sponsa, parens,
> Tu quae protrita victrix de morte tryumphans
> Manibus inuitis, Anna perenna manes,
> Quam bene præcipitis lusisti spicula mortis,
> Aucta malo, Cristo nupta, potita Deo. 6

> The[e] to invite the great God sent his starre,
> Whose freinds, and neerest freinds, great princes are;
> Who though they lead the race of men and die,
> Death seemes but to refine their majestie; 10
> For did my Queene her court frō hence remoue,
> And left of earth to be enthron'd aboue,
> Then shee's aliue, not dead: Noe good prince dies,
> But like the sun sets onely to our eyes. 14

An Epitaph of y^t second Alexander, Prince Henry,[1] that glorious daystar of Brytan's consort, too soone hid frō vs by ye cloud of God's wrath: y^t most oderiferous flower of Englands hope, too suddenly nipt by the chilling frost of heavens high displeasure.

A threefould mother God the gaue,
  O princely youth!
A royall Queene, the Church, the Graue
  Which caus'd our ruth.   4
The Church thy mother in her lappe,
  The Queene in wombe,
The Graue in clay thy corps doth wrappe
  In princely Tombe.   8
The Church the made a heauenly Saint,
  A prince the Queene,
A lifeles corps Earth doth depaint
  The to bee seene.   12
In Church eterniz'd is thy name:
  [2]She doth deplore
Thy losse. From Graue to heauens high frame
  Thou[3] once shalt soare.   16

Ex eodem ad eundem.

Henry the heate of all, ah his owne fire;
Henry braue Mars his sonne, graue Art's sweet sire;
Henry Art's Nourceling, and great Mars his Master;
Henry our glory, but by death, disaster;   20
Henry Rome's terror, whole world's admiration;
Henry our day day-star, and sun's deprauation;
Henry the glory of the Henries all;
Henry, nought grieu'd vs as thy funerall.   24
Henry the ninth was he? Nay nine in one
In Henry died, the more's our griefe and moane.   26

---

[1] For a note on this Prince, see p. 138.
[2] Queene.
[3] At ye Resurrection.

THE GOOD SHEEPHEARDS SORROW FOR THE DEATH OF HIS
SONNE P. HENRYE.

In sad and ashye weedes I sigh, I pine, I grieue, I mourne,
My oates and yellow reedes I now to ieate and ebon turne,
 My vrged eyes, like winter skies,
My fvrrowed cheekes oreflowe;
 All Heauen knowes whye; men mourne as I,
And who can blame my woe?   6

In sable robes of night my dayes of ioy apparel'd be,
My sorrowes see noe light; my light[s][1] through sorrowes
   nothing see;
 For now my sunne his date hath run,
And from his sphere doth goe
 To endless bed of solded lead,
And who can blame my woe?   12

My flockes I now forsake, that silly sheepe my griefes may
   know,
And lillies loath to take that since his fall presum'd to growe.
 I envie aire, because it dare
Still breath, and he not soe;
 Hate earth that doth entombe his youth;
And who can blame my woe?   18

Not I poore lad alone (alone how can such sorrow be?),
Not onely men make moane, but more then men make moane
   with me,
 The Gods of greenes, the mountain Queenes
In fairie-circled row,
 The Muses nine, the Nymphes divine
Doe all condole my woe.   24

You awfull Gods of skie, if sheepheards may yow question thus,
What Deitie to supplie, tooke yow this gentle star from vs?
 Is Hermes fled?　Is Cupid dead?
Doth Sol his seate forgoe?
 Or Jove his ioy he stole from Troy?
Or who hath fram'd this woe?   30

---

[1] light, singular in original.

Did not mine eyes, O Heavens, adore your light as well before?
But that amidst your seven, yow fixed haue one planet more,
  Yow may well raise now double dayes
On this sad earth below,
  Your powers haue wonne another sunne,
And who can blame our woe?   36

AGAINST THE PAPISTS: FOR THINKING IT MERITORIOUS TO
  KILL THE KING AND ALL HIS PROTESTANTS, CAUSE THEY
  BE NOT OF THEIR CHURCH—DESIRING SUBVERSION RATHER
  THAN CONUERSION.

  Rise, O my Muse, mournfull Melpomene!
  Vochsafe thine aide to thy weake Orator;
  Distill sweet streames from thy rare Deitye
  Erst too too long by him vnasked for!   4
    Vrania, take thy lute, hung vp too long,
    Let posts and stones sound out my tragicke song!   6

  O that I could in sacred Helicon,
  Or precious Nectar of Parnassus Muse
  Dip my dull pen, or from faire Citheron
  Vranias sacred skill and power could vse   10
    T' anatomize and paint to publique view
    A stratagem most horrid, strange and true.   12

  If thus[1] they hope to climbe to Heauens high throne,
  Then with Ascesius climbe to Heauen alone.
  Now how these Jesuites censures doth agree
  With Jesus doctrine, you shall plainly see: 16
  When God with sinfull flesh vouchsaft to talke,
  Did he not vnto faithfull Abraham say,
  That if in Sodome he could find ten folke
  That vpright were, his vengeance he would stay,   20
    And for their sakes on all hee'd mercy shew?
    But cruell Papists are more wise than soe.
  Did not the heauenly Husbandman decree,
  Considering how with wheat grew vp the tare,   24

---

[1] A quaint marginal gloss by the scribe: If by murthers & fornicatiõ.

How intricate a business then would be
The weed to plucke vp and the wheate to spare,
   Therefore gaue charge to let them both alone ?
   But of this husbandrie Papists will none.   28
Doth not St. Paull, doth not all Scripture teach
That none ill ought be done, tho thence may rise
A greater good ?[1]   But what tho Paul thus preach ?
Loiolae's priests are now growne far more wise,   32
   For if that any good to the Church may grow,
   They hold it lawfull to kill freind or foe.
   Our Sauior likewise said he came to saue,
   Not to destroye, whom God vnto him gaue.   36
If Christs blest kingdome of this world had bene
Legions of Angells he might haue commanded ;
But Antichrist, great Babell's man of sin,
Must here be Lord and King, and richtly landed.   40
   Peter might not once strike in Christs defence,
   But Popish priests may vse all violence.
O, saith our Sauiour, loue your enemies,
For persecutors pray, blesse them that curse.   44
But yow than Christ would seeme to be more wise,
Or rather than vnholy pagans worse,
   For Pagans loue their friends, yow would vs slaye,
   Which fauour yow, and for your soules health praye. 48
Oh is it possible such wrath should rest
In Rome's vn-erring Popes most sacred brest ?[2]   50

And tho the letter seemed most obscure,
Like great Apolloe's Delphean misterye ;
Our King a Joseph,—Daniell—was most sure
T' vntwine the twist of its obscuritye.[3]   54

---

[1] Non facienda sunt mala vt eveniant bona.
[2] Tantaene animis coelestibus irac ?   Scelestibus imo.
[3] The letter which cāe to Lord Mounteagle, Jāes our king interpreted.

That rare pare-royall of true piety,
Sweet Shedrach, Mesach, and Abednego,[1]
True worshippers of Heauen's deitye,
In whom the Lord did such a wonder show ;　　58
　And certainly such was to vs God's grace,
　And wee well nigh in as like dangerous case.　　60

The fatall sisters Latin poets call
Parcae, tho parcunt nulli, they kill all,
And Latinists the thicke wood lucus write
Ceu nunquam lucens, wherein comes no light,　　64
Bellum, fierce war is by them vnderstood
Ceu nunquam bonum, as nere being good,
And by the same antiphrasis of late
The Jesuites to themselues appropriate　　68
The sacred name of Jesus, tho their workes
Declare their liues to be far worse than Turkes.
But euen their name, and doe their workes behold
Their best part then will proue but drosse to gold.　　72
Doe thornes beare grapes ? or figgs on thistles grow ?
Or the hard oake yeild tender fruit ?　O noe.
The tree by 's fruit may manifested bee ;
On good trees good, on ill wee bad fruit see.　　76
The Jesuites doctrine who to know doth list,
It doth of five Dees certainely consist,
In daunting subiects and dissimulation
Depose, disposing kings realmes, and destruction.　　80
Whether the Jesuites come more neere to those
Which beare the armes of Christ or Mars with blowes,
It is a question, but with ease decided,
As thus, Christ's souldiers euer are prouided　　84
Of these blest weapons, Teares, prayers, patience,
These foile and spoile their foes with heauenly sence :
But daggars, daggs,[2] keene swords, poisons, deceipt,
Close fawning treasons, wiles, to couzen and cheate,　　88

---

[1] Three children that was put in the furnace by Nabuchodonezar for not kneeling to their idolls.
[2] Pistols.

These are the Jesuites armes, and with these artes,
The Pope to deifye, they play their parts.
Nor faith, nor pity, their followers haue,
They diuellishly against Truth rage and raue.   92
How fit those armes Loiolae's brats beseeme,
Brytan can witnes, and the whole world deeme.
I'le passe by sleights, all in this one,
In this great pouder treason all were showne.   96
They'le smooth and sooth, and one thing to yow say,
And yet their hart goes cleane another way.
This ambiguity was Apolloe's art,
Vnder whose name the diuell play'd his part.   100
Even Tully may these popish priests reprehend,
By whom such lamb-skin wolues are oft condemn'd ;
Who if he now liu'd, O howe 's eloquence
Would thunder out Loyolae's impudence !   104
Satan, that subtill serpent, did them teach
This lying art, they nere heard Christ soe preach.
Are not these then Rome's white deuills ? Fie for shame,
Nought but bare outsides, their best part their name. 108
What was the diuell ? a lyar, homicide,
A slie dissembler, regicide,
And with best reason, may this Jesuite deuill
Most properly be called the Kings euill.   112
If then affinity of manners vile,
If iust proportion of like fraud and guile,
If deedes so consonant and disposition
To practise greably may with prouision   116
Auaile to proue a truth ; then I Magog know,
These doe a great part of thy warfare showe,
And palpably declare to the truely wise
This offspring did from the their father rise.   120
Avant, yow locusts ! hence, yow spawne of Hell !
From whose blacke smoake yow are deriu'd full well :
If still yow will the name of Jesus take,
Let all men know yow doe it onely make   124
A cloake to hide your knauery, for yow are
But gray wolues, bearing in your front a star.
Instead of Jesus, take yow Judas' name,
Your hatefull liues will best befitt the same ;   128
For by your works wee perfectly doe find
Noe part with Christ is vnto yow assign'd.   130

Robert Cecill.

Robert Cecill was a younger son of the minister Burghley, and was born about 1565.   He was a bitter enemy, both of Essex and Raleigh, and has been previously alluded to as such in these pages.   He was made Earl of Salisbury in 1605, and died in 1612.   In him James lost a trusty friend, who had laboured much to facilitate his succession to the throne.

Vpon the death of Robert Cecill, in Queene Elizabeth's raigne Lord Treasurer and Master of the Wardes and Liveries.

Poore England ! (for how can'st thou be but poore,
Whose losses haue enricht the cope of heauen ?)
How is thy wealth decayde ?   Where is thy store ?
Who of thy treasure hath the bereauen ?
   Yet maist thou tryumph in thy povertie,
   You hadst bene rich, had heaven not robbed the.   6

Yee blessed saynts, whither haue yee convayde
Poore England's syluer-headed senatour ?
To Jove's starchamber ?   Be it never said
The highest heavens wants a councellour :
   Yet never fitter man, nor fitter place,
   Since he the heavens, the heavens him doe grace.   12

Where were ye Muses when your glory died ?
Would not your griefe endure to see his fall ?
Noe marvaile for his glory was your pride,
And those his siluer haires enricht yow all :
   Those siluer haires rich as the golden fleece,
   Which Jason with his gallants brought to Greece.   18

Then mourne, ye Muses, mourne and never cease !
Cease never till your griefe be drown'de in teares !
And when the wellspringes of your teares decrease
Make ditties of his prayses for the sphaeres ;
   Soe let the man that hath the Muses raysde,
   Or liue or dead be of the Muses praysde.   24

Twise twenty winters past, while he protected
Our ilands elder sisters nurserie;
And rose then any troubles vnexpected,
He guarded them, like as an aged tree
    From summers heate and winters cold doth cover
    The tender lamkins and their milkie mother.   30

How might wee send embassadours to Jove
To parlie for a ransome with the Gods!
O noe, yee Muses should haue overstrove
The fatall sisters, having them at odds:
    Your champione slaine yow tooke the foile, not hee,
    Yee beeing three to one, he one to three!   36

                    Ben. Hinton, Col. Trinit.[1]

The Winter-King.

THESE lines are on the death of the eldest son of Frederick the
Elector Palatine. The following account of the melancholy fate
of this young Prince is given by Mrs. Everett Green, "Lives of
the Princesses of England," vol. v. p. 468:—

"The Princess Elizabeth was placed under the care of Lord and
Lady Vere, then residents at the Hague, who watched carefully and
affectionately over her expanding talents; and the young heir,
Frederic Henry, was also brought to the Hague, to be more fully
trained in manly and military exercises. The developments of this
Prince were already very promising. He was regarded with pride
and hope, not only in Bohemia, where the people delighted to give
him the title of their Crown-Prince, but in England, where, after his
mother, he was the next heir to the yet childless King. His uncle,
Charles I., showed his approval of the intention of his parents to
train him to arms, by placing him as volunteer in the army of the
Prince of Orange. But his opening prospects were quickly closed
by a sudden and fatal calamity. On the $\frac{7}{17}$th of January, 1629, the
Prince set out with his father on a pleasure excursion, to see the
fleet returned from the West Indies, in which his mother herself
was interested, as a rich prize had been secured, of which a share
belonged to her, by the will of the late Prince of Orange. Elizabeth
parted from her son in buoyant and vigorous health. The next day

---

[1] This writer is probably the author mentioned by Allibone ("British and
American Authors"):—"Hinton, Benjamin, Eighteen Sermons. London, 1650.
4to." A Benjamin Hinton was Fellow of Trinity College, Cambridge, and
afterwards Minister of Hendon; B.A. 159⅝, M.A. 1600, B.D. 1607.

he was brought back to her palace a corpse. The circumstances of his disastrous fate have been given with much difference of detail; but the official record sent to England relates, that shortly before reaching Amsterdam, the vessel containing Frederick and his son came into collision with one of much larger make, and sustained so serious an injury that it immediately filled with water, and all on board perished, except the King, who was saved by the prompt efforts of one of the sailors. The tide of the next morning brought on shore the body of the drowned Prince."[1]

Of his studies it has been said :

"He wrote and spoke English, French, and German. Latin he understood so well that his examinations in his historical studies were conducted in that language."—Frederick Henry to Ambassador Carleton, Holland Correspondence, State Paper Office.

Frederick, a weak and incapable man, who was induced to hazard his ancestral territory for the crown of Bohemia, died heart-broken under the ban of the empire in 1632. The full record of his follies may be found in German history. While the battle of the White Mountain was raging outside of his new capital, he was entertaining the English ambassador at a grand banquet. The Winter-king faded from Bohemian history—the only record they keep of him at Prague is his Bible, preserved in the National Museum—and died a pensionary. His wife Elizabeth, daughter of James I.—"goody Palsgrave," as the unfortunate libeller called her—long survived him, dying in London in 1662. Two of her sons, Rupert and Maurice, distinguished themselves in the Civil War, and her daughter Sophia was the mother of George I.

IN OBITUM HENRICI FREDERICI MAJORIS NATU FREDERICI
COMITIS PALATINI.

Must it be soe, iust Heauens, that still the best
And sweetest flowers fierce stormes shall most molest?
Good God! can none but cedars serue to be
Th' vnhappy markes of Boreas iniurie,   4
When shrubs are safe? Must thy Lethean cup
Of direfull vengeance all be drunken vp
By thine owne servants? O yet let thy foes
Drinke vp the dregs which are begun by those.   8
Must sweet Eliza's streames of griefe still flow?
And ioyes still ebbe? Methinks the fates would owe

---

[1] True Recital of the accident happened to the King of Bohemia, $\frac{7}{17}$ Jan., 1629.—German Correspondence, Bundle 61, State Paper Office.

Some loue to vertue; or at least desist
Soe sweet a life of blacke threed still to twist.   12
Her brother's, mother's, father's death should be
Surely enough to moue or satisfie
The most revenging fates! Yet adde to these
The losse of husbands crowne and dignities.   16
Alas! 'twere well if here her woes would end,
And angry starrs no further rage extend.
She that lost freinds before must lose a sonne,
And with her age her glasse of cares must run;   20
Water must serue for sand. The earth before
Had lauishly exhausted all its store
Of hateful mischeife, and the sea must now
Conspire with earth to make afflictions flowe.   24
Yee stir-like Waues could awfull maiestie
No whit asswage your hoodwincked crueltie?
'Twas pollicie, thou trident-bearing God!
When azur'de waues thou moud'st with three forkt rod,   28
To choose the gloomie lap of clowdy night
Least else thy rage should earth and heauen affright;
Gold-haired Apollo would not daigne to showe
His earth in lightning rayes, least he should soe   32
Seeme to approue thy rage; sterne Eolus
Vnwilling seemes to loose his furious
Vnruly servants: you thy spleene to shew
Mad'st hoarie Winter arme himselfe anew   36
To further the, and mad'st blacke nighte effect
That which thy waues for pitty did neglect.
But, Neptune, thou hast done thy worst, and now
Expect the effects of angry mortalls woe,   40
Thou shalt a riuall, a new welkin see
Which brinish teares from mortalls' eyes shalbe,
Ore which new ocean thou noe rule shalt beare,
But sole Eliza shalbe governer.   44

NOTES.

P. 66. *The Learning of Queen Elizabeth.*—"Her wisedome was, without question, in her life by any unequalled. She was sententious, yet gratious in speech; so expert in Languages that she answered most Embassadors in their natiue tongues: her capacitie was therewith so apprehensiue, and inuention so quicke, that if any of them had gone beyonde their bounds, with maiestie vndaunted she would haue limited them within the verge of their dueties, as she did royally, wisely, and learnedly, the last strutting Poland messenger, that thought with stalking lookes and swelling words to daunt her vndaunted excellence."—From "England's Mourning Garment," reprinted by Mr. Ingleby in the "Shakspere Allusion-Books," p. 94.

P. 67. *For Sigismund II. read III.*—This was the Jesuit king, whose rule was so pernicious to the unfortunate country.

Ibid. *The suit of Anjou.*—Among the Ashmolean MSS., 800, 1, we have a letter from "Sr Philip Sydney to Queene Elizabeth concerning her marriage with Mounser." This has been already printed. Black, in the Ashmolean Catalogue, also quotes "A defence of the French Monsieurs desiring marriage with Q. Eliz., written by Lord Henry Howard, Earl of Northampton." This is in the Harl. MS. 180: it is noticed by Walpole in "Royal and Noble Authors."

P. 68. *Elizabeth's Lament.*—It is only fair to add that these verses are also found among the Tanner MSS., where they are asserted to have been composed by the Queen on Essex.

P. 68. *Stubbs' Gaping Gulf.*—Of this production there are two copies among Douce MSS. (XLVI.) entitled "The discoverie of A Gaping Gulf, wherinto England is like to be swallowed by another French mariage, if the Lord forbid not the banes by letting her Maiestie see the sinn and punishment therof." Also (CCLIX.) another copy, illustrated throughout with marginal notes. At the end, "Thus endeth the discovery of the Gaping

<table>
<tr><td>III.</td><td style="text-align:right">Y</td></tr>
</table>

Gulfe, seene in a dreame, allowed in a traunce, published by the autority of feareful douting, and rewarded with a common hyre to proferred servitours. Non credo." This last copy is curious, because it is supposed to be in the handwriting of the author.

P. 70. *Forman.*—I have not attempted anything like a complete account of Forman and his fellow-conjurors, as the subject would be too lengthy for a book of these dimensions. In Ashmolean MS. 802, 15, we have a long psalm composed by Dr. Forman, January 19th, 1604, "to be songe at his burialle." It begins, "Assemble now, youe people all. Finis per Forman." He was buried at Lambeth 12th Sept. 1611. The editor of the Catalogue doubts, with apparent reason, whether the mourners would have had sufficient patience to chant over the deceased doctor so lengthy and dismal a performance. Among the Ashmolean MSS. are many volumes containing the names and "cases" of persons whose nativities were calculated by him and Lilly.

P. 72. *The Partheniades of Puttenham.*—For all that can be ascertained concerning Puttenham's life, and how far it is probable that the "Arte of English Poesie" was written by him, I must refer the reader to Mr. Arber's very careful Reprint of the above-mentioned book.

P. 78. *Frith.*—Since writing my note on this word, I have met with an article by Mr. Skeat in *Notes and Queries* (4th series, vi. 573) denying its existence in Chaucer. So accurate a student of Old English cannot be wrong, and it is probably to be found in some piece by Lydgate, productions by whom are frequently to be found appended to the old editions of Chaucer.

Ibid. *iolly dame.*—In the original edition of his "Day-dream," Mr. Tennyson ventured upon the expression "he must have been a jolly king." The small wits and the reviewers of the time forced him by ridicule (we must presume) to alter this into the weaker, "a *jovial* king." Let us hope the old reading will be restored. It is certainly amusing to look at the Quarterlies on Keats and Tennyson: we see how late the real study of our own language has been. The present enthusiasm does not count many years of existence: those who promoted it could be easily specified—and their original number was very small. We may now be comforted that it is in fashion: a short time ago those who ventured in these by-paths were the subjects only of fatuous and self-admiring raillery.

P. 92. *Richard Tarleton.*—For a biography of Tarleton—the Grimaldi of his time, and a great deal more—we may also go to Baker's *Biographia Dramatica*, where we are told that his portrait was frequently made the sign of ale-houses. Baker quotes Hall, "To sit with Tarlton on an alepost's sign." See also the reference to Dr. Cave, who, speaking of him, says: "in cujus voce et vultu omnes jocosi affectus, in cujus cerebroso capite lepidæ facetiæ habitant."

P. 94. *Quotation from the Play of Henry VIII.*—Of course I have here left the question unsettled concerning the authorship of this play. For this very interesting discussion, and how far Shakespere was assisted by Fletcher—a suggestion first made by Mr. Tennyson to Mr. Spedding—I must refer the reader to the Papers of the New Shakspere Society.

P. 96. *A Poem in Praise of Queen Elizabeth.*—The first part of this piece, viz. that which was merely a translation of Simonides, did not appear worthy of transcription.

P. 100. *Sir Francis Drake.*—Ashmolean MS. 830, 17, contains some official documents setting forth the depredations committed by Sir Francis Drake as follows: "The third voyadg of Francisce Drake uppon information of ye Spa. ambassador." The indorsement is in Burleigh's handwriting, and contains official accounts of the plunder carried off by the bold navigator. So also, "A summarye relacõn of the harmes and robberies done by Frauncis Drake, an Englishe man, wth the assistauntz and helpe of other Englishmen." Thus indorsed by Burleigh, "Franc. Drakes voyadg to ye Sp. Indias." Also, 19, "An abridgement of the relation and proves made againste S^r. Fraunces Drake, k^t., towchinge his doinges in the sowthe sea, beyonde the streighte of Magalanus." The Spaniards now began to find that their *mare clausum* was being invaded, and was to become a *mare liberum* to their British rivals.

P. 114. In the emendation in the note, *for* "Britanna" *read* "Britanno."

P. 130. *To the blessed Sainct,* etc.—A duplicate of this is found in the Jackson MS. No. 9.

P. 132. *The Answere to the Libell.*—Of this piece a copy also occurs in the Ashmolean MS. 36, 37, art. 71, and in art. 72 we get "An answere to the Wiper-away of the People's teares," beginning, "Contemne not, gracious kinge, our plaints and teares."

P. 138. *Prince Henry.*—The elegies on this darling of the nation are numerous. See Ash. MS. 38, 323, "Uppon Prince Henry. Reader, wounder thinke it none." Black tells us, however, that it has been previously printed. So also another copy, 781, 75; also 96. Epitaph on Prince Henery, "I had no vaine in verse." An interesting portrait of this young man is preserved in the Bodleian Gallery: there does not appear to be any intellectual promise stamped upon the face.

P. 192. *Poems by John Lilliat.*—Lilliat has added a great many pieces on the sheets bound up with the copy of Watson's Ἑκατομπαθία, a production, let me add, of very poor merit, and in no way justifying the exuberant praise of Mr. Arber, who finds in him a second Petrarch, and speaks of his sonnets as lost pearls. Lilliat has also had his name printed in many parts of the volume: thus the preface, commencing "John Lyly to the Authour his friend," is signed John Lilliat; but ou comparing this name with other parts of the volume, we see that it has been added since. Among the pieces composed or copied out by the latter are—"A welcome to Cupid," "Dr. Goldingham his Ghost," "A Melancholy Passion;" also "Lilliat, his Confused Chaos," and "David's Dumpe." The writer was probably a Roman Catholic. As the last-mentioned poems are of no poetical merit, and deal with general topics, I have not ventured to trouble the reader with them.

P. 195. *The Earl of Essex.*—We can realize to ourselves how prominent a figure Essex was, by the abundance of fugitive poetry and other literature with reference to him. In answer to Bacon's attacks upon him, his admirers issued the following publication after his death:—"An Apologie of the Earle of Essex, against those which jealously and maliciously tax him to be the hinderer of the peace and quiet of his country. Penned by himself in Anno 1598. Imprinted 1603."

Among the Ashmolean MSS. are the following pieces relating to Essex :—

No. 767, 1. "The buzzeing Bees complaynt. There was a tyme when seylley bees could speake." Besides the different copies mentioned on page 240, we get this new version of this not very meritorious poem, and also another, 781, 56. The piece is alluded to by Ritson, and has also been published by Mr. Park, in his edition of Walpole's "Royal and Noble Authors," vol. ii. pp. 109–112. (Quoted by Black.) Tanner (Bibliotheca Britannico-Hibernica), 1748, makes "The buzzing bees complaint" to have been written by Essex. 767, 7, "By the Queene, a Proclamation declaring the treasonable attempts and practices of the Earl of Essex," etc. 781, 14. Letter from "The Lo: Keeper Edgerton to the Earle of Essex, dated 12th of October, 1599," and (15) "The Earle of Essex answere to the Lo: Keeper." 16. Letter from the Earl of Essex "To the sacred Matie of Queene Elizabeth." 20. Letter from "The Lady (Penelope) Rich to the sacred Matie of Queene Elizabeth" on behalf of her brother.

P. 196. *The Winning of Cales.*—Rawlinson MS. B. 259, 3, we have the following curious tract :—

> "An English Quid
> For a Spanish Quo ;
> God graunte one quayled
> This quarreling foe :

or a true relation of the late honorable expedition and memorable exployte (God so assisting) performed by her ma^ties moste royall navy and army at Cadez, on the coaste of Spayne, in the monthes of June and July last, this yeare of Christe oure Savyour 1596. Diligently collected, advisedly corrected, and owte of most credible advertizments newly and truly written owte, by Richard Robinson, citizen of London, anno dicto mensis Octob., fol. 47."

P. 207. *The followers of Essex.*—In Ashmolean MS. 862, 44, we have the following list of the confederates of Essex (in a hand of the time of Queen Elizabeth) :—

Earles.	Essex. Rutlond. Sussex, close prisoner. Sowthehampton. Bedford.
Lordes.	Sandes. Moountegull. Crumwell.
	Lady Riche.
Knightes.	Ferdinando Gorge(s). Charles Davers. Will^am Cunstabull. Anthone Pearsey. John Pearsey. John Davers. Gwillam Merrick. Henry Lensley. Xp'ofer Blunt. Henry Tracy slayne. Thomas West L. Delawares heyer. Henry Cari of Kent. Robt Varnam. Joh'n Haydoñ. Xp'ofer Haydoñ. Edward Bagnam. Joh'n Litelton. Yeaxley Pearsey. Charles Pearsey. Jozaphell Pearsey.

Slayn. {
George Manners.
Edward Michelboorne.
Rob't Evers.
Joh'n Throgmorton.
Joh'n Tracey.
Henry West of Kent.
Rob't Warner.
Captayn Leyceter.
Owen Salisbury.
Joh'n Salisbury.
}

P. 209. *Asked for the executioner.*—The name of this functionary has come down to us: it appears to have been Derrick. See note to "The Trimming of Thomas Nash" (p. 62), reprinted in Miscellanea Antiqua Anglicana, part ii., 1871, where the name is said to be found in a contemporaneous ballad. We never appear to have had a family to boast the hereditary honours of the Sansons.

P. 252. *The Disparinge Complainte.*—Of this a duplicate is found among the Ashmolean MSS. 36, 37, No. 10. It is alluded to by Hannah, in his "Courtly Poets," 1870, where there is a very complete account of poems by Raleigh, or attributed to him, and also relating to him. After the careful labours of this editor, there is very little for a belated worker in the field to glean. Certainly no fuller account of Sir Walter's fugitive pieces has ever appeared. Dr. Hannah has also noticed "I speak to such if any such there be," but has only quoted a small portion of it. Here also will be found printed the lines on page 269. It is a comfort to think that, although many of the pieces ascribed to Raleigh are assigned to him on such dubious authority, he cannot be robbed of the glorious sonnet on Spenser's "Faërie Queene," which is his by indubitable title. Among the Ashmolean MSS., 781, 25, we find "Letter of S^r Wa: Raleigh to his Matie before his tryall;" also, 24, "annother of his to his Matie after his condemnation;" we also have (32) "Carey Raleigh's petition to his Matie for his father."

P. 271. *When you awake, dull Brittons.*—A copy of this poem is also to be found among the Ash. MSS., 38, 14, and also in the Jacksonian MS. at Edinburgh.

P. 274. For Ellesmere, Thomas Egerton, *Bacon*, read *Baron*.

P. 290. *Verses on Queen Anne.*—Of course we must not lose the point of Anna perenna, which occurs in Ovid's Fasti, 3654, and is supposed to be an epithet of the goddess of the moon.

P. 299. *In obitum Henrici Frederici.*—The same kind of idea as that at the conclusion of this piece is also found in the following lines, copied likewise in the Jackson MS. They have been printed before, but deserve quotation on account of their grotesque quaintness. I have seen them attributed to Dekker.

"In reginam felicissimae memoriae.

The Queene they rowde from Richmond to Whitehall,
At euery stroake salt teares the oares let fall.
More clung about the boate,[1] sith vnder water
Wept out their eyes of pearle, and swōme blind after.
I thincke the Bargemen might with easier thighes
Haue rowed her thither in her peoples eyes;
Yet howsoe're, thus much my thoughts haue scann'd,
Sh' ade gone by water, had she gone by land."

The reader will observe that by an unfortunate oversight the name of Elizabeth's great minister is written sometimes Burley at others Burleigh: both forms, however, are frequently found.

---

[1] ? fish.

INDEX OF THE FIRST LINES.

GENERAL INDEX.

Rookwood, Edward, dies in prison, xxvii.

Rudolph, of Germany, one of the foreign Knights of the Garter, 129.

Sainct, to the blessed of famose memory, etc., 103.

Sampson, Dean of Christ Church, 103.

Scott, Sir W., his character of James I. in the "Fortunes of Nigel," 288.

Shakspere, his account in "Henry VIII." of the condemnation of Buckingham, 61; his praise of Elizabeth's reign, 94; he alludes to the return of Essex from Ireland in "Henry V.," 205.

Shirley, Mr., his theory as to the place where Essex and O'Neil met, 198.

Shrewsbury, Earl of, 119.

Simonides, his satire on women, 96.

Skelton, John, 153.

Slawata, the Bohemian, presents letters to Elizabeth, 69.

Southampton implicated with Essex, 208; Daniel's lines to, ibid.

Spedding, Mr., considers that Bacon was not guilty of treachery towards Essex, 207; importance of his edition of Bacon, 270.

Spenser celebrates Elizabeth, 66; his pamphlet on Ireland, 102; his account of Tanistry quoted, 203.

Spider's Web, the, or Anacharsis sayinge of Solon's written Lawes, 192.

Stalls, three vacant, among Knights of Garter in 1582, 129.

Staunton, Mr., his edition of Shakspere, 110.

Stow, his account of Candlewick Street, 142.

Strickland, Agnes, 130.

Stubbs, his "Gaping Gulfe," 68; he loses his hand, ibid.

Strype, his Annals, 105.

Suffolk, the copie of the petition of the gentlemen of, 105.

Sussex, Thomas Ratcliffe, Earl of, 117.

Sydney, Sir Henry, 122.

Synon, probably Cecil, 205.

Tanistry, explained by Spenser, 203.

Tarleton, Richard, a noted *mimus* of the period, 92; his mention in the "Marriage of Wit and Science," ibid; some of his jest books, ibid.

Teshe, Thomas, his Verses on the Order of the Garter, 115.

Thacker, Elias, hanged in 1583, 104.

Tichbourne, Chidiock, his speech on the scaffold, xv; he is decoyed by Babington into conspiracy, xxii; his letter to his wife, ibid; his last verses, xxiii.

Tresham tries to induce Catesby to abandon conspiracy, xxx; his death, xxxii.

Tytler quoted, xvi.

Vallenger, a ballad-writer, 157.

Vicars, his life, 286; his poem on Queen Elizabeth, 287.

Virginia, Raleigh attempts to found a colony in, 260.

Waad, Sir William, his account of Tresham's death, xxxii.

Waller, the poet, overhears a curious conversation between King James and two bishops, xxxvii; his boast of the spread of English influence, 111.

Walsingham, Sir Francis, his interference in the Babington plot, xiii; 128.

Warwick, Ambrose Dudley, Earl of, 120; Forman's poem in praise of, 279; he assists Frobisher, 281.

Watson's Ἑκατομπαθία, 160.

Williams, Richard, his oppressive loyalty, xxxvi; offers poems to King James, xxxvii; grant of lands to a certain, xxxix; presents a petition for increase of pay, xxxix; perhaps an old soldier who had served under Essex, 214.

Wilton, Arthur Lord Grey de, 125.

Winter accuses Lord Mounteagle of complicity, xxx.

Winter-King, the, 298.

Winthrop, John, an eminent Puritan, 104.

Worcester, William Somerset, Earl of, 123.

Wotton speaks very cautiously about his connexion with Cuffe, 241; quotations from his Reliquiæ Wottonianæ, ibid.